ANNE BENNETT

The Child Left Behind

HarperCollins*Publishers*

HarperCollins*Publishers*
77–85 Fulham Palace Road,
Hammersmith, London W6 8JB

www.harpercollins.co.uk

Published by HarperCollins*Publishers* 2009
1

A catalogue record for this book
is available from the British Library

ISBN: 978 0 00 722607 8

This novel is entirely a work of fiction.
The names, characters and incidents portrayed in it are
the work of the author's imagination. Any resemblance to
actual persons, living or dead, events or localities is
entirely coincidental.

Set in Sabon by Palimpsest Book Production Limited,
Grangemouth, Stirlingshire

Printed and bound in Great Britain by
Clays Ltd, St Ives plc

Mixed Sources

Product group from well-managed
forests and other controlled sources
www.fsc.org   Cert no. SW-COC-1806
© 1996 Forest Stewardship Council

FSC

FSC is a non-profit international organisation established
to promote the responsible management of the world's forests.
Products carrying the FSC label are independently certified
to assure consumers that they come from forests that are managed
to meet the social, economic and ecological needs
of present and future generations.

Find out more about HarperCollins and the environment at
www.harpercollins.co.uk/green

THE CHILD LEFT BEHIND

By the same author

A Little Learning
Love Me Tender
A Strong Hand to Hold
Pack Up Your Troubles
Walking Back to Happiness
Till the Sun Shines Through
Danny Boy
Daughter of Mine
Mother's Only Child
To Have and to Hold
A Sister's Promise
A Daughter's Secret
A Mother's Spirit

This book is dedicated to my sister in law Kathy Flanagan, with love and in memory of my brother Shaun, who tragically died on 5th March 2009 RIP.

ACKNOWLEDGEMENTS

I have said before that the team behind me at HarperCollins is like a security blanket and this has been so well shown this year when I developed problems for they were so understanding and full of sympathy and consideration. So I would like to say a special and sincere thank you to Susan Opie who continues to edit my books so well and my agent Judith Murdoch who has also been so supportive. Thanks also to Yvonne and Victoria and hello to my new publicist Amy Neilson and my new brand manager (now there's posh) Kate Bradley.

Thank you to all my friends for just being there and to Judith Kendall who helps me more than she knows. Thank God we all know what laughter is all about.

My family though are the most important people in my life, my eldest daughter, Nikki, her husband,

Steve and children, Briony and Kynan. Briony is eighteen this year! How scary is that? Thanks to my son, Simon, his wife Carol and their two boys Jake and Theo. And also to my second daughter Beth, my youngest Tamsin and her partner, Mark.

Love also to my sister in law Kathy, that this book is dedicated to, coping so bravely without the husband she loved. As usual, special thanks to my smashing husband Denis, who is one of the kindest people I know.

But a great and terrific thank you to all of you who read my books and often write and say something about them, which I appreciate so much. I owe you all an immense debt of gratitude.

ONE

Finn Sullivan couldn't understand his family. They had been aware of the rumblings of an unsettled Europe and so why were they surprised when Britain declared war on Germany on 4 August 1914? When the news filtered through to them, via the postman, in their cottage in Donegal, Finn's eldest brother, Tom, went to Buncrana, their nearest town, and bought a paper so that they could read all about it.

'England has declared war on Germany because they invaded two other countries,' he said as the family sat eating their midday meal.

'Well, if that's about the strength of it,' his father, Thomas John, remarked, 'it's a wonder that no one can see the irony.'

'What do you mean?' Finn's brother Joe asked.

'Well, isn't that what England has done to us?' Thomas John said. 'They invaded us, didn't they? Who rules Ireland now?'

'Not the Irish, that's for sure,' Biddy, Finn's mother replied. 'It's England has us by the throat.'

1

'Aye,' Thomas John said, 'and that means anything that involves England automatically involves us too.'

'You mean the war?' Finn asked.

'Of course I mean the war, boy. What else?'

Finn coloured in anger. He hated being called 'boy' by his father now he was over eighteen.

'So you think there will be call-up here?' Joe asked.

'Don't see how we will get away without it,' Thomas John said.

'Maybe they are hoping for volunteers,' Tom said. 'After all, young Englishmen are volunteering in droves. The recruiting offices are hard-pressed to cope with the numbers who want to take a pop at the Germans. So the paper says, anyway.'

'And why would Irish boys volunteer to fight for a country that has kept them down for years and years?' Thomas John demanded.

'The carrot that they are holding out might have something to do with that,' Tom said.

'What's that?' Joe asked. 'Have to be some big bloody carrot, for I would not volunteer to lift one finger to help England.'

'The paper claims that the government will grant Ireland independence if they get Irish support in this war.'

'Let me see that,' Thomas John said, and Tom passed the paper to his father, who scanned in quickly. 'That's what it says all right, and I don't believe a word of it. To my knowledge, England has never kept any promise it has made to Ireland

and the Irish. For my money they can sink or swim on their own. We will keep our heads down and get on with our lives. It's no good seeking trouble. In my experience it will come knocking on the door soon enough.'

Finn couldn't believe that his father thought their dull, boring lives would go on totally unaffected by the war being fought just across a small stretch of water.

To Finn, war was new and exciting. He knew that in the army no one would look down on him because of his youth and no one there would call him 'boy'.

He didn't share these thoughts, but when his young sister Nuala came in from her nursemaid's job at the Big House and was told the news later, she noted the look on Finn's face and the zealous glint in his deep amber eyes, and she shivered and hoped that her impetuous brother wouldn't do anything stupid.

War dominated the papers and Finn read everything he could about it. After the first weeks there were pictures of the first troops to go overseas waving out of train carriages, all happy and smiling. They would soon kick the Hun into touch, the papers said, and be home by Christmas with the job done. Finn looked at the pictures and ached to be there amongst them.

The following Saturday morning, he tripped getting up from the milking stool and spilled half a pail of milk over the straw on the floor of the byre. Thomas John, suddenly angered by the mess, gave him such a powerful cuff across the side of his head that it knocked him to the floor, although he had never raised his hand to any of his children before.

No one helped Finn to his feet and he was glad, because he would have hated his brothers to see the tears he brushed away surreptitiously.

'Don't worry about it, Finn,' Tom said quietly as they walked back to the house. 'You know Daddy's temper flashes up out of nothing and is gone in an instant. He will be over it in no time.'

But I won't be, Finn thought, but he said nothing.

When he set out for Buncrana later that morning with Tom and his mother, he was as angry as ever. This anger was increased as Biddy took out her purse as they pulled into the town and, dropping some coins into Finn's hand, told him to go to the harbour and buy some fish for their dinner.

Finn never got to the harbour, however, because as he turned down Main Street he heard a military band and saw the line of soldiers at the bottom of the hill. In front of this company was a tall officer of some sort, in full regalia, and so smart, even the buttons on his uniform sparkled in the early autumn sunshine. He held a stick in his left hand.

Suddenly the band behind him began to play and the officer led the soldiers up the hill to the marching music, the beat emphasised by the young drummer boy at the front. The officer's boots rung out on the cobbled street, the tattoo of the soldiers' tramping feet completely in time.

Shoppers and shopkeepers alike had come to the doorways to watch the soldiers' progress. As they drew nearer, though, Finn was unable to see the officer's eyes, hidden as they were under the shiny peak of his cap, but his brown, curly moustache fairly bristled above the firm mouth in the slightly red and resolute face.

Finn felt excitement swell within him so that it filled his whole being. Tom, brought out of the Market Hall to see what was happening, saw the fervour filling his brother's face and he was deeply afraid for him, but the press of people made it impossible for him to reach Finn.

And then the company stopped, and while the soldiers stood to attention the officer talked words that were like balm to Finn's bruised and battered soul, words like 'pride', 'integrity' and 'honour' to serve in the British Army, whose aim was to rid the world of a nation of brutal aggressors. The army would crush the enemy who marched un-invited into other counties, harassing and persecuting innocent men, women and children, and they would deal swiftly and without mercy to any who opposed them.

Many, he said, had already answered the call and now he wished to see if young Irishmen had what it took to join this righteous fight. He wanted to see if they felt strongly enough for the poor people of Belgium and France, their fellow human beings, who were prepared to fight to the death for freedom. Any who felt this way should step forward bravely.

At the time, freedom and liberty were what many Irish people longed for, and so those words burned brightly inside Finn. And if he were to join this company, like he saw more than a few were doing, then Ireland would gain her freedom too; wasn't that the promise given?

His feet stepped forward almost of their own volition and he joined the gaggle of young Irish men milling around, unsure what to do, until the company sergeant came forward to take them in hand.

'Finn, what in God's name are you doing?' Tom cried. He had broken through the crowd at last and now had his hand on his brother's shoulder.

Finn shook him off roughly. 'What's it look like?'

'You can't do this.'

'Oh yes I can,' Finn declared. 'You heard what the man said. They need our help and if enough Irishmen do this, Ireland will be free too.'

'This is madness, Finn . . .'

'Now then,' said the sergeant beside them. 'What's this?'

'I want to enlist,' Finn said firmly. 'My brother is trying to prevent me, but I am eighteen years old and the decision is my own.'

'Well said,' the soldier told Finn admiringly. He

turned to Tom. 'As for you, fine sir, you should be ashamed at trying to turn your brother from what he sees as his duty. As he is eighteen he can decide these things for himself. It would look better if you were to join him rather than try to dissuade him.'

Finn shot Tom a look of triumph, then said rather disparagingly to the sergeant, 'Tom can't join just now, for he has an urgent errand to run for our mother.' And he dropped the coins their mother had given him into Tom's hand. 'I'm going to be busy for a while, Tom, so you must get the fish for Mammy.'

He turned away before Tom could find the words to answer him and followed behind the sergeant to find out what he had to do to qualify to join the battles enacted on foreign fields not that far away.

If Finn were honest with himself, he had joined more for himself than for anyone else. He was fed up being pushed around, barked at to do this or that because, as the youngest boy, he was at the beck and call of everyone. Yet he couldn't seem to do anything to anyone's satisfaction and he never got a word of thanks.

Even if he expressed an opinion, it was often derided and mocked. His father in particular seemed have a real downer on him, and then to knock him from his feet that morning for spilling a bit of milk – it was not to be borne.

According to the army he was a man and could make a decision concerning his own future. He was pleased when he saw that his best friend, Christy Byrne, had enlisted too. They had been friends all through school and they were of like mind. Both lads wanted excitement and adventure and were sure that the army could provide it.

By tacit consent, Tom never told their mother what Finn had done. Later that day Finn looked at his family grouped around the table eating the fish Tom had bought in Buncrana. He loved his father, whose approval he had always sought and seldom got. He loved his elder brothers too. He saw Tom was nervous because he knew what Finn was going to say and he hated any sort of confrontation and unpleasantness. Joe, on the other hand, was eating his dinner with relish, totally unaware of the hammer-blow Finn was going to deliver, and Nuala was at work. He wondered how his mother would react. She was often so bad-tempered and unreasonable, about little or nothing, and sometimes no one but his father seemed able to please her.

Still, he knew he had to get the announcement over with. There was no point in beating about the bush. 'I joined the army this morning,' he said, as soon as there was a break in the conversation. 'I enlisted,' he emphasised, in case there was any doubt. 'I'm in the Royal Inniskilling Fusiliers, and I am to report in the morning.'

Biddy and Joe sat open-mouthed with shock,

but Thomas John leaped to his feet, his face puce with anger. 'Are you, begod?' he snapped, thumping his fist on the table. 'Well, you are not. You will not do this. You are just a boy yet and I will accompany you tomorrow and get the matter overturned.'

'This is the army, Daddy, not school,' Finn said loftily. 'And I am not a boy any more, not in the army's eyes. I signed my name on the dotted line of my own free will and there is not a thing anyone can do about it.'

Thomas John sat back in his seat defeated, for he knew that Finn spoke the truth.

'But why, Finn?' Biddy cried out.

'I am surprised that you can ask that, Mammy,' Finn said, 'for nothing I do pleases anyone here. And I began to ask myself why I was working my fingers to the bone anyway for a farm that one day will be Tom's. I shall have nothing, not even a penny piece to bless myself with, because it seems to be against your religion to actually pay us anything like a wage.'

'Finn,' Biddy rapped out, 'how dare you speak to me like that? Thomas John, haven't you a word of censure for your son?'

Thomas John, however, said nothing. He knew he no longer had any jurisdiction over Finn, whom he loved so much, though he was unable to show it. Well, it was done now. The boy had stepped into a man's world, only he had chosen a dangerous route and Thomas John knew he would worry about him constantly.

His brothers had a measure of sympathy for Finn, although Tom expressed concern for him.

'Why worry?' Finn said. 'They say they fight in trenches, and a French or Belgian trench, I would imagine, is very like an Irish one, and those I am well familiar with. And if I pop off a few Germans along the way, so much the better.'

'You don't know the least thing about fighting.'

'Neither do any of us,' Finn said. 'We'll be trained, won't we? And after that, I expect I'll be as ready as the next man to have a go at the Hun. And there's something else, Tom. They say the French girls are very willing. Know what I mean?'

'Finn!' Tom said, slightly shocked. 'And how do you know, anyway? Just how many French girls do you know?'

'God, Tom, it's a well-known fact,' Finn said airily. 'Don't get on your high horse either. A fighting man has to have some distraction.' And Finn laughed at the expression on Tom's face.

Much as he could reassure his brothers, though, Finn dreaded breaking the news to Nuala when she came home. He had missed her when she began work, more than he had expected and more than he would admit. She had always listened to him and often championed him. She did the same that day in front of her parents, but later she sought Fin out in the barn.

'You will be careful, won't you, Finn?'

'Of course I will. I have got a whole lot of living to do yet.'

'Will you write to me? Let me know that you're all right?'

'I will,' Finn promised. 'And I will address it to you at the Big House. That way I can write what I want, without worrying about Mammy possibly steaming it open.'

Nuala nodded. But she said plaintively, 'Finn, I don't think I could bear it if anything happened to you.'

Finn looked into his sister's eyes, which were like two pools of sadness. He took hold of her shoulders. 'Nothing will happen me. I will come back safe and sound, never fear. And it's nice to have someone even partially on my side as I prepare to dip my toe into alien waters.'

'I'll always be on your side, Finn,' Nuala said. 'You know that.' She put her arms around her brother's neck and kissed his ruddy cheek. 'Good luck, Finn and God bless you.'

The next morning, Tom told his father he was going with Finn as far as Buncrana. When Thomas John opened his mouth as if to argue the point Tom said, 'He is not going in on his own as if he has no people belonging to him that love him and will miss him every minute till he returns.'

'As you like,' Thomas John said. 'But remember that the boy made his own bed.'

'I know that, Daddy, but it changes nothing.'

'So be it then. Bid the boy farewell from me.'

'I will, Daddy.'

Tom watched his father and Joe leave the cottage for the cow byre before going to see if Finn had all his things packed up.

Finn was ready and glad that Tom was going in with him and Christy, for his insides were jumping about as they set off up the lane.

'This is real good of you, Tom,' he said.

'Least I could do for my kid brother,' Tom replied easily.

Christy was waiting for them at the head of the lane and the two boys greeted each other exuberantly and then stood for a few moments to look around them at the landscape they saw every day. The September morning had barely begun. The sun had just started to peep up from behind the mountains but it was early enough for the mist to be rising from the fields. In the distance were rolling hills dotted with sheep, and here and there whitewashed cottages like their own, with curls of smoke rising from some of the chimneys, despite the early hour.

Finn knew soon the cows would be gathering in the fields to be taken down to the byres to be milked and the cockerel would be heralding the morning. Later, the hens would be let out to strut about the farmyard, pecking at the grit, waiting for the corn to be thrown to them just before the eggs were collected, and the dogs in the barn would be stretching themselves ready to begin another day.

It was all so familiar to Finn and yet wasn't

that the very thing that he railed against? Didn't he feel himself to be stifled in that little cottage? Maybe he did, but, like Christy, he had never been further than Buncrana all the days of his life. As he felt a tug of homesickness wash over him he gave himself a mental shake

Christy was obviously feeling the same way for he gave a sigh and said, 'I wonder how long it will be until we see those hills again?'

Finn decided being melancholy and missing your homeland before you had even left it, was no way to go on. He clapped Christy heartily on the shoulder.

'I don't know the answer to that, but what I do know is that joining the army is the most exciting thing that has ever happened to me.'

Christy caught Finn's mood and he gave a lopsided grin. 'I can barely wait. People say that it's all going to be over by Christmas and all I hope is that we finish our training in time to at least take a few pot shots at the Hun before we come home again.'

'I'd say you'd get your chance all right,' Tom said as they began to walk towards the town. 'And maybe before too long you'll wish you hadn't. War is no game.'

'Sure, don't we know that,' Finn commented. 'When we decided to join up, we knew what we were doing.'

Tom said nothing. He knew neither Finn nor Christy was prepared to listen, and maybe that was the right way to feel when such an irrevo-cable decision had been made. The die was cast now and it was far too late for second thoughts.

Finn and Christy were part of the 109th Brigade, 36th Division, 11th Battalion, and they began their training at Enniskillen. The recruits had all been examined by a doctor, prodded and poked and scrutinised, and both Finn and Christy were pronounced fit for the rigorous training.

They were fitted with army uniform which Finn found scratchy and uncomfortable, but the discom-fort of the uniform was nothing compared to the boots. He had been wearing boots most of his life, but the army boots were heavy, stiff and difficult to break in, even though route marches were under-taken on an almost daily basis, often carrying heavy kit.

Finn couldn't see the point to some of the things that the recruits had to do and he wrote to his family complaining.

There have to be proper hospital corners on the bed sheets each morning, as if anyone cares. And there has to be such a shine on your boots that the sergeant says you will be able to see your face in them. Now what is the use of that? Unless of course we are supposed to dazzle the enemy with our shiny boots and will have no need to fire a shot at all. And the marching would get you down. We are at it morning, noon and night, and I have blisters on top of blisters. The tramp of boots on the parade ground can be heard constantly because we are not the only company here.

Finn was looking forward to target practice with rifles, which he anticipated being quite good at. Both he and Christy, the sons of farmers, were used to guns.

However, Finn had never fixed a bayonet to a rifle before, nor screamed in a blood-curdling way as he ran and thrust that bayonet into a dummy stuffed with straw. He did this with the same enthusiasm as the rest, though after one such session he told Christy he doubted that he could do that to another human being. 'In war you likely don't have time to think of things in such a rational way,' Christy replied. 'They're not going to stand there obligingly, are they? They more than likely will be trying to stick their bayonets in us too.'

'I suppose,' Finn said. 'God, I'd hate to die that way, wouldn't you?'

'I'd hate to die any bloody way,' Christy said. 'I intend to come back in one piece from this war, don't you?'

'You bet,' Finn said. 'And at least when we are in the thick of it, they won't be so pernickety about the shine on our boots.'

'Yes,' Christy agreed, 'and if I looked anything like our red-faced sergeant, and had that pugnacious nose and piggy eyes, I wouldn't be that keen on seeing myself in anything at all, let alone a pair of boots.'

'Nor will they care about the way the beds are made,' Finn said a little bitterly, remembering how the sergeant, angry at the state of his bed one day, had scolded him with his tongue in a manner that resembled Finn's mother in one of her tantrums. And then he had not only upended his bed, but every other person's in the hut too and Finn had had to remake them all.

He had been so keen to join up because he was fed up being at the beck and call of his father and brothers and was never able to make his own decisions. In the army he soon found it was ten times worse and a person had practically to ask permission to wipe his nose, and he realised that he had probably jumped from the frying pan into the fire.

It soon became apparent as 1914 gave way to 1915 that this was no short skirmish, and soon, with his training over, Finn would be in the thick of it. The family always looked forward to his letters, which arrived regularly. He wrote just as he spoke so it was like having him in the room for a short time.

In early January he mentioned he had a spot of leave coming up.

I won't make it home as it's only for three days so I am spending it with one of my mates. They say we're for overseas afterwards,

16

but no one really knows. I can't wait because it is what I joined up for. Bet we're bound for France. Them French girls better watch out. Ooh la la.

The tone of Finn's letter amused Tom, Joe and Nuala, but it annoyed Thomas John, who said the boy wasn't taking the war seriously enough.

'God, Daddy, won't he have to get a grip on himself soon enough?' Tom said.

Biddy pursed her lips. 'War or no war,' she said, 'Finn has been brought up to be a respectable and decent Catholic boy, and I can't believe he talks of women the way he does. Of course you get all types in these barracks. I just hope he doesn't forget himself and the standards he was brought up with.'

Joe sighed. 'Do you know what I wish? Just that Finn keeps his bloody head down. That's all I want for him.'

'Don't speak in that disrespectable way to your mother,' Thomas John admonished.

'I'm sorry,' Joe said, 'but really, isn't Finn's survival the most important thing?'

'Anyway,' Tom put in, 'it's likely this is the way he copes. He's probably a bit scared, or at least apprehensive.'

'Doesn't say so,' Thomas John said, scrutinising the letter again. 'According to this he can't wait.'

'Well, he would say that, wouldn't he? Joe said. 'That's how he was: always claiming he wasn't scared, even when we could see his teeth chattering.'

'None of this matters anyway, does it?' Nuala said, her voice husky from the tears she was holding back. 'All this about how he feels and the words he writes in a letter. I agree with Joe. All I care about is that Finn will come home safe when all this is over.'

'That's all any of us care about, cutie dear,' Thomas John said gently. 'We just have different ways of expressing things. Didn't know myself how much I would miss the boy until he wasn't here. He would irritate the life out of me at times and yet I would give my eyeteeth now for him to swing into the yard this minute, back where he belongs.'

By the end of April, Finn and Christy's training was complete, and they were ready and anxious to take on the Hun. In Belfast on 8 May they were all paraded in front of City Hall before the Lord Mayor and were warmed by the cheers from the watching people.

How proud Finn felt that morning as he donned the uniform he now felt he had a right to wear. He had got used to the scratchiness of it and thought, as he looked in the mirror, that he had seldom been so smart. His dark amber eyes were sparkling; in fact his whole face was one big beam of happiness, though his full lips had a tendency to turn up at the corners as if he were constantly amused. He had polished his buttons and belt, as

18

well as his sparkling boots, and his peaked cap sat well on his head as his dark brown hair had been shorn by the army barber.

The whole battalion moved together as one, their boots ringing out on the cobbled streets and their arms swinging in unison. Finn could seldom remember feeling so happy.

'This must be it now,' he said that night to Christy. 'Surely we will soon be on our way to France.'

However, it was July before the troops were on the move again, and though they crossed the water, once on dry land they found themselves in England, not France, just outside a seaside town called Folkestone.

The camp was called Shorncliffe, and situated on a hill, from where, on a clear day, the outline of France could be seen. One of the men lent Finn his field glasses, and Finn was startled to find he could actually pick out the French coastal towns and villages.

'Brings it home to you just how close it is,' he remarked to Christy. 'Here, see for yourself.'

'Course it's close,' Christy answered, taking the glasses from him. 'We wouldn't hear the guns if it wasn't close.' And Christy was right because the distant booms could be heard quite distinctly. 'They are making sure that they won't reach here, anyway,' he went on. 'Look at all the destroyers out at sea. Searching for torpedoes, they are.'

'Aye,' said Finn. 'And those new flying machines are doing that too.'

'I'd like to have a go in one of those, wouldn't you?' Christy asked.

'Part of me would,' Finn admitted. 'It looks exciting all right, but I think that I would be too nervous. I would rather ride in an airship. They look safer somehow.'

Christy stared at him. 'You're a soldier and we are at war, man,' he said, 'in case you have forgotten or anything. You shouldn't be bothered that much about safety.'

'War doesn't mean we can throw all caution to the wind,' Finn retorted. 'We're here to fight the Hun, not throw our lives away.'

'And I think fighting the Hun will be no picnic,' Christy said. 'Look at those poor sods being unloaded from the hospital ships in the harbour.'

Finn took a turn with the glasses and he too saw the injured soldiers and felt his stomach turn over with sympathy for them.

At last, in October, the orders to move out came. Finn was glad to go. Camp life had been boring, the only distraction the favours of the camp followers. Initially Finn and Christy had been staggered by how far the girls were prepared to go. At the socials in Buncrana, even if the girls been semi willing to do more than hold hands, they were overseen by anxious mothers, often belligerent older brothers, and of course the parish priest, who endeavoured to do all in his power to keep marauding young men and innocent young girls as far from each other as possible. That girls might be even keener to go all the way than they themselves were had been a real eye-opener to Finn and Christy. These girls often took the lead, and that again was strange, but Finn was more than grateful that they knew what to do, at least in the beginning. However, he soon got the idea and readily availed himself of what was on offer, like most of the other men.

Finn was glad to be on the move. Bedding girls, pleasant though it was, was not really what he had joined the army for. Whatever awaited them in France, he told himself as he marched along-side Christy that autumn morning, so early that it was barely light and icy damp air caught in the back of his throat, he was well enough trained to deal with it.

Despite the inclement weather and the early hour the people of Folkstone lined the way, cheering and waving, wishing all the soldiers well.

The autumn winds had set in by the time they reached the harbour. The relentless waves crashing against the sides of the troopships made them list drunkenly from side to side as the soldiers climbed aboard.

As they pulled out into the open sea, Finn looked back. 'Look at those white cliffs,' he said to Christy. It was a sight that neither of them had seen before.

'That's Dover, that is,' one of the British Tommies remarked. 'By God, won't them cliffs be a great sight to feast your eyes on when we have the Krauts beat and we are on our way back home again?'

Christy agreed. Finn didn't say anything at all because he was too busy vomiting over the side. Nor was he alone. He could only be thankful that the crossing was a short one.

TWO

Once across the Channel, Finn soon perked up. He was surprised by the landscape, which, even in the murky gloom, he could see that the fields were as green as Ireland. The region itself, however, was as unlike craggy, mountainous Donegal as it was possible to be, for the whole area was so flat that he could see for miles. Now he understood the reason for fighting in trenches.

'At least we are in France at last,' he said to Christy, 'though my family probably think I have been here this long while.'

'Why should they?'

'Well, I thought when we were paraded in front of City Hall that time that it was embarkation for us and so did they. I could tell by the tone of the letters they wrote, urging me to keep safe, keep my head down and stuff like that.'

'Didn't you put them right?'

'I tried to, but the censor cut out any reference to my location, which means most of the letter

23

was unreadable. Point is, to tell you the truth, I feel a bit of a fraud.'

'Why on earth should you?'

'Well, we joined up not long after this little lot started,' Finn said, 'and yet, for all our training, we haven't seen hide nor hair of the enemy. Yet look at the injured we saw getting unloaded at Folkestone.'

'I heard they're saving us for the Big Push.'

'What Big Push?' Finn cried. 'And how do you know that when they tell us nothing?'

'One of the chaps at Shorncliffe overheard a couple of the officers talking.'

'And where is this Big Push to be?'

'He didn't catch that.'

'Well, I hope it comes soon,' Finn said, 'otherwise I will feel that I have joined up for nothing.'

'You told Tom that was the most exciting thing that had ever happened you,' Christy reminded him.

'It was,' Finn said, 'but it all falls flat when nothing happens.'

'Well, something is happening now,' Christy said consolingly. 'Let's see where we end up tonight.'

The family, back in Buncrana, did think Finn had been involved in the battles in France for some time and hadn't been able to make head nor tail of the letter he had sent telling them where he really was. In the newspaper they read with horror of the machine guns that could rip a platoon of soldiers to bits in seconds and the new naval

24

weapon – the submarine that floated below the water.

They'd been horrified by the bombs that had landed on innocent people in the coastal towns of England in December 1914. And that wasn't all, for in May of 1915 they read about air raids on London from something called a Zeppelin.

Unfamiliar words and places became part of the Sullivan language as 1915 unfolded, words like Gallipoli and Ypres and the Dardanelles, and the battles in these places and the terrible casualty figures. One hundred and twenty-five thousand Irish had volunteered for war, and by the summer of 1915 some of those whose bodies had not been left behind in a foreign field began to arrive back on Irish soil. People were shocked to see many of the young, fit men who had marched off return with missing limbs, blinded, shell-shocked or wheezing like old men, their lungs eaten away with mustard gas.

Each day, Thomas John woke with a heavy weight in his heart, waiting anxiously for the letters that told them that Finn was still alive.

Finn's letters to Tom and Joe were in a different vein altogether. Remembering his time in Folkstone he described the camp followers offering a man everything for a packet of cigarettes, and he couldn't help boasting about it all to his brothers, who had thought him a young boy the day he had left home. This would show them he had become a man. Finn knew they would think he was talking of French girls but he couldn't help that. He couldn't mention where they had been for the censor would cut it out and so he just wrote,

> You scoffed at me, Tom, but you wouldn't scoff now, for these girls that hang around the camp are wild for it, if you get my meaning. God, I didn't know what I was missing when I was in dear old Ireland and the Catholic Church had me seeing sin in even thinking about a girl. I wonder what they would do to me now, when it doesn't stop at thought. If I was ever daft enough to confess it, I would spend the rest of my life in prayer, I think.

Tom folded up the letter with a smile. Finn was sowing his wild oats right and proper, a thing not even Joe had ever had the opportunity to do. He was glad, though, that his young brother had something else to focus his mind on sometimes, 'distractions for the fighting man', he had described it before he left, and God knew distraction of any sort had to be welcomed because the death toll continued to rise. It was estimated that as many as 250,000 men had died by the summer of that year. In Ireland there were many Masses said for those serving overseas, or for the repose of the souls of those who hadn't returned, and Tom's constant worry about Finn was like a nagging tooth.

* * *

The soldiers camped that first night at a place called Boulogne-sur-Mer, not far from the coast. However, the following morning Finn and Christy were part of a sizeable section that was detached from the original company and marched off without any indication of where they were heading or why.

Once they had set up camp beside a wide and very picturesque canal, overhung with weeping willow trees, and had a meal of sorts brought to them, which mainly consisted of bully beef and potatoes, they were free until reveille the next morning.

'Fancy going into the town and having a look about the place?' Christy asked Finn.

'Hardly much point is there?' Finn replied. 'We might be better hitting the sack. We'll probably be off tomorrow before it's properly light.'

'No, I think we're set here for a while,' Christy said.

'How the hell d'you know that?'

'Well, I was talking to one of the other men here and he told me that he had volunteered to be a machine gunner,' Christy said. 'Apparently this town, St-Omer, runs a school here to teach them, and I don't suppose you learn to be one of them in five minutes.'

'No,' Finn conceded.

'And they've set up a cookhouse,' Christy went on. 'The meal was at least warm. Anyway, he said that there are some mechanics here as well, and they will be working in the repair shop because

27

it's the major one in this area. He told me they send the broken stuff down by canal.'

'Yeah, but I have no wish to fire a machine gun and neither of us is a mechanic,' Finn said. 'So what are we doing here?'

Christy shrugged. 'Can't answer that. The general neglected to discuss all his plans with me,' he added with a grin. 'Now are we going to explore the town tonight, or have you a better idea?'

'No, not really,' Finn said. 'And if we are here for a bit, it would be better, I suppose, if we could find our way about.'

So, side by side, the two men left the camp and crossed over the bridge into the town, noting the strange-sounding street names. They tried pronouncing them and pointing out the little alleyways between the buildings.

'I don't know if this is typical of a French town or not,' Finn commented, 'but I bet you that it's a thriving place in the daytime when all these shops are open.'

'I'd agree with that,' Christy said. 'And I'd say half as big again as Buncrana.'

'Rue Dunkerque,' Finn read out the road name as they turned into it.

The night was still and quiet, and there were few people about. Their boots sounded very loud as they tramped along the cobbled streets.

'Rue must mean road,' Finn said. 'God, we'll be speaking French like natives if we stay here long enough.'

Christy laughed. 'I doubt it. I think I'd have to get by with sign language and gestures.'

'I know the type of gestures you'll be making,' Finn said, giving his friend a dig in the ribs. 'And they do say the French girls are very willing.'

'Have to go some way to beat those trailing around the camp just outside Folkstone, I'd say,' Christy said.

'Yeah, but we can have some fun finding out, can't we?'

'Don't you ever think of anything else?'

'You can talk. Are you any better?'

Christy didn't answer because just then the road opened on to a square ringed with shops, closed for the night, and bars, which were open. There was a large building on one side of the square, looming out of the darkness, and they went forward to have a closer look. In the light from the moon they could see arched pillars holding up the second storey, and Christy said he thought he had seen a dome on top but he wasn't sure in the darkness. The name was written in the archway over the main entrance.

'*Hôtel de Ville*,' Finn read. 'Least I think that's what it says.'

'So it's a hotel then?'

'Maybe not,' Finn said. 'Probably "*hôtel*" means something different in French. I mean, it doesn't look much like a hotel, does it?'

'No,' Christy agreed. 'Not like any hotel I ever knew, anyway.'

'I'd like to see it in the daylight,' Finn said.

'Well, until you can do that, we can always try our chances of getting a decent pint in one of those French bars,' Christy said. 'I have a terrible thirst all of a sudden.'

'Don't think you stand a chance,' Finn said. 'People say they drink wine in France.'

'Not all the bloody time, surely,' Christy said. 'Anyway, you can please yourself but I am going to see if any of these places serves anything at all that's drinkable Are you coming?'

'Course I am,' Finn said. 'It isn't as if I've had a better offer.'

The next morning, Finn and Christy were assigned as porters to help the medical corps with the wounded that came into St-Omer on the troop trains. For some of these soldiers, the town was just a clearing station and they were later sent on to the coast and taken to Britain. 'Like the poor sods we saw off-loaded at Folkstone,' Finn whispered to Christy.

For others, though, from Canada, Australia and New Zealand, St-Omer was the end of the road, and the sight of those wounded young men sobered Finn. For the first time he experienced the nauseous smell of blood in his nostrils, the putrid stink of scorched human flesh and the repulsive odour of festering wounds. Though the sights and smells shocked him to his very soul, he never allowed himself the luxury of being sick for too many were relying on him.

He wasn't pleased then that after a week he and Christy were among those taken from hospital duty. They were told to report the following day to the BEF Headquarters, also in the town, where they were to be employed as temporary batmen to the officers stationed there.

'Playing nursemaid to a crowd of toffs,' Finn said disparagingly as they were leaving the hospital. 'At least here I felt I was doing something useful.'

Christy was more philosophical. 'One thing I have learned in my time here is that you do as you're told, when you're told. Anyway, we might find this is all right, especially if the officers are the decent sort.'

'Huh . . .' Finn began, then suddenly jabbed Christy in the ribs. 'Will you look at that,' he said softly, jerking his head to the other side of the street. 'Isn't she the most beautiful girl you've ever seen in your life?'

There were two girls walking with a man Finn presumed to be their father. At Finn's words, the elder raised her head and their eyes locked for an instant. Finn, his heart knocking against his ribs, lifted his cap and grinned broadly. The girl lowered her eyes, but not before Finn had seen a tentative smile touch her lips and a telltale flush flood over her cheeks.

Her father, striding in front, was not aware of this, but the younger girl sneaked a look to see what had caught her sister's attention and smiled innocently at the smartly dressed British soldiers.

31

Christy watched them go and then said with a shrug, 'She's all right, I suppose.'

'All right?' Finn exclaimed. 'She is just magnificent.'

Christy laughed. 'Well, Finn, however you feel about her you'll never get near her. If you want, there's a couple of fellows billeted with us who could fix us up.'

However, just the day before the young soldiers had been warned off that sort of encounter by their sergeant major who told them camp followers were often riddled with diseases that they could and did pass on to the soldiers. 'If you don't believe me,' he'd said, 'see the men always waiting in line for the doctor.'

Finn had talked to these men and been horrified to learn what their symptoms were. Remember we were told women like that can leave you with more than you bargained for.'

'That never bothered you before.'

'I didn't know before.'

'I think that I might be willing to take a chance on that if we're here for very long,' Christy said.

'You do as you please,' Finn said. 'But I think I will leave well alone.'

'Oh, you good little Catholic boy,' Christy said mockingly. 'Wouldn't your mother be proud of you?'

'Shut up, you,' Finn said, giving Christy a punch on the arm. 'Anyway, whoever that girl is, I'd give my right arm just to talk to her. I wouldn't think of her that way.'

Christy fairly chortled with mirth. 'Course you would,' he said. 'That's how any man thinks of a woman – and a bloody fine soldier you would be with your right arm missing.'

The next day Finn got his wish to see *hôtel de ville* by daylight because the BEF Headquarters were next to it. He found it even more imposing now. The arched stone columns were ornately carved and the windows on the first floor were also beautifully arched, some with stained glass. Above it all was a blue-grey dome with a clock atop that.

'That's far too posh to be just a hotel.' Christy said, and Finn agreed it looked like a really important building.

'Maybe we'll get to find out,' he said. 'Just now, though, I suppose we should go and meet our new bosses.'

The two men really seemed to have fallen on their feet. Finn's officer was Captain Paul Hamilton. He was a tall man – half a head taller than Finn, who wasn't considered short – and stood straight as a die. He had a full head of hair though the brown was shot through with silver, as was the moustache above his full lips, but his eyes looked kind enough and he greeted Finn and told him that he had been a soldier all his life. Christy's officer, Captain Leo Prendagast, was a younger man, and clean shaven. Neither was a particularly hard taskmaster and both were fairly free and easy with the young soldiers.

Increasingly preoccupied with the girl that had so entranced him, Finn was all fingers and thumbs on his first day as Captain Hamilton's batman and didn't seem to hear when the captain spoke to him.

In the end Hamilton said with irritation, 'Sullivan, is anything the matter? You seem very distracted.'

'No, sir. Sorry, sir.'

'And you have such a dreamy expression on your face that I suspect you maybe in love,' the captain continued.

Finn bent his head to hide the blush, but he was too late and Hamilton burst out, 'By Jove, that's it, isn't it? I've hit the nail on the head. You've fallen for someone.'

'Oh, no, sir. Nothing like that,' Finn said rather forlornly. 'I have just seen a girl I think is so very beautiful. She was with a man I presumed to be her father, but I haven't spoken to her or anything.'

'So you don't know who it is you've lost your heart to?'

'No, sir.'

'Describe her to me,' the captain commanded.

'Oh, sir, she is just wonderful,' Finn cried. 'She has dark hair and it hangs down her back and it rippled and shone in the autumn sunlight, and she had a pert little nose, and her eyes set her face alight, and her blushes only make her more attractive.'

34

Hamilton laughed gently. 'You have got it bad,' he said. 'Did you take any notice of the man?'

'Oh, yes, sir,' Finn said. 'I took particular note of him because I couldn't see how he had fathered such a good-looking girl.'

'He wouldn't win any beauty contest then?'

'No, sir,' said Finn with a chuckle. 'He is quite tall and portly, and he has a fine head of hair though it is steel grey, but his face has a sort of forbidding look about it. His eyes look almost hooded, his nose is long and his mouth wide, though not much of it could be seen because he sported a large moustache that was as grey as the hair on his head.'

'Now,' said Hamilton, 'a word of warning. You steer well clear of that girl and you can take that look off your face, man. I was young myself once and I know what it is to yearn after a woman who is unattainable – and believe me, Gabrielle Jobert is as unattainable as they come.'

'Gabrielle,' Finn breathed, thinking the name suited that lovely creature so well.

Hamilton nodded. 'I am pretty certain that is who she is from the description that you have given me of her father. Pierre Jobert is an unpleasant and ugly kind of character and he rules those girls – even his wife, Mariette, so it's said – with a rod of iron. I have seen that for myself. The girls are seldom out alone and what he is protecting them from are the lusty British soldier boys strutting about the place. Lay a hand on

35

Miss Jobert, and her father, in all likelihood, would tear you from limb to limb.'

'Believe me, sir, I mean her no harm,' Finn muttered earnestly.

'Of course you do, man,' Hamilton said. 'What you would really like to do is take her out for a tumble in the nearest available cornfield.'

'No, sir.' Finn was shocked.

'Then you are not the man that I took you to be,' Hamilton replied. 'I recognise the feeling running through you well. The point is, Sullivan, frustration doesn't bode well in a soldier. You have to have your wits about you on the battlefield. There is no place there for mooning over a girl you have a fantasy about.'

'No, sir.'

'Isn't there another you can take up with?'

'I was warned not to touch those girls, sir.'

'Not the camp followers, no,' Hamilton said. 'But there might be others in the town not so well guarded or regarded, who might welcome a dalliance with a soldier. Believe me, when you have a real live girl in your arms you will get over this fixation on Gabrielle Jobert.'

'Yes, sir,' Finn said. He knew, though, no matter what he said, he wouldn't go looking for any girl in the town. When a person has seen perfection first-hand, he is not likely to settle for second best.

'Anyway,' Hamilton went on after a while, 'Jobert may be no oil painting, but I have it on good authority that he just happens to be the best

36

baker in the town and so that is where I want you to go now. His shop is on Rue Allen and his name is above the shop, along with the word "*Boulangerie*", which means baker. See, I have written it down for you, and I've written down what you must say too.'

'*Bonjour. Avez-vous une ficelle?*' Finn read out.

'Not bad,' Hamilton said approvingly. 'Off you go then. I want that bread today, not tomorrow.'

Once out in the streets, Finn's pulse quickened at the thought that he might see Gabrielle again. She might even serve in the shop. He deliberately hadn't asked the captain if she did, because he guessed, by the amused smile on Hamilton's face, that he had been waiting for him to do just that.

Gabrielle did serve in her father's shop. Just to be near to her caused Finn's heart to thump almost painfully against his ribs. His mouth was so dry that he wondered if he would be able to speak. He didn't want to hand the piece of paper over as if he were a deaf mute. He had practised the sentence on the way so that he wouldn't make an utter fool of himself and he continued to practise as he stood in the queue waiting to be served.

Though she made no sign, Gabrielle was only too aware that he was there. She couldn't understand her attraction to the young soldier, who she could tell by his uniform served in the British Army, but she studied him surreptitiously as she served the other customers. He wasn't as tall as her father, or as broad, but he looked fit, and his shoulders were well muscled. He wore no greatcoat that day and he looked so smart in his khaki uniform. His boots shone and his putties too were spotless.

He had removed his cap when he entered the shop and stood twisting it between his hands nervously. Gabrielle saw his hair was dark brown, his eyes were encircled with long black lashes, and his brow above them was puckered as if in concentration. Then the last customer left and the shop was empty except for Gabrielle, her mother and Finn. The mother turned to Gabrielle, said something to her and walked through to the back. Then Gabrielle faced Finn and smiled as she said, '*Bonjour, Monsieur. Vous desirez?*'

Her voice was just as melodious and charming as Finn had imagined it would be, and though he hadn't understood what she said, he assumed that she was offering to serve him and so he replied, '*Bonjour, Mademoiselle. Avez-vous une ficelle?*'

Gabrielle clapped her hands in delight. '*Très bon*,' she said, and added in an accent that totally bewitched Finn, 'Very good, but we can talk in English, soldier, if it is easier for you.'

'That's fantastic,' Finn cried. 'I am so impressed. I never expected . . .'

'Most of the townspeople speak only French,' Gabrielle said, reaching for the bread he had asked for. 'And they have never seen the need to learn other languages, but my maternal grandmother was half-English. She lived with us until she died, and though she spoke French most of the time, she

38

spoke in English to me and my sister, Yvette. She always said learning another language was a good thing. It has been so useful now with so many English-speaking soldiers in the town.'

'I can well imagine that,' Finn said, taking the bread from Gabrielle. Their fingers touched for a brief second and a tingle ran through Finn's arm.

'Will that be all, soldier?' Gabrielle asked.

Finn wanted to say no, say he wanted to stay and talk, but he was mindful of the captain's warning about the girl's father. Also the captain would be waiting for the bread, so he said regretfully, 'I'm afraid it is, so I must say goodbye.'

'Oh, not goodbye,' Gabrielle smiled. 'We are sure to meet again. Shall we say *au revoir?*'

Just the way that she said it and the way that she was looking at him was causing Finn's heart to flip over and only willpower kept the shake out of his voice as he said, '*Au revoir* it is then.' He left the shop and floated on air all the way back to Headquarters.

Every day that week, Hamilton sent Finn to the baker's and every day he was increasingly charmed and bewitched by Gabrielle. He was surprised that she never seemed to hear the thump of his heart in his breast at the sight of her.

On Saturday, on his way to the baker's, he had to weave his way through the crowded market that was held in the square in front of the *hôtel de ville*, which Captain Hamilton had told him was

39

the town hall. Produce of every description was piled high on carts, barrows and trestle tables, and it reminded Finn of the Saturday market at Buncrana. It was a day such as this that he had stepped forward to enlist in the British Army, and for a moment he thought of them all at home and a wave of homesickness took him by surprise.

As he was making ready to return to his company on Saturday evening, he asked if he had leave in the morning to attend Mass.

'Should have guessed you were a Catholic,' Hamilton said.

'Yes, sir,' Finn said. 'I didn't get to go last week because we were just so busy transporting the wounded, but I thought—'

'You thought that as all you are doing is attending to my creature comforts, you feel justified in leaving me to my own devices and attending to your immortal soul, is that it?' Hamilton asked with a wry grin.

Finn wasn't sure whether he was angry with him or not, though he knew that he was often sarcastic, so he said hesitantly. 'Well, sir, it's just . . . You see, sir . . . a Catholic is expected . . .'

Hamilton decided that he had enjoyed Finn's discomfort long enough. 'I am joking, Private Finn Sullivan,' he said with a broad smile. 'I wouldn't like to be held responsible for you committing a sin by missing Mass and so if you make my breakfast, then you are free for the rest of the day.'

'The whole day, sir?' Finn said delighted. 'Thank you, sir.'

In their brief forays through the town, Christy and Finn had decided to attend Mass at the cathedral, Notre Dame des Miracles, which was on Rue des Tribunaux towards the edge of town, and so the following day they made their way there. The cathedral was an imposing building, built of grey brick and approached up a set of stone steps.

'It isn't all that big, though, is it?' Finn said. 'I always thought that cathedrals were bigger places.'

'How many cathedrals have you seen, then?'

'Well, not that many,' Finn replied with a grin. 'None, in fact.'

'Exactly,' Christy replied. 'Anyway, things are probably different here. Let's go and have a look anyway.' As they ascended the steps he said, 'One of the lads in the mess was telling me about some tale of the shoes left on top of the tomb of some saint or other in this church.'

'A patron saint of shoes?' Finn asked incredulously.

'No, you dope.' Christy said. 'Parents who have children with walking problems pray to him and leave shoes on his tomb.'

'Was he having you on?'

'Don't think so.'

'Well, it's a very odd thing to do,' Finn said. 'I can't wait to see that for myself.' He opened the door as he spoke and stepped inside.

The cathedral was very beautiful. It was held up by gigantic pillars, and many flickering candles illuminated the elaborate golden screen above the ornate altar, while autumn sunshine shone through the domed stained-glass windows bathing the interior in shafts of vibrant colour.

Finn spotted, among the tombstones set around the edges of the church, the gilded tomb of St Erkembode, a collection of shoes of all shapes and sizes lining the top. The strains of the organ began and the two soldiers hurriedly entered a pew. But then all the beauty and splendour of the cathedral mattered little to Finn as he had spotted the Jobert family just two pews in front of him.

After that, he went through the Latin responses in an almost mechanical manner, anxious to get the Mass over and done with so that he could gaze on Gabrielle's beautiful face once more. Her family were taking Communion ahead of Finn and Christy so that they were going to the rails as she was returning. Her eyes met Finn's and once more she gave him that shy, tentative smile before bending her head over her joined hands.

Finn felt his heart skip a beat. Her smile was so wondrous he thought as he kneeled down at the rails to receive Communion; it was just as if she had bestowed a gift on him.

When the Mass was over, Finn led Christy out of the side door, knowing that that way he would be out before the Joberts, as people would probably mill on the steps outside the front door, as they did in most churches.

Christy, who hadn't noticed the Joberts in the congregation, was surprised by the unseemly haste in which Finn was leaving, and a bit annoyed. He wouldn't have minded taking a look round as the church emptied, and as they reached the alleyway the side door opened on to, he said, 'What's your hurry, Finn?'

Finn didn't answer but continued to move up the alleyway, from which he could see the main doors of the church without being observed himself.

'So what are we now hanging about here for?' Christy said. 'We should head back, shouldn't we?'

'In a minute,' Finn said, because he had seen Gabrielle framed in the doorway and his heart had started to turn somersaults.

Christy followed his gaze and sighed. So that was it. Finn and his fixation on the Jobert girl. 'You are heading for bloody trouble, if you ask me.'

'Well, I haven't asked you,' Finn said. 'Weren't you the one that said soldiers should take risks? And this is the time to take them, because you are a bloody long time dead.'

At that moment a group of chattering girls, running round the corner at speed, almost cannoned into him. There was a flurry of apologies before Finn realised that one of the girls was Gabrielle's young sister. He saw that Gabrielle was now out of church and on the steps beside their parents, who were in conversation.

Yvette Jobert recognised Finn at the same time and bobbed a little curtsy. '*Bonjour, Monsieur.*'

'*Bonjour, Mademoiselle,*' Finn replied, raising his hat.

The girls giggled at Finn's response and the sound drew Gabrielle's attention. She turned and, spotting her sister, came towards them. When she saw Finn and Christy she coloured bright pink before turning to her sister and speaking sharply to her in French.

'Don't scold her,' Finn said. 'We only greeted one another, that was all.'

'That is enough,' Gabrielle said. 'Believe me, if my father caught her near a soldier, let alone talking to one, he would be very angry.' There was a pause and then she added, 'Let us hope that he hasn't noticed our absence.' And then turning to include Christy she said, 'I bid you *au revoir*, gentlemen.'

'*Au revoir, Mademoiselle,*' Finn replied, his voice slightly husky with emotion.

He watched her stride back to her parents with her chastened sister trailing behind her.

'See. Do you want it spelled out any more clearly than that,' Christy said. 'Even to stand near you is a sin in their father's eyes, so your fantasy will just have to stay a fantasy. Now let's go back to the camp and get something to eat before I fade away completely.'

THREE

Finn was so agitated by seeing Gabrielle that he found it hard to settle down when they got back to the camp and after dinner in the mess he decided to go for a walk, though the early promise of the day being a fine one was false. The sky was now gun-metal grey, with a nip in the air that showed winter wasn't that far away.

'Are you coming?' he said to Christy.

'Might as well,' Christy said good-naturedly. 'Though, God knows, you are the Devil's own company. Let's walk into the town and see if a few drinks will put a smile on your face.'

The canal was a busy thoroughfare through the week because as well as carrying produce in from the farms, it transported broken military equipment. On Sunday, however, the water was quiet and still, and the ground the other side of it was a carpet of fallen leaves. Finn was morosely kicking them in front of him when suddenly, coming down Rue de Dunkerque, Finn saw the two Jobert girls dressed in the matching blue coats, bonnets and muffs that they had worn to Mass, and they were alone.

At Mass he hadn't dared look at Gabrielle directly; now, as he drew nearer, he noticed just how fetching she looked in the bonnet that framed her pretty little face, and the blood ran like liquid fire in his body as he said with a smile, '*Bonjour*. May I say how very fine you both look?'

'We cannot speak to you,' Gabrielle said with a panicky look around her. 'If word was to get back to my father, it would be too terrible to contemplate.'

'We mean you no harm,' Finn said.

Before Gabrielle was able to answer, Christy added, 'I hope you didn't get into trouble for speaking to us this morning.'

'No, neither of us did, thankfully,' Gabrielle said, 'but only because my father was unaware of it. But to tarry here is madness, and if word got to my father, my mother would be in trouble too.' And so saying, she pulled Finn into the relative shelter of a large weeping willow at the water's edge.

Finn looked at her in puzzlement. 'Why?'

'Because Maman is supposed to guard us,' Gabrielle said almost bitterly. 'You see, my father retires each Sunday not long after dinner because he has to be up in the early hours to put on the ovens to bake the bread. My mother is supposed to accompany us on our walk, but she is tired from working in the shop all week.'

'She usually has stomachache too,' Yvette said.

'Yes,' Gabrielle said. 'Our poor mother is plagued with indigestion and it is always worse after a Sunday dinner, for all she eats so little of it. Anyway, I am seventeen years old. I can look after myself, and Yvette too. My father would like us both locked up in a dungeon with him as the gaoler. But we must go now. I'm sorry.'

'We could meet you in the *jardin public,*' Yvette said. 'We normally go there anyway when the weather is fine. We only came here today because Gabrielle thought it was going to rain.'

'Yvette, what are you suggesting?' her sister scolded.

'Nothing,' Yvette said.

'We can just meet to walk and talk together,' Finn said hopefully.

'Come on, man,' Christy said irritability. 'You must see that this is crazy.'

Strangely it was Christy's words that lit the small flame of defiance in Gabrielle's soul. What was wrong with walking and talking with two respectable young soldiers far from home, and Roman Catholic soldiers, no less? Some of her old school friends were engaged to be married, despite the war that had taken many young men away. It was no shame now to walk arm in arm with a British soldier about the town and she had seen many who did. They were, after all, allies of the French, and if she was to agree to meet with them again Yvette would be with her as her chaperone.

If her father got to hear, she decided, then she would deal with it, though she felt a little icy finger of fear trickle down her spine at the thought because her father's rages did frighten her. And yet she knew that if ever she was to have a life of her own, she had to learn to stand up to him.

'Yvette is right. We could meet at the *jardin public* next Sunday, if the day is a fine one.'

'I think you are both courting danger,' Christy said. 'Anyway,' he turned to his friend, 'doesn't it depend on whether we have time off or not? We are in the army, unless it has escaped your notice, and our time is not our own.'

Gabrielle shrugged. 'If you cannot come, there is no harm done,' she said. 'If it is fine Yvette and I will be there at about half-past two. It is what you English call a park,' Gabrielle said, 'and it is at the other side of the town, not far from the cathedral where you were this morning. Do you think you could find your way there?'

'I think so.'

'Well then, wait at the bandstand,' Gabrielle said. 'You will have a full view then of the main entrance. We will not come over to you or acknowledge you in anyway but make our way to the woodland further in. You wait a few minutes and join us there.'

She saw Finn's eyes open wide in astonishment. She grabbed hold of his hands and he felt the tingle from her touch run all through his arms as she said earnestly, 'Believe me, I am not being overdramatic.

This – oh, what do you call it? – this subterfuge is necessary to protect us both.'

'All right,' Finn said, reading the fear in Gabrielle's eyes. 'It will be done just as you say.'

'You're a fool, Finn Sullivan,' Christy said as the two girls left them.

'You can only say that because you have obviously never felt this way about anyone,' Finn said as he watched them walk away.

'No, I haven't,' Christy said. 'And I'll take care to see that it stays that way. Seems like a mug's game to me. Now, are we going for this drink or not?'

The following Sunday afternoon the sky was overcast, the air felt cold and there was a bristling wind. 'I hope we're not too late,' Finn said to a reluctant Christy, as they hurried towards the park.

'How could we be?' Christy answered. 'We set off from the camp at two o'clock sharp and it doesn't take more that fifteen minutes to walk here – less at the pace you set.'

'I just wanted to be sure we were on time.'

'What you want is to have your head examined,' Christy commented wryly. 'But we have already gone down that road and you don't listen to reason. Now settle yourself. If they have decided to come out today, despite the fact that it would be far more comfortable to sit by their own firesides, they'll be along shortly. If there is no sign of them in about fifteen minutes or so, I am going to find myself a nice warm bar somewhere and have a drink, and you can please yourself.'

'They'll be here,' Finn said firmly. 'I've been almost daily to the shop. If Gabrielle wasn't going to turn up for some reason then I'm sure that she would have found some way of telling me.'

He had been very careful to try to keep his excitement in check that morning when he served Captain Hamilton his breakfast, but he was unable to keep the smile from his face.

In the end, Hamilton said, 'What the devil is pleasing you so much, Sullivan?'

'Nothing, sir.'

'Something damned well is,' Hamilton snapped. 'You're grinning like a Cheshire cat. Got a fancy for a woman or what?'

The blush that flooded over Finn's face gave Hamilton his answer and he laughed. 'So that's it, you sly horse. Glad to see that you have taken my advice and got over Gabrielle Jobert. I hope the girl you're seeing is a decent sort.'

'Oh yes, sir.'

Finn knew that the captain would be singing a different tune entirely if he had been aware who he was waiting for that bleak Sunday afternoon. He might easily have him transferred back to his battalion, and in disgrace too. Gabrielle wasn't the only one who wanted the liaison kept secret.

A few minutes later, from his vantage point on the bandstand, he saw Gabrielle and her sister cross the road and enter the park. They didn't approach, or even look in his direction, but followed the path round, and Finn thought five minutes had never passed so slowly before he could set off to meet up with them. '*Bonjour, Mademoiselles Jobert,*' Finn said as he approached them.

He spoke to them both, but his eyes were fastened on Gabrielle and when she blushed Finn thought she was more beautiful than ever.

Yvette laughed. 'My name isn't Mademoiselle Jobert. I'm just Yvette and my sister is Gabrielle.'

'And I am Finn Sullivan,' Finn declared, as they began to walk on through the trees. 'And this is my friend, Christy Byrne.'

'Well, I am very pleased to meet you both,' Gabrielle said. 'I was surprised to see you at Mass last Sunday and then again this morning. I don't recall ever having seen a man from the British Army at Mass before.'

'Well, although I am in the British Army, Christy and I are from Ireland,' Finn said. 'And that, like France, is a Catholic country.'

'Ah, yes,' Gabrielle said. 'I wondered what the accent was. I couldn't quite place it.'

'We are in the Royal Inniskilling Fusiliers,' Finn explained. 'We have a fair few Catholics in our regiment.'

'Then I am surprised there were not more soldiers at Mass,' Gabrielle said.

'Well, there are other churches in the town and Mass at different times,' Finn pointed out.

'But probably some, now that they're away from home, will risk their immortal souls for a few extra hours in bed.'

'Besides, only a relative few were sent here for special duties,' Christy said.

'And what are those special duties, soldier boy?' Gabrielle asked with a coy smile.

Finn gave a quiet chuckle as Christy said, 'We look after the creature comforts of the officers at the British Headquarters, for the moment at least.'

'And what do you both do in your spare time?' Gabrielle asked.

'Well, our free time is governed by the officers we are assigned to,' Finn said. 'When we are at the camp some of the lads might be playing football, others will be playing cards or dominoes or reading, and I would probably be cleaning my kit and especially my rifle, lying on my bed sleeping, or writing letters home. It's pretty boring, really.'

He smiled at her and then in the bantering tone she had used, he asked with a sardonic grin, 'And what do you do with your free time, Mademoiselle Jobert?'

'I really don't have much free time,' Gabrielle said, 'what with serving in the shop and helping my mother. Sunday is my one free day and then we love to go for a walk.' She grinned mischievously at Finn and added, 'I find it a most agreeable pastime.'

'And so do I,' said Finn.

Gabrielle's eyes met Finn's and she saw the

yearning in them that she knew would be mirrored in her own. For a split second it was as if time had stood still and they were alone. Everyone else had ceased to exist.

Then Finn tore his gaze away. His heart was banging and his mouth felt unaccountably dry. He knew then that he loved Gabrielle Jobert heart, body and soul, although he had not touched her and he barely knew her. None of that mattered.

What did matter, though, was that he was a soldier from a country at war, who any moment could be ordered away. He wondered whether it was wise to begin any sort of relationship with this wonderful girl or whether it would be kinder to her to nip it in the bud. Yvette's voice brought him back down to earth, saying how brave she thought all the soldiers were.

He was unable to answer straightaway and he was grateful to Christy, who said, 'I don't know whether either of us have earned that title or not, Yvette, for we have yet to meet the enemy, though we joined up last year and have done months of training.'

Yvette's eyes were puzzled as she said in surprise, 'Do you want to fight then?'

Finn had recovered himself sufficiently enough to say, 'It's not the fighting for fighting's sake that I regret, but when my brothers write that there are boatloads of injured Irish boys arriving home just now, and I am here high and dry and never near a bullet, it makes me feel a bit of a fraud.'

'I can understand you feeling that way,' Gabrielle said, 'but I am very glad you came here for a time.' Again there was that attractive flush to her face that caused Finn's heart to beat faster as she asked, 'Do you think me very forward?'

'Why should I?' he asked.

'It's not seemly for a woman to speak of such things.'

Yvette suddenly walked ahead and Gabrielle knew that it was to give her and Finn some privacy. Christy, seeing the way the wind blew, followed Yvette.

Finn continued, 'Of course it's seemly. Yvette sort of suggested we meet today and if you hadn't agreed then I would probably never have plucked up the courage to ask you myself. I would consider it too presumptuous.'

'What is this word, presumptuous?'

'It means not my place to do that sort of thing,' Finn said. 'For one thing, your father owns a shop and I am a common foot soldier, and then you are French and I am Irish, and you are still very young.'

'And how old are you, Finn?'

'Nineteen,' said Finn

Gabrielle laughed, but gently. 'Such a great age,' she said with a wry smile. 'And prepared to lay down your life for France and Great Britain. That you have not done this yet is not the point. You will when the time comes and in my mind that makes you a great man.'

'There really is nothing great about me,' Finn said. 'I am very ordinary.'

'In my eyes you are great and so you must indulge me in this,' Gabrielle said. 'This town has been flooded with soldiers for over a year now, and of all nationalities, helping to fight in this terrible war, and never have I had the slightest desire to get to know any of those soldiers better, though I had plenty to choose from. What I am trying to say is that the way I behaved towards you is not the way that I would normally behave. I would hate you to think that I have approached other soldiers, because you are the only one. That first day I saw you standing there with your friend, I don't know what happened to me. It was just as if you had reached across the road and laid your hand upon me.'

'Oh, Gabrielle . . .' Finn breathed. He had the urge to clasp her to him and kiss her long and hard, but their relationship was too new and tenuous for such intimacy yet. So he dampened down his ardour sufficiently to be able to say, 'I too felt that certain pull between us, but any day I may be forced to leave this place. Maybe after today it would be better if we do not meet again.'

Gabrielle stopped walking. 'If you hadn't been in the British Army and sent to this town then we might never have met anyway. I know that we are on borrowed time. When you are gone, the memories of what we shared, even for a short time, will warm me and I will never regret a minute of it, I promise you.'

Finn was not convinced. 'Are you sure?'

'I have never been surer of anything in my life.'

'All right,' Finn said. 'We will do it your way. Now let's walk on because I can see you shivering with cold.'

Gabrielle hid her smile. It would be far too bold to say that it wasn't the cold that had made her limbs shake, but the nearness of Finn beside her, but she did walk on quicker and they caught up with Yvette and Christy.

Then Gabrielle said, 'We must leave you here till we meet again.'

'So soon?'

Gabrielle nodded. 'I am afraid so. My mother could not see the attraction of coming out today at all. Last week, although the rain was only drizzling after you left us, Yvette and I were soaked by the time we reached home. All week our mother waited for us to go down with colds, or worse, and she didn't want us to venture out at all today.'

'She didn't forbid you?'

'Maman never forbids,' Gabrielle said. 'She says we have enough of that from our father.'

'And we do,' Yvette put in grimly.

'She's right,' Gabrielle said with a smile. 'Our father is a very hard man and so Maman is more gentle with us, but she did ask me not to stay out too long and so I really must go now,'

'So, when will I see you again?'

'As I said, Sunday afternoon is the only time that I'm free.'

'They will be the longest seven days of my life,'

Finn said. 'And yet my time isn't my own either, though at the moment at least most of my evenings are free.'

'Till we meet again then,' Gabrielle said, and she stood on tiptoe and kissed Finn on both cheeks in the French way, and laughed at the look on his face.

Later, as he and Christy made their way into the town, Finn acknowledged that the captain was right. If he was honest with himself, what he really wanted to do with Gabrielle was roll her in the first available cornfield and show her how much he desired her. Not that he would ever even hint at such a thing. He would not debase her in that way.

He felt that he had been reborn, that his life before had been sterile and meaningless, and he knew that at that moment he wouldn't change places with anyone in the world.

The following week, when Finn met Gabrielle in the park he went alone. Christy had to work, although he admitted to Finn that he hadn't tried that hard to get the time off. 'I value my hide more than you obviously value yours,' he said. 'Anyway, last time I was hanging about like a spare dinner.'

Finn could see his point, but there was no way he was passing up a chance to see Gabrielle and so he set out the next Sunday, which was dry and fresh, though extremely cold.

When Finn joined them in the woods, Yvette

moved on ahead to give them privacy and Gabrielle smiled as she said, 'You may hold my hand if you wish to.'

Finn was only too happy to do that. 'But we must walk quickly lest you get cold,' he advised.

Gabrielle hesitated. There was an urgency about their time together rather than a normal courtship, when she could invite Finn to the house and walk out openly. And so, though she wouldn't normally have admitted such feelings on such a short acquaintance, she said in a voice barely above a whisper, 'Don't worry about me being cold, for I feel as if I have a furnace inside me, just because I am near you.'

Finn's heart soared with happiness, and he pulled her closer. 'Ah, Gabrielle, those words fill me with such joy. Now tell me about yourself. I want to know all about you.'

Gabrielle smiled as she told him about her life in the small French town not that unlike Buncrana, where Yvette went to school and she herself helped in the shop.

'Your eyes cloud over when you speak of your father,' Finn said. 'Are you so afraid of him?'

'Yes,' said Gabrielle. 'Sometimes I even think that I hate him because he is so intractable and stern. I can't see when he is going to give me some freedom and allow me to live like other girls my age. Even dressing me in the same clothes as my sister is his way of controlling me further. No seventeen-year-old girl wants to dress in clothes that suit her sister, who is four years younger. We are never allowed out alone and apart from Mass the only time we go into the town is when we are being bought clothes by my father, and then he escorts us. That is where we were going that first time that you saw me in the town. We were on our way to buy winter coats and dresses.'

'I think his character is well known amongst the townsfolk,' Finn said. 'My captain warned me not even to try speaking to you.'

'Finn, he is suffocating me,' Gabrielle said. 'And how could we help being drawn to one another?'

'I didn't think things like this happened.'

'I've read about it in romantic novels,' Gabrielle said. 'I was never allowed such books, but when I was at the school, the other girls would have them and I would smuggle them home.'

'Your father isn't the only one we have to be worried about, though,' Finn said. 'I think if the Army knew of this they'd probably post me some-where else.'

Gabrielle shivered. 'I know one day that this will happen anyway. But I want these stolen moments with you to last as long as possible.'

'And I do,' said Finn.

'If my father was a kinder, softer man,' Gabrielle went on, 'I could probably feel it in my heart to feel sorry for him because he is a baker, like his father and grandfather and great-grandfather for generations. He wanted sons to follow on from him and all he got was two girls.'

'Surely it is not too late,' Finn said. 'He may yet have sons.'

'No,' Gabrielle said. 'My mother was damaged giving birth to Yvette. There will be no sons for my father. She feels that she has failed him.'

Finn could understand only too well what a blow that would be. Farmers felt the same about sons. They often wanted a fine rake of sons to ensure continuity on the farm and yet only the first son inherited. On the death of the father, the others, who had often grafted all their lives, had to then make their own way in the world, and yet to have no sons at all would be hard on any man.

'My father says that Yvette and I will have to make good marriages,' Gabrielle continued. 'What is even scarier, he keeps hinting that he has some-one in mind for me already. Isn't that a dreadful thought?'

'It is indeed,' Finn said. 'Surely your husband is your choice.'

'He should be,' Gabrielle said. 'But six days a week I am either in the shop with my mother, or else in the bakery with my father. I see no one but customers, and apart from going to Mass my only outing is a walk with my sister on Sunday afternoon if the weather allows. We go to bed at half-past eight,' she added contemptuously. 'What sort of time is that for a girl of my age?'

'Well,' said Finn, 'we don't keep late hours in the country, with cows to milk early, but half-past eight seems ridiculous. Why have you to go to bed at such an hour?'

'Because my father goes at that time so that he is up before dawn to light the ovens,' Gabrielle said. 'When he goes to bed, we all have to go to bed. Even Saturday night, when he goes into the town himself, as the bakery is closed on Sunday, he still wants us in bed at the same time. We stay up a bit later with Maman, but not too long, for she would get in trouble if he found out and we are never sure when he will be in.'

'I can understand how frustrating you would find that,' Finn said.

Gabrielle went on, 'In the summer with the windows open I can often hear the sounds of merriment in the streets below and sometimes I long to join in and meet up with people my age. I could easily, for there is a tree just outside my window I could climb down. I wouldn't dare, of course, because Father would be bound to find out. Sometimes, though, I am so restless and the room so stuffy I have climbed into the branches of the tree to feel the breeze on my face. I always wait until Yvette is asleep to do this.'

'You must be careful that you don't fall.'

'Oh, no, it is a safe old tree.'

'You must keep safe always,' Finn said in a voice made husky with emotion. 'I would hate anything to happen to you.'

'My dear, darling Finn . . .' Gabrielle said softly. Then she added, 'Just think, if I hadn't met you almost accidentally and we had set up these meetings, we would never had got to know each other.'

'That is a dreadful thought,' Finn said. 'Because I am sure that I love you. If there was no war on, then I would take you away from here and we could get married.'

'And I would go with you anywhere,' Gabrielle said.

'I don't feel I have the right to ask you to wait for me till the war is over, though,' Finn said, and a frown creased his forehead.

'Why ever not?' Gabrielle asked.

'Well, you are young and—'

'Haven't you listened to a word I've said?' she demanded. 'I know what it is to love someone and that someone is you. I will wait for you as long as it takes. All I ask is that you come back to me safe and sound and I will go to the ends of the earth with you if you ask me to.'

'What of your father?'

'He can plot and plan all he likes, but he cannot make me marry anyone if I refuse, and I promise you with all my heart that I will only ever marry for love, and my love is you, my darling, Finn.'

Finn kissed Gabrielle that day when they parted, but though it was on the lips it was a chaste kiss. His desire for Gabrielle was mounting daily but he knew that he had to proceed carefully. She was pure and innocent, and totally without any sexual experience. He was convinced of her love for him, though, and that was all that mattered. As long as he was stationed in St-Omer, he would let nothing come between them.

Finn had reckoned without the weather. The next day was the first of November and it arrived with torrential rain that fell in sheets day after day, driven by bone-chilling, gusty winds. Eventually, the camp field resembled a quagmire, the air they breathed seemed moisture-laden, the beds were damp and all the men found it hard to sleep deeply, however tired they were. Everyone was in low spirits, worn down by the constant grey skies, the steadfast drip, drip, drip of the relentless rain and the raging wind that hurled itself at anyone who stepped out of the minimal shelter of the drenched and billowing tents.

Those like Finn and Christy, who worked in the Headquarters all day, were considered the lucky ones. Never was Finn so glad of his greatcoat, though it was usually sodden each morning by the time he got to the Headquarters, and he would leave it steaming before the fire he made up for Captain Hamilton.

The first Sunday of November passed and then the second. Finn was desperate to see Gabrielle again though he didn't know how it was to be achieved. It was torturous now when he went into the bakery, or caught sight of her at Mass.

The third Sunday loomed with no solution, and he knew that as the winter really took hold, the weather would probably get considerably worse before it got any better. It might be weeks before he could see Gabrielle. In fact he could be marched away before he got the chance at all. He knew he would go clean mad if that happened

Christy knew what was eating him and coming upon him one evening in the mess tent, staring miserably at a mug of tea, he said, 'You're mad if you have developed more than a mere fondness for Gabrielle. You're a soldier, for Christ's sake.'

'I know that,' Finn spat out. 'I know it's not sensible, but it just happened. And now with this bloody weather I don't know if I will ever see her again. We need somewhere where we can be alone.'

'Oh, is that all?' Christy said sarcastically. 'Ten a penny, places like that are around here.'

Finn's eyes blazed. 'Bugger off, Christy!' he yelled, leaping to his feet.

'Now where are you going?'

'For a walk,' Finn snapped. 'On my own.'

'It's dark, man.'

'Yeah, well, I'm not afraid of it,' Finn said, pushing off Christy's restraining arms, and he set off into the night.

It was like pitch, for the rain had eased to a drizzle that ensured there was no moon to light his way. Sounds from the camp trailed after him, growing fainter as he turned away from that and plunged into the darkness.

His eyes did adjust slightly, but not enough to stop him slipping in the mud underfoot. He heard the ground sucking at his boots as he slurped and slopped his way through thick and glutinous slurry, or slid into quagmires where he nearly lost his boot on more than one occasion. He went doggedly on, however, knowing that he needed no company that night and especially not people trying to cheer him up.

In the end, though, he was thoroughly chilled, wet through and more miserable than he had ever felt in his life before, and he decided to go back. And then, in front of him, rising out of the darkness he saw a building. He didn't recognise it, but he decided to investigate and he made his way over cautiously.

It was built in a hollow, which he didn't see in the dark night and he nearly went head over heels as he approached. He didn't know whether the place was occupied or not. It could well be, and the people in bed. He lit one of the matches he kept in the inside pocket of his tunic and by its light could see the building was very dilapidated. But that signified nothing, he thought as the match burned down to his fingers and he dropped it. He crept around the sides until he came to the front door.

There was no sign of life at all, no irate farmer appeared to challenge him and no dog erupted barking from the barns. He risked another match and in its light he saw the single-storey building had a sort of battered, neglected look about it. The door was slightly open and hanging on one set of hinges, and Finn knew the place was deserted.

Another match showed him that the odd dark shapes in front of the house were trees, and past those he saw there was a wooden bridge over the canal, which ran by the side of the house. He wanted to jump for joy because he had found the perfect place for him to bring Gabrielle.

He turned and made for the camp as quickly as he could. He would say nothing to her until he had looked inside the house and he intended to do that as soon as possible.

That night Finn hardly slept and he was up hours before the bugle call. Everyone else slumbered on as he struggled into his damp clothes. This time he took a torch, for it was still dark.

He went quicker with the torch playing before him, but still the house was a fair way from the camp.

He pushed aside the ill-fitting door, stepped inside. He was not surprised to see the whole place was dust-laden and festooned with cobwebs, nor was he surprised to hear rats scuttling away. The air smelled musty and sour, but there was no sign of the roof leaking. He crossed to the fireplace. There were ashes in the grate and even kerosene in the lamp on the mantelshelf above it.

All right, he thought, so it isn't a palace; it is in fact a very Spartan house, but it has four walls, a roof, and a grate where I could light a fire.

There was plenty of wood around that he could use. He would clean the place up before he let Gabrielle see it and light a fire to warm the place.

He began making plans in his head. He was sure that he could wedge the door shut, and the one window, though filthy dirty, was unbroken. He would bring blankets from his own bed to cover the battered sofa and they would be totally alone for the first time.

His limbs shook at that thought and he told himself that he was no marauding beast and that just because they would be alone there was no reason to forget himself and take advantage of his beloved Gabrielle. Just to hold her in his arms properly would be enough. A thrill of excitement ran through him and he was whistling as he returned to the camp.

FOUR

Gabrielle too had been trying to think of a way that she could meet Finn secretly, but her mind drew a blank, particularly while the weather remained so foul. She knew too that even if the rain eased off, winter was setting in and if she suggested going for a walk in the freezing cold, or with snow underfoot, even her mother might be suspicious for her need to be outdoors.

It wasn't fair to drag Yvette out with her either. She couldn't see any way around the problem and she began to dread seeing Finn come into the shop, or glimpse him at Mass, because to see him and not be able to communicate with him in any way was terribly hard for her.

The day after Finn had checked out the farm-house Captain Hamilton sent him to the baker's shop again. Gabrielle was alone because her mother had been struck down with her chronic indigestion and had gone to bed. Finn, looking through the shop window, decided to risk Hamilton's anger at his tardiness and he hung about outside until the last customer left.

Gabrielle's eyes leaped at the sight of him and he was by her side in seconds.

'Where's your mother?' he whispered urgently.

'In bed with her old stomach problem,' Gabrielle said. 'Oh, Finn, how I have longed to see you.'

'And I you, darling,' Finn said. 'But we might have little time to talk and the point is I have found a place we can go.'

'Where?' Gabrielle cried incredulously.

'Ssh,' Finn cautioned. He explained where the house was and the condition of it, then went on, 'It's far enough away from the camp to be undiscovered. Most of the service men go straight into town and not over a muddy field. It has a little copse in front of it, which means a ready supply of wood for the fire and even a plank over the canal.'

'I know where it is,' Gabrielle said, remembering back to a time before the war. 'That place belonged to a taciturn old man called Bernard Reynaud. He was hardly ever seen in the town and he seemed to have no family. He died in the winter of 1913, and when war was declared the land was commandeered by the army. I'm surprised that the farmhouse is still standing.'

'We could meet there after you are supposed to be in bed at night,' Finn said.

Gabrielle didn't hesitate. Her need to see Finn was greater than respectability, or even caution.

'To get out unseen and unheard,' she said, 'I will have to climb down the tree.'

'Would you be prepared to do that?' Finn asked. 'Wouldn't you be frightened?'

'I would go to the ends of the earth for you,' Gabrielle said. 'I thought you knew that. I will probably be a little afraid, but I would still do it if you are there to help me,'

Finn suddenly noticed a man studying the bakery shop window and he said quickly, 'Of course I'll be there to help you. I'll be in the yard by the tree tonight at half-past nine.'

He was halfway back to Headquarters when he realised that he had forgotten to buy the bread and pastries he had been sent for and had to return for them. By then, though, the shop was crowded and he had no opportunity to say anything further to Gabrielle. But what do I care? he thought. I have tonight to look forward to.

Gabrielle had no chance to speak to her sister privately until they reached their bedroom that same evening and then she told her quickly about Finn's earlier visit to the shop and the deserted farmhouse that he had found. Yvette was excited at the news initially, but then thoroughly alarmed when Gabrielle told her that she was meeting him that night and climbing down the beech tree outside their window to do so.

'It is the only way,' she told Yvette, seeing the worried look on her sister's face. 'If I tried to creep down the stairs I would be heard, you know that.'

'But you can't climb down a tree,' Yvette cried. 'And what if Papa finds out?'

'He won't,' Gabrielle said confidently. 'They sleep on the other side of the house.'

Yvette crossed to the window and looked out. 'It's an awfully long way down.'

'I have climbed into that tree before,' Gabrielle said. 'On summer nights, when I am too hot to sleep, I will often sit out in the top branches, but I always waited until you were asleep before I did that.'

'Yes, but I bet you have never climbed all the way down, and in the dark.'

'No I haven't,' Gabrielle admitted. 'And I won't do it now until I hear Finn arrive in the yard below. One day you will probably meet a boy or man that you will love with all your heart and soul, and if you were kept from him, you'd feel that your life was not worth living.'

'I can't ever imagine my life not worth living,' Yvette said. 'Is that how you feel about Finn?'

'Yes, Yvette, it is,' Gabrielle said. 'And remember, Finn is a soldier. Any day he could be snatched away. We must take any chance we can to be together.'

Yvette sighed. 'I can see that you have no alternative, but you needn't worry: even if I don't like what you're doing, I'll never betray you.'

'I know that. You are a lovely little sister and

if Papa ever finds out, you must deny all knowledge and I'll back you up.'

Before Yvette was able to reply they heard the sound of feet on the gravel in the yard below and a low whistle.

Gabrielle tied her cape around her waist, opened the window and shivered as the cold night air tumbled in.

'*Au revoir, Yvette,*' she said as she swung her legs over the sill and, catching hold of the branches, pulled herself into the tree. There was no moon or stars visible through those thick, rain-filled clouds, but the light from the bedroom lit the top of the tree and the heavy beam of Finn's army-issue torch illuminated the lower branches.

In a moment Gabrielle was down and in Finn's arms, and kissing him hungrily.

Though their need for each other was great, Gabrielle and Finn knew better than to linger or make any sound in the yard. They stopped only long enough for Gabrielle to rearrange her clothes and put on her cape, and then they were away, stealing through the darkened streets of St-Omer.

Yvette sighed again and closed the window, but did not fasten it so that Gabrielle could open it when she returned. Then she surveyed the room critically. Gabrielle's bed was so obviously empty; should their mother peep in on them, as she very occasionally did, she would see that immediately.

So Yvette made a mound of clothes in Gabrielle's bed, shaped just as if she was in it. And if she pretended to be asleep too then she didn't think her mother would risk rousing them by taking the lamp further into the room. Yvette undressed and got into bed, but though she snuffed out the lamp she intended to stay awake until Gabrielle returned.

Finn and Gabrielle took the back roads and alleys through the town to avoid meeting people. They longed to scurry along quickly, but held back, their senses alert to any noise that would mean they should hide themselves.

However, they reached Rue Therouanna, at the very end of town, without incident. At the bottom of the road the canal was in front of them.

As they walked the deserted banks, leaving the town further behind, Finn thought they were far enough away from being overheard to whisper to Gabrielle, 'It's just a little further to the bridge and it comes out by the little copse of trees near the house. Take care how you cross because it's a bit rickety.'

When Gabrielle saw the bridge, it had obviously seen better days she thought it safe enough, and the two of them crossed with no trouble. In the shelter of the trees, Finn put his arms around Gabrielle and she leaned against him with a sigh.

'You're shivering,' he said. 'Are you cold?'

'No, said Gabrielle, not really cold. I think I'm shivering with excitement.'

'Come on then,' Finn said. 'Let's go. My insides are churning too. Good job I've got such a powerful torch. The ground is boggy and the potholes are filled with icy water.'

'I've brought a torch too.'

'Keep it safe for later,' Finn advised. 'Mine is probably more powerful and using one will give me an excuse to hold you closer.'

'Ah, yes, please,' Gabrielle laughed and she snuggled so close against Finn that he could feel her heart thudding.

Gabrielle was quite enchanted at the cosiness of the house. A bright fire was burning in the grate, the place was lit by the kerosene lamp and Finn had a grey army-issue blanket over the sofa.

'Oh, Finn,' she exclaimed, 'I never expected it to be so nice!'

'I have cleaned it up a bit,' Finn admitted. 'Take off your cape and let us sit by the fire. I so desperately want to kiss you.'

Gabrielle knew that by creeping out of the house to meet a man, let alone allowing that man to hold and kiss her, was very wicked and if she was found out she would be beyond the bounds of respectable society. And yet she had agreed to come with Finn to this lonely farmhouse because she loved him so much she was prepared to risk everything and she gave herself over to the excitement she felt when Finn's lips met hers.

She didn't know that the feelings running through her body were the awaking of her sexuality. In fact, the only thing she was sure of was that she loved and trusted Finn. He said he would never hurt her and she believed him.

Finn didn't kiss her properly, fearing that it might frighten her. When he eventually pulled away before he forgot himself completely, Gabrielle groaned in disappointment, for she had wanted the kiss to go on and on.

'Tell me about yourself,' she said to Finn later as she lay in his arms. 'You know about my life and I need to know about yours.'

'Not that much to tell, to be honest,' Finn said. 'My life up until now has been anything but exciting.'

'You said before that you were from Ireland.' Gabrielle said, 'What's Ireland like? Did you have a farm?'

'Oh, aye,' said Finn, and he told Gabrielle about the little cottage on the farm in Buncrana, County Donegal, where he had been born and raised. 'As for Ireland, I can't describe it all to you, but just the place where I was born,' he went on. 'Donegal is totally different countryside from this. It's far more hilly – mountainous even, in places. The hills of Donegal are famous. People write poems and songs about them and until the day I marched away with the army I had never left it.'

'That's how it is, though, isn't it?' Gabrielle said. 'You never leave the place of your birth in the normal way of things. I have never left St-Omer because I have never had any reason to.'

'Have you never wondered what is beyond the town? Wanted to find out, explore?'

Gabrielle shook her head. 'No, not really.' Then she added, 'I have an aunt in Paris whom I wouldn't mind visiting. She is lovely, and promised me that when I was older I could stay with her for a holiday. She has suggested it a few times but my father has always refused.'

'Why?'

'He said my help was needed in the shop.'

'Is it?'

'Sometimes, when Maman is ill,' Gabrielle admitted. 'She can do little then, but my life will probably get easier when Yvette leaves school in the spring, when she will be fourteen. Apart from that I have never had any desire to go anywhere.'

'Oh, I always wanted to find out about other places,' Finn said. 'I used to become irritated with my brothers sometimes, especially Tom. Though I suppose as the farm will be all his one day he has reason enough to be contented.'

'Have many brothers have you?'

'Two,' Finn said. 'Tom is the eldest and Joe is two years younger. When I was small they used to play Irish music. Tom played a violin, though we used to call it a fiddle, and Joe would play a tin whistle.'

'What sort of music was it?'

'Most of it was jolly enough stuff,' Finn said, 'tunes that have been performed for years, and my sister Aggie would dance.'

'You have a sister too?'

'I had two sisters,' Finn said, 'but the elder, Aggie was a fine dancer. Everyone said it and she was at it every spare minute.' He smiled at the memory. 'Tom said he wouldn't be surprised if she danced in her sleep.'

'It all sounds so nice,' Gabrielle smiled.

'It was,' Finn admitted. 'I was sorry when it all stopped. I would hear the music through the walls when I was in bed, and the slap of Aggie's feet on the floor.'

'Why did it stop?'

'Oh, that's a long story,' Finn said. 'I mustn't keep you long from your bed either because you have to get up early and my bugle call is earlier still.'

'You mean we must go home already?'

'Not quite,' Finn said. 'I haven't been kissed enough to satisfy. And remember, my darling love, this isn't just one stolen moment. We can come here as often as we like, though I work with a company of soldiers who would think it mighty odd if I was to disappear every night and not tell anyone where I was going, and suspicion is something that we must not raise in anyone's mind.'

'Oh, but—'

'Gabrielle, listen to me,' Finn pleaded. 'You are so protected that you may not be aware of this, but the town is far more crowded on Friday and Saturday evenings.'

Gabrielle nodded. 'My father goes out on Saturday evening.'

'There you are then,' Finn said. 'And Friday

night is just as busy. All my fellow soldiers go into town on those nights, unless they are on duty, and many locals are abroad too. It's too risky to come here then. We could easily be spotted by someone.'

'And tomorrow is Friday,' Gabrielle said. 'I will miss you.'

'I will miss you too,' Finn smiled. 'But we must be careful. 'Dream about Sunday, when we will make for here again and I will kiss you until you are breathless.'

'Maybe we should practise that?' Gabrielle said coquettishly.

Finn gave a gurgle of laughter as he gathered Gabrielle into his arms and wondered if a person could die through sheer happiness.

'So, where did you slope off to last night?' Christy asked Finn the next morning as they made their way to work.

'That's my business.'

'Come on, Finn. I thought we were supposed to be mates.'

'We are,' Finn said. 'Me wanting to keep certain things to myself doesn't alter that. Let's just say that I had bigger fish to fry last night.'

Christy looked at him in astonishment. 'That sounds like you have found yourself a woman.'

'Well, what if I have?'

'You're a bloody quick worker, that's all I can say. For weeks you went round snapping the head off everyone because of some devotion to Gabrielle Jobert.'

'And you thought I was crazy and told me so.'

'I did,' Christy said. 'I'm glad that you have come to your senses. I don't suppose that this new woman of yours has got any sisters or friends that you could introduce me to?'

'I'm not introducing you to anyone,' Finn said. 'Get your own woman, like I did.'

'Well, that's a mate for you,' Christy said, slightly affronted. 'Anyone decent would take pity on me and put in a word.'

'Good job then that I don't consider myself the decent sort.'

'What's her name then?'

'That really is my business,' Finn said, as they went up the steps of the Headquarters. 'Anyway, we're here now. See you tonight.'

Finn was glad that, without him having to say much, his friend had jumped to the wrong conclusion about the girl that he was seeing, as Captain Hamilton had.

The captain was glad to see a smile on Finn's face for once. 'Good God, man,' he said, 'I thought your face was set in that glum expression you've carried around for weeks now.'

Finn had a large grin on his face as he said, 'Yes, sir. Sorry, sir.'

'You don't look in the slightest bit sorry,' the captain said with a smile. 'Did the constant rain get you down too?'

'A bit, sir. Sometimes the clothes I put on each morning were not what you might call bone dry, and that sort of starts the day off all wrong.'

'All well,' the captain said, 'the weather is the one thing that none of us can do the slightest thing about. Now, tonight I am going to a dinner with the top brass. Between you and me, something big is afoot. Anyway my dress uniform must be spotless.'

'I'll deal with that directly, sir,' Finn said. 'By the time I have finished you will be the best dressed man there, sir.'

Christy had lost no time in telling the whole camp that Finn Sullivan was seeing a girl from the town. Consequently, Finn came in for a fair bit of teasing, because he was one who had spurned the camp followers and now the dirty sod was having it away with some French piece.

'What's she like?' one of Finn's comrades asked. 'I've heard these little French damsels like a little bit of the altogether.'

Finn could hardly blame him for thinking that way. He himself had thought the French girls ripe for sex. However, he had found that most of the ordinary girls in St-Omer seemed very like the ones in his home town, and just as hidebound by the Catholic Church. But he was not going to share details of his love life with his jeering fellow soldiers, though he did say, 'You are altogether too anxious to get your leg over and the girls sense that. No wonder few of them will give you the time of day.'

There were hoots and howls of derision at Finn's words and another man called out, 'Now he is going to try and have us believe that all he does with his little French number is hold hands.'

Finn hid his smile for he had done little else. He knew that holding a girl in his arms and kissing her luscious lips would be considered incredibly tame by his comrades. However, he wanted to spend the rest of his life with Gabrielle and so, whatever it cost him, he would respect her until he placed that very special ring on her finger. But he said none of this, and he bore the ribaldry directed his way.

Eventually, they tired of it, as he knew they would, and then he remarked quietly to Christy, 'Do you fancy doing something together this evening?'

Christy eyed him speculatively. 'Haven't you got bigger fish to fry tonight?'

'No.'

'Had words, have you?'

'No, we haven't had words,' Finn said. 'Her parents don't want her to go out at the weekends because there are too many marauding soldiers about.'

'Funny then that they let her go out with you.'

'Maybe they think that I am not the marauding type,' Finn said.

Christy gave a wry chuckle. 'If they really believe

that, then I think they must be truly stupid, for you're as lusty as any other man.'

Finn laughed and he clapped Christy on the back. 'No change there then. So do you want to go out with this lustful man this evening or don't you?'

Christy put his head on one side as if considering the proposal, then said, 'D'you know, I don't mind if I do.'

Finn did, however, tell at least something of his relationship with Gabrielle in his letter to his brothers, which provoked much interest and speculation between Tom and Joe.

> I have to tell you both, I have met the most wonderful girl and her name is Gabrielle. She is the most beautiful girl in the whole world. She isn't a camp follower, I don't want you to think that, but a respectable girl from a decent Catholic family in the town. I saw her and her younger sister, Yvette, walking through the town with their father a few weeks ago. He hardly lets the two girls out of his sight and I can't say I blame him, with the place teeming with soldiers, but I did manage to sneak a word with her and we are in love and I can't tell you how happy I am.

'Well, well, well,' Joe said, folding up the letter and handing it back to Tom. 'I thought that the purpose of our young brother going to France was to fight the Hun, not try and bed every girl in the whole country.'

'He has never said he loved anyone before.'

'You know what?' Joe said. 'All that means is that this Gabrielle has held out longer than the others.'

'You think that's all it is?'

'Don't you?' Joe said. 'He's a boy. What does he know of love?'

'Huh! What do any of us?'

'Well, that's true, I suppose,' Joe conceded. 'I expect you know when it hits you. But you need to have more experience than Finn.'

Tom laughed. 'To judge from his letters he has had more experience than both you and me together.'

'I still don't see where he has the time,' Joe grumbled.

'Well, they have free time sometimes.'

'In the middle of a battle? It isn't a matter of saying to the advancing German armies, "Hold your hand, chaps, while I have a quick dalliance with a French damsel."'

'Sure this isn't just sour grapes?' Tom asked.

Joe sighed. 'You know. Tom, you could be right. Don't get me wrong. I know war is a serious business and I do miss Finn and worry about him, and I know he can tell us very few details, but he does seem to be leading the life of Riley at the moment.'

Nuala knew that her brother was in love,

because in his letter to her he had poured out his heart, knowing that she wouldn't laugh at him. She would be sixteen in the spring of 1916 and it thrilled her that her brother Finn, who she loved dearly, was beginning his very own love story.

She guessed he would not have said face to face what he committed to paper, for he spoke about his limbs trembling when he was near Gabrielle, the way his heart turned over when she smiled at him and the tingle that ran between them when they held hands. Her romantic soul drank it in eagerly and she wrote a supportive letter back to him.

Nuala would have liked to have discussed Finn's letter and his declaration of love for Gabrielle with her brothers. She wouldn't have divulged all the romantic things that she guessed were for her eyes only, but it was difficult to talk to them about anything without her mother hearing and it would never do for her to learn about Finn's romance. That would be the very last thing Finn would want.

It wasn't that they never talked of Finn; sometimes Nuala thought they talked of little else, for her mother would almost dissect every word he wrote to her and they would talk about him as a happy young child. They remembered that he usually went about the place with a smile on his face and his laughter often used to echo around the yard.

'He would talk nonstop sometimes,' Thomas John said one night. 'And plague me to death with

84

questions wanting to know the whys and where-fores of every damned thing. I would often tell him to stop his blether and give me some peace, but what I'd give now to hear him chuntering away.'

They all knew what Thomas John meant. They missed Finn and when he had been gone some months Thomas John began to look forward to the end of the war and Finn coming home. He'd say things like, 'When Finn is back where he belongs, I'll look to getting a few more cows.' Or, 'When the lad's back home, I've a mind to till that top field that's lying fallow just now.'

The end of the war seemed as far away as ever as 1915 drew to a close. Finn and Gabrielle's love-making grew more ardent as the days and then weeks passed. If they met in the park, they were as respectable as they had been in the beginning. It was different in the confines of the farmhouse though December was halfway through before Finn kissed Gabrielle properly.

She was astounded at first, and quite perturbed by the strange yearnings coursing through her body and the moan she let slip. When she felt Finn feeling her clothed body, it felt so right, so good that she let him continue.

Afterwards, in her bed, she remembered what Finn had done and how it had made her feel, and she grew hot with shame. Yet she knew she would do it all again, for when she was with him all form of reason, even what was wrong or right, didn't seem to matter any more. Further than this, though, Finn refused to go. He was more experienced than Gabrielle and knew just how easy it was to lose control, but he was aware that it got more difficult and frustrating every time he pulled away.

Finn often talked of his family and Gabrielle loved hearing of them all.

One night, as they snuggled together, Gabrielle said, 'You told me all about your sister Aggie a while ago. You said everyone had a good time with the music and everything. Why did it stop?'

'Well,' said Finn, 'that was a mystery and a half. You see, one day Aggie just disappeared.'

'Disappeared?'

'Aye,' Finn said. 'She was fifteen and they say she ran away with the gypsies. I was only five and I was scared of gypsies for some time after that. But as I grew up, I was less and less sure, because it would be such an odd thing for her to do. Tom never believed that story either, and he and Aggie were close. Not that we could talk about it openly, because our mother disowned her and we were forbidden to speak her name, but I would sometimes hear my brothers talking about her when they didn't know I was there.'

'So what do you think did happen to her?'

Finn shook his head. 'I don't know, and likely never will.'

'That is awful,' Gabrielle said. 'She was only

two years younger than I am now, and to just disappear like that . . .'

'I know,' Finn said. 'I remember the Guards coming and all, and no trace could be found of her. The point was she had nowhere to go. She had apparently taken clothes, not that any of us had many, but she had no money at all.'

'What a terribly sad story.'

'Aye,' Finn said. 'Aggie brought me up nearly as much as my mother did and was very much nicer and kinder altogether, and I remember crying for days. I kept getting into trouble because I kept forgetting we weren't supposed to mention her name.'

'But you were only a little boy.'

'That didn't matter to my mother,' Finn said. 'She used to fly into the most terrifying rages. I tell you, Gabrielle, they would scare the stoutest of hearts. We are all scared of her, Tom most of all, and she has a cane hanging up by the fire that we have felt the sting of. She beat me with it one day when I mentioned Aggies's name by mistake, but my father put a stop to it when he found out.'

'So he was kinder?'

Finn considered this. 'I suppose,' he said at last. 'Fairer, maybe. He is the only one Mammy listens to, but except for Nuala, hugs and kisses were just never part of our growing up.'

'No, they wouldn't have been in mine if my father had had his way,' Gabrielle said. 'But in that at least my mother defied him. My life seems so dull in comparison to yours, though. Is that the end of the story?'

'Almost,' Finn said. 'In Ireland many people can make a story out of nothing and memories are kept alive by being spoken about from one to another, often for years. Aggie's disappearance, though, and the speculation surrounding it was overshadowed, because only a few days afterwards, a man called McAllister, who taught the boys to play the tunes and the girls the dancing, was found dead.'

'Was that a mystery too?'

'No,' Finn said. 'He was apparently thrown from his horse. It was spoken about and discussed, and was quite the news for a while.'

'What of your other sister?' Gabrielle asked. 'The one you said got all the hugs and kisses. Is there a story about her too?'

'Not much of a one,' said Finn, smiling at the thought of Nuala. 'Maybe because she is the youngest my parents spoiled her terribly. She is four years younger than me and pretty as a picture and, despite my parents, she has a lovely nature. She is nurse-maid to the children of the big Protestant family beside us and loving every minute of it.' He looked at Gabrielle and smiled. 'She knows all about you, for I write and tell her, and I would love you to meet her.'

'I would like to meet them all,' Gabrielle said.

'And so you shall, my darling,' Finn said. 'Just as soon as the war is over, I am out of the army and the world is a safer place.'

FIVE

Gabrielle's Parisian relatives were coming to spend the festive season with the Joberts, as they had done many times before.

'They are nice,' Gabrielle told Finn. 'Really nice. Uncle Raoul is a dear, and Aunt Bernadette is such fun. She's always up to the minute with fashion though she is older than Maman.'

'When are they due to arrive?'

'Christmas Eve,' Gabrielle said. 'And they usually stay until New Year. The thing is, it will be almost impossible to see you while they are here.'

'Why?' Finn cried.

'Well, for one thing, my aunt thinks it's quite monstrous that Yvette and I should be expected to go to bed at half-past eight in the evening. It doesn't happen when she is here, because she always says she wants to see more of her nieces, and after the evening meal we all sit and talk or even play games. Anyway, I couldn't risk my slipping out because the guest bedroom is on the same side of the house as our room, and Aunt Bernadette is always saying what a light sleeper she is.'

Finn resigned himself to not seeing Gabrielle for the rest of the year, but he tried to keep any resentment out of his voice or his manner; it wasn't Gabrielle's fault.

He'd bought her a silver locket for Christmas. It had cost him a great deal of money, especially as he had had it engraved 'F loves G Christmas 1915'. He had no photograph to put in it so instead enclosed a lock of his hair, and he gave it to Gabrielle as they sat on the sofa in front of the fire in the farmhouse the evening before Christmas Eve.

She was surprised and enchanted with her present. It was beautiful and she knew Finn must have had to save up for it because soldiers were not highly paid.

'Don't worry about the cost of it,' Finn said when she expressed concern about him spending so much. 'That's not how to receive a present. You are worth more than fifty thousand lockets, and if I had the means I would shower you with jewellery.'

Gabrielle smiled. 'I should not want that. I am content with this locket bought with such love. Thank you so much. I will wear it beneath my clothes always,' she promised as Finn fastened the chain around her neck. 'It will lie against my heart. I am only so sorry that I have nothing to give you in return.'

'You don't give a present to expect one back,'

Finn said. 'Just thinking of you wearing the locket is present enough for me. It will remind you of me when I am gone from this place.'

'I don't like to think of that time,' Gabrielle said, her voice forlorn. 'I know one day it will come, but when it does I shall have no need of any locket to remind me of you. You are ingrained in my heart and you will take a sizeable piece of it when you leave. Have you any idea when it will be?'

'Nothing official,' Finn said. 'They don't tell soldiers useful things like that, but I am concerned for you because you told me that your father would want a good marriage for you and your sister because he has no sons.'

'It is not my fault that my father has no sons,' Gabrielle said. 'And I told you already that I would only ever marry for love, and the only man I love is you.'

'It might be ages before I am able to return for you,' Finn told her. 'Years even, because there's no time limit on war.'

'I will wait for you for however long it takes,' Gabrielle said simply. 'I love you with all my heart and soul, and that will never change.'

Finn felt a lump rise in his throat. He took Gabrielle into his arms and when she snuggled tight against him he felt that his heart would burst for love of this beautiful girl. When his tongue slid into her mouth between her opened lips, he heard her gasp of pleasure. He let his tongue dart backwards and forwards until Gabrielle was unable to stop herself groaning in desire.

That night, maybe the thought they wouldn't see each other for days, or the gift of the locket and their declaration of their love for one another, conspired to make Gabrielle ready for more. Finn could feel it in every line of her body. When he began stroking her clothed body she moaned with the sheer pleasure of his touch. He began to open the buttons on her blouse, thinking any moment that she would stop him, but instead she helped him. He slipped his trembling hands inside and when he cupped his hands around her plump, firm breasts for the first time she gave a sigh of contentment.

Finn felt as if he was on fire, and when Gabrielle arched her back to make it easier for him to reach every part of her, he knew that she was ready. He could take her here and she would do nothing to stop him.

But how could he do that to the woman he loved and then leave her unprotected and un-supported? The effort it took for Finn to pull back was immense, especially when Gabrielle clung on to him.

'Stop, Gabrielle!' he cried, disentangling himself with difficulty.

'I don't want to stop.'

Finn sighed. 'Neither do I,' he admitted.

'Then . . .'

'Gabrielle, you don't know what you're saying.'

Finn said. He pulled away from her slightly; to touch her again now would be madness. 'I love you and desire you so much and yet I know I must show you respect because I can offer you nothing. But if we go on with this much longer, then there will come a point when I will be unable to stop. Do you understand what I am telling you, Gabrielle?'

'I think so,' Gabrielle said, but really she was ignorant of the sexual act and only knew that she had thoroughly enjoyed what Finn had been doing to her and had wanted it to go on much longer.

Finn saw her confused face and suppressed a smile as he leaped to his feet and pulled her up with him. 'Come on,' he said, as he fastened her blouse. 'Let's get you home before I forget all about my principles and ravish you totally.'

Gabrielle wasn't sure what ravish meant, but she was sure that she wouldn't mind if it was Finn doing it, and so she smiled demurely and said, 'Yes, please,' and Finn's laughter rang around the room.

Despite missing Finn, Gabrielle enjoyed her aunt and uncle's visit. The minute they stepped over the threshold, the air in the house seemed lighter. She couldn't remember having a happier Christmas Day. What really made an impression on Gabrielle that year was the laughter around the table as they all tucked into a truly sumptuous meal, and the silly party games they played afterwards.

She realised, possibly for the first time, that pleasure wasn't a sin and that life didn't always have to be the austere, sterile one demanded by her father and followed blindly by her down-trodden mother. Her life would not be like that, she resolved. When I marry Finn our life together will be full of happiness. I shall see to it that it is.

She got ready for Mass the first Sunday after Christmas, knowing that, surrounded as she would be by her aunt and uncle as well as her parents, she would dare not even sneak a look at Finn. It had been the same on Christmas Day, and so she felt rather than saw the melancholy surrounding him, but could do nothing to ease it.

The following morning Gabrielle dressed to go into the shop, because never before had her father allowed the visit of her aunt and uncle to upset her work at all. She had no idea that her aunt had decided to try to do something about this.

Bernadette went straight into the bakery kitchen where Pierre was working. He looked up in surprise, for she had never done such a thing before.

'Is anything the matter, Bernadette? he asked. 'Are you all right?'

Bernadette was a carbon copy of his wife, Mariette, though her features were firmer somehow. She and Pierre had always got on well, so she smiled as she said, 'I am perfectly well, thank you, Pierre. But I feel I do need to speak to you about your daughters.'

'What about them?'

'Well, the girls should be allowed to go into town sometimes,' Bernadette said. 'What can happen to them in their own town in broad daylight?'

'You don't know the worry of trying to rear daughters decently these days,' Pierre said morosely. 'More especially now that the town is teeming with soldiers and some of the girls' morals very lax because of it. Anyway, Gabrielle has her duties in the shop and Yvette is at school all day.'

'Ah, that is something else I need to talk to you about,' Bernadette said. 'Surely Gabrielle deserves time off sometimes, and isn't Yvette on holiday now?'

'Gabrielle's help is needed,' Pierre said doggedly.

'Surely not all day and every day,' Bernadette said. 'While we are here at least, Raoul can give you a hand, and if Mariette would take a turn in the shop it would free Gabrielle for a few hours. The girls, and especially Gabrielle, need some fun in their lives.'

'Life is not one long entertainment, Bernadette, whatever you think,' Pierre growled, and his eyebrows puckered in annoyance. 'And did you not hear me tell you about the soldiers?'

'Of course I heard you,' Bernadette said. 'I would have to be deaf not to hear you, but do you really think that some soldier is going to leap on them as soon as they leave the shop, especially as they will be in my charge?'

'No,' Pierre had to admit. 'I suppose if you were with them it might be all right.'

95

'I would like their company,' Bernadette said. 'You don't know how I envy your two fine girls like that.'

Pierre thought daughters were all very well, but sons would have done him far better. Bernadette and Raoul, however, had neither a chick nor child to call their own and he acknowledged that that must be hard.

'All right,' he said with a sigh. 'You win. While you are here, Bernadette, Gabrielle will have lighter duties and you may take her out now and again, and Yvette too.'

'Thank you, Pierre,' said Bernadette. She thought it was a start at least, and she scurried off to tell the girls the news.

She found Gabrielle fully dressed, but still in the bedroom, sitting on the bed and staring fixedly out of the window. She was so preoccupied that Bernadette stood for a few moments on the threshold and Gabrielle was unaware of her. 'Gabrielle,' she said softly and then, as the girl turned towards her, she was staggered by the bleak look in her eyes before she recovered herself and replaced her sadness with a smile of welcome.

Bernadette told her what had transpired between her and Pierre. Even as she did so she wondered if Mariette or Pierre had ever really looked at their elder daughter. It was obvious to her aunt that the girl was burdened over something. Small wonder, Bernadette thought, when she was almost a prisoner in her own home.

Gabrielle wished that she could have confided in her aunt, but much as she loved her and her uncle Raoul, a large and jovial man, she knew she couldn't. However, she was very pleased at the thought of time away from the shop and outings with her aunt, and she began to get ready while Bernadette went off to find Yvette.

Finn, of course, did not know this, so when the captain dispatched him for bread on Monday morning, he went eagerly. He thought if Gabrielle was alone he might manage a word or two with her at least. However, Gabrielle was nowhere to be seen, and though Finn hung about outside for as long as he dared, eventually he had to buy the captain's loaves from her mother.

The next day was the same. But returning to the Headquarters, he spotted Gabrielle with her sister and a woman he presumed to be her aunt. They were ambling through the town, laughing and joking together, and looked as if they hadn't a care in the world, while he felt as if his heart was breaking.

Captain Hamilton took one look at him when he returned and said, 'Good God, man, what the hell's the matter with you? You look as if you've lost a pound and found a penny.'

'Yes, sir,' Finn said. 'Tell you the truth, sir, I feel a bit like that.'

'Woman troubles again, I suppose?'

'Yes, sir.' Finn said. 'Sort of, anyway.'

'Ah, well, no doubt it will resolve itself,' the captain said. 'And if it doesn't, well, you're not going to be here much longer so it will hardly matter.'

Although Finn had known that the day would come when he would leave St-Omer, he suddenly felt sick to the pit of his stomach. He didn't expect to be told anything, but he asked, 'Have you any news of when, sir?'

'Nothing definite,' the captain said. 'I know that some units are moving out by the end of January. You won't be going then, because you won't move until we go, but I reckon we will all be left here by the spring.'

He caught sight of the woebegone look on Finn's face at his words and he laughed. 'Now what's up with you?' he demanded. 'You knew it was only a matter of time until it came to this. You are here to fight a war, and while a carnal liaison with a young French maid is a great attraction, it must be no more than that for a soldier going to war. You don't need me to tell you this, do you?'

'No, sir.'

'Well then, let's have no more long faces and heartfelt sighs,' the captain said. 'You get on with the job you came to do and in this instance that means brewing me up some tea.'

'Right away, sir,' Finn said.

Finn tried, but his heart felt heavy, and at the turn of the year he looked forward to 1916 with no enthusiasm whatsoever.

* * *

98

Bernadette and Raoul were to return to Paris on Monday 3 January.

The day before, as they tucked into their large Sunday dinner after Mass, Bernadette said to Gabrielle, 'If your parents are agreeable, how would you like to return to Paris with me and your uncle? We would love to have your company for a while.'

'We would indeed,' Raoul put in. 'A pretty young woman about the house is just the thing for chasing away the winter blues.'

'And you would see all the sights of Paris. What do you say?'

Before she had given her heart to a soldier that she loved and longed to see again with every thread of her being, Gabrielle would have thought she had died and gone to Heaven to receive such an offer, but now it was too late. She couldn't leave. She honestly thought if she didn't see Finn soon she would die of a broken heart.

She could see by her father's heavily furrowed brow and his eyes full of indignation that he was seriously displeased by the bombshell that Bernadette had dropped and before she was able to voice any sort of opinion her father snapped out, 'I would have thought it good manners, Bernadette, to discuss this with me and ask my permission, before voicing it in front of Gabrielle.'

'It only occurred to Raoul and me as we walked home from Mass,' Bernadette said. 'Mariette had no objection and so I thought I would see what

Gabrielle thinks about it. I have so enjoyed her company, and that of Yvette too, this holiday.'

'And what do you think, my dear?' Raoul said. 'You haven't said a word yet.'

Gabrielle knew that she had to be careful. To refuse this offer point-blank or show the slightest disinclination at all would probably evoke suspicion, as well as hurting the feelings of her aunt and uncle, and so she said carefully, 'it is awfully kind of you and I would love to do this, but I feel my father would miss me in the shop just now. If my parents are agreeable I could perhaps go to Paris in the spring when the weather will be warmer. By then, Yvette will have left school and can take my place in the shop.'

'I still don't want my daughters being trailed across the country,' Pierre said. 'They are far better at home and then I rest easier in my bed. You must put this ridiculous notion out of your head.'

Mariette seldom argued with her husband – she was well used to his autocratic ways – but she had seen the disappointment flash across her sister's face and so she said, 'I don't see how you can say the idea's ridiculous, Pierre. Bernadette and Raoul will look after our daughter as if she was their own. And it would be good for the girl to see more of life before she settles down. I don't see what harm it will do, though Gabrielle spoke good sense when she said that waiting until the spring would be better.'

Pierre was dumbfounded that his wife had questioned his authority.

'Is a man not to be master in his own home now?' he spluttered eventually.

'Of course,' Mariette said rather impatiently, 'and I'm sure if you think this through you will see it is the best solution all round.'

Pierre looked around the table and saw them all ranged against him, though Gabrielle didn't look as pleased as he thought she would. Maybe she didn't want to get her hopes up in case he forbade the trip. However, he acknowledged that she was a good girl, she worked hard and had never given them a minute's bother, and as long as Bernadette and Raoul looked after her like a hawk, he really couldn't see what he had to worry about.

He thought too that it might bring the bloom back to Gabrielle's cheeks because she had looked decidedly pasty for days. 'All right,' he said at last after the silence had stretched out between them. He looked at Bernadette and Raoul. 'Gabrielle can visit you in Paris in the springtime and I trust that you will look after her well.'

'You have my solemn word on that,' Raoul said, and stood up to shake Pierre's hand.

Bernadette and Raoul returned to Paris and Gabrielle took her place behind the counter in the shop. Finn was hardly able to believe the evidence of his own eyes when he saw her standing there. He felt as if his heart had actually stopped beating because he had wondered if Gabrielle's love for him had waned. He approached hesitantly.

'Hello, Gabrielle,' he whispered and he raised his eyes and met her love-filled ones. The ache in his heart disappeared and was replaced by joy that seemed to fill every part of him. He needed no further words to know how Gabrielle still felt about him. It was written all over her face.

'I couldn't get away sooner,' Gabrielle said. 'But my uncle and aunt are gone now and so I could meet you this evening,'

'Oh, yes, my darling. I can barely wait that long.'

'Nor I.' Gabrielle gave a gasp as Finn reached over and took her hands from the counter and kissed her fingers. Shafts of desire ran down her spine and she bit on her lip to suppress the groan.

'Till tonight, my darling,' Finn said, and Gabrielle hoped the hours would speed by until she could be in Finn's arms again.

But they dragged as they do for anyone in such circumstances, and by the time the Joberts sat down to their evening meal, she was on tenterhooks. She was unable to eat, for she wasn't hungry for food.

'Are you upset because your aunt and uncle are gone?' Mariette asked.

'Not really,' Gabrielle said.

'Well, something is wrong with you,' Pierre said. 'For you have been unable to settle all day.'

Gabrielle was desperate to get away from her parents and their watchful eyes and so she said, 'I am just so tired. I'm not used to late hours and I am feeling very weary. I think I will seek my bed before long.'

'You do right, if that is how you feel,' Pierre said. 'Bed is surely the place for tired people, and I will probably do the same thing myself soon.'

Gabrielle, though, wasn't in the least bit tired. She had never felt more awake. She lay on the bed and tried to wait patiently until it was time to climb down the tree into her beloved's arms.

'You're meeting Finn tonight, aren't you?' Yvette said when she came up to bed not long after Gabrielle.

Gabrielle nodded. 'Is it so obvious?'

'Yes, it is,' she said. 'Even Papa noticed.'

'I can't help it,' Gabrielle said. 'I haven't seen Finn alone for ten days.'

Yvette asked, 'What are you going to do when he leaves, because he can't stay here for ever?'

'I truly don't know,' Gabrielle said. 'I suppose I will cope as well as anyone else if I have to.'

Yvette doubted that. She remembered her sister's behaviour throughout the festive period and that it had been tempered slightly only because of the presence of her aunt and uncle. But it was a problem that Gabrielle had to deal with on her own and so Yvette said nothing more.

*   *   *

103

As usual, Finn was waiting for her beneath the tree, his arms outstretched, and she snuggled into them. As they kissed Finn felt Gabrielle's body yielding against his and he felt himself harden as his own desire rose. Eventually he pulled away from her and as they began walking through the alleyways of the town, he knew he would have to be very strong that night – maybe strong enough for both of them if he wanted to protect Gabrielle.

To take his mind off his own emotions he asked her about her uncle and aunt, and their visit.

'Ooh, it was lovely,' Gabrielle said. 'Their visits before were sometimes curtailed because Uncle Raoul was busy running his business in Paris, but he sold that last year. He has a weak heart and said he wasn't killing himself for a business that would die with him anyway.'

'Have they no children to hand it on to?'

'No,' Gabrielle said. 'That's why they think so much of Yvette and me. I do love them very much, but all through their visit all I could think of was how much I was missing you. As I said, Aunt Bernadette said that it was ridiculous for us to be sent to bed at eight thirty, but if my father didn't insist on that, then I would never have been able to sneak out and see you at all.'

'No, that's true enough,' Finn agreed. 'The way he goes on, though, is not fair to you. You go nowhere. Even back home in Buncrana, my brother Joe and I used to go to the socials run by the Church on a Saturday evening. Mind you,' he said, with a rueful grin, 'I had to fight for the right to do that. Mammy couldn't believe that I wanted to go when I turned sixteen. But sometimes you have to fight for what you want in this life. I told my young sister the same, for she used to sway like the wind, do whatever Mammy wanted. She stood against her too in the end, because she wanted to be nursemaid to the people in the Big House.'

'I never defy my father.' Gabrielle said. 'I do whatever he wants and so does everyone else in the house.'

'That worries me a little,' Finn admitted. 'You have said that your father wants you to make a good marriage and I am afraid that—'

Gabrielle came to a sudden stop and, facing Finn, took his face between her hands. 'Listen to me, Finn,' she said. 'I love you with all my heart and soul. My life is nothing without you and if I cannot have you then I will have no one.'

'But if your father—'

'If I ever felt that I couldn't stand against my father, then I would go to my aunt and uncle in Paris,' Gabrielle said. 'I know they would help me.'

'I saw you with your aunt in the town a couple of times.' Finn said. 'You looked so carefree.'

Gabrielle was a little irritated by what Finn said. 'How shallow you must think me,' she answered. 'That carefreeness was an act I was putting on; to behave any other way would have been unkind to my aunt and uncle, and also would make my parents angry and suspicious.' She looked at Finn and cried, 'My throat was so constricted with love of you I could barely eat.'

'You're not crying?' Finn said, appalled.

'I'm trying not to,' Gabrielle said brokenly. She gave a sigh and went on, 'But I'm hurt that you could think so little of me.'

They had reached the farmhouse and Finn kicked the door open and pulled Gabrielle inside.

'Oh, my darling, I'm so sorry,' he said, unfastening Gabrielle's cape as he spoke. He let it fall to the floor as he kissed the tears from her face. He couldn't believe he had made his beloved cry and he didn't know how he could make it up to her. He drew her towards the sofa before the fire and lit the lamp. 'I deserve to be hung, drawn and quartered for upsetting you so,' he said.

'You have no reason to distrust me,' Gabrielle said. 'My uncle and aunt were all for taking me back to Paris with them. Before I met you I would have loved to go, but all I could envisage were more weeks before I could see you and I knew that I couldn't have borne that.'

'How did you get out of it?'

'I told them that it would be better for me to go in the spring when Yvette has left school and will be able to take my place in the shop.'

'Captain Hamilton says that we will be gone from here by the spring,' Finn said. 'Some are moving out at the end of January, but I'll not leave until the officers do. So it might be a good thing for you to go to Paris for a while.'

Gabrielle fell as if a tight band was squeezing her heart at the thought that in a few short months Finn would be gone. What was Paris to that?

She knew when he went from here it would be as if he had disappeared from her life, for there was no way that they could communicate, and she knew that that would be really hard for her, for them both; she didn't imagine that it would be any easier for Finn to bear. She tried to bite back the sob, but Finn heard it and he held her even tighter as she said forlornly, 'Every moment must count from now, my darling, because these are what I must commit to memory until you come back to claim me.'

Finn too felt a lump in his throat as he bent to kiss Gabrielle, and that kiss unlocked fires of passion in both of them. The poignancy of their situation and the threat of parting so soon – and maybe for years – were in their minds, and Finn felt as though desire was almost consuming him.

Gabrielle made no move to stop him as he kissed her neck and throat. Her sobs turned to little gasps of pleasure as he unbuttoned the bodice of her dress and fondled her breasts. Even when he eased her bloomers from her and slid his hands between her legs while his lips fastened on her nipples she wanted him to go on and on, and do something to still the feelings coursing through her. She wasn't afraid, because she was with Finn and she knew he would never harm her.

There was a sudden sharp pain as Finn entered

her and then the rapturous feeling as they moved together as if they were one person. She felt enveloped in total bliss that rose higher and higher in waves of exquisite joy, so that she cried out again and again.

Eventually their movements slowed and then stopped. Finn slipped off Gabrielle and on to the floor beside her, and she lay back on the sofa in sated satisfaction with her eyes closed.

Suddenly she realised that Finn was crying. 'My darling! What is it?'

Finn turned a tear-washed face to her. 'Gabrielle, do you know what we have just done?'

Gabrielle nodded. 'I'm pretty sure that you have done what you threatened to do to me before.'

'What was that?'

'Ravish me,' Gabrielle said, smiling at Finn, who looked so ashamed of himself.

'Yes,' said Finn. 'Dear God, I deserve horse-whipping. How could I have been so stupid?'

'Don't,' Gabrielle said. 'It's the most wonderful experience I have ever had.'

'You don't understand,' Finn said. 'I wanted to protect you. My feelings for you just overwhelmed me. I am so sorry.'

'It isn't all your fault,' Gabrielle said. 'I could have put a stop to it if I had wanted to. Maybe when two people love as we love, it's impossible to wait.'

Finn got up and began to dress. What if she was to have a child? That would be the very worst thing to happen to an unmarried woman. And it wasn't as if he would be there to share the burden with her. That thought brought him out in a cold sweat.

Gabrielle seemed not in the least bit worried about that and she looked into Finn's eyes as she said, 'With or without marriage I now belong totally to you, Finn Sullivan. My lover and my very own British soldier.'

Finn felt his stomach give a lurch as the passion rose in him at Gabrielle's words. He knew, however, that he must never let himself be overcome in that way again, and he pushed her from him gently and said, 'Get dressed, my darling, before you catch your death of cold.'

SIX

Gabrielle knew that Finn's family would worry about him as much as she did when he left, but they at least would have letters to sustain them. Maybe, she thought, she could write to them for news of Finn. His parents might not be that understanding, but his sister or brothers were probably more approachable. So one evening she said, 'What are your brothers like? The only thing I know about Tom is that you consider him to be a plodder.'

'He is,' Finn insisted, 'and he would be the first to admit that there is little else to say about him. He doesn't mind in the least that each day is like the one before it and he knows that tomorrow will be just the same. The only thing that disturbs him is the milk yield being down. Yet he is the kindest man that walked the earth and it would be very hard to dislike him. It's just that he won't stir himself to do anything, not even to come to the socials with me and Joe.'

'So Joe is not like Tom?'

'No,' Finn said, 'he is more like me, though maybe not as determined. He has been saying for a few years now that he doesn't want to stay in Buncrana all his life. Once he told me that he wouldn't mind trying his hand in America. I suppose the war has put paid to that, but I sometimes wonder if he will ever leave the farm. Yet after my father's day, everything will go to Tom.'

'Joe would do well to leave then,' Gabrielle said. 'Otherwise he will be left with nothing, though it hardly seems fair.'

'I suppose not,' Finn agreed. 'Though in this case it seems so, because Tom suits the work much better than Joe or me. Particularly me. My father always said I was too impatient to be a good farmer. I didn't care about that because I didn't want to be a farmer all my life, but I tried my damnedest just the same because I loved my father dearly.'

'More than your mother?'

'I'm not sure what I feel about my mother,' Finn admitted. 'I was afraid of her for so long.' He gave a rueful smile. 'I suppose that I have tried to respect her, but, hand on heart, I can't say I love her. Biddy Sullivan, I would say, is a hard woman to love.'

'What a shame,' Gabrielle said, and then added, 'Biddy is a strange name. Is it Irish?'

'I suppose it is,' Fin said. 'Her full name isn't Biddy, of course, it's Bridget.'

'Bridgette,' Gabrielle said. 'That is like the French name Brigitte, and it is a shame to shorten it to Biddy.'

Finn laughed. 'It's lovely the way you say it.'

'And isn't it a tragedy for people who never experience love in their lives?' Gabrielle went on. 'My father is the same. Somehow, I cannot imagine my mother ever loving him.'

'From what you say,' Finn said with a broad grin, 'I imagine that my mother and your father would suit one another. Maybe we should maroon the two of them on a desert island somewhere.'

'Oh, yes,' Gabrielle giggled. 'Maybe your mother loves your father, though. You said before that he is the only one that she listens to.'

'That's right, but I don't know whether that is love or not. My father is a good man, and one I always tried to please, and yet nothing I did was quite good enough. In a way it is my father's fault I enlisted.'

'Did he want you to?'

Finn laughed. 'Just the opposite. I did it, in a way, to spite him.'

'Do you regret it?'

'No,' Finn said, putting his arms around Gabrielle as they sat on the sofa, 'though I did think that a soldier's life is more exciting than it is. I also thought I might get treated more like a man, after being at the beck and call of my father and brothers, only to find that in the army I am at the beck and call of all and sundry. But then I came to St-Omer and I met you, and my life was turned upside down because I love you with everything in me.'

112

'I am the same,' Gabrielle said. 'Without you my life is worth nothing.' She lifted her face as she spoke and their eyes locked for a moment, then their lips met in a kiss that left Gabrielle gasping for more.

Since they had made love that one time, their lovemaking had got more daring so that as January gave way to February and then March – coming in like the proverbial lion, gusting through the streets of St-Omer – not only did Finn know every area of Gabrielle's body, she had began to explore his too. Finn had wanted her to do this and she had begun tentatively and timidly, hardly able to believe that she was actually touching the most private parts of a man.

In the cold light of day afterwards, just the thought of doing so had embarrassed her so much she grew hot with shame. In the heat of passion, though, it was different, and anyway, when she saw how much pleasure she gave Finn, she persevered. Her one desire in life was to please him. They did come dangerously close to making love again a few times, but Finn always made sure they stopped short of it and although this made him as frustrated as hell, he would not go any further.

Gabrielle, however, was still remarkably naïve about how babies were conceived, or how they got out once they were inside a woman, because she had been told nothing. She didn't have the advantage of girls reared on a farm who might see the animals mating and, later, the birth of the babies, and she had no friend with a confiding married sister or young aunt who could have put her right about things.

She knew the Church had said it was wrong to go with a man until a woman was married, but no one had told her what that actually meant. She had no doubt, though, that they would say what she and Finn was doing was a sin, because the Church semed to see sin in everything enjoyable and she certainly had no intention of telling in the confessional anything she and Finn were doing. How could you explain things like that to a man, even if he was a priest?

She didn't know either why the bleeding that used to happen every month had stopped. When it had begun two years before and she had thought she was dying, her mother just told her that it was something that happened to women. It wasn't to be discussed, and certainly not with men, and there was no need to make a fuss about it. She hadn't been told that it had anything to do with fertility, and so when she didn't have a monthly show of blood, she didn't automatically associate it with what she and Finn had been doing.

Neither did Mariette, who knew nothing of her daughter's nocturnal sojourn with a British soldier. She did know, however, that there had been no bloodied rags in the bucket she had left ready and she said to Gabrielle, 'Funny that your monthlies should have stopped. Do you feel all right?'

'Yes,' Gabrielle said. 'In fact I have never felt better.'

'Well, you certainly look all right,' Mariette said.

And Gabrielle did. She had developed a bloom on her skin that had not been there before because she was thoroughly loved by a man she loved in return. Even her not very observant parents noticed in the end and remarked on it, and many of the customers said the same, while Finn thought she had never looked more beautiful.

'We'll leave it for now then,' her mother said, 'but if they don't return then I will ask the doctor to have a look at you. Just as well to be on the safe side.'

However, other matters took precedence. At the end of March, Yvette was fourteen and would be leaving school at Easter. In early April, Aunt Bernadette wrote to Gabrielle, repeating the invitation she had made at Christmas.

'I don't really know how I can refuse this time,' Gabrielle confessed to Finn.

'When are they arriving?' Finn asked.

'After the schools are closed, and that is less than two weeks away.'

'Darling, I might be gone before then,' Finn said. 'The camp is on high alert. Any day we expect orders to move out.'

'Oh, Finn . . .'

'Go on with your uncle and aunt to Paris,' Finn urged. 'It might make it easier for you.'

Gabrielle tossed her head impatiently. 'Nothing will make the loss of you easier.'

Finn put his arm around her and gave her a squeeze. 'My darling,' he said, 'in many ways I wish you and I had not met and fallen in love because it will be harder for us to part. But part we must and our lives must take different paths for some time. When the Army says "March", then I must march.'

Distressed though Gabrielle was, she knew Finn spoke the truth, and she wished she could hold back time, even for just a little while. Once Finn left St-Omer she would be desperately worried about him. As so many soldiers had already left, he and Christy had been drafted in to help with the wounded again. She was aware that more and more came every day and the hospitals were filled to breaking point.

The talk around the Jobert table at night, and often in the shop too, was of the number of Allied soldiers, and especially British, that had been killed or injured on the battlefield so far, of the disbanded camp, and more and more troops going off to join the carnage being enacted in many areas of France.

Gabrielle never contributed in such discussions. In fact, if she could have done so she would have stopped up her ears so that she didn't hear such things. She wasn't stupid, and knew that when Finn left here he would probably soon be in danger, and could well become one of the casualties, but her love was so deep and all consuming that she imagined he could fold it around him like a cloak and it would protect him from any German onslaught.

Bernadette and Raoul arrived in the middle of April, and wished to return the following day. That shook Gabrielle, who thought that she might have another few days' grace and, despite the risks, she had to see Finn one more time. She communicated this to him in a note that she gave him with his change in the bakery that morning.

It was late that night when Gabrielle went to bed. Yvette was already asleep and Gabrielle forced herself to lie and wait until she heard everyone settle for the night and the house grow quiet.

Then she opened the window carefully. She knew Finn would be waiting for her, though she couldn't see him for she dare not turn on her torch, her aunt and uncle's bedroom being only a few feet away. She had never before climbed down the tree with such care, especially as she had the cape in a bundle under her arm.

In the bakery yard Finn had waited so long that he was worried that something had happened to prevent Gabrielle meeting him. He had begun wondering how long he should stay before returning to camp when he heard the distinct rustle of the tree.

Then she was above him, and the next minute in his arms and kissing him, and the next fastening her cape about her. Not a word was spoken until they were in an alleyway well away from the bakery.

Then Gabrielle said, 'Oh, Finn, have you had to wait a long time?'

'No matter. You are here now,' he said.

'I didn't think they would ever stop talking and go to bed,' Gabrielle said. 'I had already—'

'Hush,' said Finn. 'It is of no consequence. I would wait for you till the end of time. Don't you know that? Now, let's hurry. I can barely wait to hold your body close to mine.'

Once inside the farmhouse there was no hesitation. They didn't light the lamp and so they only had the flickering light of the fire. As Finn began to caress Gabrielle, she helped him remove all her clothes for the very first time. Finn tore off his uniform, and when he too stood naked Gabrielle gasped as even in the dim firelight she could see how aroused he was.

Finn pushed her gently back on the sofa and lay on top of her, skin to skin. She shivered in delicious anticipation, and Finn knew he wanted Gabrielle more than he had ever wanted her before. Yet when she said, 'Love me, Finn,' he shook his head.

'I mustn't; I dare not,' he said, though his hands continued to stroke her gently.

'I will go mad if you do not make love to me tonight,' Gabrielle said. 'How can you be so cruel? Can't you leave me one beautiful memory of you to hold against my heart, until you return for me?'

'Gabrielle, you know I can't,' Finn said huskily.

'You can, you must,' Gabrielle said frantically.

'I tell you, I will die if you do not make love to me tonight.'

'And I,' Finn might have said, because he felt as if he was burning up inside, such was the intensity of his desire. He was also well aware that this was the last time, perhaps for years, that he would hold this girl in his arms.

His fingers and hands stroking, caressing and gently kneading were followed by his lips kissing and nuzzling all over Gabrielle's body. She felt as if she were being consumed by lust for this wondrous man she loved with all her heart, and when he kissed her lips, his tongue darting in and out, her need was so great that she felt as if her body was melting under his touch.

And then came unbidden into Finn's mind a vision of him marching away and Gabrielle behind and alone, carrying his child in her belly. It took every ounce of his willpower to pull back.

'What is it?' Gabrielle said, her voice still husky with desire.

'Gabrielle,' Finn said, 'I do love you so much. Far too much to do this to you.'

'Oh, no, my darling Finn. Please?' Gabrielle pleaded.

Finn hesitated. How he wanted to do as Gabrielle was begging him. Shafts of acute desire were pulsating through him, and Gabrielle's body was all of a tremble. She cried out to Finn again and the picture he had had danced before his eyes again. Then his hands lay still on her body, and he pulled his mouth from hers and he got to his feet, staggering slightly.

'Don't you love me any more, Finn?' Gabrielle asked, and there were tears in her eyes.

'Love you?' Finn repeated incredulously. 'You might as well ask me if the sun never shines. I love you so much that I cannot risk leaving you with a child.'

'I would love to carry your child,' Gabrielle said. 'I would be honoured.'

'And you will, my darling,' Finn said. 'When this war is finally over and we are married. We will have the rest of our lives to make love and each day we will love each other more. Think on that, my darling, darling Gabrielle. Now please, get dressed before I forget myself entirely.'

Gabrielle was still a little upset and very frustrated, but in her heart of hearts she knew that Finn was thinking of her and so she began to put on her clothes.

It was as they were walking back towards the town that she mentioned something that had been worrying her, talking in little above a whisper for sounds carry further in the night.

'Finn, I hate to think of anything happening to you and that is why I have said nothing until now, but it may, for I know war is no game. But how would I ever know? Would it be all right if I write to your family – if not your parents then your brothers, or your sister?'

Finn could just imagine how such a letter would

be received, especially by his mother, and that would probably colour her opinion when he brought Gabrielle home after the war. If she refused to accept her then he would take her somewhere else, but he would hate to be estranged from his father, his brothers and Nuala, and he knew that could so easily happen if his mother took umbrage.

'My parents know nothing about us as yet,' he said.

'Wouldn't they approve either?'

'As I said, my mother really is one on her own,' Finn said. 'And in all honesty, she finds it hard to approve of anything. As I said, I have told Nuala all about you and my brothers too know a little, but if you wrote to them at the cottage my mother would not be above steaming open the letters.'

'My father would do that too,' Gabrielle said.

'I would have to think very carefully about a letter to my parents telling them about us,' Finn said. 'And I think the first approach must come from me, but I will ask the priest.' Lowering his voice still further as they approached the bakery yard, he went on, 'Father Clifford was assigned to our battalion as soon as we passed out last spring in Belfast. He is fairly young and one of the worldliest priests I have ever met. I am sure if anything happens to me, he will get word to you, but maybe you will still be in Paris.'

'I doubt that,' Gabrielle said. 'My father says I can stay one month, but no longer, and you haven't had orders to go anywhere yet, have you?'

'Not yet.' Finn whispered as he put his finger to his lips. 'Now, not another sound. We're getting too close.'

They crept along holding hands, and once in the yard underneath the tree, Finn drew Gabrielle into his arms.

She felt tears start in her eyes. She knew this was goodbye. She wasn't sure that she could exist without Finn, but she knew the forces pulling them apart were stronger than they were. As she kissed Finn with such intensity it seemed to come from the very essence of her being, and she couldn't help the little moans that escaped from her mouth. Then, very gently, Finn lifted her into the tree.

Her aunt Bernadette didn't sleep very well or deeply, and at that moment she was lying in her bed wide awake and imagining the treats in store for her niece. As for her just saying a month, she would stay as long as Bernadette wanted. There was nothing Pierre could do about it. He could hardly leave his precious bakery and come to fetch her.

Telling herself that she would never sleep with all these thoughts running around in her head, she tried to clear her mind and relax, and that was when she heard the sound in the yard below. She listened intently. There were no further sounds, and Bernadette told herself she had imagined it. She knew if she got out of bed to look she would be thoroughly wakened. She closed her eyes, but a few minutes later she heard rustling coming from outside. She lit the lamp beside the bed and saw that it was past two in the morning.

She waited a few more minutes to ascertain that she wasn't imagining it and then, thoroughly alarmed because she thought someone might be trying to break into the room where the girls were sleeping, she got out of bed. She wondered for a moment if she should try rousing Raoul, but he could be difficult to wake, and anyway, she wanted to satisfy herself first that there was something worth shouting about.

However, Gabrielle was now adept at climbing the tree, and by the time her aunt got to the window the girl was not only in her room but almost undressed.

Bernadette returned to her bed, smiling to herself. She had became really citified if she allowed a rustling tree to worry her, she thought, and was glad she hadn't woken Raoul and she cuddled against him and went fast asleep.

Gabrielle was also trying to sleep as she knew that they had an early start in the morning, but all she was aware of was the ache in her heart that grew bigger and bigger. Whether she was in Paris or St-Omer she knew she would miss Finn every waking minute. In fact she was missing him already, and as the tears started in her eyes she muffled her face in the pillow.

The following day, as he walked with Christy in to work, Finn felt it hard to lift his mood and yet he knew he must. It might be months, even years, before he would see Gabrielle again and he had to deal with that just as she had to do.

Christy cast a glance at his morose face and, risking a rebuff, he said to him, 'What's up, mate? You look as if you have the weight of the world on your shoulders.'

Finn sighed. 'Nothing,' he said. 'At least nothing that anyone can do anything about. Last night I bid my girlfriend goodbye, that's all.'

'Well, I suppose it was as well,' Christy said. 'To delay only puts off the inevitable.'

'I know,' Finn agreed. 'Anyway, she was going to relatives in Paris for a while, so it seemed the right time. It would suit me now though if we started moving out. It would be something positive to do.'

'Can't be too long now,' Christy said. 'I overheard yesterday that we are part of the New Army held back for something special.'

'Well, I for one can't wait,' Finn said.

However, day after day passed on with no further orders, and by the time Gabrielle had been gone over a week there was still no sign of the company moving on. Meanwhile, thoughts of her filled Finn's mind by day and disturbed his sleep at night. He didn't think it was possible to miss anyone as much as he missed Gabrielle, and without her he was often so sunk in melancholy that he didn't hear if someone spoke to him.

This had caused Captain Hamilton to yell at

him a few times, and in the end he had said, 'I don't know what ails you, Finn Sullivan, but I will give you a word of advice. Snap out of it. Before long you will be on the battlefield and then you'll need to focus your mind on the enemy and keep your wits about you or you will be blown to kingdom come, or else end your life on the tip of a German bayonet. Do I make myself clear?'

He did, of course, and yet still Finn found it hard to lift his despondency.

'Can't you write to her or something?' Christy said, one morning as he and Finn set out for Headquarters, and then slapped his head as he added, 'Oh, that's stupid of me. How can you write to a French girl? It's hardly likely she could read English.'

'She can read and speak as good English as you and me, though with a really lovely accent,' Finn told Christy. 'But writing to her has never been an option'

'Why not?'

'It just isn't.'

'Why?' Christy said. 'And who is she, for God's sake?'

There was no need to keep her name a secret any more and so Finn shrugged. 'I don't suppose it matters now. Her name is Gabrielle Jobert.'

Christy stopped dead on the road. He looked at Finn incredulously as he said, 'You are joking? Tell me that you are joking?'

'It's no joke,' Finn said. 'It's the truth.'

'I bet her father doesn't know that you were seeing his daughter,' Christy said, 'and that's why you can't write to her.'

'That's it exactly,' Finn said, as the two men strode on again.

'But, I've seen you at Mass,' Christy said, 'and the whole family has been there, and you haven't even looked at her. I spotted more than one hopeful young Frenchman lusting after her, but I never thought you felt that way too.'

'Well,' Finn said, 'd'you think I should have carried a banner advertising the fact that I love Gabrielle Jobert?'

'No, but—'

'It wasn't just her father we had to worry about either,' Finn said. 'It was the army. When I admitted at first how I felt about her to the captain he warned me away from her. He said the town was full of girls more than willing, with fathers not as formidable as Pierre Jobert, but when you have your eye on the main prize you don't settle for second best. We both knew, though, that if the army got a hint of any sort of romance between us, I could be whisked away to join the rest of the company before I had time to draw breath.'

'Well,' Christy said, 'if it was all this cloak-and-dagger stuff, where the hell did you meet? You could hardly be out of doors in the depths of winter, however hot with passion you were.'

'If I tell you that, then you are not to mention

it to another soul,' Finn said. 'It would sort of spoil it then.'

'Don't see why it should,' Christy said, 'now your affair is over and your bird flown away to Paris.'

'We didn't have an affair,' Finn retorted. 'And it isn't over. Although I will probably have left here by the time she returns from Paris, she has said she will wait for me.'

'Oh, yes?' Christy said sneeringly. 'Were you born yesterday or what? Her father probably has some person he feels suitable for her to marry and he will have a fair choice, for the girl is a looker and set to inherit the bakery, I suppose, as she is the eldest.'

Finn remembered Gabrielle saying her father wanted her and her sister to make what she termed 'good' marriages, and her reaction to that. 'Maybe her father will have some ideas that way, but Gabrielle has sworn to me that she will only marry for love, and that she loves me, and that she will wait.'

Christy looked at his friend pityingly, certain that he was heading for one massive disappointment if he thought that was actually going to happen, but what he said was, 'All right then, where did you conduct this great love affair? And you are all right, I shan't tell a soul where your love nest was.'

'A farmhouse I stumbled on one night,' Finn said. 'It is quite a way from the camp though some of the land the camp is on belonged to the owner, but Gabrielle said when he died there was no one to inherit and so the house is lying empty. I cleaned it up because it was filthy, and we used to have the fire alight, and it was real cosy. I even brought a blanket from my own bed.'

'But how did she get out of her father's house?'

'She climbed out of the bedroom window and down a convenient tree there,' Finn said. 'Because her father has to get up so early, the whole house retires at eight thirty every night. She would wait until it was all quiet and creep out. Her sister was the only one to know because they shared a room.'

'God!' Christy breathed. 'I wouldn't have said she had enough gumption.'

'Oh, she has gumption enough, believe me.'

'And did you . . . you know?' Christy said, nudging Finn with his elbow.

'That's none of your bloody business.'

'Maybe not,' Christy said, 'but I bet you didn't go to all that trouble to bloody well hold hands.'

They had reached the Headquarters and as they went up the steps Christy caught sight of Finn's face, with a smile playing around the corners of his mouth. Suddenly he knew with absolute conviction that Finn Sullivan had lain with Gabrielle Jobert and was remembering their nights of passion. Oh, how he envied him. He would have sold his soul for such an experience himself.

SEVEN

With the casualty lists rising in Ireland and no sign
of the promised Home Rule, an insurrection began
in Dublin on Easter Monday. The postman told
Biddy about it the following morning and when
the men came in for breakfast they could scarcely
believe what she related.

'Surely not,' Thomas John said. 'They would
not be so stupid as to take on the might of the
British Army.'

'I don't know so much,' Joe said. 'There are
plenty of stupid fellows in that Irish Republican
Brotherhood, or whatever they call themselves
these days.'

'Well, I think we need to know what is happening in our own country,' Thomas John said
decidedly. 'Someone of us must go to Buncrana
and buy a paper.'

Tom went in on the old horse, and when he got
home, regardless of the jobs awaiting attention on
the farm, Thomas John spread the paper on the table.

'Just a thousand of them,' he said in disgust. 'What on earth can a scant thousand men achieve? Connolly and Pearse are leading them to be slaughtered.'

'They have both sides of the Liffey covered, though,' Joe put in, impressed despite himself. 'And taken over the GPO in Sackville Street like the postman was after telling Mammy.'

'Hoisted up the tricolour flag too,' Tom said. 'It might be ill timed, stupid or whatever you want to call it, Daddy, but isn't it a fine sight to see the tricolour flying in Ireland again?'

'Aye it is, son,' Thomas John said rather sadly. 'And take joy in it, because it won't flutter there for long. It wouldn't hurt to get a paper each day though and keep abreast of things.'

That night Tom wrote to Finn telling him all about the uprising.

The worst thing is, there are so few of them pitted against the might of the disciplined British Army. Daddy thinks the whole thing is doomed to failure and I am inclined to agree with him. In fact the rebels might have hindered, not helped, the peace process.

Finn tried to be concerned, but the uprising seemed far removed from the war in France. It was as if Buncrana was in his distant past, almost another life, a life that hadn't Gabrielle in it.

The day that he received Tom's letter he met

Father Clifford in St-Omer. He was really pleased to see him and he greeted him warmly. 'But what are you doing here, Father?' he asked.

'I am here to tend to the injured in the hospital,' the priest replied. 'Father Kenny has been taken ill himself and I offered to take his place for a while.'

'So have you left our battalion then, Father?'

'No, not at all,' Father Clifford said. 'This is just temporary. I am moving out with you.'

'No one knows when that will be yet?'

'The next forty-eight hours, I heard,' Father Clifford said.

Finn knew that once he moved from St-Omer there would be no way that Gabrielle could find him. In his reply to Tom that night he mentioned not one word about the uprising, but said that the whole company was on the move, no one knew where, and he was heartbroken at leaving behind his beloved Gabrielle.

Before Tom even received Finn's reply the rebellion was over. Britain's response had been immediate. Thousands of troops had arrived in Dublin, field guns were installed, and by Wednesday a gunship had sailed up the Liffey and began shelling the place to bits. And as Dublin began to burn all those shops not shelled or burned to the ground were closed up. The Dublin people were starving, and looting became commonplace, with the British Army shooting anything that moved.

By Saturday, it was all over and the rebels marched off to Kilmainham Gaol, apart from de Valera, who had an American passport and was taken to Richmond Barracks. Tom didn't tell Finn any of this. Instead he wrote back to him in conciliatory tone, though he wasn't too worried about his brother. He was young and impetuous and, though he seemed very fond of the French girl, it was likely that he would fall in love many times before wanting to settle down

In Paris, Bernadette was seriously concerned about her niece, who seemed filled with sadness. In an effort to amuse her, her aunt and uncle had taken her to concerts and theatres, as well as private parties and soirees. Her aunt had taken her shopping and bought her beautiful gowns, and they paraded the streets of Paris dressed in their finery, stopping to talk to this one and that, or taking a break at a café for coffee and cake, or a reviving glass of wine, which Gabrielle had never tasted in her life before.

She thanked them for their kindness, was polite and solicitous to her aunt's friends, and answered their many questions without a hint of annoyance. Bernadette noted, though, that Gabrielle's smile never reached her eyes and she never saw them dance with delight as they had once used to. Even her movements seemed slow and heavy and she held herself stiffly, even when she submitted to her aunt's embraces. And that was the word – submitted.

'It's almost as if she's frozen inside,' Bernadette said to her husband as they made ready for bed. 'I remember how she used to hug and kiss us both when she was a child, and even last year she was the same. I have never seen such a change in a girl before.'

'I have noticed it myself,' Raoul said. 'Why don't you send a note in the morning to ask the doctor to call to look at the girl? What if there is something radically wrong and we haven't sought medical advice?'

'You're right, Raoul,' Bernadette said. 'I'll see to it.'

The following morning after breakfast, Gabrielle retired to her room with a book, but she didn't even attempt to read. She knew by now something was the matter with her and it occupied all her thoughts.

She hadn't seen her monthly bleed since before Christmas, and she had noticed the other night that her nipples were brown when they had once been pink. She had let her nightdress fall from her, and studied herself in the mirror. She saw that her breasts had definitely changed. They looked slightly larger, though she wasn't sure about that, but they definitely had blue lines on them that she had never noticed before.

She knew what she and Finn had done just that one time could have resulted in a baby because Finn had said so and that had been why he had refused to do it again, though when she remembered how he had made her feel inside, she couldn't wholly regret it. In fact, if Finn had transplanted a seed inside her that would grow into a child, his child, whom she would rear and nurture until he came back from the war, she would leap up and down with delight, but she knew that no one else would see her situation in the same light. Most people would consider it just about the worst sin that a girl could commit. She dreaded telling her father, yet if she was right, there was no way she could get out of telling him.

This was her mood then when her aunt knocked on Gabrielle's door.

'Ah,' Bernadette smiled. 'Here you are.'

'Do you want me, Aunt?'

'No, my dear,' Bernadette said. 'But it's just that the doctor has called to have a look at you, for you are not yourself, are you?' Bernadette met her niece's eyes.

Gabrielle knew she wasn't, and she shook her head. Now it was all out of her hands and there wasn't a lot she could do about it. So when her aunt said, 'Shall I ask him to come in?' she nodded her head and said glumly, 'You may as well.'

Downstairs, waiting to hear what the doctor had to say, Bernadette ran through in her mind the symptoms that Gabrielle had displayed almost since the day she had brought her to Paris, and came up with all manner of ailments that Gabrielle could be suffering from, except the right one. She castigated herself for not contacting the doctor sooner, but she had thought it was some sickness of mind, some form of depression, due partly to the way that she had been raised, and she'd been convinced that the freedom and gaiety of Paris would soon sort her out. It hadn't, however, and so she waited anxiously for the doctor's verdict.

The doctor had been the Dufours' physician for many years and they had become friends, and so he came down the stairs with a heavy tread. He knew that he was about to deliver a hammer blow to these good people. Bernadette had made it clear over many years the feeling she had for her sister's children, and especially the elder, Gabrielle, who truly was a very beautiful girl. He wondered how she would feel about her when he delivered his news.

Bernadette came hurrying to him when she saw him descending the stairs, wringing her hands with anxiety. 'What's the matter with her, Doctor?' she asked. 'I blame myself for not consulting you sooner.'

'Calm yourself, dear lady,' the doctor said. 'My diagnosis would have been the same in any case, and I am afraid that you must prepare yourself for a shock.' He saw Bernadette's eyes open wide in concern and confusion as he continued, gently, 'I am very much afraid that your niece is expecting a baby.'

Bernadette stared at him almost in disbelief. Her mouth opened but no sound came out, and she staggered in shock. The doctor steadied her and he led her into her sitting room to the sofa. Then Raoul poured them each a glass of wine with hands that shook.

Bernadette sipped the wine gratefully as she looked steadily at the doctor. 'Are you sure of this, André?'

'I am, Bernadette,' the doctor said. 'And I wish from the bottom of my heart that it wasn't true, but Gabrielle is more than three months pregnant.'

'But her father is like a gaoler with the girls,' Raoul said, shaking his head in disbelief. 'I'm sorry, and I don't doubt you for a minute, but it seems incredible. The girl goes nowhere and sees no one, and she is sent to bed at eight thirty each night. Remember we have spoken about it before with your wife?'

The doctor nodded. 'There is someone special in her life, though.'

'I don't see how there can be,' Bernadette said.

'Ah yes, this much she has told me,' the doctor told her. 'Only she wouldn't say who the man was. You see, all will not be lost if there is some arrangement between them. They can be married speedily and the problem solved.'

Bernadette shook her head. 'St-Omer, like Paris, has few young men left. They are mostly enlisted in the army, and she has been given no opportunity to meet anyone, though the town has plenty of British soldiers.'

'She would never have been given the opportunity to meet any of those, though,' Raoul said.

'Well, she met someone,' the doctor said. 'And it needs only one to put her in the state she's in.'

'Then I intend to find out who the man is,' Bernadette said, 'and, if possible, take the girl back to St-Omer and see if the man will do the decent thing by her. That little lady,' she added grimly, 'has some explaining to do.'

Gabrielle was sitting on her bed waiting for a visitation by her aunt, and when she saw her framed in the doorway, her face so full of sadness and disappointment, she cried, 'Oh, Aunt Bernadette, I am so sorry.'

Bernadette crossed the room. 'What possessed you, child?'

'Auntie, we couldn't help ourselves.'

'Tell me, was it one or several men you lay with?'

Gabrielle was truly shocked. 'One man only, Aunt, and one I love with all my heart and soul. What sort of girl do you take me for?'

'You know, Gabrielle, a year ago that wouldn't have been a hard question to answer,' Bernadette said, disappointment being replaced by anger. 'But now I don't know what sort of girl you have turned out to be. A girl who lies down and offers herself like some repulsive harlot is not the sort of person I would wish to be related to.'

Gabrielle recoiled from the harsh words, and

yet she tried to defend herself. 'It wasn't like that, truly it wasn't!' she cried desperately, yet she knew that is how everyone would view it. The love she and Finn had shared in the farmhouse would be tainted and spoiled, and she could almost feel a coldness between her and her aunt that had never been there before.

'And who is the boy or man who took you down in such a manner? Was he from the town?'

'No,' Gabrielle said, and when she saw the look of repugnance sweep over Bernadette's face, she lifted her head higher. 'His name is Finn Sullivan and he is an Irishman in the British Army.'

'A common soldier!' Bernadette cried. 'How could you lower yourself like that?'

'He wasn't. He isn't!' Gabrielle exclaimed. 'You don't know him. I don't care what you say either because I love him and he loves me.'

'And what would you know about love?' Bernadette sneered.

'I know how I feel.'

'I know how you felt as well,' Bernadette said. 'Full of wantonness. How did you meet this common soldier you say you love?'

There was little point in concealment. It would all come out in the end, but when Gabrielle began explaining how she climbed down the tree, even she was aware how sordid it sounded.

Bernadette suddenly remembered the sound of rustling she had heard outside her room the night before she and Raoul had left for Paris, and she said, 'You even crept out to see him the night before we brought you here, didn't you?'

Gabrielle nodded. 'I had to do that,' she whispered. 'It was to say goodbye. I don't know when I will ever see him again.'

Bernadette's face was full of disgust. 'You shouldn't have seen him in the first place, you stupid girl. You behaved little better than a common tramp, Gabrielle. To think I felt sorry for you, cooped up in that house. I see now that your father was right. He must have known that he had a slut for a daughter.'

'I am no slut,' Gabrielle cried. 'We didn't intend this to happen and it happened the once only when we forgot ourselves. Finn is a fine man and will marry me willingly, I know, and he is a Roman Catholic.'

'Then that is the only good thing about all this,' Bernadette said. 'At least it is not some heathen you will be married to.'

'And we should be grateful to him and men like him because he is fighting for France,' Gabrielle said, lifting her chin in the air. 'I'm proud of what he is doing.'

'You can take that haughty look off your face before I take it off for you,' Bernadette said sharply. 'You have nothing to be so high and mighty about, and the idea that he and his kind are fighting for France is nonsense. They are fighting for themselves. But that is neither here nor there. He has got you in the family way and he must be made to marry you.'

'We wanted to marry,' Gabrielle said. 'I said I would wait for him, but he might not be at St-Omer now.'

'Why not?'

'Because they were awaiting orders for moving out when I came to Paris.'

'Well, if they are gone someone will know where. He will have to be found and made to do his duty,' Bernadette said. 'We must make plans to return as soon as possible. Raoul will go to find out when the next train is and we must send a telegram to your parents so that they will expect us.'

A shudder went right through Gabrielle's body and she said to her aunt, 'I'm afraid of facing Papa.'

'I'm not surprised,' Bernadette said. 'You have done your best to shame him – shame the whole family, in fact – but you should have thought of that sooner.' As she got up she looked at Gabrielle disparagingly. 'I will tell my maid that there is sickness in the family and you are needed at home, and send her in to help you pack. And we won't bother taking any of the fancy gowns I bought for you. You will hardly fit into them for much longer anyway.'

They travelled to St-Omer that same day and arrived in the evening. The Joberts had already eaten, but when Mariette offered to make them a meal, Bernadette shook her head.

'We had something before we left and I have news that cannot wait,' she said.

Mariette nodded. The telegram had just said that they were returning unexpectedly, and news like that was bound to make a person anxious until it was explained.

'I need to speak to you privately,' Bernadette went on, looking at the puzzled faces of Pierre and Mariette. In the train Gabrielle had begged her aunt to break the news to her father, hoping it might soften the blow. Bernadette agreed to try, though she felt sure there was no way news like that could be softened.

Gabrielle sat in the adjoining room and listened to the murmur of the voices and the ticking clock, which seemed inordinately loud, and waited. She heard a cry from her mother and a roar from her father. Then he was at the door, his face puce with such temper he was like an enraged bull, and he was across the room in seconds. Grabbing the bun at the nape of Gabrielle's neck, he pulled it with such force that grips spilled out all over the floor and Gabrielle's hair loosened. Then he pulled her into the room and slammed her so hard against the wall that she felt as if all her bones had loosened.

'Tell me it isn't true, you strumpet,' he bellowed.

'I'm sorry, Papa . . .'

'Sorry,' snorted Pierre. 'And you will be sorrier before you are much older.' The punch he powered at Gabrielle caught her full in the face and knocked her from her feet, and she folded to the floor with blood spurting from her nose.

'This isn't the way,' Bernadette said, helping the disoriented and weeping girl to her feet.

'I haven't started yet,' Pierre said, drawing his belt from his trousers as he spoke. 'I have never lifted my belt to either girl before, but then neither has presented me with a full belly before.'

'Haven't you listened to a word I said?' Bernadette said. 'Time is of the essence. Gabrielle said this man was awaiting orders to leave and you say some have already gone. We need to go up to the camp early tomorrow morning and find this man wherever he is, and Gabrielle needs to be in a fit state to do that, not beaten senseless.'

'She's right, Pierre,' Mariette said. 'The only way to make any sense out of this and make it a bit more respectable is to get Gabrielle married off as quickly as possible.'

Pierre knew that what Bernadette and his wife said made sense, but he was so angry with Gabrielle he had wanted to beat her to pulp. He had no place in his heart to feel any measure of sympathy for her or guilt for the mess he had made of her face. In his opinion she had got what she deserved.

He wagged a finger in front of Gabrielle's eyes and said, 'You thank your lucky stars that your aunt and mother pleaded your case because it saved you from the beating of your life.'

Gabrielle knew they had and she knew it might happen yet if they couldn't find Finn at the camp.

'God, I wish we could get a move on,' said Finn, with the company assembled to move out. 'Despite the fact it is the first of May today it's chilly enough this early.'

'I'll say,' Christy agreed. 'Still, can't be much longer now. We've had roll call and kit inspection and everything. I can't think what they are waiting for.'

Many thought the same. Some had begun to kick a football around, others became involved in an impromptu game of cards, and Mikey Donahue drew out his mouth organ and began to play the haunting tunes of their homeland. Others, like Finn and Christy, were anxious to get going and were milling around aimlessly waiting for orders.

Suddenly Christy said, 'Uh-uh, here comes trouble.'

Finn turned and saw Sergeant Lancaster approaching them. Like the sergeant who had trained them initially, this one had a voice like a foghorn. In fact, every sergeant he had ever met appeared to enjoy yelling. Finn remembered in his early days in the army he had often prayed the sergeant assigned to them would have a bout of laryngitis to give them all some respite.

'Looks as if one of us is for the high jump,' Christy said out of the corner of his mouth. 'What you done?'

Finn couldn't think of a thing and, anyway, there was no time to say anything before the man snapped out, 'Private Sullivan, follow me.'

Finn's time in the army had taught him that it was pointless to ask questions. You might as well talk to a brick wall. And so with an almost imperceptible shrug to Christy, he marched behind the sergeant many of his fellow soldiers stopped what they were doing and watched in surprise.

Sergeant Lancaster halted outside the tent occupied by Lieutenant Haywood, who was Finn's platoon commander. 'Wait here,' he told Finn, and he entered under the flap, leaving Finn outside wondering what it was all about. He heard the sergeant announce him and the lieutenant saying to send him in, and he entered tentatively. He couldn't see who was in the tent until he had gone past the second flap. When he saw sitting across the table from a stern-faced Lieutenant Haywood was Gabrielle, beside her thunderous father and her agitated mother, his gasp was audible.

He felt as if a piece of cold steel was in his stomach and then Gabrielle turned and looked at him, and he gasped anew at the sight of her battered face. He guessed then what they had come about. Somehow, they had learned about his association between him and Gabrielle.

But surely there had been no need to abuse Gabrielle in such a way. He felt anger coursing through him and he glared at her burly father

144

beside her, his face suffused with rage, and had the urge to rush across the room and take the man by the throat.

'D'you know what this is all about, Sullivan?' the lieutenant rapped out.

Of course he knew, but still he said, 'No, sir.'

'Monsieur Jobert says that his daughter is with child and she has named you.'

Finn looked at Gabrielle in total shock. The nightmare scenario of him marching away and leaving Gabrielle alone and pregnant was going to come true. It was the future he hadn't wanted for her and it was all because he had forgotten himself just the once and made love to her properly. His face was lined with sorrow and regret, and he didn't have to ask if it was true. It was evident in Gabrielle's face, even though it was so swollen and discoloured.

He saw something else too. Though her eyes were little more than slits, he could see the slight fear behind them. Surely she knew he would never let her down?

'Do you deny it is your child?' the lieutenant asked.

'No, sir, I don't deny it,' Finn answered firmly.

At this, Pierre growled out something in French and Gabrielle's mother put a hand on his arm. Pierre shook her off and got to his feet, and it was Sergeant Lancaster that restrained him.

When he was seated once more, the lieutenant said, 'Are you willing to marry the girl, Sullivan?'

'Oh, gladly, sir. More than willing.'

'St-Omer,' Pierre said in broken English. 'We go back.'

'Oh no, sir,' the lieutenant said. 'There is no time to go back to St-Omer. We have already held the company up over this and they must move out shortly. Can you understand any of this?'

'I can translate, Lieutenant,' Gabrielle said.

'Then please do so,' the lieutenant answered.

Gabrielle spoke to her father and then he leaped up from his chair and banged his chest and announced, 'I Catholic.'

'We have a Catholic priest on the camp, the name of Clifford, who can officiate,' the lieutenant said. He turned to Gabrielle. 'Can you tell him that? Assure him it will be done properly and tell him also that it's the only thing we can offer. We do after all have a war to fight and have already been delayed long enough.'

When Gabrielle spoke to her father, this time impressing on him that it was that or nothing, he seemed to calm a little. The important thing was that his daughter would have marriage lines, and where the ceremony was carried out, and by whom, mattered much less. So he nodded and sat back heavily in the chair.

The lieutenant said to the sergeant, 'Can you find Father Clifford and ask him if he would be so kind as to come here?'

'Yes, sir.'

'And there is no reason to delay the company

any longer. They can move out now and the rest of us can follow later.'

'Could I have Christopher Byrne as my witness, sir?' Finn said.

'You are hardly in a position to make demands, Sullivan.'

'No, sir,' Finn said. 'Sorry, sir. It's just that he is the same faith as myself.'

'And that's important, is it?'

'Yes, sir.'

Lieutenant Haywood sighed and then glanced over at the sergeant. 'See to that as well, will you?'

'Yes, sir.'

'You are a bloody nuisance, do you know that, Sullivan?' the lieutenant burst out as the sergeant left. 'The whole regiment has been put on hold because you couldn't control your carnal urges.'

'Yes, sir. Sorry, sir.'

'I should put you on a charge for this, and if we weren't all set to move out immediately I would do just that.'

Gabrielle suddenly felt very sorry for Finn. 'Could Finn and I have a few words alone?' she asked. And then, as he hesitated, she pleaded, 'Please. It might have to last us years.'

'All right,' the lieutenant said. 'But a few minutes is all you will have.'

Pierre had been watching the interchange with interest, understanding little of it, and then as Gabrielle stood up, he grasped her wrist and she spoke to him in French. Finn thought he was about

147

to protest and not let Gabrielle go, but her mother spoke up too and he released Gabrielle and she crossed the room to Finn.

They were shown into another smaller tented area off the main one and as soon as they were out of sight they were in one another's arms.

'Oh, my darling girl, how you have suffered,' Finn said brokenly, kissing her face gently. 'What a brute your father must be to abuse you so.'

'I angered and shamed him,' Gabrielle said. 'My father is not known for his gentleness but I think many fathers would have reacted so. I almost expected it, for all I asked my aunt Bernadette to break the news to him. She found out, you see. She was worried about me and called the doctor when I was just coming to terms with the truth myself, and when I told her who the father was and said the camp might have already moved off, she couldn't get me home fast enough.'

'Good job she did,' Finn said. 'In a few minutes we will be husband and wife. How do you feel about that?'

'I am pleased about it,' Gabrielle said, 'but I would be just utterly delighted if you were able to go home with me.'

'One day, when the war is over, I'll be able to do just that,' Finn said. 'And at least this way, if anything should happen to me . . .'

'I don't want to think about that sort of thing.'

'I know, but all I'm saying is that as my wife you would be informed first. Say I was injured or something. I could be passing through St-Omer and maybe you could come and see me.'

'I don't want to think of you injured.'

'Then I won't be,' Finn declared stoutly. 'I will tell you what I told my brothers. I will catch the bullets in my teeth and spit them back.'

Finn was gratified to see the ghost of a smile playing around Gabrielle's bruised eyes and she said, 'You are a fool, Finn Sullivan.'

'I know this,' Finn said with mock humility. 'It isn't so bad, I always think, if a person is aware of it.'

'Ah, Finn!' Gabrielle said, cuddling against him. 'I love you so.'

'And I you, my darling girl.'

'What will your family say, d'you think?'

'Well, I don't know till I write and tell them,' Finn said. 'My mother is a queer kettle of fish altogether and would hardly welcome the Pope if he came knocking on the door. But Joe and Tom would love you almost as much as I do, and my wee sister, Nuala, would I'm sure be delighted to have a new sister. You will see all this for yourself one day, for I will take you home to meet them just as soon as I can.'

Their time was up. There was no way that Finn could kiss those inflamed lips, but the love light shone from both their eyes as Gabrielle held Finn close once more. 'Please be careful,' she said earnestly. 'You have more to lose now.'

Finn knew he had for he had found the love of

his life and he would soon have a child to provide for. Just the thought of holding a child of his own made him quiver with excitement. He said to Gabrielle, 'You must write to me often, for we can do that now. I want to hear all that you are doing, and when the child is born I want to hear all about him or her too. Tell me everything.'

'We haven't got all day, Sullivan,' the sergeant remarked sarcastically, and Gabrielle and Finn went towards him hand in hand.

Father Clifford and Christy were already there, and Finn suddenly realised that he hadn't a ring. However, Gabrielle's mother understood this and she slipped a gold ring from one of her own fingers and passed it over to Gabrielle.

'This was given to Maman by her mother on the day she married my father,' Gabrielle said, dropping it into Finn's palm. 'She has told me often that I would be given it on my wedding day.'

'And it will do perfectly,' Finn said. 'But I intend to get you a proper wedding ring as soon as I can.'

EIGHT

To Finn, the wedding felt almost like a nonevent, because Gabrielle returned to St-Orner with her parents, and Christy, Father Clifford and Finn himself set off to catch up with their battalion, who were regrouping at Lille.

'You a married man,' Christy said to Finn as they walked along. 'I can scarcely believe it.'

'Neither can I,' Finn replied. 'I mean, it doesn't really feel any different. Whenever I thought of marrying someone I never imagined it like this.'

'That's because there was no Nuptial Mass and we weren't able to celebrate it in any way,' the priest said. 'That's often how it is in wartime. But you are still just as much married, so don't you forget it.'

'You have no need to remind me of that, Father,' Finn said. 'I have no need of any other woman when I have such a prize waiting for me in St-Omer, and one too that is carrying our child. I am concerned about Gabrielle, though. Whatever she said, her father must be a vicious bully of a man to batter her the way he did and I'm not there to ensure it doesn't happen again.'

'You have to see things from his point of view,' the priest said. 'That must be the very worst news a daughter can give her father.'

'Yes,' Finn conceded. 'But, Father if he had been a more reasonable man in the first place, I could have called at the house and asked to walk out with Gabrielle, in the normal way of going about. Then we wouldn't have had such a hole-in-the-corner relationship, and maybe if they had allowed us to get engaged, she wouldn't be in this situation now.'

'These things happen, Finn,' Father Clifford told him. 'And at least you did your duty and married the girl.'

'I never had any intention of letting her down,' Finn said. 'I just wish, at least, until the baby is born, she was away from her father and maybe give him time to get over it.'

'Perhaps she will go back to her aunt in Paris,' Christy suggested.

'She didn't say so,' Finn said. 'But I would feel happier if she did that.'

Pierre Jobert too would have felt happier if Gabrielle had gone back to Paris, and in fact he almost expected that to happen but Bernadette and Raoul, who had stood in for them at the bakery that morning, refused to take her.

Pierre was quite surprised, but Bernadette said, 'She would be the talk of the place and that would impinge on Raoul and me. Respectable doors would be closed to us.'

'But she has marriage lines now.'

'And what would be the good of those in Paris?' Bernadette said. 'People would think it odd that there was no talk of marriage when she was there just a few days ago. And when her stomach begins to swell, they will know the real reason we returned to St-Omer in such a hurry. You know very well the most stupid people in the world can count up to nine when it matters.'

Pierre sighed. He had hoped to hide Gabrielle away so that he wouldn't have to think of what she had done. Now, it seemed, he was stuck with her. Well, there was no way he was going to have her at the front of the shop, proclaiming her shame for all to see. Yvette had done well enough when Gabrielle had been in Paris and she could carry on in the shop, and Mariette could lend a hand when they were busy. Gabrielle could work in the bakery with him where he could keep an eye on her.

'Go out and buy a big coat for that brazen hussy to cover herself when she goes to Mass,' he told his wife that night. 'I'll see to it that she will go no other place and the first thing I will do tomorrow is fit bars to the bedroom window and have that tree cut down.'

Mariette was upset and disappointed at what

Gabrielle had done, but she knew that it had hit Pierre harder. He'd had plans for Gabrielle, though she wasn't sure what they were, but whenever they discussed the future for their daughters he would always say that Gabrielle was intelligent, charming and very beautiful. She could have the pick of the town. But Mariette knew what Pierre meant was that he would have the pick of the town, choosing someone who might be beneficial for him in the business.

Now Gabrielle had pre-empted him and married a man of her own choice, someone of a different nationality and a different culture, and a common soldier, he considered that she had thrown her life away. Mariette didn't know whether she had or not. Only time would tell, but the deed was done now and Gabrielle and her Irish soldier were married for life, whether Pierre liked it or not. She sighed and could only hope that he would get over it soon because when he was in a bad mood they all suffered.

Pierre had had someone in mind for Gabrielle and the man's name was Robert Legrand. He was a big, beefy sort of man, fifteen years Gabrielle's senior, a widower with a small son called Georges, who was being raised by his late wife's parents thirty miles away. This meant that Robert seldom saw the boy. He was after a wife who was easy on the eye and who would be a new mother for the child so that he could have him back again, and he had a fancy for Gabrielle.

154

He had confided all this to Pierre when they met in the bars in the town on a Saturday evening. Pierre knew that it must be terrible for a man to be separated from his own son. At first he wasn't sure that he was the man for Gabrielle. Then one night Legrand said that if he were to marry Gabrielle, he would move into the bakery where Pierre could teach him all about making the bread and cakes he was so famous for. Then he would sell his house and that money could be used to modernise the place.

Pierre was sold on the idea, but he advised Robert to wait until Gabrielle was eighteen at least before he approached her. 'Gabrielle is gone to her aunt's house in Paris at the moment,' he had told Legrand just days before. 'When she returns I will speak to her.'

When she returned, however, it was to find that she was carrying another man's child and the dreams Pierre had for the bakery crumbled away like dust. And he still had Legrand to face. He felt that he could never hold his head up again.

Rumours about Finn's marriage had spread amongst the other Inniskilling Fusiliers and many were amazed by it, and told him so when they all met up again in Lille. As they were preparing to make camp for an early start in the morning, Lieutenant Haywood sought out Finn.

Finn stood to attention by his bed.

'Well, Sullivan,' the lieutenant said, 'I have been

talking to Captain Hamilton, and he told me that he made it clear to you that you were to give Mademoiselle Jobert a wide berth.'

'Yes, sir. He did, sir,' Finn said.

'He said he would have soon put a stop to that if he had known.'

'Yes, sir,' Finn said.

'Got her in the family way too,' the lieutenant snapped, giving vent to opinions he'd been unable to express before, with the Joberts themselves present. 'Damned fool thing to do in wartime.'

'Yes, sir,' Finn said. 'It wasn't meant to happen, sir.'

'What's that got to do with anything?' the lieutenant said sharply. 'The point is that has happened and you don't need much imagination to know how her family and maybe the entire town will make her suffer for this. You saw her face.'

Finn didn't say anything, because every word the lieutenant said was right. The blame was always laid at the girl's door.

'Well, the damage is done now,' the officer said. 'And you must do the job that you came to do, because what do you think will happen to your wife and child if the Germans are allowed to reach St-Omer? You know of the atrocities that they committed in Belgium. Do you think the people of France will fare any better?'

Of course they wouldn't. Finn knew he would gladly lay down his life for his beloved Gabrielle and the child that she was carrying. So he squared his shoulders and faced the lieutenant as he said, 'I enlisted to fight the Germans, sir, and I will do whatever I am asked to do to the best of my ability.'

'And so will I, Sullivan,' Lieutenant Haywood said. 'May God be with the pair of us.'

'Are you writing to your parents?' Christy asked Finn that night, seeing him put pen to paper.

Finn shook his head. 'Writing to my parents will need careful thought. I don't know how they'll take the news at all.'

'They'll likely not be pleased.'

'Well, no, but it's more than that,' Finn said. 'I'm under age. I won't be twenty-one until next year. I gave a false age to Father Clifford because if I hadn't I wouldn't have been allowed to marry Gabrielle. I couldn't think of anything else to do. So is the marriage legal or not?'

'I don't know,' Christy said. 'Does it matter?'

Finn shrugged. 'I don't know, but it might. If it ever comes out.'

'That would be just awful for Gabrielle.'

'You're right, it would,' Finn said. 'My parents were totally against me enlisting, and now if I just write to say I'm married and they realise that I didn't ask permission, then they could easily make a fuss. That would be catastrophic for Gabrielle, and our child would be a bastard.'

'So what are you going to do?'

'Not write to them until I have to,' Finn said.

157

'When we are going for this Big Push they keep talking about, I will write then in case anything happens to me. I'll tell them all about Gabrielle, and when Europe is a safer place maybe she can go over and see them and take our child to be reared where I was.'

'What are you on about, talking that way?' Christy said. 'You and I are going to get through this in one piece. You will be able to take your Gabrielle home on your arm, and I will be there along with you.'

'I hope you're right,' Finn replied. 'But in case . . .'

'Don't even think that way.'

'I must,' Finn said. 'I have Gabrielle and a child to think about. And so I will leave that letter and my marriage lines with Father Clifford to send to my parents. Should anything happen to me the authorities will inform Gabrielle, as she is my next of kin, but I would like Father Clifford to write to her too.'

'Won't he think it odd that you haven't written to your parents before?'

'How will he know?' Finn said. 'I will let him assume they know everything. He won't open any letter I give him to keep.'

'No, of course not,' Christy said. 'So you think that this is the way to play it then?'

'God, Christy, I don't know,' Finn sighed. 'But it is the best that I can do for the moment.'

*   *   *

158

By the middle of May the company were on the move again, heading further south, according to Finn's compass. The spring had been quite wet and cold up until then, but the morning that they set out, the sun was already up, despite the early hour. The sky was blue with little fluffy clouds scudding across it, driven by the breeze that riffled through the fields and hedgerows. Finn was glad of the breeze by mid-morning. Without it the heat could have been quite uncomfortable, as they kept up a steady marching pace, hard enough to do with a heavy kitbag on his back.

The only blot on this beautiful spring day was the muffled sound of gunfire, which had been an almost constant backdrop, and got louder with every step they took. The increased sound caused a knot of nervousness to form in Finn's stomach. He knew that their period of inactivity was coming to an end. Soon he would meet the enemy for the first time and he was a little afraid.

He knew many might be feeling the same way, but no one spoke of it and he would hate to let this fear take hold of him or, worse still, display it and mark himself out as a coward. That was something that he had never considered before.

As they camped that night he wrote a few lines to his family explaining the route march and the countryside he had passed through; painting a picture of where he was but leaving out any names of places they passed, for he knew the censor would cut them out. He didn't mention the gunfire at all.

Gabrielle got a similar letter, but in hers Finn expressed again how much he loved her and longed for them to be together, and he urged her to take care of herself.

She always wrote cheerful replies and she never mentioned the fact that her father was making her work from dawn till dusk and seldom spoke at all unless it was to bark out an order. She didn't tell him either that she wasn't allowed across the door unless to Mass, and even then she would be marched to the cathedral and back and forbidden to exchange pleasantries with anyone. It was the thought of Finn's letters that kept her going, and the realisation that soon she would be holding his child in her arms.

Finn was worried that he had made no financial provision for Gabrielle and now, with the child, it was even more important. However, he had no idea how to do this and sought out Father Clifford.

'I see what you say, Finn,' he said. 'As soon as we are settled somewhere, as far, that is, as anyone can be settled in war, I will find out for you. I think there is something like a separation allowance that the wives in Britain get, and money for the child when it is born, though I don't yet know how this works in France.'

'We won't be here long then?'

'No,' the priest said. 'This is more a collection point. You must have noticed the battalions of soldiers that are arriving regularly. By tomorrow we will be on our way further south. I am no military man, but

160

I think this is all for the Big Push the officers have been talking about for weeks.'

'I should say you have a good grasp of it, Father,' Finn said. 'The sound of the artillery fire is certainly closer than it was.'

'And it will be closer yet, I should say,' Father Clifford said grimly.

The priest was right. Neither Christy nor Finn had seen so many soldiers gathered together in one place.

'And what do you think of these pals' brigades?' Christy asked Finn one day.

'I'd never heard of them before now,' Finn said. 'I met some from a place called Barnsley and they were telling me that they are called pals because they take all the young men from that area. I suppose,' he mused, 'if they had introduced conscription in Ireland, like they threatened to do, they could have rounded up all the men from Buncrana and the farms and villages and such.'

'Maybe they did it that way so that they could look out for one another,' Christy suggested.

Finn shook his head. 'I'd like to think that,' he said. 'I mean, I would like to think that you and I will watch out for one another. It's what we said, isn't it? But I have a feeling that when we are sent over the top, it will be every man for himself.'

'You could be right.' Christy added, 'Anyway, I am hitting the sack. The word is we are all setting out early tomorrow.'

'So what's new?' Finn said with a grin. 'We always set out early. I'm not sure that bugler goes to bed at all.'

And they did set out early the next morning, but still the sun was well up and the day a very pleasant one. They kept up a good pace and by the second day they realised the area was slightly different from the flat land they had seen when they had first arrived in France, more undulating and wooded in places. It was easier on the eye and more interesting to walk through, and the following day they marched through a town called Albert.

It was obvious that the small town had been shelled heavily. Many buildings had been destroyed and there were piles of masonry or gaping holes. People came out into the streets to see the soldiers pass, and while there were some who gave a desultory wave, others just looked resigned. Finn thought he could hardly blame them. More soldiers to them probably signified more fighting, more loss of life, and perhaps more heartache for them all.

With the town in the distance, however, Finn and Christy had their first sight of mile upon mile of trenches, scorching into the green fields before them, like gigantic white snakes, illustrating how chalky the soil was. Finn remembered the white cliffs of Dover they had seen from the boat when they had first sailed.

162

He thought he knew all about trenches, but Ireland's trenches were mere ditches to these monstrous constructions. Sergeant Lancaster said the chalky soil meant the trenches would be easy to dig, but, he imagined, they would be easier to crumble away too.

Eventually they stopped for the night, and after a meal of stew and potatoes, which everyone was ready for, Finn and Christy went to inspect the nearest trenches and saw they were reinforced with hundreds of sandbags and wood with wooden duckboards laid down to walk on. There were intersections too where one trench joined another, making little bays, and ladders at intervals along the length. Finn wondered how he would feel when he had orders to go up one of those ladders.

The next day, 108th and 109th Brigade were marched further on still until a halt was ordered west of a village called Thiepval. There Finn and Christy saw dugouts for the first time, which they found were living and sleeping quarters built underneath the trenches.

Finn's stomach quailed at the thought of entering the dark tunnel that opened up at the side of a trench, for he was no lover of confined or enclosed places. But he swallowed his panic and followed the others. The steps appeared to go on and on until he felt as if he was descending to the bowels of the earth, and when they emerged into a sort of corridor Finn wasn't the only one to sigh with relief.

Lieutenant Haywood, leading them, said, 'This is not your journey's end. Your billet is on a lower level yet. The accommodation here is for officers.'

So they went further down and eventually, they reached another corridor with rooms off. Lieutenant Haywood opened the first of these doors and Finn saw that the room had six bunks to either side, each with folded bedclothes on the pillow, and there was a small table between each set of bunks.

'Make your beds up,' Lieutenant Haywood ordered, lighting the lamps already set on the tables from his own. 'Then make your way to the canteen where you will be fed and given your issue of candles.'

'I'll never settle to this,' Finn said, looking around the room with distaste, when the lieutenant had left.

'I don't think I will either,' Christy agreed.

But they were to find that however grim the surroundings, they were sometimes glad to reach them when the depth of them meant the noise of any bombardment was more muffled and they felt moderately safer. The hundreds of tons of soil above their heads was then a comfort rather than something to be feared. They also found much camaraderie between the other men in their billet and if any got parcels from home or anywhere else, they were always shared out among them all. The twelve men soon drew very close.

Like all the Irish they could make a story up about anything, but the best of them all was Dinny McColl. His stories about his large and extended family were legion. They couldn't all be true, but what did that matter? Whatever your mood, Dinny could always put a smile on your face. Finn respected the young man: he was not stupid and he knew what they were up against, and probably had moments of doubt or apprehension, even fear, but if he had there was no sign of it in his demeanour.

Finn was taught card games for the first time in his life. All the Sullivan men had been turned off the idea of gambling away their hard-earned money by their father. He had often told them that he had seen gambling have such a hold on some men that it had badly affected their wives and children's lives, and so Finn hadn't a clue how to play anything. He soon learned, though, and as none of the soldiers had any spare money they only played for fun. Their card games did help to fill the times of inactivity and prevented Finn thinking of what lay ahead.

The front-line trenches had a sort of parapet to them that was made by the soil dug out to make the trench in the first place. Finn was shown how to use the trench periscope to see over the top without raising his head.

Sometimes the sides of the trenches did crumble away, as Sergeant Lancaster had warned they might, and chalky flakes would sometimes line the back of a person's throat or fill up his nostrils, but the men learned to cope with that like everything else. The trenches weren't heavily guarded, even those in the front line, unless they were told to 'Stand ready'. There were more soldiers drafted in at dawn and dusk because that's when an attack was more likely, and the trench intersections were always manned heavily.

The trenches were just as uncomfortable and dismal as Finn and Christy expected them to be, especially as the month, which had been warm and quite sunny, became overcast, cold and wet. Finn was often drenched and thoroughly chilled, and the food was sparse, cold or nonexistent. He was usually more than happy to return to the drier quarters of the dugout to rest his weary bones and close his smarting eyes.

Rats were another bugbear of the trenches and their size had to be seen to be believed. Finn had grown up on a farm where rats were commonplace, but he had never seen rats like these. They were as plump and big as any cat, and totally unafraid as they scurried along the duckboards. One of Lieutenant Haywood's favourite sports was shooting them with his pistol. His men cheered when he got one and yet it seemed there were another two to take the place of any he killed.

They had been there for over a fortnight when, one night, Finn bumped into Father Clifford, who had been working with brigades further down the line. Finn asked him again about finding out how he was to make some allowance for Gabrielle, and Father Clifford told him that he would enquire.

The priest, however, was given short shrift when he asked. By then, the whole area was on high alert, officers running hither and thither, issuing orders and then rescinding them, and the priest was told sharply that the middle of one of the largest campaigns of the war was no time to be dealing with personal issues.

Father Clifford didn't tell Finn this, because he knew he might fret about it. A fighting man didn't need to have other concerns on his mind. He told him instead that the matter was in hand and Finn was satisfied with that. He also wrote the letter to his parents telling them of his marriage to the beautiful Gabrielle, which he left with Father Clifford, and sent another to Gabrielle herself, telling her that things were hotting up and assuring her of his love.

And then the barrage began. Finn knew – they all knew – that it was a technique designed to wipe out the German defences. It certainly cheered him, Christy and many of the others, who thought that when they eventually 'went over the top' German resistance would be minimal. The news reporters and film crews allowed into the battlefield were recording it all for the people back home, as day after day the bombardment and shelling went on. Their dugouts at least gave them some respite from the full force of the ear-splitting noise, which could be heard across the Channel.

It had been going on for almost a week when Lieutenant Haywood came to talk to his men. They had been delayed for two days already, he told them, because of the atrocious weather, but the weather reports for the following day, Saturday 1 July, promised to be dry and fine so the Big Push was set for the morning.

'The Ulster regiments are to be in the forefront of the attack,' he said. 'But 108th and 109th Brigades will attack from the side ten minutes after the main onslaught. So on the whistle you will leave your trenches, make for the woods and assemble there. It has been shelled already but will afford you some shelter. In fact, we have pounded Jerry so hard that we have probably wiped out most of any resistance.'

'What is our objective, sir?' Sergeant Lancaster asked.

'To gain control of Schwaben Redoubt,' the lieutenant said, pinning a map on the wall and pointing with his stick. 'Reinforcements from other regiments should also have broken through by then and will join you there. You will proceed to St Pierre Divion and Beaucourt Station.'

Finn felt his mouth go suddenly dry. He knew this was the real thing, what he had joined the army for nearly two years earlier. Now he was to find out what he was made of.

'Thieoval village itself will be attacked by the Salford Pals,' the lieutenant went on. 'It has already been heavily shelled, most of the buildings razed

168

to the ground and the people long gone. However, many of the houses have strong cellars and there may well be Germans holed up in there. They are to be rooted out.

'We go over the top tomorrow,' he continued, his eyes raking up and down the lines of men. In a voice as cold as steel he continued, 'And remember, if your comrade falls, you step over him and go on, even if the man is related to you. Your duty is to go forward.' He saw the men were uncomfortable with such orders and so he went on, 'To do anything else could be seen as cowardice and you could end up being shot. Have you all got that?'

Finn and Christy exchanged glances. Oh, they had got it, all right, and Finn thought it left a nasty taste in his mouth. But they were in the army and that army made up its own rules, they had to obey them or else.

NINE

They were in the trenches ready for the signal. Father Clifford was moving among the company, hearing confessions, giving Communion, just simply praying, or putting his hand on a man's shoulder in a gesture of support, and didn't seem to mind about his soutane trailing in the mud.

'Would you like him to hear your confession?' Christy asked.

'Are you kidding?' Finn said. 'My nerves are jumping about all over the place and I might come out with anything. Anyway, he heard my confession only a few days ago. I haven't had a chance to sin at anything yet. Now isn't that a sad admission to make?'

Christy was unable to reply for the priest was at his elbow. 'Are you set?' he asked them both.

'As set as we ever will be,' Finn said. 'Is anyone ever ready for war?'

'It is a righteous war,' the priest said. 'And you will win through with God's help.'

170

'Yes, Father,' Christy and Finn chorused, knowing it was always safer to agree with a priest. He blessed them both, made the sign of the cross on their foreheads then moved on. Christy and Finn watched him go as the trench mortar batteries ceased firing. Finn's muscles tensed because he knew the orders to go over the top would come soon, and fear of what was to come trailed down his spine. In the eerie quiet he adjusted his rifle, checked his bayonet was secure, and he waited.

When the whistle sounded into the early morning, there was no room for fear or hesitation of any sort as the men scrambled up the ladders. Once out of the trench they were running for the relative shelter of the woods. They were hardly able to see anything as a smoke screen had been set up to conceal the advancing Ulster troops.

The swirling smoke caught in Finn's throat and made him cough, but he thought that far better than being shot to pieces; if he couldn't see the enemy then they wouldn't be able to see him.

He drew to a halt in the wood and flung himself beside Christy on his stomach in the partial shelter of the trees.

'This is the one day when I would have preferred cloudy skies or even rain,' he told his friend.

'Why?'

'Don't you see?' Finn cried. 'If that smoke screen disperses we will be at a disadvantage because our direction is uphill and to the east, into the rising sun.'

'Aye, I see,' Christy said. 'We'll be like sitting ducks.'

'That's about the shape of it,' Finn replied. 'Now we must wait here until it is our turn and see if we are both right.'

The wait was agonising, and though they couldn't see much they could hear plenty. The German guns were barking out relentlessly towards the advancing troops and they heard cries and screams as some evidently reached their marks.

After a few minutes, Christy's horrified eyes met those of Finn. 'Can you hear those bloody guns?' he said in a shocked whisper. 'I thought that they expected opposition to be minimal.'

Finn could read the fear in Christy's face and heard it in his voice. He was no better for the blood ran like ice in his veins.

'It's what we were led to believe. We'll likely find out the right of it soon enough because Lieutenant Haywood is on his feet, look.'

The men stood up, all eyes on the lieutenant, who was scrutinising his watch. 'Right men. Stand ready,' he said. 'Just a few minutes longer.'

Finn's body was tense. He felt as if every nerve was exposed and tingling. And then came the order.

'Charge!'

There was no time to think or feel. Finn went on with the rest, but when he burst from the cover of the wood he knew no words to describe the scene. The whole field beyond the barbed wire was littered with dead and wounded. Some of them

172

were crying out, but their voices could barely be heard above the sound of battle, the barking of the rifles, the whining shells exploding and the constant tattoo of machine-gun fire. Some were still twitching, and others, with limbs blown off, were lying in pools of their own blood. He was shocked by the enormity of such tragedy.

They had no time to stand and stare, however, for the lieutenant was urging them on. They slithered under the barbed wire, and then Finn and Christy were crossing no man's land side by side.

The swirly smoke had disappeared and so the enemy had a clear sight of them from the top of the hill. They dipped and dodged around their stricken comrades, hoping to escape the bullets whining past their heads and the shells erupting all round them, but the sun was in their eyes, as Finn had prophesied that it would be.

They hadn't even reached the first enemy trench when the lieutenant was struck. The first bullet struck his shoulder and he staggered, a second found his chest. He sank to his knees and then keeled over. His eyes were shut, but he was breathing.

'Sir!' Finn cried. 'Lieutenant Haywood!'

The man's eyes opened and his voice was little above a whisper as he said. 'Go on, Sullivan, damn you. Go on.'

Finn still hesitated and the lieutenant croaked out. 'That's an order, Sullivan.'

'But, sir . . .'

Christy was pulling his sleeve. 'Come on, man. He's gone anyway.'

Finn saw that Christy was right. The lieutenant's head had fallen sideways and blood was dripping from his mouth. Finn didn't need to feel for the pulse in the neck.

'Let's be at them and avenge his death,' Christy said. 'And all those fine boys and men left lying here.'

Finn nodded. He started to run, Christy beside him, bending low and from side to side, and while men in front and to either side of them were hit and fell, no bullets touched them. They stormed the first German trench, Finn fighting like a mad man. He had once expressed doubts about ever sticking a bayonet in a human being but he had had no doubts now. He seemed invincible and so did Christy, and Dinny McColl was just ahead of them.

Prisoners were taken and sent back to the British lines under guard. The Inniskillings went on to three support trenches with similar success. They continued to advance now led by Sergeant Lancaster, and they entered the southern end of the Schwaben Redoubt where they overwhelmed the German resistance and four hundred prisoners were taken and sent back to the British lines. Finn felt adrenalin pumping through his body.

However, as they proceeded up the Redoubt they met with heavy fire and many were hit. Eventually they were forced to withdraw to the earlier captured trenches.

'I wonder where the promised reinforcements are,'

Christy said. 'There are too few of us to hold this for very long.'

But the hours ticked by and no reinforcements appeared. Finn found the waiting getting to him. 'We can't just sit here all day, Sarge,' he said at last.

'What do you suggest, Sullivan?' the sergeant asked testily. 'An attack with so few will just massacre the rest of us.'

'Yes, sir,' Finn said, 'if we go in all guns blazing. I don't know if they have more men than we do, though. I mean, just a handful of soldiers could hold this because they are in a far better strategic position at the top of the hill. How about small groups going up either side and surprising them?'

'It's madness.'

Finn shrugged. 'We better wait then, Sarge,' he said. 'But didn't the 36th Division promise no surrender?'

The sergeant knew he had to make a decision. It was beginning to look as if there was not going to be any further support. If they did nothing they would have to stay where they were until night-fall and then retreat.

Retreat stuck in the sergeant's craw. So many men had died or were injured already, and if he and his men just retreated those comrades would have died in vain. He knew too that it would be doubly hard to retake this position later because the Germans would reinforce it. Sullivan could be right: little more than a handful of men could control that hill. What if that proved to be the case? Would his failure to advance be cowardice?

'All right,' he said at last. 'The German guns and attention will be focused down the hill and they probably think that if we were going to attack we would have done so by now and may have relaxed their guard a little. Two groups of us will attack the side trenches.' He picked up a stick and drew on a stone. 'We will creep right to the back if we can,' he said. 'That will be the last thing they'll expect and when we have them engaged, the rest of you attack the front trenches.'

Finn wasn't the only relieved one. It was much better when a plan of action was devised and they were doing something, even if it was risky. The sergeant chose two teams of eight men. Finn, Christy and Dinny McColl were in the sergeant's own team.

They began to make their way slowly and stealthily down the hillside avoiding any patches of scree that might crunch beneath their boots and betray their positions. When they reached the back end of the trenches, the sergeant gave them his thumbs up.

The Germans had posted a sentry, but he was looking the other way. The sergeant withdrew his knife and killed him virtually silently. Then one by one the British slipped into the German trench. The Germans were taken totally by surprise, but the other group of Inniskillings were running up the hill before they had time to position their rifles. The fight was fast and furious, and the Ulstermen were gaining the upper hand when suddenly Finn saw the silver flash of a bayonet and called out a warning to Dinny. He turned, but too late, and the German drove the bayonet into Dinny's side. He slithered to the muddy ground, his life blood pumping from him.

'You murdering bastard!' Finn cried, intent on avenging Dinny's death. He failed to notice another German soldier creeping up on him. Christy screamed as he saw the bayonet slice into Finn's body and, too close to shoot him, he smashed his rifle down on the German's head.

Around him the day's fighting was drawing to a close. The remaining Germans surrendered and were disarmed, but Christy had eyes only for the mate he had known for ever. He felt as if a lump of lead was in his stomach as he remembered Finn saying that he would hate to end his life on the end of a bayonet. Finn's eyes were glazed, but still open. Christy kneeled beside him.

'Go on,' Finn said weakly. 'You know the rules.'

'Bugger the rules.'

'You can bugger them all you like. But you still have to obey them, you know that,' Finn said.

'I could pull you back to the bottom of the Redoubt and try and find you some shade. It might be ages before the medics come,' Christy said.

'No, you couldn't,' Finn croaked. 'You could be shot for disobeying orders and I wouldn't make it anyway.'

'What rubbish are you spouting now?'

'No rubbish,' Finn said slowly, his voice beginning to slur. 'This is the end of the road for me, Christy.'

'Ah, no, man,' Christy said. He was unable to see the glistening of Finn's eyes because of the tears in his own. 'You're my best mate. We've been together through thick and thin. You can't give up on me now.' Tears spilled over and trickled down his cheeks. But he knew just by looking at the waxen pallor of Finn's skin, and the trickle of blood seeping through his blue-tinged lips, that he spoke the truth. He felt sick to his very soul.

'Take my dog tag,' Finn said, and Christy had to strain to hear every painful word he was gasping out. 'Look out for Gabrielle and the child for me, and tell Gabrielle I died still loving her with all my heart and soul.'

He closed his eyes and suddenly there was a rattle in his throat followed by a sudden gasp and then silence.

There was a roaring in Christy's head too and a soundless voice screaming denial that Finn should be dead.

But he was gone, the boy and then the man he had known and loved all his life, and he didn't know how he was going to bear the loss of him. Already, he was feeling as if he had a hollow pit of pain in his stomach. He unfastened Finn's dog tag, told his name, serial number, brigade number and regiment, and he put it in his own tunic

178

pocket and lay for a moment almost overwhelmed with grief. Then, because there was nothing else to do, he began to slither after his comrades.

He had reached the other side of the hill and was hurrying to catch up when a shell came from nowhere. Instinctively Christy rolled into a ball, but it lifted him into the air and he landed in a crater and knew no more.

The Ulster battalions captured the redoubt in vain. Their reinforcements had been beaten back by the Germans and they were given orders to retreat under cover of darkness. The medical orderlies were hard at work in no man's land, taking the casualties to the infirmary on stretchers.

Father Clifford, who had been shaken by the tragic savagery of that first day, worked alongside them, almost overwhelmed with sorrow. Never in all his life had he seen so many corpses. Some had even been killed as they left the trenches, had tumbled back into it and lay spread-eagled on the duckboards. Some were impaled on the wire, but no man's land was a sea of bodies and parts and pieces of bodies.

The short summer night was almost over, there was definitely a lightening of the sky, and he was just leaving the infirmary to collect more casualties when they brought in Christy's unconscious form. The priest gasped when he saw him and the stump of his left leg that the orderlies had tended to in the field to try to stem the bleeding.

'Someone you know?' the doctor asked as he cut the clothes from him.

The priest nodded. 'Yes, but then I know so many of them. His name is Christopher Byrne and he is with the Royal Inniskillings.'

'Odd,' the doctor said, reaching into Christy's tunic pocket. 'There is a tag here that says his name is Finn Sullivan. 'And he showed it to the priest.'

'That's his best mate,' the priest said. 'They have been bosom buddies since they were small.' He knew the only reason Christy would have removed Finn's dog tag was if he was dead, and he told the doctor that. 'Will Christy make it?' he asked.

'Probably,' the doctor said. 'But he needs to be prepared for surgery.'

Father Clifford left them to it and returned to his tent, beaten down by heartache. He thought of Finn's pretty little wife and the child she was carrying, and Finn's parents, whom Finn had once told him hadn't wanted him to enlist in the first place. After what he had seen that day, he didn't blame them either.

They would likely be prostrated with grief at the loss of their son and he could guess many parents would be the same. There would be grieving families all over England and Ireland he imagined. And then there would be parents like Christy's, who had seen their fit young man march away, and would welcome him home maimed and mutilated. War surely was a terrible catastrophe altogether.

*   *   *

180

It was two days before the priest was able to see Christy, and then only for a few minutes because they stressed he was still very ill. The priest saw the pain reflected in the glazed eyes that were turned to him.

'Hello, Christy,' he said gently, his heart turning over in pity to see him in such a state. 'How are you feeling?'

'You don't want to know, Father,' Christy said. 'You want me to say I'm grand and I'm bloody well not. In fact, I don't know whether I will ever feel grand again.'

'That doesn't surprise me. Really it doesn't,' the priest said. 'Did Finn—'

'Finn's dead, Father.'

'Ah, Christy, I'm sorry. I know how close the two of you were.'

Christy's eyes were dulled as he said, 'You know, Father, I wouldn't have minded joining Finn, for I will never have such a good friend however long I live. Maybe you think that wicked of me?'

'Not at all. You are still coming to terms with his death.'

'I don't think I will ever come to terms with it,' Christy said with a sigh. 'There is another that needs to be told too, of course, and that is Gabrielle.'

'Won't the authorities have informed her?'

'I don't know,' Christy said. 'No one knows officially about Finn's marriage, do they? Finn asked me to remove his dog tag and they told me that when they found it in my tunic, with me unconscious and not able to put them right, they

181

gave it in like mine so that the army could inform our families. I think, according to army records, Finn's next of kin will still be his parents.'

'But they will know that the news of his death should have gone to Gabrielle and will tell her.'

Christy shook his head. 'Unless you have already sent the letter he left with you, his parents don't even know of Gabrielle, never mind that he was married to her.'

'He told me that he had informed them.'

'I don't care what he told you. They don't know.'

'Dear, dear,' said the priest, distressed at the state of affairs. 'I will sort this out, because the girl must be informed.'

The priest went away quickly to attend to this and Christy felt his spirits sink. What was it all about? he asked himself. Their first day on the battlefield, and Finn's body still lay there, and he himself would go through the rest of his life with one leg. Life was a bloody bitch all right. And he turned his face to the wall and wept.

Father Clifford went into his tent, sat down at the desk and put his head in his hands. In front of him was a writing pad. He made no move to pull it nearer, though he knew he had many letters to write. Finn's parents needed to know of his marriage. That was of prime importance, and according to what Christy said, the letter Finn had left in his keeping was the one informing his parents of that. If he sent it now, as he must, of course, it would follow hot on the heels of the telegram informing his parents of his death. Surely that was a lot for them to cope with, yet it had to be done. He had the marriage lines to enclose with the letter so that they could see it for themselves.

He also had to write to Gabrielle, informing her of her husband's death and trying to explain why she hadn't been informed by the military. He groaned aloud. So distracted was he that he didn't hear the whistle of the rogue shells until it was too late. The first one ripped into the cookhouse, killing the cook his three helpers, and some surviving soldiers nearby, having a meal, but the second was a direct hit on Father Clifford's tent so that his body, together with all the letters and documents relating to Finn's marriage, were blown into a million pieces.

Christy was unaware of this for some time, because after the shell attack, the hospital was moved back to what was considered a safer location. Christy was actually too ill to be moved and he developed an infection from which his life hung in the balance for weeks.

In Buncrana, they were aware of the Battle of the Somme, and for the first time could read with horror of the colossal loss of life and look at the heart-rending grainy newspaper photographs.

'It says twenty-one thousand Allied soldiers were killed in the first hour,' Tom said. 'It's hard even to visualise so many.'

Thomas John's face was grey and lined with

worry. 'Aye, and if there were that many killed in the first hour, how many were killed in the first day, and the day after.'

'This wasn't a battle,' Biddy said. 'It was a massacre and they'll just go on massacring people.'

No one said anything, because there was nothing to say. The photographs showed the scale of the tragedy all too clearly as there were many pictures of no man's land littered with mangled bodies.

Along with accompanying pictures the reporter had written,

The dead were left on the field, but any who have a chance of survival are carried away to the field hospital on stretchers by the medical orderlies. Some of these men are horrifically injured, and many have missing limbs, but the doctors and nurses are working tirelessly to save them.

'Of course there's no saying that Finn was involved in any of this,' Joe said.

'That's right. He might be in a different place altogether,' Tom said, his tone matching Joe's. He was worried about the affect the report of the battle was having on his parents.

Thomas John looked from one son to the other. He knew what they were doing. Worry for his youngest son was clawing at his innards, but he knew he had to put a brave face on it for the sake of his wife. He sighed heavily as he got to his feet.

'If Finn is involved then no doubt we will know soon enough,' he said, patting Biddy's trembling hand. 'And people say no news is good news.'

The following Sunday morning the three Sullivan men were just finishing the milking when Tom, glanced up through the open door of the byre, saw a boy in a uniform of sorts clatter across the cobblestones on a bicycle. He saw him throw this down before the cottage and take a telegram from the bag around his shoulders.

None of the Sullivans had ever received a telegram, but Tom remembered Joe had said that was how the army informed the relatives if a man was missing or dead. His mouth suddenly felt very dry.

He looked back into the byre where his father and brother were tipping milk into the churns, and he called out, 'There's a boy here with—'

He got no further, for they all heard Biddy give a sharp cry of distress and Tom, bursting into the yard, saw the boy standing apprehensively before the open cottage door. He looked thankful to see Tom, and he said, 'She sort of fell over when I gave her the telegram.'

'It's all right,' Tom assured him. 'I will see to her now,' and as the relieved boy mounted his bike again, he turned to his mother.

She was kneeling on the floor, keening in deep distress, the tears pouring from her eyes and a crumpled buff telegram clutched to her breast. His father and Joe were at his heels.

'What is it?' Thomas John cried, but in his heart of hearts he knew what it was all about

Tom didn't answer, but instead lifted his mother to her feet and, putting his arms around her, led her to one of the easy chairs pulled up before the fire, saying as he did so, 'Come on, Mammy, don't take on like this.'

He was moved by the bleak expression in his mother's dark and saddened eyes. She didn't answer but handed him the telegram and he scanned it quickly.

'It's Finn,' he said to his father and Joe standing staring at him.

'Well, of course it's Finn,' Thomas John snapped. 'I haven't a rake of sons in the British Army. Is he dead?'

Tom nodded and Thomas John felt a deep and intense pain inside him. 'Ah God,' he cried. 'What a tragic waste of a young life.'

Biddy began crying afresh and Tom busied himself making tea so that none would see his own wet cheeks. As the eldest, he remembered Finn from the day that he was born. He recalled the cheeky grin he had and how funny he had been as a wee boy. He would trail after him all the time, and plague him to death with questions. What he wouldn't give to hear those same questions now, he thought as he set out with the cups, noting that Thomas John's eyes were glittery with unshed tears and even Joe's were brighter than normal.

No one went to Mass that Sunday, but sat on and talked of Finn, their memories punctuated with Biddy's sobs.

'I will have nothing of his,' she said suddenly, 'not even a grave to tend.'

'Well, that's the way of it in wartime,' Thomas John said. 'And you won't be alone either. There will be many families, both sides of the Irish Sea, mourning the loss of a loved one this day, I'm thinking.'

'Maybe, but that doesn't help me.'

'Nothing will help,' Thomas John said. 'Nothing but time.'

In the end, because Biddy was incapable, Tom and Joe made a stab at getting some breakfast for them all, though his mother could eat none of it and even Tom had little appetite.

Eventually he could stand the atmosphere no longer, and when he lifted his jacket from the hook behind the door, Joe said, 'Where you off to?'

Tom shrugged. 'Nowhere in particular. I just want to try and walk some of the sadness out of me.'

'Do you want company?'

'Aye, come along if you want to.'

For a while, the two brothers walked in silence, and then Joe said, 'It's unbelievable really, isn't it? Finn seemed so alive, had more about him than either you or me.' He gave a sad little smile. 'D'you know what the little fool said to me when I told him to be careful? He said not to worry about him.

That he would catch the bullets in his teeth and spit them back.'

'Aye,' commented Tom wryly. 'Maybe he found that more difficult to do than he anticipated. When a person joins the army, especially if the country is at war at the time, you take on board the risks, or you think you do. It was the first thing crossed my mind that day in Buncrana when Finn stepped forward to answer the recruiting officer's call. Inside, though, you hope and pray that your loved ones will come home safe and sound.'

'Aye,' Joe said. 'And now we know that that is not going to happen I think Nuala should be told. Daddy won't want to go today and leave Mammy on her own. I wish her employers hadn't asked Nuala to go in as a favour today.'

'Yes, and wasn't she upset enough at the reports of this battle when she read all about it in the paper?' Tom said, as they began to walk towards the Big House. 'Of course any normal human being couldn't fail to be upset.'

'Huh, if Mammy had got her own way she would never have let Nuala see those papers,' Joe said.

'I know,' Tom said, 'but you can't protect people from this. It's too big and too tragic.'

'Anyway, didn't she tell us that they talk about the war all the time at the house because the mistress's brother is in the army as well?' Joe said. 'Mind you, she'll know something is amiss with none of us at Mass today.'

'Yes,' Tom agreed. 'And I don't mind telling you I dread doing this. Nuala will be heartbroken for she and Finn were very close.'

Nuala was in the window of the nursery rocking the fractious baby and wondering why none of her family had been at Mass that morning. She should have gone up after Mass and seen that everything was all right, but she had promised Nanny Pritchard that she would be straight back. The point was her master and mistress were out for the day, and it meant that Nanny Pritchard had charge of all the children on her own and there were four of them now. This was more than enough for anyone, especially with the new baby, wee Sophie, teething and letting everyone know about it.

Suddenly, she saw her two brothers turn into the gravel drive from the road. They had never called at the house before, and at the look on their faces and their determined strides, she felt her spine suddenly tingle with alarm.

'My brothers are here, Nanny,' she said, turning from the window. 'Will you have the baby? I must see what they want.'

'Aye, give the child to me and get yourself away,' Nanny Pritchard said. 'I know you have been fretting that something was wrong at home.'

She watched Nuala leave the room, biting her bottom lip and hoping that she wasn't going to hear bad news.

Nuala flew through the house and arrived in the

kitchen where the preparations for dinner were in progress and delicious aromas wafted in the air.

Nuala wasn't a usual visitor in the kitchen and the cook had just turned from the stove to ask her if she wanted something, when there was a knock at the door. That too was an unusual occurrence. Grumbling slightly, she went to open it.

Tom had just asked if he could have a word with Nuala and she was there before him, her eyes full of foreboding as she said in a voice that trembled slightly, 'What is it? What's wrong?'

Tom's heart felt like lead. He said gently, 'It's Finn, Nuala. We had the telegram this morning.'

'Dead?' Nuala said, her voice little more than a whisper. 'Are you telling me he is dead?'

'Aye.'

She looked at Tom and Joe with eyes so full of pain that Tom had to look away. 'Finn assured me that he would be all right,' she said in a small voice brittle with anguish. 'That any bullets would bounce off him.'

She suddenly covered her face with her hands. 'Oh God, I can't bear the thought that he is dead,' she cried. 'I really can't bear it.'

The cook left down her spoon and she put her plump and motherly arms around Nuala while she wept.

'Take her home,' she said to Tom, when she was calmer at last, and to Nuala she said gently, 'You need to be with your own at a time like this and be some support to your poor mother.'

190

'But Nanny Pritchard . . .'

'Amy here will go up and give a hand,' the cook said, indicating the kitchen maid. 'And we will cope. You go on home, for the loss of that poor boy will be a grievous one for you all.'

Nuala knew the cook was right. She stopped only to fetch her coat from the nursery and tell Nanny Pritchard the news, and then she walked home, a brother either side of her, so numbed by the tragedy that no one could think of a word to say. Nuala had never experienced the death of anyone before and didn't know how to cope with the loss of her very dear brother. She remembered the time when they had been playmates when they were children, the only one of her brothers her mother had allowed her to play with, and they stayed close as they grew up. Nuala had known Finn better than any of them.

She remembered too his letters enthusing about the girl Gabrielle, who he had claimed was the love of his life. She had wondered if Gabrielle's love for Finn was just as ardent and if she had been as distressed as he had when his regiment had been deployed. She thought it hard on her that she might never know what had happened to him. She wouldn't have minded writing to her, but all she knew was that her name was Gabrielle and she lived in France and so she had to accept that there was nothing she could do about it.

Everyone was saddened by the news of Finn's death and the commemorative Mass for him was well attended, but life had to go on. Nuala returned to work and the farm still had to be tended, although Tom and Joe shouldered most of the work, for Thomas John had seemed to have aged twenty years.

'There is a pain in my heart every time I think of Finn,' he said to Biddy as they sat together one evening. 'It's like I've strained it in some way.'

It was so odd for Thomas John to speak of his feelings this way that Biddy just stared at him.

'I loved him, you see,' Thomas John said. 'Better than the other two, and I was so afraid of showing that favouritism that I was even harder on him. I think of every bad thing I have said to him – and over the years there has been a fine collection of them – and now they come back to haunt me.'

'Don't do this, Thomas John,' Biddy said. 'You are a grand father, none better. Finn was always a happy child and he died doing something he had chosen to do.'

Thomas John sighed. 'Aye, I have to accept that I know, though I doubt any of the boys really knew what they were going into. The whole thing, all those deaths, and they are still dying daily. It's almost obscene.'

TEN

It was early August before Christy was declared to be out of danger and then he enquired about Father Clifford, surprised that he hadn't been to see him.

'I'm not sure what happened to him,' said the young nurse whom he asked, 'but I'll try and find out for you.'

Two days later, Christy found out that Father Clifford had been killed in the shell attack. He was sorry about that because the priest had been a fine man and a brave one. He knew that the likelihood was that Father Clifford had been killed before he could write the letter to Finn's parents about Gabrielle because he had been receiving regular correspondence from his mother in which she had gone on about the tragedy of Finn's death, even told him about going to a Memorial Mass in his memory, but had never mentioned news of any sort of marriage between Finn and a French beauty.

Christy didn't know what to do. He could hardly write and ask his mother. That would set the cat amongst the pigeons right and proper. In the end he decided to do nothing until he was home again and then he would be able to see the setup for himself. However, it was halfway through August before arrangements were made to get him to the coast and ship him home.

The people of St-Omer were well aware the Battle of the Somme was still raging. They heard the boom of the guns and they read reports of the fighting in the French newspapers, and scrutinised the photographs as they were coming to terms with the horrifying list of casualties.

Finn had just been one of two thousand from the Ulster battalions killed on that first day. It was they who launched the first assault and so lost a great many men. A Captain William Spender, who witnessed the carnage of that first day, wrote in his report

The Ulster men have lost half the men who attacked and in doing so have sacrificed themselves for the Empire, which has treated them none too well. The much-derided Ulster Volunteer Force has won a name which equals any in history. Their devotion, which no doubt has helped the advance elsewhere, deserves the gratitude of the British Empire. It is due to the memory of these brave fellows that their beloved Province should be fairly treated.

Many of the surviving Ulster battalions returned to the old camp at St-Omer to rest and recuperate. News of this was given to Gabrielle by Yvette because Gabrielle couldn't leave the bakery.

'Shall I try to find out if Finn is one of them?' Yvette asked her sister.

'No,' Gabrielle said. 'If Papa found out he would be angry with you. Anyway,' she said assuredly, 'if Finn is camped here, he'll get word to me somehow, or even come and see me, and Papa could do nothing about it, because Finn is my husband.'

Finn did not come, but then neither did any telegram.

'Are you worried Finn might be injured or something?' Yvette asked Gabrielle about a week later.

'No,' Gabrielle said confidently. 'Nothing can have happened to him or I would have heard of it.'

'Are you sure?' Yvette insisted.

'Ah, yes. I am quite, quite sure,' Gabrielle said. 'Finn explained it all to me. Once we married I became his next of kin, and that means I would be informed by the Military if anything had happened to him.'

Yvette looked at her sister dubiously. She wasn't at all sure that she was right. With the carnage and mayhem that she had read about in the paper, it was not inconceivable that a body might lie unidentified for some time.

She didn't say this, though. She reckoned that Gabrielle was going through a hard enough time without her adding to it, because their father had never forgiven her. Yvette, though, couldn't help feeling excited about the coming baby. She was eager to hold her niece or nephew and was delighted that Gabrielle had already asked her to be godmother.

Gabrielle was glad that Yvette was there too because she was the only one who had a kind word for her. Mariette, mindful of her husband's temper, virtually ignored her, and her father treated her much as she imagined he would a stray dog. He expected Gabrielle to rise when he did in the morning, and then he kept her hard at work all day long. There was no chance for her to rest at all, no allowance made for her pregnant state.

In the beginning, she had thought that working with him in the bakery, she might be able to win her father round about Finn and maybe even to look forward to the birth of his grandchild.

'And how can I take any joy or pride in any grandchild you are carrying?' he had thundered when she had mentioned the baby. 'It will be little more than a bastard and a constant reminder of the shame you have brought upon this house.'

His eyes seemed filled with hate as he regarded her and she ardently wished for some sort of communication from Finn to reassure her that this wasn't going to be her life for always, that soon her father's feelings would have no bearing on their life together.

*   *   *

She was over eight months pregnant when she collapsed in the bakery at the end of August. Mariette looked at her child in a crumpled heap on the floor, her hair plastered to her head, her face wet with perspiration and lined with fatigue, and she felt ashamed of herself.

'She needs her bed,' she said to her husband. 'And we should send for the doctor.'

Pierre pursed his lips. They hadn't sought the services of a doctor about Gabrielle. Pierre had claimed that she was young and healthy, and when the time came she'd make do with the old woman who did as a midwife in St-Omer. Mariette knew, though, that really he hadn't informed the doctor because he wanted to keep Gabrielle's pregnancy a secret as long as possible.

She seldom argued with her husband, mindful of the overpowering rages he could fly into if she tried to oppose him in any way. This time, though, concern for her daughter had to transcend her caution and she said impatiently, 'You must help me take her to her bed and go for the doctor immediately. This is no time to think of yourself. She could easily lose the child. Would you have that on your conscience?'

In Pierre's opinion, Gabrielle losing the child would be the best outcome all round, but not if he had any sort of hand in it, for that would be a mortal sin. So he gave Mariette a nod and said, 'Make the bed ready. I will carry Gabrielle on my own.'

Dr Marc Gilbert was a fairly young man to be

in charge of the town's health and he had heard the rumours of the pregnancy of the baker's daughter, but he did wonder if rumours were all they were because there had been no news about a marriage, and he knew the Joberts to be a respectable family. The father, it was well known, was a force to be reckoned with, especially when it concerned his daughters.

He was surprised therefore to find Pierre Jobert at his door, who explained not only about his daughter's pregnancy, but also about her collapse in the bakery. When later he looked down on the unconscious form of Gabrielle with her face as white as the sheets she lay upon, he noted the swell of her stomach as he examined her gently. 'When is the child due?' he asked.

Mariette answered, 'Almost four weeks yet. Towards the end of September.'

The doctor turned to Pierre. 'What was a girl so advanced in pregnancy doing in the bakery?'

'She was working,' Pierre said shortly. 'Her sister, Yvette, is too young and I cannot cope alone.'

'How you manage your affairs, Monsieur Jobert, is up to you,' Dr Gilbert said angrily. 'But this young girl had no place in that bakery when she is so heavily pregnant.'

'She is my daughter and I will treat her as I see fit,' Pierre blustered. 'You have no right to talk to me like this.'

'I have every right,' the doctor said. 'Gabrielle is now my patient.'

'See to her then,' he almost snarled, red-faced with temper, as he crossed the room and yanked the door open. 'I at least have work to do.' He slammed the door so hard that it juddered on its hinges.

The figure on the bed didn't move, though, and the doctor, noting the ring on Gabrielle's finger, looked quizzically at Mariette.

'I didn't know Gabrielle was married,' he said.

'You may as well know it all doctor,' Mariette sighed. 'Though I should hate the news spread abroad.'

'A doctor is used to keeping secrets.'

'Of course,' Mariette said. 'But you see, Doctor, Gabrielle was married at the British Army camp by the Catholic priest and she had to be married, because we found out that she was expecting a baby.' She looked the doctor full in the face. 'Now I imagine that that has shocked you to the core.'

'Very little shocks me now,' the doctor said. 'So her husband is a soldier?'

Mariette nodded. 'He is an Irishmen but in the British Army.'

'That explains your husband's attitude a little,' the doctor said. 'You must remember that these things happen, and especially so in wartime, I believe, and at least you say that she married the man.'

Mariette nodded. 'Yes, she did, but Pierre is still having a very hard job coming to terms with it. You needn't worry, though, Doctor,' she went on,

'I am as much to blame for not sticking up for Gabrielle more. I am just so used to doing things my husband's way, but this time I have let my daughter down. Things for Gabrielle will change for the better from now on.'

'Glad to hear it,' the doctor said, getting to his feet. 'I think she is wakening. She should be all right now. I would let her stay in bed for a day or two and I'll look in then and check that all is well. If you want me before that you know where I am.'

Gabrielle opened her eyes slowly as if they were very heavy and looked from the doctor to her mother, her face showing her confusion. 'What happened?' she asked.

Mariette smiled at her. 'Let me see the doctor out,' she said. 'And I will explain everything.'

Mariette apologised to Gabrielle for not supporting her more, but Gabrielle didn't blame her. She knew that it was a brave person who would stand against her father. Now, however, with her doctor's words ringing in her ears, Mariette felt quite strong, and the first thing she did that day was something Gabrielle thought she'd never do, and that was to ask about the Irishman that she had fallen in love with.

Mariette watched her daughter's face light up as she told her about the farm Finn's family had, and the nearest town a place called Buncrana, which sounded not all that different to St-Omer. She knew from Gabrielle's voice and the look in her eyes that she truly loved this Finn Sullivan. She suddenly understood how two people in love could forget themselves when they knew they were soon to be parted and maybe for years. Every minute would have to count.

'Maman,' Gabrielle said suddenly, 'I know what I did was terrible for you all, and I am very sorry about that. I had no wish to shame you, but Finn and I loved each other so much that we forgot ourselves just the once and I would love it if you could forgive me for that one slip?'

Mariette kissed her. 'I do, my dear,' she said. 'Now you lie down and rest yourself, and I will go and tell Yvette you are all right. You gave us all a fright, you know, and she will be longing to come up and see you for herself.'

'Let her, Maman.'

'You won't be too tired?'

'No, not for Yvette,' Gabrielle said. 'Let her come up.'

She listened to her mother going down the stairs and felt even her toes curl up with happiness. The only thing that would make it complete would be a letter from Finn.

Two days later, Mariette took the post in from the postman and extracted a letter addressed to Gabrielle. She knew it wasn't from Finn because she knew his writing. She knew more or less everything else about him too, because Gabrielle had told her, delighted that she was able to confide in

201

her mother. She hoped that the doctor would see the improvement in her because she was expecting him to call in that morning.

As she took the letter upstairs, she noted that it had been sent from Ireland, where Finn's family lived. Maybe they had written to Gabrielle at long last. She had thought it odd that they hadn't written before this and welcomed her to their family. She had blamed the war and thought maybe Finn hadn't had the chance to get word to them. No matter, it was here now.

'It's from your husband's people, I think,' Mariette said to her daughter as she passed the letter over. Gabrielle took it from her eagerly and tore open the envelope, anxious to hear what it said. However, it wasn't from Finn's family, but from Christy Byrne, Finn's best friend. He told Gabrielle that Finn was dead, that he had died on the first day of the battle, 1 July, the same battle in which Christy himself had lost his left leg and he had been too ill to write sooner. 'He said that I was to tell you that he died still loving you with all his heart and soul,' Christy finished.

There was more, but Gabrielle threw the letter from her with a shriek. Tears spilled from her and ran down her cheeks.

'What is it?' Mariette cried, but Gabrielle could only look at her and shake her head helplessly.

She seemed incapable of speech, unable to say that she would never see her beloved Finn again, never hear his lilting voice, his infectious laugh, and never feel his arms encircling her, his lips on hers. She felt like a shell of a person, as if there was nothing inside her but a dark hole filled with grief and heartbreak, with an agonising band of pain encircling her heart. She wrapped her arms around herself and howled like a wounded animal might. Mariette was alarmed and almost in tears herself seeing her daughter's distress. She tried to put her arms around her, but Gabrielle fought her off.

The primeval sounds permeated down to the shop and the bakery, and Pierre and Yvette came pounding up the stairs.

'What is it?' Pierre cried.

'How do I know?' Mariette said. 'She won't let me near her. But whatever it is, it's bad. Fetch the doctor, Pierre, and quickly,'

Gabrielle was unaware of any of this. It was as if she were enveloped in a cloak of sadness and sorrow deeper than she had ever felt before, where no one could reach her and where her tears and her gulping sobs were blocking her throat and threatening to choke her.

She wasn't aware that Dr Gilbert came, for she could neither see nor hear him. In the end, he had no option but to administer a draught to sedate her. When eventually she was quiet and those anguished eyes closed, he took the letter from the floor.

Though Mariette could speak English, she had never learned to read it, and as she passed the

203

letter to the doctor she asked, 'Can you read English?'

'Yes, a little.'

'Well, it was something in the letter she received this morning that brought this on.'

The doctor scrutinised the letter, got the general gist of it, and told Pierre, Mariette and Yvette what it said.

'So, why didn't the Military inform her, as Gabrielle said they would?' Yvette asked.

'Oh, this Christy Byrne explains that too,' said the doctor. And he went on to tell the Joberts of the company moving off straight after the marriage. 'I think it was just general lack of communication, which often happens in wartime. According to his friend, this Finn left a letter with Father Clifford, the priest who had married them explaining everything to his parents if anything should happen to him. But the priest was killed before he could send the letter.'

'So the Army would have contacted Finn Sullivan's parents?' Mariette said.

'Yes,' the doctor said. 'They did. That's what this man Christy says.'

'So as far as the Army is concerned, and the Irish family in Donegal, Gabrielle doesn't exist and neither does the child she is carrying?' Pierre asked. 'And the only proof she married him at all is her marriage certificate?'

'That's the way it looks,' the doctor said. 'That is something to go into later when Gabrielle is more able to cope with it. But now we have another problem on our hands.'

'What's that?'

'Well, unless I am very much mistaken, Gabrielle's child doesn't want to wait any longer,' the doctor said. 'And her body will be sluggish because of the draught I administered. She might be safer in hospital.'

'Doctor,' said Mariette, 'Gabrielle isn't just having a baby; she's also coping with the news that the baby's father is dead. A hospital who knows nothing of her heartbreak will do her no good at all.'

'You're right,' the doctor conceded.

'So can you do it if I help you?'

'Yes,' the doctor said. 'I need hot water and towels.'

'I'll see to it,' said Mariette. 'And, Yvette and Pierre, be about your business while we get on.'

Pierre went willingly enough. It wasn't a place for any man, except for a doctor. Yvette would have liked to linger but she had to be in the shop. She'd had the foresight to put the bolt on the door before she had sped up the stairs and she wouldn't be at all surprised if she had a queue of people down the street.

At first, Gabrielle was able to sleep through the contractions because of her drugged state, and the doctor felt confident to leave her in the capable hands of her mother and attend to his

205

other patients. By the time he returned in the early evening, the contractions were strong enough to have jerked Gabrielle awake.

She was still disoriented, however, and in more pain than she could ever remember. It was invading every part of her. She cried and screamed and writhed on the bed, and Mariette, who had seldom left Gabrielle's side all day, mopped her glistening brow.

'Hush, child, it will soon be over.'

'What's happening, Maman?'

'You're in labour, *ma petite*. The baby is in a hurry to be born.'

Gabrielle lay silent. She was giving birth to the baby and soon she would hold in her arms part of her beloved Finn and feel closer to him because of it. She no longer wanted to die, but live to cherish the child made with the rapturous passion that they had shared for such a short time.

She groaned with the power of another contraction. 'Does it always hurt like this, Maman?'

'Yes,' Mariette said. 'But afterwards you will not think of it. Trust me. Hold tight to my hand. You are doing so well.'

Gabrielle held on so tight that when the next contraction was at its height Mariette's bones crunched together. Suddenly, Gabrielle cried, 'I want to push.'

Mariette glanced at the doctor, sitting towards the end of the bed, and when he nodded, she said to Gabrielle, 'Then push, *ma petite*. Push with all your might.'

The doctor cried out, 'Good girl, go on. One more push. Come on, Gabrielle. I can see the head.'

Gabrielle feeling like she was giving birth to a cannonball, gave another almighty push and another and another. Suddenly Gabrielle felt the baby's body slither out from between her legs, and newborn wails filled the room. She was exhausted, yet filled with elation, and she exchanged a weary smile with her mother as the beaming doctor said, 'Well done, Gabrielle. You have a beautiful, bouncing baby girl. Slightly small, but she will grow and she certainly looks healthy enough.'

Gabrielle's emotions rose and plunged in the few days after the birth. One minute she was in black despair because of the death of her beloved Finn. Then she would lift her daughter and hold her close and feel the love for her seeping into her very being, until she remembered that Finn would never see or hold his baby daughter, and then she would sink once more into despondency.

On the fourth day the doctor called to see her. As he examined her he could almost feel her inner sadness, which was reflected in her large dark eyes.

'Have you a name for the baby?' he asked.

Gabrielle nodded. 'I want to call her Bridgette, for Finn's mother, though I daren't tell my father why I want the name, but I am determined on it despite him. I know my mother will support me. I have never known her stand against my father before, but I'm sure she would wrestle with the fiercest lion for the sake of Bridgette.'

The doctor smiled. 'I often find that a small and quite helpless baby born into a family suddenly has immense power over the adults,' he said. 'And who have you in mind for the godparents?'

'Well, Yvette is to be the godmother,' Gabrielle said. 'And because you have been so kind to me I was going to ask you, Doctor, if you would consider being the baby's godfather? I know that's asking a lot of you.'

The doctor was surprised at the request. 'No, it's not asking a lot,' he said. 'I would consider it an honour, but haven't you someone in the family who might be a better choice?'

Gabrielle shook her head, 'The only male relative I have is my uncle Raoul, but he is older than my aunt Bernadette, and she is some years older than my mother. There is truly no one else, and you have been more understanding than I expected.'

The doctor knew too that if he were to agree to be godfather to the child it would put a veneer of respectability on the occasion and that would help the girl in the bed and probably her parents too. So he said, 'Then I will be delighted to be little Bridgette's godfather when the time comes. When were you thinking of?'

'Oh, I hadn't thought,' Gabrielle said. 'Is the time a problem for you?'

'Not if it is close,' the doctor said. 'But after reading about the injuries at the Somme and the like, I have volunteered to join the Medical Corps of the French Army.'

'Oh,' said Gabrielle a little dismayed at the news. 'So when will you go?'

'I must report the end of next month,' the doctor said. 'That gives me time to find a replacement doctor for the town.'

'And time to be godfather to Bridgette Mariette Sullivan,' Gabrielle said with a smile.

'That too,' the doctor agreed.

'We must get on with organising the christening without delay,' Gabrielle said. 'Just wait until I tell my mother that you have agreed to be my baby's godfather.'

Mariette was surprised when Gabrielle told her who the godfather was to be, but Pierre was completely shocked.

'I wouldn't have thought the doctor would want to be godfather to a child like that,' he said.

'A child like what?' Mariette snapped. 'A child without a father. She won't be the only one in France when this war is over.'

'You know I didn't mean that.'

'Yes, I know exactly what you meant,' Mariette said. 'And I would say in agreeing to do it, the doctor has proved that he is a better and bigger man than you.'

With the godparents sorted out, Gabrielle invited her uncle and aunt from Paris to the christening. She wasn't sure they would come, but she needn't have worried. She was to find, like many before her, that the birth of a baby, however it was conceived, healed many wounds. Gabrielle was pleased that the animosity between herself and her aunt appeared to be gone.

Pierre had told the priest all about the hasty marriage conducted at the camp and the reason for it, and that the young soldier concerned had later died at the Somme. The priest found himself feeling sorry for Gabrielle rather than outraged, as Pierre had expected.

The girl had done wrong. There was no denying that, but the man had at least married her so her shame was minimised, and it was tragic that he had been killed so soon after. But then that was war for you. Meanwhile the girl had to bring up the child and in that house, and he didn't envy her at all for he found Pierre Jobert aggressive in his speech and manner, and he guessed that he had made Gabrielle's life a misery over this business.

Pierre had still not come to terms with what Gabrielle had done. He had been aware that rumours about her condition had been circulating for some time and he had seen speculative glances in her direction as he had scurried the family home from Mass. His brusque manner had meant that no one had said anything out loud, and certainly wouldn't dream of asking him such a thing, and the all-enveloping coat Pierre had insisted Mariette buy for Gabrielle, and the girl's own slim form, had hid her shape very well.

210

Now the subterfuge was over and he knew the fact that Gabrielle Jobert, or whatever she called herself these days, had had a baby with no man in sight would be the topic of many discussions in people's homes that day.

Just after the christening, Gabrielle thought she really ought to write a reply to Christy. He did, after all, have problems of his own with his injury, yet he had written to her and told her of Finn's death. She thought it must have been a very hard letter to write, for Finn and Christy have been friends all their lives, and so she took her time over the letter,

Dear Christy,
Although it wasn't news I welcomed, I must thank you for telling me about Finn's death for if you hadn't I might never have known what happened to him. I am very sorry that you were so badly injured too. It really is a dreadful war, with so many young lives cut short or damaged in some way. All we can hope is that right will triumph in the end and we might have a more peaceful world for, in that way, those lives lost won't have been totally in vain.

Having said that, there isn't one day goes by when I don't miss Finn. I feel only half a person because he is not by my side. I know that you will feel this loss as well because you were his very best friend and that bond too is a precious one.

211

When you sent me news of Finn's death I went into labour and have given birth to a baby daughter, who I love very much. She is part of Finn and so I have called her Bridgette after Finn's mother because I thought that might please him. I am forbidden to speak his name in my father's presence and yet I am determined that my daughter should know the fine man her father was. Thank you once more, Christy.

    Best wishes,

    Gabrielle

Gabrielle had to ask her mother for the money to buy a stamp and to post the letter for her. She had explained before how important Christy was in Finn's life and Mariette was certain that Gabrielle had done the right thing in commiserating with him: he must have felt the loss of such a friend grievously. It also pleased her that, in the middle of her own sadness, Gabrielle should have such feeling for another's suffering.

'I'll post it, my dear,' she said, 'never fret, though I will have to take the money for the stamp from the till. Don't worry,' she said, seeing the startled look flash over Gabrielle's face. 'I have had to do this on occasion because I am given no money of my own, just as you were never paid a wage. Your father will not miss a few coins for a stamp.'

*   *   *

Christy was surprised and pleased to get the letter from Gabrielle, though he wondered how gratified Finn would be that his innocent baby daughter had been named after his virago of a mother. They had talked about the coming child often after the wedding, and Finn had even asked him, his oldest and closest friend, to be the child's godfather.

He brushed the tears away impatiently. It was nice of Gabrielle to write, yet he had no intention of replying. That was a period in his life that he would rather forget.

ELEVEN

Not long after she returned to Paris after the christening, Bernadette sent Gabrielle a large and commodious pram that she said was the height of fashion in that city, wartime or not. It was black and sprung, with large wheels on the front and slightly smaller ones at the back. Gabrielle folded back the hood, with its brass hinges, and ran her hand over the padded cream lining of the interior and Yvette pointed out the white porcelain handle. Gabrielle had never seen anything so fine, and it was so large her mother declared it would accommodate four babies with ease.

She had sent clothes too: the softest little vests, everyday dresses of cotton, and others of silk and satin decorated with lace, ribbons and smocking, lacy knitted jackets to go over them and outer coats with bonny little bonnets and bootees.

'With a pram like that Bridgette can be taken out each day whatever the weather,' Mariette said. 'And you can take that look off your face,' she said to Pierre. 'Gabrielle cannot do any strenuous work in the bakery as her milk will dry up, and much of the day she will be attending to her baby.'

As the weeks passed Bridgette became even more enchanting and she had a ready smile for everyone. Gabrielle began to feel sad for Finn's parents, who knew nothing about their grandchild in France. Maybe, she thought, they had a right to know about Bridgette.

She was still running these thoughts around in her head when a second letter came from Christy. Christy hadn't wanted to write again, but he remembered Finn had asked him to look out for Gabrielle and the child if he could. After Gabrielle wrote to him it had begun to bother him that she might write to the Sullivan family, telling them about the marriage and the child. Finn had been underage, so when the truth came out the losers would be Gabrielle and that innocent little baby. He decided to write to warn her.

He thanked her for her letter and said that Finn was the best mate he had ever had or was likely to have. However, the real reason for writing the letter came later.

Finn's brother Tom has been to see me twice since I came home. He's a good man in that way, Tom, for time hangs heavy on me. I know to my cost that cobblestones and crutches do not go hand in hand and I have

215

fallen more than once, so I am always glad to see him.

I never told him about you or the baby, though, and the reason I haven't is because Finn confided to me after the marriage that he was underage to marry you without his parents' permission. He wouldn't have been twenty-one until June of this year but he told Father Clifford that he was older.

So on your marriage lines, Finn's date of birth is false. He was never sure whether that meant your marriage is legal or not.

Gabrielle didn't know either, but if it wasn't then she wasn't properly married, and her child was a bastard. She knew Finn had lied to protect her, and now she must do all in her power to protect her child. She would not allow the slur of illegitimacy to lodge between her shoulders and so she wrote back and told Christy that it was probably better to let sleeping dogs stay sleeping and she put out of her mind the idea of contacting the Sullivan family again.

By the end of March, Gabrielle was sure that her mother was ill. Her bouts of indigestion became even more frequent, although she always said she was fine. Gabrielle wasn't convinced because Mariette also appeared to tire easily and her face had taken on a greyish tinge. Eventually, though, the week after Easter, Mariette admitted that she was in a lot of pain with indigestion.

'Don't you think, Maman, it is about time to see the doctor?' Gabrielle asked.

'How can I bother the doctor with something that has plagued me for years?' Mariette asked. 'It always goes off again and it will do the same this time, I'm sure.'

'But maybe he could give you something to ease it?'

'Don't fuss, *ma petite*,' Mariette said.

'Yes,' Pierre said, uncharacteristically. 'Leave your mother be.'

Gabrielle and her mother, and even Yvette, stared at Pierre. He had seldom made any comment about Mariette's complaint other than to moan about it now and again.

However, Pierre did not want Mariette to be sick just then because, surprisingly, Robert Legrand was as keen as ever to marry Gabrielle. He was well aware that if he married Gabrielle, he would inherit a thriving bakery when Pierre retired. He would also have a good-looking wife, who would, he was sure, be good in bed, and a mother for his son. He was as anxious as Pierre for the marriage to take place as soon as possible.

So the next day, Pierre waited until his family were all sitting around the table, eating their Sunday dinner before he announced to Gabrielle, 'Last night Robert Legrand asked my permission to marry you, and I have given it.'

Gabrielle gave a gasp, hardly able to believe the words that had come from her father's mouth.

'I have no desire to marry Legrand, or anyone else, either,' she snapped. 'And it is my permission should be sought, not yours.'

She had lifted her chin in the air almost imperceptibly as she spoke but Pierre noticed the movement and it angered him. He thought Gabrielle had no reason for pride of any sort and he banged the table with his fist. 'You, my girl, will do as you are told,' he said firmly.

Gabrielle's innards were quaking but she faced her father squarely, 'No, Father, I won't, not in this instance.'

She turned to her mother for support and saw the grimace of pain pass over Mariette's face. 'Oh, Maman, what is it? Are you ill?' she said, moving towards her.

Mariette waved her away as she said to Pierre, 'Now what's all this nonsense about Legrand?'

'I don't happen to think that it is nonsense,' Pierre said. 'Best solution all round, I would say.'

'Pierre, the man is too old for Gabrielle and they say he was less than kind to his late wife,' Mariette said.

'What people say is based on rumour and gossip,' Pierre replied dismissively. 'And who do you think will have her if Robert won't?' His eyes raked over Gabrielle with disgust. 'Once she could have the pick of the town, but that is now in the past. Most men wouldn't touch her.'

'I don't want any man to touch me,' Gabrielle

218

cried. 'I have no need for any man in my life. I can bring my daughter up alone.'

'Of course you can,' Pierre said sneeringly. 'But you are not bringing her up on your own, are you? You are living on our bounty. And I am tired of providing for another's brat, while Robert is willing to take on you and the child.'

'Are my wishes of no account, Papa?' Gabrielle asked. 'I do not even like Robert Legrand.'

Pierre looked at Gabrielle with distaste as he said, 'You ceased to be my daughter when you went behind my back to meet a soldier and then let him lie with you. You can redeem yourself by marrying a man of my choosing.'

Gabrielle was pained by her father's words for she knew they were considered and spoken calmly.

Mariette too was shocked at Pierre's words and she had opened her mouth to reply when she suddenly doubled over with pain and slid from her chair onto the floor in a dead faint.

'Maman!' screamed Gabrielle and Yvette in unison, and they fell to their knees beside her. Gabrielle wiped spots of blood from her mother's mouth with her handkerchief as Pierre pushed between them.

'Go for the doctor and tell him it's urgent,' he said to Yvette, as he lifted Mariette in his arms. 'And you,' he said to Gabrielle, 'come with me and attend to your mother.'

Gabrielle went gladly and she was sitting by Mariette's side, wiping her face with tepid water, when the doctor, walked in. Dr Fournier was a replacement for Dr Gilbert, and a much older man. He knew little of the Jobert family, for they did not often need his service, but he was shocked at Mariette's appearance. He guessed she had been ill for some time and she verified this as he examined her. She was very thin and he could feel the tumour in her stomach. When their eyes met Mariette said, 'I thought it was indigestion at first, but then I knew.' She shrugged and went on, 'I nursed my mother with a growth like this. I hoped I was wrong.'

'You have reached the crisis point,' the doctor said gently. 'I believe that it has ruptured inside you. Anyway, as you probably know, there is no cure.'

'I know,' Mariette said with a sigh. 'I know what I face.'

'I can keep the pain at bay.'

'Well, I'll be grateful for that,' Mariette said. 'My own mother suffered terribly towards the end. But I would like a little more time. Yvette is just a child yet and I would have liked to have seen Bridgette grow up.' Her voice broke and tears seeped from between her lashes and she wiped them away impatiently. 'This is not the time to cry,' she said. 'I imagine the girls will do enough of that, and I must be strong for them.' She looked the doctor straight in the face and said, 'I haven't long, have I?'

'It's impossible to be specific.'

'Come, come, Doctor, I am not a child,' Mariette said sharply. 'At this stage I deserve the truth, surely?'

'You do, of course,' the doctor said. 'I'm sorry. In my opinion you have only weeks to live.'

'Well, Easter is passed. Will I make it to Whitsun?'

The doctor avoided her eyes. 'You may do.'

'Look at me, Doctor,' Mariette commanded. 'You don't think so, do you?'

The doctor shook his head sadly and said again, 'I'm sorry.'

'Thank you for your honesty, Doctor,' Mariette said. 'Will you tell the girls and Pierre for me? I don't feel up to that yet.'

'Of course,' the doctor said. 'And if one of the girls could come to the pharmacy later today I will have medication made up for you.'

'Thank you, Doctor. I will be glad of it.'

Gabrielle and Yvette were both distraught and stunned when the doctor told them they were soon to lose their mother, but when a weeping Gabrielle went to see her later, she knew that the doctor spoke the truth. She castigated herself for not noticing before that her mother was so ill, and now there was so little time left.

'Oh, Maman,' she cried, 'I can hardly bear to lose you.'

Mariette's eyes were very bright and she took Gabrielle's face between her hands, and said, 'You must bear it, *ma petite*, for I must. I am looking

221

to you to care for Yvette and your father as well as Bridgette. It will be up to you now.'

'I will look after them, Maman, don't doubt it,' Gabrielle said sadly. 'But it is you that I will miss. Oh, Maman, I'm heartbroken.'

'I too would like to have had longer,' Mariette said.

Gabrielle heard the slur in her mother's voice and guessed that that was probably the result of her medication, so she got to her feet. 'Sleep now, Maman,' she said, and she kissed her gently on her cheek as her eyes fluttered shut, and she turned the lamp down low as she left the room.

The whole ethos of the house changed with the illness of Mariette. Gabrielle knew that she would be bereft when her mother breathed her last, but she tried to lift the burden of sadness for the sake of her little daughter and her sister Yvette too, who was often awash with tears.

As the news filtered through the town, people came to offer not only their condolences but practical help too, though there was little that they could do. The priest called every few days as well, and he was deeply troubled to see how ill Mariette was.

Sometimes, Gabrielle sat with her mother, or read to her if she had the time to spare, or sometimes Yvette would do this. Mariette ate very little, and was sometimes sick, and had lost so much weight her cheeks were sunken, and her paper-thin skin was tightly stretched across the bones of her ashen face.

This was the Mariette Raoul and Bernadette saw when they had been summoned from Paris. They were shocked to the core, Bernadette dreadfully upset, and yet Gabrielle was glad they were there. Her uncle, she thought, was looking quite frail himself.

'Has Uncle Raoul been unwell?' she asked her aunt.

'No, my dear. He's just getting old, like the rest of us,' Bernadette said. 'And the winter was a hard one. If the next one is as bad, we might spend the worst of it with friends who moved out of Paris and are now living just outside Marseille. But that is a possibility only, and for the future. Just now our place is with you. You have a heavy load placed on your shoulders.'

'I'm glad you're here,' Gabrielle said. 'I know Maman has very little time left and it will break my heart when she dies.'

'And mine,' Bernadette said. 'But you have looked after your mother so well, you will at least have nothing to reproach yourself for when the time comes.'

Pierre, on the other hand, thought that there was plenty for Gabrielle to feel guilty about.

That night he said to her, 'I asked the doctor today what caused this disease that is eating away at your mother. He said there are many factors; that we all have the potential to have such a disease and anything could start it off. Some think even a shock or an upset might do it. Wouldn't surprise me in the least if you hadn't made your mother worse with the shock that you gave her when you said you were pregnant and with a soldier's baby.'

The room was suddenly very still. Gabrielle was looking at her father with terrified eyes. Only Bridgette, in the highchair beside her mother, seemed oblivious to the charged atmosphere and continued to bang her wooden spoon on the table. Pierre continued, 'How does it feel to be responsible for your mother's death?'

Bernadette and Raoul immediately leaped to their niece's defence, 'Don't be silly,' Bernadette said. 'Mariette has suffered for years. Our mother had the same complaint.'

'That's right,' Raoul said. 'I remember that well. None of this can be blamed on Gabrielle.'

'Well, I think it can,' Pierre said firmly, and he turned to face his daughter. 'You will die with your mother's death on your conscience.'

Gabrielle said nothing. It was true her mother had had the condition for years, though it had just rumbled on, giving her pain now and again, and it might have gone on that way for years more.

She, however, remembered the look on her mother's face when she had gone into the room after Bernadette had broken the news of her pregnancy. Maman had been more than upset – she had been distraught – and that shock to her system could have caused the tumour eventually to swell

224

so much that it had ruptured inside her. Her father was right: she had made her mother's condition worse, and she knew that she would blame herself to the day she died. First thing tomorrow, she vowed, she would beg her mother's forgiveness.

However, Gabrielle was not able to do that. By morning Mariette had lapsed into a coma and she died three days later. Gabrielle was almost inconsolable, and also filled with guilt. She knew she should be caring for her woebegone sister and her bereaved aunt, but she was wearied by all she had to do and those dependent on her for emotional support.

The funeral was well attended, and Gabrielle was gratified to see how well liked her mother was. She got more than one glowering look from her father, but she was well able to cope with that and she was just glad that he didn't blurt out that it had been her wickedness and the shock to her mother's system that had shortened her life.

When she said this to Bernadette the morning she was leaving, she took Gabrielle by the shoulders and looked deep into her eyes. 'Listen to me, Gabrielle,' she said. You are not responsible for what happened to your mother. Your father is not the only one to speak to the doctor and he told me that this had probably been festering for years and that this eruption could have happened any time. Your mother, my dear girl, was like a walking time bomb. Don't let your father bully you or lay guilt upon you.'

'Oh, Aunt Bernadette . . .'

'Courage, my dear girl,' she said, and she put her arms around Gabrielle. 'If you want me, you know where I am.'

'Thank you,' Gabrielle said, but inwardly she sighed because she knew that she would miss her aunt and uncle greatly.

Gabrielle found that each day it seemed to get harder rather than easier to live without her mother, but her father gave her no time to grieve. He told her he had had enough of her lying around the house and she had to get back to the bakery and earn her keep. Gabrielle didn't bother complaining: it would have done no good.

Bridgette had to come with her, strapped into the big pram with things to amuse her, but Pierre resented any time that she spent seeing to the child. She also undertook the bulk of the washing and cooking, and as the spring gave way to summer she felt very melancholy. The loss of her mother was like a big black hole in her life that seemed one long drudge, and all she saw ahead of her was more years of the same with nothing to look forward to.

Bridgette reached her first birthday and Gabrielle would have liked to mark it in some way. She risked her father's displeasure by asking if he would bake the baby a small cake, but she got a curt refusal and as neither she or Yvette received wages there was nothing that they could do about it.

Though there were cards and presents from Paris, the girls could provide little in the way of celebration in the bakery.

'It won't always be like this,' Yvette told her crestfallen sister.

'How will it be different?' Gabrielle asked. 'For you it may, because you'll probably marry, but I never shall.'

'How do you know?'

'I just do,' Gabrielle said firmly. 'Anyway, I could hardly leave Papa to fend for himself.'

'There's always Monsieur Legrand,' Yvette said with an impish smile. 'He can't seem to keep his eyes off you.'

Yvette was right. The man was staring at her before and after Mass each Sunday in a way that was barely decent.

'He is wasting his time,' Gabrielle told her sister. 'I gave my heart to Finn Sullivan. There's nothing left for anyone else, and certainly not for Robert Legrand.' She gave a slight shudder. 'No, I could never marry a man like that.'

Six months after Mariette's death, and a Sunday, Pierre faced his daughter over the dinner table and told her that Robert Legrand would be calling to see her that afternoon.

'You remember that I spoke about it before? He has waited this long out of deference to your mother.'

Gabrielle stared at him. 'But I told you then that

227

I don't wish to have anything to do with Robert Legrand – or anyone else either.'

'Just who do you think you are that you can dictate to me?' Pierre asked. 'You will do as I say while you are living under my roof, or you and the brat can leave and just as soon as you want.'

Gabrielle looked at her father's malevolent eyes and felt a cold shiver run all through her. She had never received a penny piece from him and everything she and the baby owned had been paid for by her father, often reluctantly, though he would not let either her or Bridgette go to Mass badly dressed, for that would reflect on him. But however was she to provide for herself and her child without money?

Her thoughts flew to her aunt in Paris, but just a couple of weeks before, she had written to say that Raoul had been taken to hospital and was seriously ill with pneumonia and she was very concerned about him.

Pierre watched his daughter's face and knew she was thinking of alternatives. He also knew that there were none, and she would come to realise that eventually, and so he went on, 'As the day is a fine one, you may walk out with him.'

Gabrielle knew there was no way to change her father's mind once he decided something. He didn't listen to any arguments. The only alternative that she could see was to agree to go out with Legrand, which would appease her father, and she would explain to her suitor that she could never love another man after Finn. Surely he would see her point of view. No man liked to be thought of as second-best, and so she nodded her head and said, 'Very well then.'

Yvette was surprised by Gabrielle's decision until she told her what her father had threatened. Then she understood her sister's dilemma and readily agreed to look after Bridgette. Gabrielle waited for Legrand with her stomach knotted in apprehension and yet when he did arrive she was pleasantly surprised both by his smart appearance and his manner. She stopped only to kiss the baby in Yvette's arms before stepping out into the street beside Robert. She didn't object when he took her arm, though she was aware of the curious glances the two had from many of the townspeople.

'Did you not see the people looking at us as we passed?' Gabrielle asked as they reached the canal.

Legrand had been well aware of them, but he said, 'What about them?'

'It's just that they assume, don't they?' Gabrielle said. 'They'll have us married off by the time we return.'

'You could do worse,' Legrand said.

Gabrielle was taken aback. 'Robert, I—'

'That can't have come as a total surprise,' Legrand said. 'I had mentioned it to your father before, when your mother became ill that time.'

Gabrielle thought she had to put Robert right about the impossibility of her marrying him or anyone, but while she was still forming the words he spoke again.

'I am most incredibly fond of you, Gabrielle and you are one of the most beautiful women I've ever seen.'

Gabrielle, not used to such praise, coloured. 'Please, Robert . . .'

'What? Surely you have been told this before. Didn't your husband tell you how beautiful you are?'

'Yes, he did. And that's it, you see. I still love Finn. I gave him all of my heart. There is none left for anyone else, not in that way.'

'There is a lot of nonsense spoken about love,' Legrand said dismissively. 'We just need to get to know each other better. And with or without love, I want to marry you.'

'No. I've told you.'

'That's a real pity because your father is all for it.'

'It really is nothing to do with him,' Gabrielle said heatedly. 'He can't force me to marry anyone.'

Legrand told Gabrielle's father what she had said about her first husband as they sat in the bar the following Saturday evening. Pierre could hardly believe his ears.

'You mean the stupid girl still fancies herself in love with that dead and useless soldier who married her only because he had been forced to?' he asked incredulously.

'That's what she said,' Legrand said resignedly.

Rage burned within Pierre and he said between clenched teeth, 'Leave her to me. When you come tomorrow she will be a changed girl, believe me. Let's have another drink, for we've other things to discuss.'

Later that night, Gabrielle heard her father come home, but she was in bed and preparing to settle down for the night. She heard him stumbling around the kitchen and was glad that it was Saturday and there were no ovens to light in the morning.

She was surprised, though, to hear him call to her to get up. He had never done such a thing before, but she knew better than to defy him, especially when he had been drinking. She slipped out of bed, and checked that Yvette and the baby were fast asleep, before pulling her robe around her.

Her father, she saw, was very drunk and angry, though for the life of her she couldn't think what she had done to annoy him. He left her little time to wonder, though, for he launched into her straight-away.

'I have been drinking with Legrand tonight –' he said – 'Robert Legrand, who you went walking out with last week – and he was telling me a strange tale.'

Gabrielle was silent. She guessed what was coming.

With a sneer her father went on, 'Are you not interested in hearing it? No matter, I will relate it to you anyway. It appears that this man asked the father's permission to walk out with his daughter and the father agreed, and then he finds that the daughter tells him that her heart belongs to a man who never did her a moment's good in her life. You fancy yourself in love with a ghost, while Legrand is offering you marriage.'

Gabrielle felt as if there were a tight band around her chest, restricting her breathing, so afraid was she of the irascible look in her father's eyes. 'I can't help it,' she cried desperately. 'It's how I feel. I thought it best to be honest. I can't marry Robert Legrand, really I can't.'

'Now you listen to me,' Pierre growled. 'Tomorrow you will either welcome Robert as a woman welcomes the man she is going to marry, or you will pack your bags and be gone from here. Do I make myself clear?'

Gabrielle gasped in shock. She saw her father meant every word and she was unable to keep the repugnance out of her face and her voice as she said through gritted teeth, 'Abundantly so.'

She was unprepared for the two punches her father levelled at her face, which knocked her to the ground. 'You are in no position to be clever with me,' he said. 'You brought shame on the whole family and in doing so hastened your own mother's death, and don't you forget it. Now get to your bed and think on my words.'

Gabrielle got to her feet gingerly and, trying to stanch the blood streaming from her nose with a handkerchief she had found in the pocket of her robe, she made for the stairs and the relative safety of her room. Once there, she was too agitated to rest, and crossing to the window she let the tears fall from her eyes.

'Gabrielle, what's the matter?' Yvette whispered from the bed.

'Nothing. Go to sleep.'

In answer, Yvette got out of bed and, with her robe around her, went to her sister. 'How can I sleep when it is obvious that you are unhappy? What is it, Gabrielle?' she said, putting her arms around her.

Gabrielle sighed, glad of the concealing darkness that hid her face from Yvette as she said through her tears, 'Papa has given me an ultimatum. It is as if I am standing on the edge of a bridge and I can either cross it to Legrand on the other side, or turn back and begin packing up my possessions and those of Bridgette. If I take that course I may just as well jump into the canal and let the water submerge the two of us.'

Yvette gave a gasp. 'Don't even say words like that.'

'It will soon be winter,' Gabrielle said. 'How long do you think that I would survive on the streets, and how could I condemn Bridgette to that?'

'Papa wouldn't really throw you out, though, surely?' Yvette said.

'I don't know,' Gabrielle told her sister. 'At the

moment he seems to hate me and still blames me for Maman's death.'

Yvette was silent because she knew that their father's animosity towards Gabrielle had become even more entrenched since their mother had died. He did blame Gabrielle and probably always would.

'In a way he has a point,' Gabrielle said. 'I might not have caused Maman's illness, but I certainly think I helped worsen it. Maybe this is my penance.'

'Gabrielle, Maman had suffered for years – you know that,' Yvette replied firmly. 'This is just something Papa has put in your head.'

Gabrielle shrugged. 'I can't get over the feeling that I am somewhat responsible, but anyway, I can't risk defying Papa, especially now Aunt Bernadette has let out the house in Paris and taken Uncle Raoul to spend the winter in the South of France. I can't even turn to her.'

'But how well do you really know this Legrand, Gabrielle?'

'You don't really know any man fully until you marry him,' Gabrielle said. 'It's all a bit of a lottery. Anyway, none of this matters. For better or worse my future lies with Legrand, and I must accept it.'

Yvette was flabbergasted the next morning to see the state of Gabrielle's face and though she did what she could to repair it before Mass, she couldn't work miracles. Gabrielle had many odd looks from the townsfolk, and when Legrand came to speak to them all after Mass, he noticed straight-away that something very unfortunate had hap-pened to Gabrielle's nose and her eyes were definitely darkened too.

He was delighted by the change in Gabrielle, though, who greeted him quite pleasantly and even agreed to take his arm. He didn't know whether he fully approved of Pierre's methods to make Gabrielle see sense, and yet he knew from his late wife how irksome and annoying women could be at times. Sometimes they needed firm handling, and he guessed that Gabrielle had a stubborn streak in her at times that he too might have to curb once they were married.

TWELVE

As soon as Gabrielle's marriage to Robert Legrand was agreed, he began bringing his son, Georges, with him to the house at the weekends. Gabrielle thought the child was completely undisciplined and when she said this to Robert he explained that his late wife's parents had indulged him and he didn't want to be the one to be reprimanding him all the time.

This attitude was also adopted by Gabrielle's father. His eyes softened when he first caught sight of the little boy, and she knew Robert had given him what both she and her mother had failed to do: the son or grandson he had craved. As far as Pierre was concerned, Georges Legrand could do no wrong.

The child was allowed to be as noisy and as rude as he wanted. What he really enjoyed, though, was being spiteful and downright nasty to Bridgette, but Pierre had never taken to the baby girl, and Gabrielle knew that Robert merely tolerated her. Only Gabrielle and Yvette minded Bridgette being treated this way, but as no notice was taken of their protestations, Georges soon realised that they held no power in that house.

Gabrielle became quite agitated as the day of the wedding drew closer. She had thought that she would be moving out of the bakery, away from her father, and she was astounded when she learned that wasn't going to happen.

'What do you mean?' she asked.

'Robert is moving here,' Pierre told her. 'I will teach him all he needs to know in the bakery, and he will help me. I'm not getting any younger.'

Gabrielle's heart sank. That really was the last thing she had thought would happen.

As far as Pierre was concerned, 26 January 1918 was Gabrielle's first proper wedding. If it wasn't for Bridgette, he could pretend that that was really so, and he supposed that was why the child irritated him.

Never mind, he thought as he took hold of Gabrielle's arm in the church porch, there would soon be a houseful of children, with plenty of sons.

The organ began to play, the congregation rose to their feet, and Pierre and Gabrielle began the slow walk down the aisle, Yvette following behind. Pierre delivered Gabrielle into Legrand's keeping and they stepped forward under the carrel. It was believed that taking wedding vows under that silken canopy before Nuptial Mass was protection against bad luck in the marriage.

The reception back at the bakery was exceptional, as might be expected. The table groaned with food and the centrepiece was the wedding cake, a magnificent croquembouche: a glazed pyramid of cream-filled pastry puffs.

Gabrielle had expected bad behaviour from Georges but she burned with embarrassment as he grabbed food from the table the women had spent hours arranging, spilling or knocking things over in the process. Then he ran around like a dervish, smearing women's dresses and the men's suits with the food he clutched in his hands, knocking glasses from people's hands without a word of apology, and pushing Bridgette over whenever he had the opportunity.

As the night wore on he was still running madly around, insulting any person who said anything to him and kicking out at both Gabrielle and Yvette. Gabrielle knew he was over-tired but her father had said that Georges should go to bed when he wanted, though Bridgette had been tucked up only slightly later than normal. Robert and Pierre seemed amused rather than embarrassed by Georges's outrageous behaviour.

'They're drunk,' Gabrielle said to her sister, who was rubbing her shin where Georges had kicked her again 'What do you expect?'

'I expect Legrand to act as a father to his own son,' Yvette said in a hissed whisper.

'How could he tonight?' Gabrielle whispered back. 'Look at the state of the pair of them.'

238

Really she hoped that Robert would drink so much that he would pass out and she would be spared his attentions – for that night, at least. Every time she thought of his hands upon her she felt sick. But she could hardly share that hope with her young sister.

But by the time the guests had left and Gabrielle and Yvette had begun to tidy up, Legrand was still on his feet, still drinking, and the over-tired and belligerent Georges sat on his shoulders.

When Gabrielle returned to the room to collect more dishes he said, 'Leave that now. It's time for bed.'

Gabrielle felt her stomach give a lurch and she glanced at Georges.

Robert said, 'Leave Georges to me. You just get into bed and wait for me. Don't worry about a nightdress. That will only get in the way. I want you naked.'

Gabrielle's face flamed with embarrassment. She looked from her father, beaming approval, to Yvette, who was obviously uncomfortable. Georges was also listening, and though the sexual connotations were lost on him, he understood naked-ness and giggled at the thought of Gabrielle having no clothes on. She would have remonstrated with her new husband but one look at his licentious, drunken face told her that she would be wasting her time. So without a word, she turned away and went upstairs.

She was very nervous at the prospect of sharing

a bed with Legrand, and felt self-conscious as she slipped between the sheets. She had never gone to bed naked before and she trembled from head to foot as she waited for her new husband. Her nervousness increased as she listened to his measured tread on the stairs. She heard him first go along the passage to Georges's room and then she was filled with apprehension as she watched the door knob turn and he was there, his broad frame almost filling the space.

'You looked lovely today,' he said, crossing the room, almost tearing off his clothes as he spoke. 'And I can't wait to love you properly.'

He snuffed out the lamp and threw back the covers. A blast of cold air hit Gabrielle's naked body and she gave a sudden shiver as he slid in beside her.

'And,' he said huskily, 'I am ready for you. See?' He grabbed her hand and pressed it down on his hard penis.

Gabrielle felt sick, but this she told herself was real marriage. She longed to pull her hand away but she allowed Legrand to hold it there and even moved it up and down as he instructed while he groaned with pleasure. Suddenly he rolled on top of Gabrielle, crushing her down on the bed and began mauling her breasts with his big rough hands, then sucking them with such intensity she wriggled in discomfort and bit her lip lest any cry of pain escaped to annoy him.

He continued to suck at her breasts, but she felt

his hand on his penis, and when he entered her she felt as if he was ripping her in two and she cried out in pain.

Legrand slapped a hand across her mouth. 'Shut up, you stupid bitch,' he cried. 'You knew what it was all about.'

'It wasn't like this,' Gabrielle wanted to say, but with his hand over her mouth she was hardly able to breathe, never mind say anything. As Legrand thrust himself inside her again and again she tried to ride the pain.

After what seemed an eternity, it was over. He he took his hand from her mouth and rolled on his side. Gabrielle lay rigid in the bed, her nerve ends tingling and every part of her aching, but she was loath to move and disturb him in case he was still aroused enough to attack her again.

Then in the quiet room, where the ticking clock was the only noise, she heard Legrand's even breathing and occasional snore and she knew that it was safe to move. She curled into a ball in an effort to ease her battered body and throbbing breasts as far from him as she could get. Tears trickled down her cheeks and she muffled her sobs in the pillow.

Next morning, Gabrielle got a grip on herself. She knew if that was the way Legrand was, she had to learn to put up with it, as she knew many other women did.

She heaved herself out of bed. It was Sunday and there was a lot to do, though only breakfast to make for the children, for she imagined everyone else would be taking Communion. She had Bridgette dressed and sitting eating her breakfast in no time, but Georges was a different matter.

He was tired that morning and even worse tempered than usual. He didn't want to get up and when Gabrielle coaxed him to do so, he said he was too tired to get dressed but determinedly refused all help and dawdled over his breakfast. Robert and Pierre, both nursing hangovers, were no help at all and Gabrielle felt she really needed the peace of Mass that morning.

In church she let the familiar Latin words wash over her and prayed for God to give her the strength and wisdom to cope with her husband and his difficult son.

Legrand declared that though he had no intention of adopting Bridgette legally, he was providing for her and as such she was to be known by his name and to call him Papa, as Georges did. Knowing that her marriage to Finn might not have been legal, Gabrielle was agreeable to this. It would be better for the child anyway, she reasoned, because in all probability there would soon be a houseful of children and it would be easier if everyone was known by the same name.

The war that had claimed so many lives rumbled to a close in November of that year. The town was in carnival mood and Gabrielle and Yvette took both children out into the streets so that they could drink in the atmosphere. Gabrielle could well understand the joy and relief of the carousing people, even if the peace had come far too late for her and Finn.

It had been an immense war, with much loss of life. But it was the war to end all wars, people said. Now everyone could get on with their lives in peace, and Gabrielle looked forward to the future.

There was just one fly in the ointment. Despite Legrand's desire for a son, the first Christmas of their marriage passed with no sign, and then the second. He became impatient and short-tempered with Gabrielle. She understood his frustration and even shared it because she too longed for a child; it would be some consolation for her in a marriage that she knew was less than ideal.

Legrand had begun to drink far more than was good for him, and so did Pierre. Where once he had frequented the bars only on a Saturday evening, now they went out together most evenings and were always well oiled or worse when they returned.

Regardless of his drunken state, Legrand often demanded sex. Many times Gabrielle was woken with his weight on top of her, fumbling at her nightdress, and more than once, befuddled by the fastenings, he had ripped the nightdress down the front.

Eventually, despite her embarrassment, Gabrielle went to see the doctor. Dr Fournier had been good with her mother, but he had aged somewhat since then and become quite feeble-looking. She wouldn't have minded seeing the doctor half so much if it had been Dr Gilbert, whom she had liked, but he had been killed when his field hospital had been shelled just six months after he joined up.

But Dr Fournier listened to all she said, and examined her sensitively, and told her that as far as he could tell, she was perfectly healthy and there was no reason why she couldn't conceive; that it was often a waiting game.

Gabrielle returned home and told her husband this, but he continued to taunt her about her barren state, which upset and angered her.

She knew that it wasn't a child Legrand wanted but a son. If she were to give birth to another daughter, he would ignore her, as he did Bridgette.

As time had passed, though, while Legrand redoubled his efforts to beget a second son Pierre put all his energies into the one male child he had. He indulged Georges atrociously, even more than his father did, and Georges soon learned that the man he called Grandpapa would give him anything he wanted and allow him to do what he liked. Knowing this, he behaved like a little prince in the home, where he did as he pleased. Any discipline that Gabrielle and sometimes Yvette tried to exert over Georges was never supported by either of the men and so Georges took no notice.

Pierre Jobert died in the October 1921 when Bridgette was just passed her fifth birthday. There was no warning to his death. He got up from the table one day after his lunchtime meal saying he didn't feel very well, and he was dead before he fell into the armchair he was making for.

When Gabrielle told Bridgette of the death of her grandfather she seemed remarkably unconcerned, and Gabrielle couldn't blame her. The little girl often bore the brunt of his bad temper. She was frightened of Georges too, who thought nothing of pinching, kicking or scratching her, or pushing her over. He was also fond of taking whatever she happened to be playing with, if he took a fancy to it, and Pierre had seemed even to encourage him. Bridgette had learned not to make a fuss, because that only made things worse.

So when Gabrielle told her young daughter that her grandfather had died and gone to live with Jesus, she was glad. She didn't tell her mother but, as far as she was concerned, Jesus was welcome to him.

Gabrielle learned the real cruelty of her father after the funeral when she found that he had disinherited not only her but Bridgette and Yvette too. He had left everything to Legrand, and to Georges on his death, unless Gabrielle were to have a son, in which case the inheritance would be split between them.

The ownership of the bakery changed Legrand, but not for the better. Gabrielle wasn't surprised when Yvette elected to go back to Paris with her aunt and uncle after the will had been read. She was, however, totally unprepared for what Legrand told her after they had gone, which was that he had no wish for them to return and that they were no longer welcome in 'his' bakery.

'Robert, please, you cannot do this,' Gabrielle said. 'They come at least once a year. This is my family that you are banishing.'

'And you are my wife.'

'And as such do I have no say in any of this?'

'No,' Legrand said. 'Before God and half of the town you made a promise to obey me, and this is how I want things. You will be too busy to miss them for, as you cannot give me the sons I crave, you must earn your keep in another way. I have engaged a boy but he will not start until eight and so I want you up at five to help me. When he takes your place you will have plenty of time to see to Georges and Bridgette, make a bite for me and still be in the shop for nine o'clock.'

Gabrielle knew that she would, because there was nothing else that she could do. The future she had once looked forward to unnerved her totally.

Every day when Georges and Bridgette came home for school, Legrand would get out of bed to sit and talk to his son while Gabrielle returned to the shop with Bridgette. There, Bridgette would practise the English words Gabrielle had been teaching her. Bridgette knew instinctively that she had to keep this a secret from her father, but she was keen to learn because she loved pleasing her mother.

And Gabrielle was relieved as well as pleased. She knew that there would be no secondary education for Bridgette, because Legrand had made it plain that he would not pay to keep Bridgette at school a moment longer than necessary. She would have just the basic education and leave at twelve. Gabrielle reasoned that English, which was, after all, the language her real father spoke, might stand her in good stead when she would have to make her own way in the world.

Gabrielle was always glad, though, when the clock showed six o'clock and she could thankfully lock the door, draw down the blinds and go into the kitchen to prepare the evening meal. By the time she had eaten, Gabrielle was usually very tired, but while she insisted on an early bedtime for Bridgette, she could not seek her own bed until Georges decided to retire.

Legrand, rested from his nap, would go out to the bars of St-Omer while Gabrielle would fall asleep as soon as her head hit the pillow. She knew that when her husband came in, however late it was, he would demand his conjugal rights.

One night, a fortnight or so after her aunt and uncle had returned to Paris, she felt that she had scarcely laid down before she felt the weight of Legrand on top of her. Suddenly, she was angry. There was no consideration or tenderness in the man at all. He worked her half to death through the day, and then expected sex every night. And that's all it was: sex for his own gratification.

For a fleeting moment she remembered the exquisite joy she had experienced with Finn when they made love together, and then she was grappling with Legrand, trying to shift the weight of him and crying, 'Leave me alone, can't you, for pity's sake?'

Legrand was so surprised that he stopped trying to lift her nightgown over her head. She gave an almighty push and he fell out of bed and onto the floor. She was out the other side in seconds.

Legrand got to his feet and stood swaying slightly and staring at her. 'What are you on about?' he growled angrily.

Gabrielle was afraid of the temper smouldering in Robert's eyes. But she still said pleadingly, 'Please leave me tonight, Robert. I am so very tired and hadn't been long in bed when you arrived home.'

'Is that my fault?' Legrand demanded. He caught her by the neck of her nightgown. 'Do I have to remind you that you are my wife?'

Gabrielle had been half expecting the punch that landed between her eyes and knocked her to the ground because she had long sensed the aggression running through Legrand. She lay stunned by the blow, blood streaming from her nose with a pain that made her groan.

'You asked for that,' Legrand said, lying on top of her on the floor. 'You are my wife and as such you cannot refuse me, though some wife you are. I made a bad bargain with you because you turned out to be a barren bitch in the end.'

Gabrielle was too frightened to protest any more. She didn't even flinch when he ripped her nightgown right down the front, though she couldn't help the cry of pain that escaped her as he entered her roughly. She heard his guttural grunts as he jabbed into her again and again, and she bit on her lip as tears seeped from beneath her throbbing eyes, which she kept closed.

When it was over, she breathed a sigh of relief. Her eyes had swollen but she opened them as far as she could. Legrand shook his head from side to side before he climbed off her, got to his feet with difficulty, staggered to the bed and almost fell into it. Then Gabrielle made for the bathroom. Her eyes were bloated, bruised and tender, and she knew that they were probably going to be black in the morning, and there was dried blood from her nose smeared all over her face.

Hatred for Legrand rose in her as she began to bathe her face gently. He had said she was a barren bitch. She hadn't been barren when she had lain with Finn and she had Bridgette to prove it, but she was glad that he'd not been able to give her a child. She was sure any child of his would be corrupt and tainted, like Georges.

But however she felt, she was chained to him for life. It was a depressing thought because although that night was the first time Legrand had hit her, she knew with dreadful certainty that it wouldn't be the last.

THIRTEEN

Bridgette was preparing breakfast when her mother came up from the bakery. When she saw the graze on her cheek that she had tried to cover with powder the girl knew that her father had hit her mother again. Maman would say she bumped into something, because that was what she always said. When Bridgette had been a child she had believed her.

She was a child no longer however. It was October 1932, and she had just passed her sixteenth birthday. She knew the truth now. Over the years she had even heard her mother cry out in pain, and her stomach would be tied into knots and her toes would curl in the bed in anticipation of what that brute was doing to her. Many times she had wanted to go in and try to put a stop to it, and had even got out of bed to do just that on more than one occasion. It was only the thought that her mother would hate her to see her in that state, added to the fact that she might make things worse for her later, that had made her stay put.

250

Her father was cruel in other ways too. He had not allowed her mother's aunt and uncle and her sister to visit, though Maman loved them dearly and missed them very much. She had not even been allowed to travel to Paris to her sister's wedding – to Henri Dellatre in 1921 – nor to attend her uncle Raoul's funeral three months later. In May 1923 Yvette gave birth to a baby boy, whom she called Raoul after her uncle, but Legrand said that Gabrielle could not be spared from the bakery to go to the christening, and he said the same when Raoul's brother, Gerard, was born in April 1925.

But Yvette did not forget her niece growing up in a household where she was denied a secondary education. Every so often she would send Bridgette books from the bookshops in Paris. There were a variety, and Bridgette devoured them all. When Bridgette had written to tell Yvette she was trying to master English, some were in that language, which by now she could speak so well.

Robert never knew about this because the post was all delivered to the shop, and Bridgette always made sure the books were hidden away in her mother's room because Georges seemed to like nothing better than foraging amongst her things. He was a thorn in her side all right, and one that she detested with all her heart and soul. She was afraid of him no longer, though, and she remembered well the day that she had lost her fear two years before.

She had entered the living room to find Georges

had been into her bedroom and he was holding her doll, dangling it by its feet and he waved it tantalisingly in front of her. She loved that doll. It was the finest thing she had ever owned. Her auntie Yvette had sent it from Paris for her thirteenth birthday the previous year. 'To celebrate you reaching your teens. A pretty lady to adorn your dressing table,' she had written on the accompanying card.

She wasn't the sort of doll to give a young child to play with. She had the prettiest china face and a wig of natural hair the colour of chestnuts, which hung in curls past the shoulders. Her body was soft, but firm enough for her to stand, and she was dressed like a Victorian lady. She had proper clothes, from the finest lawn underwear to the ball gown topped by a fur-trimmed coat, and the muff around her neck matched the leather boots on her feet. To see that wonderful doll in Georges's big bearlike hands enraged Bridgette.

'What are you doing?' she'd cried. 'Give that back to me.'

'You are far too old to play with dolls,' Georges said.

'That isn't a doll to play with,' Bridgette said disparagingly. 'Anyway, it's mine. Give it to me.'

'No, I don't think I will,' said Georges. 'You don't need things like this any more.'

Bridgette thought of trying to snatch the doll from Georges, but she knew she would be no match for him, so instead she said, 'Come on, Georges,

252

I don't go rummaging around in your things. That's a special doll because Aunt Yvette sent it to me from Paris.'

Georges knew that, of course, but Yvette never sent him anything half as good as the things she sent Bridgette. Thinking this, he suddenly hurled the doll across the room towards the fireplace. Bridgette heard the crack as the doll's head hit the hearth and saw it smash into pieces before she opened her mouth and screamed, darting to the fireplace as she did. Her screams were so loud that they brought her father from the bakery and her mother from the shop to see what had happened.

Bridgette, ferreting about in the grate with the poker, didn't need to speak. Gabrielle could plainly see the doll's china head smashed to bits in the hearth while the flames licked and consumed the rest of it. 'Georges,' she cried, 'what have you done?'

Bridgette flew at Georges and pummelled his chest with her fists but Robert strode across, pulled her away and slapped her hard across the face. 'Stop that hysterical nonsense.'

Bridgette was shocked into silence and then her mother's arms were around her. 'There was absolutely no need for that,' she said grimly, through tightened lips.

'There was every need. The girl was hysterical,' Robert countered.

'And can you wonder?' Gabrielle said. 'Your son threw her doll into the fire. Have you never one word of censure for him?'

Robert ignored this and said, 'Bridgette's far too old to play with dolls, and I was surprised at Yvette sending it to her in the first place.'

Bridgette had known that was how it would be. For as long as she could recall she had been subjected to punches, pinches, slaps and shoves from Georges, who also delighted in stealing and often breaking her toys. If she told her mother, things just got worse, and she would lie on her bed and tremble in fear at the anger she had unleashed. Then the next morning she would see fresh marks on her mother's face so she soon learned to keep her mouth shut.

But this time Bridgette felt rage fill her body, so powerful it replaced all fear of Georges, which had dogged her childhood, and she sprang out of her mother's arms and hit Georges full in the face with her fist. The attack was so unexpected that Georges hadn't time to protect himself, and he staggered under the blow as his nose spurted blood.

Robert reached for her but Gabrielle pulled her into the shelter of her arms. 'You shall not lay one finger on her ever again,' she said to Robert. 'You will have to kill me before I would let that happen.'

Bridgette hadn't finished, however, and she sprang in front of her stepbrother. 'Listen to me, Georges Legrand,' she spat out. 'You lay one hand on me again and you will get the same back, even if I have to wait until you're asleep to do it. You would never again be able to sleep easy in your bed.'

Both Georges and his father were surprised by Bridgette's defiance, although Georges wasn't letting her see that. He looked at her scornfully before saying, 'Oh, yes?'

But Bridgette was not the slightest put off by either Georges's attitude or his words. 'You have had it all your own way for too long because you have bullied me all my life,' she said. 'But now you have gone too far. Leave me alone, or suffer the consequences.'

Legrand took a step forward and raised his fist but Gabrielle pushed Bridgette behind her. 'Don't you dare! What Bridgette did to Georges was perfectly justified. You have raised a monster, Robert.'

Legrand lowered his arm. 'If you have finished your hysterics now, you have a shop to run,' he said.

'No I haven't, because I'm closing early tonight,' Gabrielle replied. 'The townsfolk can go else-where for their bread and cakes, and I am taking Bridgette with me to close up.'

In the refuge of the shop she had told Bridgette of the terms of her grandfather's will. Bridgette had been stunned that her grandfather had disinherited her. It was bad enough that Robert was to be in charge of everything, but to think that after his death Georges would inherit it all was monstrous.

'Georges!' she cried, unaware that her lips had curled back in disgust. 'He isn't even a blood relative.'

'My father was trying to punish me,' Gabrielle said, 'because I hadn't given him a grandson.'

Bridgette was silent for a few moments, thinking about this. She was remarkably naïve about how babies were conceived. She had an idea that it was something parents did in the bedroom, though she wasn't sure what. But she was certain that it took two people, so she said, 'Well, that wasn't all your fault, was it?'

'No,' Gabrielle said. 'But that wasn't how he saw it.'

Bridgette shook her head in puzzlement. 'But to just give away the bakery like that . . . Hasn't it been in our family for generations?'

'Yes, but we no longer own it You will have to make your own way in the world. I want you to leave the bakery and find work that pays a wage. If you don't, should you annoy Robert in some way, or certainly when Georges inherits, he would take pleasure in getting rid of you and you won't have any money to fall back on. And,' she added, 'I even know of a place that might suit: the Laurents' milliner's shop.'

Bridgette had known Marie Laurent's daughter, Lisette, well at one time. When she first went to school, she had sat beside the little girl with black curls that bounced on her shoulders and dark dancing eyes, and they had become friends. Sometimes Bridgette had gone home for tea with Lisette after school and so she had met her parents, Marie and Maurice. She envied Lisette her big brother, Xavier, who was invariably kind to both of them and only teased in a gentle way that was never cruel.

Bridgette had loved the time she'd spent in that friendly house, so unlike her own where violence always seemed to bubble just under the surface, to be unleashed by the slightest remark.

Legrand had soon put a stop to her going to the Laurents and demanded that Gabrielle find her something useful to occupy her. Of course, Bridgette was never allowed a friend round to play – not that she would have liked to take anyone into her home – and so their friendship had petered out a little.

Then when Bridgette left school at twelve, Lisette had stayed on. Now she saw Lisette only fleetingly at Mass, or if she came into the shop for bread or cakes.

'Marie has had an extension built onto the shop and she is opening up as ladies' outfitters,' Gabrielle said, breaking in on Bridgette's thoughts. 'She is looking for a smart girl to train up and she thought of you.'

'What about Lisette?'

'Well, she is at school at least until the summer,' Gabrielle said. 'And when she does leave it seems she has a flair for the hats and will be working with her father at that side of the business. Would you like to work with the Laurents?'

Bridgette felt excitement fizz inside her. She would just love to work with such nice, kind people. But then a shutter came down over her thoughts and she stated flatly, 'Papa will never allow it.'

'Leave your papa to me,' Gabrielle said, and Bridgette noted the steely glint in her eyes. 'I will fight to give you a future, and it is a fight that I am determined to win.'

She did win the fight, though she carried the marks on her for weeks afterwards. Bridgette had been so concerned for her mother's safety that in the end she had threatened her father with the poker if he didn't leave her alone. She knew by the look he threw her that he believed her, and not even Georges would tackle her with the poker held tight in her hands and the murderous look on her face.

Bridgette soon found that working at the Laurents' dress shop was even better than she had thought it would be and, anxious to please, she picked up the business very quickly. She thought the customers were lovely. Most of them she had met at Mass, and many had been to the bakery. Some expressed surprise that she wasn't still working there. She just told any who asked that she fancied a change, for very few were aware of the details of her grandfather's will, and she had no desire to tell everyone else and show them how little the man had thought of her.

Each day, at lunchtime, the shop was closed and they all sat down to a meal that Marie Laurent cooked. Xavier came home most days because the tile factory, where he worked, was not far away. There was usually lively banter around the table and often a great deal of laughter. It was all so different from Bridgette's home, but she soaked it all up eagerly.

In such an atmosphere she blossomed. Most people would have agreed that, at sixteen, she was as pretty as a picture. She was slight, like her mother, and also took after her in looks in the main, though she had inherited her father's dark amber eyes, ringed by long black lashes. Although her mouth wasn't as large as her father's, it turned up at the corners, as his had done. She had the same flawless skin her mother had had at the same age, with just a dusting of crimson on her cheekbones and her long dark brown hair had natural waves.

She received many a lustful look at Mass, but she never encouraged any of her admirers in the slightest way. Marie guessed that was because she loved Xavier, and though Bridgette had never said a word about it, it would be hard not to know how she felt about the young man. And yet Marie didn't know if Bridgette loved him as a woman truly loves a man, or loved him in an almost brotherly way, and she didn't know how Xavier felt about the girl.

She knew he liked her – a person would be hard to please if they didn't like Bridgette – but liking wasn't enough for marriage, which had to last a lifetime. Nothing would please Marie more than if he were to marry the girl, for she was more than fond of her, but she refused to scheme and plan. Xavier would choose his bride without any interference from her and marry for love, as she had.

In early November, Bridgette woke late one night to find Georges sitting on the bed and stroking her arm. She was instantly wide awake.

'Get off!' she cried, shaking his hand away. 'What are you doing?'

Georges didn't answer. He lit the lamp before turning to her and saying, 'I like it when you're angry. Your eyes flash.'

Bridgette sighed. He was very drunk and she knew there was no reasoning with him when he was in that state. 'Georges,' she said as forcibly as she could, 'get out of my room!'

'Actually,' Georges said in a drunken slur, 'it's my father's room because he owns all this. So I have a right to be here.'

'Not while I'm in the room you haven't,' Bridgette said. 'So you'd better go before I call him.'

Georges sniggered. 'As if he'd care about you.'

Bridgette knew that indeed he would care very little, and she gave a little shiver of apprehension. Georges was over twenty now, a very large man, like Legrand, and if he took it into his head to rape her, or hurt her in some other way, what could she do about it? No one would come to her aid but her mother, and if she tried to intervene she would likely be subjected to the same abuse.

'Come on, be nice to me,' Georges urged, throwing back the covers as he spoke. 'You know what I want.'

As he slid into the bed, Bridgette was out the other side of it in seconds. 'What you doing over there?' George protested, climbing out after her.

Bridgette was pressed against the wall. There was nowhere else to go, Georges was between her and the door, and even in his drunken state she doubted that she'd get past him. What was she to do? Just wait for him to attack her?

She could feel her heart banging against her ribs almost painfully, and she suddenly thought maybe if she jumped on to the bed, taking Georges by surprise, she could perhaps reach the door. She made a leap and Georges lunged for her clumsily, clouting her head with such force she was knocked on to the bed, where she cracked her head on the bedpost and cried out in pain.

Before she had her wits about her Georges was on top of her. 'We can do this the hard way or the easy way,' he said as he straddled her. 'Makes no odds to me.'

'Georges, please . . . !' Bridgette pleaded, now thoroughly frightened. She began to writhe and struggle to free herself. She stopped, though, when she saw the licentious way he was staring at her, a smile of smug satisfaction on his face.

'That's it,' he said huskily. 'You know what it is all about.'

'No I do not,' Bridgette said. 'Nor do I want to. Let me go, Georges.'

261

'I will,' Georges said, 'when I have tasted your wares.' With that, he took hold of her nightdress by the collar and ripped it all down the front.

Bridgette shrieked as the cold air hit her bare skin, and then Georges was on top of her, his weight near knocking the breath from her body. She felt him fiddling with his buttons and she screamed for all she was worth.

'Shut up, you stupid bitch,' he cried and he clamped a hand across her mouth so tightly she felt her teeth rub against her lips.

She was looking straight into his black hate-filled eyes as he breathed stale alcoholic fumes all over her and spat out, 'I'm going to take you tonight and there is nothing that you can do about it. And I will do the same again any night I feel like it.'

Bridgette knew he was enjoying seeing her so powerless. But then she felt the pressure of one of his fingers with her tongue because she had been in the middle of a scream, her mouth open, when he had clapped his hand over it. She bit down as hard as she could. Georges gave a roar and released her. She just glimpsed his finger dripping blood before his other fist slammed into her face and she pushed him off the bed as she screamed and screamed and screamed.

'What in God's name is going on?'

Bridgette's eyes were mere slits, but she saw her father in the doorway and she could almost see the raging temper he was in. Behind him was her mother, a shawl wrapped over her nightdress. Gabrielle was angrier than Bridgette had ever seen her.

'I shouldn't think you need ask what has happened here tonight,' she said, crossing to the bed and putting her arm around her weeping daughter. 'Your despicable son has obviously tried to have his way with Bridgette and when she wouldn't comply, he has beaten her senseless. Take him away, out of my sight, for I have a great desire to find the heaviest pot in the kitchen and hit him over the head with it. But this isn't over, so don't think it is. We will discuss this tomorrow.'

'It was all Bridgette's fault,' Georges said, as his father led him from the room. 'She asked me in and was all for it, and then she suddenly turned nasty.'

Gabrielle shut the door with a resounding slam and returned to Bridgette. 'Did he violate you? You know what I mean by that?'

'Yes, I know, Maman,' Bridgette answered. 'He didn't, but he would have done. That was why I bit him.'

'Has he ever done anything like this before?'

'No, but he threatened to do it in the future any time he felt like it.'

'He won't ever do anything like this to you again,' Gabrielle promised.

'How can you be so sure?'

'Trust me he won't,' Gabrielle said determinedly. 'Now if the coast is clear, I will get a bowl of water to clean you up.'

*   *   *

263

The next day Bridgette was far too battered and bruised to go to work and Gabrielle went out early to explain what had happened. Had it been anyone else, she would never have told the truth, but Marie was a very good friend, and Gabrielle wanted her advice on how to keep her daughter safe.

Marie was furious that Georges should have so abused and hurt Bridgette in the way Gabrielle described – so angry that her voices penetrated through to the kitchen, where Xavier was having his breakfast, and he heard every word.

'D'you mean Robert and Georges refuse to discuss it,' he heard his mother ask Gabrielle incredulously, 'just as if it never happened?'

Gabrielle shrugged. 'More or less. All Robert said was that Georges was drunk and he had made a mistake. He also said that Bridgette had to take some of the blame, for if she hadn't encouraged Georges and then played hard to get, she wouldn't have ended up so battered and bruised. But I know Bridgette would not ask Georges into her room if he were the last man on earth.'

'I know she wouldn't as well,' Marie said. 'She makes her feelings for Georges Legrand abundantly clear and always has. Xavier has little time for him either.'

By now Xavier was seething with temper. He didn't let on he had heard anything but slipped out of the door and made his way to work. He was determined that he would make Georges Legrand pay, both for what he had done to

264

Bridgette and for what he had attempted to do. And all he needed was time to decide just how he was going to do that.

Later, when Gabrielle had left, Marie went in search of her son but found he had already gone out. She was glad that he hadn't heard the exchange, and she had no intention of telling him the real reason Bridgette wasn't at work that day because she didn't know how he would react.

Bridgette languished in bed all day, glad to be there because she didn't want to see Georges or her father, but she was unable to sleep as the time drew near for the men to come home. She felt as if every nerve ending was standing out in her body as she lay wide-eyed, alert to every noise.

She heard them both come in and listened to Georges's stumbling progress up the stairs, encouraged by his father, and she assumed that he had had more to drink than usual.

The next day Gabrielle told Bridgette that she had to go down to the bakery to help until the boy Legrand had engaged should arrive.

'Why?' Bridgette asked. 'What's up with Georges?'

'He was set upon by a crowd of ruffians,' Gabrielle said, with a smile, 'and beaten up quite badly. I couldn't be more pleased, though I have to hide that from his father, of course.'

'Of course,' Bridgette said with an answering grin, and despite her aches and bruises went down quite cheerfully to the bakery to help her father.

She insisted on going to work after that, though. Gabrielle did her best with her face and Marie said she would keep her in the back for a few days till it healed a little. Lisette was agog with curiosity, but it was only later that day, as they walked out with Xavier after lunch, that Bridgette was able to tell her friend the real reason why she hadn't been at work the previous day.

Lisette was appalled. Then they fell to discussing what gang of ruffians had done the world a favour and assaulted Georges Legrand, and suddenly Xavier laughed.

'There was no gang of ruffians,' he said. 'I attacked him.'

'You did?' Bridgette said in horror.

'Yes. For all I hate him with a passion, I hit him with nothing but my fists and have skinned knuckles to prove it. Look.'

Xavier spread his hands and Bridgette looked at the broken and bruised skin. 'You should have them seen to,' she said.

'Oh, no,' Xavier assured her. 'They'll be all right in a day or two.'

'Good job that Maman didn't catch sight of them,' Lisette said with a giggle. 'Oh, there would have been all sorts of questions then, and she would have got to the bottom of it in the end.'

'I was in no danger,' Xavier said. 'Like most bullies, Georges Legrand was a coward when it came down to it. To tell you the truth I have wanted to punch that man for some time. He is

266

crafty and a sneak, and has been that way since we were at school together. It's a wonder no one has done it before. But the final straw for me was when he abused you, Bridgette.'

'How did you know?' Bridgette asked. 'Did your mother tell you?'

'Not exactly,' Xavier said, and explained how he had overheard.

'I knew something was wrong as soon as I saw you,' Lisette said, 'and I think what Georges tried to do to you was dreadful.'

'You don't think less of me because of what happened, do you?' Bridgette asked Xavier and Lisette worriedly.

'Why would we do that?' Lisette replied.

'You might feel that I was somehow to blame.'

'How could you even think that?' Xavier asked. 'We have known you since you were a little girl. The whole family knows the kind of girl you are.'

Bridgette gave a sigh of relief. Then she said, 'You won't get into trouble for hitting Georges like this, will you?'

'I doubt it,' Xavier shrugged.

'Did he recognise you?'

'Of course. But if he complains, he also has to admit that it was one man alone that attacked him, and then he will have to say why, which I told him before I laid a hand on him. He'd hardly want that spread around the town, would he?'

'No, I don't suppose he would.'

'But I think I had better tell Maman and Papa anyway.'

'Why?'

'Look, Bridgette', Xavier said. 'At the moment Georges is frightened and he will leave you alone, but how long d'you think that will last?'

'He might never touch me again after what you did to him,' Bridgette answered confidently.

Xavier shook his head. 'You forget, I know this man. He'll wait until the furore dies down and then probably, with his wits affected by far too much wine, he will attack you again. You are unprotected in that house and he knows that.'

Bridgette gave a shiver. 'I suppose I could ask for a bolt to be fitted on my door,' she said tentatively. 'What else can I do?'

'I have been thinking about that. You could always move into our house.'

Bridgette stared at him. 'Xavier, I can't just go moving into other people's houses.'

'Yes you can,' Xavier insisted. 'You could share a bedroom with Lisette. You wouldn't mind that, would you, Lis?'

Lisette clapped her hands with delight. 'Mind? I would love it. It would be like having a sister.'

Bridgette shook her head. 'Papa would never allow it.'

'I bet your mother will,' Xavier said. 'She can threaten to expose Georges if your father plays up.'

'She would never do that,' Bridgette said. 'And my father will know that.'

'Well, he won't be so sure of me,' Xavier said. 'He wasn't there when I beat Georges but Georges is sure to have told him. Would he take the risk that I might tell everyone of my beating up Georges Legrand if he makes a fuss about you coming to live with us?'

'No, I don't think he would,' Bridgette said. 'He would hate to be snubbed or ridiculed, and if people were incensed enough it could affect the business, though I know my mother will be the one who bears the brunt of his ill humour.'

'Bridgette, your mother would want you to be safe, wouldn't she?' Lisette said.

Of course she would – Bridgette knew that – and only if she put some distance between her and Georges would she feel safe. She sighed.

'All right, tell your mother and see what she says,' she told Xavier.

Marie and Maurice agreed straightaway, and Gabrielle could see the sense of it too, though she knew she would miss her daughter sorely. When she tried to tell Legrand what was proposed, however, he was flabbergasted and said that he would never allow Bridgette to leave the bakery.

He roared and he bellowed about it, and when Gabrielle tried to change his mind, he lashed out at her. In the end, Xavier and his father went to talk to him and Xavier threatened to tell everyone of Georges's behaviour if he refused to let Bridgette move into the Laurents' house.

As Bridgette prophesied, her father didn't want rumours spread about him, and though he still blustered and grumbled they all knew that was just for show and the battle had been won. Bridgette moved into the Laurents' without delay.

Marie insisted that Bridgette keep in regular contact with her mother. She knew Gabrielle was tortured by the thought that, to ensure Bridgette's happiness and safety, they had to live apart. Gabrielle said none of this when her daughter came to visit, but just cherished the time that they had together. The afternoons, while the men slept, were usually quiet at the shop, and Gabrielle would make coffee and put a cake by for each of them, and Bridgette looked forward to these occasions as much as her mother did.

FOURTEEN

For years Bridgette had liked and admired Lisette and wished Xavier had been her brother, but by the time she had passed her seventeenth birthday, she was very glad he wasn't, for just the sight of him caused her heart to beat faster, her hands to become clammy and her mouth to feel dry.

Many times she and Lisette had talked of falling in love, like all young girls longed to do, and how they would know when it happened. That was the topic of conversation one late November day in 1933.

'I mean, it must be a very odd thing,' Lisette said, lying full stretch on her bed. 'It's what most of the songs are about, and poems and many stories, and yet . . . how does a person know?'

Bridgette shrugged, thinking of her own situation, for Xavier surely saw her just as his sister's friend. 'And what if you are madly in love with someone and he doesn't even know that you exist?' she asked.

'Ah, yes,' said Lisette. 'Unrequited love. Wouldn't

that be the most dreadful thing? I hope that doesn't happen to either of us.'

The phrase 'unrequited love' ran round and round in Bridgette's head all morning and as she sat down opposite Xavier for lunch that day her heart was thumping so hard against her ribs, she felt sure that everyone could hear it.

She suddenly felt very miserable and the meal tasted like sawdust in her mouth. And then she reached for the salt cellar at the same time as Xavier, and as their fingers met, a tingle ran all through Bridgette's arm and her startled eyes met those of Xavier. She felt her limbs had suddenly turned to jelly and her throbbing heart leaped with joy, and yet not a word had been exchanged between them.

Bridgette was surprised that the wondrous thing between her and Xavier had not been noticed by anyone else and that ordinary life was going on around them.

Someone else had seen the spark between the young couple, and that was Marie. When the meal was over she waved away Bridgette's offer of assistance to wash up.

'Why don't you and Xavier take a walk out?' she suggested to Bridgette. 'You don't get many dry, fine days like this in November. Make the most of it. Lisette will give me a hand.'

Lisette was about to protest, for they had always walked out together, until she saw the wink her mother gave her, and then she followed her gaze and saw Bridgette and Xavier gazing at one another as if they were the only people on earth. She felt a sudden pang of loss for she knew that soon someone else would be closer to Xavier than she was, but she was ashamed of herself almost at once, for how could she begrudge such happiness to the two people she loved best in all the world?

Outside in that chill November day, Xavier was holding Bridgette close. He could hardly believe that he had her in his arms, the girl he had thought loved him only in a fraternal way, as Lisette did.

Almost in wonderment he told her, 'I never dreamed . . . I mean, I never knew that you felt like this.'

'Loving you like this sort of grew on me,' Bridgette explained. 'I didn't know you felt the same. I thought you saw me as Lisette's friend.'

'Oh, I felt much more than that for you,' Xavier answered. 'My heart has ached for you for some months now, but I was afraid to speak. You are so young.'

'Oh, Xavier, I am old enough to know my own heart,' Bridgette murmured, snuggling closer.

'Darling, just to hear you whisper my name sends tremors down my spine. I love you from the very core of my being. My heart and soul belong to you.'

'I love you the same way,' Bridgette said. 'Isn't it wonderful?'

'It is.' Xavier swung Bridgette round to face him. 'But this is better.'

Bridgette watched his face coming towards her and she clasped him tight, and when their lips met she closed her eyes with a groan of desire she barely understood. She knew that Xavier was kissing her in the street in open view of anyone passing, but she didn't care. It was her very first kiss, and just about the sweetest thing she had ever experienced.

When Xavier released Bridgette eventually she said to him, 'Shall we go back to the house and tell them?'

Xavier laughed. 'I don't think that it will come as any sort of surprise.'

'Why?'

'Well, Maman is very aware of it. I saw it in her eyes. Why d'you think she wangled for us to come out alone today?'

'I did wonder at that,' Bridgette admitted.

'Come on,' said Xavier. 'Let's go and tell her that she is right, as usual.' And they ran hand in hand along the street.

'I suppose I should go and see Robert Legrand and ask his permission to marry his daughter,' Xavier said morosely to his mother that same evening. 'I don't relish that, I can tell you. I mean, he cannot stop us walking out together because Bridgette lives here, but he can stop our marriage. I may as well tell you, Maman, that while the man never thought much of me, he hates me now because of what I did to his son that time. I guessed that Georges would have admitted to him what really happened that night. If looks could kill I would have died on the floor of the cathedral many a time already, for the way he looks at me sometimes is positively venomous.'

'Oh, Xavier!'

Xavier gave a grim laugh. 'I'm not frightened of the man, Maman. Anyway, for all his talk, he is as cowardly as his son. I'm sure, though, he would take great pleasure in withholding his permission for Bridgette to marry, especially me. But I am twenty-one, old enough to take a wife, and neither of us wishes to wait for four years, until Bridgette is old enough to please herself.'

'Well, don't go near Legrand,' Marie advised. 'Speak to Gabrielle.'

'She has no voice or influence in that relationship. You have said that yourself.'

'She has where Bridgette is concerned.' Marie said. 'Legrand is not her father.'

Xavier's eyes showed his astonishment. 'Not her father?'

'No,' Marie said. 'Gabrielle told me that Bridgette's father was an Irishman in the British Army, stationed here in the early part of the Great War, and they fell in love. Well, you know how it is? She felt for that young soldier the same burning love that you have for Bridgette. Gabrielle was young too then and the affair was a clandestine one because she had to sneak out to meet her lover without her father's knowledge. There was the added pressure that her soldier could be shipped out at any time.'

'Are you telling me that Bridgette is illegitimate?' Xavier asked. 'It will make no difference if she is.'

'No, Gabrielle married her soldier,' Marie said. 'But, of course, Bridgette was born not that long after the wedding.'

'And her father?' Finn said. 'What happened to him?'

'He was killed before the baby was born.'

'Then why did she marry a man like Legrand?' Xavier asked. 'It has always puzzled me. He is so much older, for a start, and uglier, apart from being a right nasty piece of work.'

Marie nodded. 'I agree with you. Gabrielle told me that her father wanted to marry her off quickly, and to anyone who would have her. When Legrand offered marriage Pierre threatened to put Gabrielle and the child out on the streets if she didn't marry him.'

'Would he really have done that?'

Marie shrugged. 'Who knows, but could she take that risk?'

Xavier shook his head. 'That poor woman has suffered all her life.'

'Yes,' Marie said. 'Gabrielle did confide to me that, had she produced a son, her life might have been easier. But the man is brutal and he beats Gabrielle like he did his previous wife.'

'I despise men like that,' Xavier said contemptuously.

'So do I,' Marie said. 'But it does mean that in this case Legrand has no jurisdiction over Bridgette, though she has no idea that he is not her father.'

'Why doesn't Gabrielle tell her the truth? Bridgette would probably be glad that she isn't related to Legrand. I know I would be.'

Marie nodded. 'All this secrecy is no good for anyone, but Gabrielle told me that it was how Legrand wanted it when she married him, and her father was all for it too. I suppose she just went along with it and is still doing what Legrand wants for an easier life. He never adopted Bridgette – she did tell me that – and so it is Gabrielle that you have to see in this instance. The big fellow might roar and bellow all he likes but he has no legal power over her.'

Xavier gave a brief nod. 'I will leave work early tomorrow and see Gabrielle in the shop before it closes. She should give her permission before we spread the news abroad.'

Gabrielle was surprised to see Xavier in the shop, but when he told her of his love for her daughter, which Bridgette returned, she thought for a moment that her heart had stopped beating, because those were words she never expected to hear. She knew of Bridgette's love for him only because she had seen it in her glowing face and sparkling eyes every time she spoke his name.

Gabrielle had prayed that the daughter she loved with all her being would have a much better life than she had had, and part of that better life was to love and be loved by a young man such as Xavier Laurent. It was no matter to her that Bridgette was young. She herself had loved Finn as deeply as if she had been a woman ten years older. It was what was in the heart that mattered.

She caught Xavier's hands in hers and told him how happy he had made her. She gladly gave her permission for him to marry her daughter, although secretly she knew that she would suffer for it when Legrand got to hear.

He soon did, of course. The beautiful diamond ring that Xavier bought Bridgette was soon noticed and commented on by customers in the shop, and Bridgette was only too happy to tell anyone who wanted to know about her wonderful Xavier. The news of the engagement flew around the town. That first Sunday after Mass, the priest went out of his way to congratulate the young couple. Then Bridgette was hugged and kissed by men and women alike, and Xavier had his hand pumped up and down many times. She was soon surrounded by girls admiring the ring, and oohing and aahing over the whole romance of it.

Xavier was on the steps talking to the priest, and as the crowd around Bridgette thinned she almost felt her father's malevolent eyes boring into her. She turned slowly.

He and Georges were side by side, and his smile was disdainful as he said. 'I believe congratulations are in order, though it would have been nice for my permission to be asked. That is the normal order of things, or don't good manners apply here?'

Xavier had been expecting a confrontation of some sort and when he saw Legrand approach Bridgette, he broke off his conversation with the priest and walked quickly down the steps to stand at her side. It was he who answered.

'There is nothing wrong with my manners, Legrand, and permission to marry Bridgette was asked and given. If you have a problem with that, then it is yours alone, and if you want to discuss it I would be agreeable to meet with you to do that, but this is neither the time nor the place.'

How proud Bridgette was of her young husband-to-be who had spoken to her hated father so assertively. She could see that he didn't know how to answer. A few passing had stopped to listen, and even the priest paused on the steps. In the end Legrand turned away.

'Come away now, Xavier,' Maurice said to his son.

Bridgette said, 'Oh, please wait, just two minutes?'

She ignored her father and Georges, and went to her mother. Gabrielle had already seen the ring and shed tears of joy over it. She'd said she had never seen such a fine thing in the whole of her life. She had been so happy for her daughter and still was happy, but Bridgette saw the bruising on her mother's face and her darkened eyes, and knew that she had paid the price, and dearly, for giving her permission for the two young people to marry.

With a sigh she put her arms around her as gently as she could. 'I'll be up in the week,' she whispered into her ear as she held her close.

As she released her Gabrielle squeezed her hands tight before turning away with tears in her eyes.

All the way home, Bridgette burned with rage. She barely waited until she was inside before bursting out, 'Did any of you see what that maniac did to my mother?'

'Yes,' Marie said. 'There is nothing to be done about it because, as far as your mother is concerned, when a person marries it is for better or worse. She is prepared to put up with the worse as long as she can content herself that you will have the better.'

'As you will, my darling,' Xavier said, catching hold of Bridgette and swinging her into his arms. 'I have never raised my hand to a woman yet, and never would, and I will love you with all my heart until the breath leaves my body.'

'Well,' said Maurice with a throaty chuckle, 'I would say that a man can't say fairer than that.'

Bridgette knew Maurice was right. She knew how lucky she was and she longed to be married to Xavier so that she could show him just how much she loved him. She wished she could make things right for her mother but knew that she couldn't, and the only thing she could do was let her share in her happiness.

The wedding was set for 14 April 1934. Bridgette wanted the days to speed by because it seemed like each day she loved Xavier more, and her longing for him sometimes overwhelmed her. Through the winter they were allocated the parlour to do their courting, and Bridgette appreciated the consideration of Maurice and Marie Laurent in allowing them to use that lovely room. It was cosy cuddled together on the sofa with the fire warming them and the lamps lending everything a rosy hue.

Over time, their kisses grew more ardent and demanding, and when Xavier teased Bridgette's mouth open for the first time she groaned at the delicious feelings stealing all through her body. Christmas passed and the year turned, and their lovemaking grew more impassioned and sensual. By early February, Bridgette was surprised at the places on her body she was allowing Xavier to touch and explore and caress, and that she was relishing it as much as he was.

In late March, Gabrielle had a talk with Bridgette about what would probably happen on the wedding night. She drew on her experience of the one time she slept with Finn, the night that Bridgette was conceived and she explained the feelings of desire that were almost uncontrollable. She also told her of the gentle and considerate husband who would wait until she was ready.

Bridgette was quite embarrassed to hear her mother talk like this, and she didn't really need the advice. Xavier, not wishing her to approach the wedding bed in total innocence, had already explained things to her. She didn't say any of that to Gabrielle, though she was glad when she finished and they could return to discussing the wedding itself.

'Are you sure that you won't mind living with the Laurents after your marriage?' Gabrielle asked.

Bridgette shook her head. 'It makes sense. I want to continue working at the shop. At least until the babies start arriving.'

'I hope you have better luck in that department than me,' Gabrielle said. 'I will pray that your marriage might be blessed with children.'

'Ooh, yes,' Bridgette said. 'Xavier and I have discussed it and we want a houseful. By then, of course, we shall have a place of our own. And,' she added, 'you would hardly recognise the room we have. It is Xavier's old room, which is plenty big enough for the two of us, but Marie said it needed redecorating for newlyweds, and Xavier moved out to stay with his friend Edmund Gublain while the whole place was done over with new curtains and even fluffy rugs to match. We ordered a double bed and a bedroom suite, and with that in place it looks like a little palace. I know we will be more than comfortable. I would love you to see it.'

'Maybe I will come with Yvette,' Gabrielle said. 'I am so longing to see her.'

Bridgette knew how much her mother had missed her family and wanted to invite them to the wedding. She could barely remember them, but she wanted to thank Yvette for her kindness

282

to her as she was growing up, and let them see her fine young husband. And so she wrote to her aunt.

But it was Henri, Yvette's husband, who wrote to Legrand and asked permission to come to celebrate Bridgette's marriage to Xavier. He grudgingly gave it, fearful of alienating such a rich and influential man. Gabrielle was like a dog with two tails at the thought of seeing her sister again, although Yvette had written to say that Bernadette was too old and frail to make the journey.

'Almost everything is sorted now,' Bridgette said to her mother. 'But who am I going to ask to walk me down the aisle?'

Gabrielle went cold inside. It was obvious that Bridgette didn't want it to be Legrand, and she couldn't blame her. She knew that was the point when she should have told Bridgette who her real father was, though she could guess what her reaction would be if she did that. She would probably ban Legrand from even attending the wedding. Gabrielle could guess his fury if Bridgette did that and she was afraid because she had to live with the man after the wedding was over.

'Your father would probably be very angry if you don't ask him,' she said quietly.

Bridgette was about to retort that she didn't care how angry he got, and then she looked into her mother's eyes and knew who would bear the brunt of her father's temper if she were to make this stand against him. So for her mother's sake she said, 'I had better ask him then,' and she heard her mother's sigh of relief.

'What else could I do?' Bridgette said to Xavier later. 'If I do not ask my father then he will take it out on her. It was there in her eyes.'

It was on the tip of Xavier's tongue then to tell Bridgette that Legrand wasn't her real father but he stopped himself. Nobody would benefit from that knowledge spurted out now. Bridgette could not help but be disturbed by that revelation and it would also almost certainly cause further trouble for Gabrielle, and he couldn't risk that. Really, regardless of how he felt, it had to be her decision to tell Bridgette the truth when she thought the time was right.

'I do understand,' he said. 'Don't fret over it. Nothing else matters but our love for each other and so I can put up with your despicable father for the short walk down the aisle. Once I stand beside you and the priest pronounces us man and wife, my joy will be complete.'

The following Sunday morning, after Mass, Bridgette suppressed a sigh as she said to her father, 'It's a simple question. Do you want to walk me down the aisle or don't you?'

'I just expressed surprise that I was being asked to do anything at all,' Legrand commented sourly. 'So far this wedding seems to be going on without me being involved in any way.'

'Fathers usually aren't involved in wedding

284

preparations,' Bridgette said dismissively. 'But most fathers walk their daughters down the aisle and I just wondered if you wanted to do the same?'

Most fathers also pay for their daughters' weddings, Bridgette might have said but she knew there would be no point. Instead she chivvied her father. 'Yes or no?'

'Yes, I suppose,' Legrand said in the end. 'It would seem mighty odd to the townsfolk, not to mention Yvette and her fancy husband, if I refused.'

So, he was only doing it because it was the expected thing to do, and he didn't want to risk making a show of himself in front of Yvette and Henri. But Bridgette didn't care, if her request might have saved her mother from further misery.

Then Legrand further surprised her. 'I will make the wedding cake too, and all the pastries for you and your guests if you give me the numbers invited.'

Bridgette couldn't believe her ears. She was preparing most of the wedding food, together with Marie and Lisette, and as they were all working, two girls had been hired from the town to help. The centrepiece was always the delicious croquem-bouche, which was difficult to make well, and so she thanked her father sincerely.

'What else could he do?' Lisette said when Bridgette told her afterwards. 'Wouldn't it look very odd if we had ordered the croquembouche from another baker?'

'Yes, I know why,' Bridgette said. 'He is trying to impress our Parisian relations, Henri in particular.'

'He doesn't seem to like women, does he?'

'I think he sees them as good only for bedding and producing sons,' Bridgette said.

'Shame, isn't it?' Lisette said. 'I wouldn't mind if I had boys or girls.'

'I wouldn't either,' Bridgette replied. 'Good job really, seeing that we have no choice on the matter. But if I were you I wouldn't have any at all until you're married.'

'Oh, you!' Lisette gave Bridgette a push and the two girls fell upon each other laughing.

Bridgette was delighted to see Yvette again. She was incredibly smart and although there was a likeness to her mother, her aunt's hair was much darker and cut in a bob, quite an unusual sight in St-Omer but, Yvette said, quite the thing in Paris, and enabled women to wear the cloche hats which were all the rage too.

She looked the perfect companion to her tall, handsome and very distinguished-looking husband, Henri. Despite his appearance though, Henri was friendly and had eyes that twinkled, and Bridgette guessed that he could be fun and got on with him very well. She loved their two sons too: black-haired Raoul, who was nearly eleven, looked the image of his father, and was very aware of his position as the elder son, and Gerard, who was just nine and had lighter hair and a resemblance to his mother. He was always striving to do things as well as his brother and

Yvette joked they should have called Gerard, 'and me'.

The arrival of the Dellatres meant that Legrand was on his best behaviour, so when Marie issued an invitation to Yvette and her family to go for a meal, Gabrielle was able to go too because Robert had hired a girl to work temporarily in the shop. It was a lovely meal and they did it justice, and afterwards Xavier and Maurice took Henri and the boys down to the canal, Lisette said she would help her mother with the clearing up, and Bridgette took her mother and her aunt up to show them the bedroom done out for her and Xavier.

She even let them have a peep at the wedding dress. It was a marvellous creation, made of thick white satin with lace decorating the neckline and the puff sleeves. The sequined bodice was fitted; the skirt, covered with tiny seed pearls, billowed out from the waist, helped by layers and layers of lace petticoats, and it was scooped up at intervals and fastened with tiny blue and pink rosebuds. It had been the dress Marie wore at her wedding, but it had been professionally cleaned.

Lisette's dress of pale blue satin had been made by the local dressmaker to match Bridgette's, only less elaborate and with fewer petticoats. Yvette declared that Bridgette and Lisette were going to dazzle all the men in the town.

Bridgette smiled at her aunt. 'I thought the dress was the something borrowed – you know you have to have something old, something new, something borrowed and something blue – but Marie said that the dress could be something old, though it hardly looks it. She has a deep amber necklace that she was given by her mother on her wedding day, which she says will match my eyes perfectly, so she will let me borrow that.'

'What about something new?' Yvette asked.

'That's my veil,' Bridgette said, pulling it from a bag on the shelf of the wardrobe, 'and the blue is the garters that will hold up my silk stockings.'

'You know I am so pleased to be here on your wedding day,' Yvette said. 'And let me say that you are as beautiful on the inside as you are on the outside, Bridgette, and are a true credit to your mother. I hope that this Xavier knows what a gem he is getting.'

Bridgette laughed. 'Believe me, I am no gem. Xavier is much nicer than me sometimes. Anyway, I love him to bits, and for me the wedding can't come soon enough.'

'Well,' said Yvette, 'I would say that is the best way to feel about something that's a life-long commitment.'

Gabrielle said nothing. She hoped and prayed that it would stay that way for her daughter. At least there was no chance that she would have her husband stolen away from her by war, and that was one thing to be thankful for.

Lisette and Marie helped Bridgette dress on the morning of the wedding. As she put her arms into her sleeves she heard the delicious rustle of the many petticoats as they slid down her silk-clad legs before billowing around her like cloud of lace. Just the tips of her white shoes were visible. Then Marie fastened the bodice, and Lisette put the veil in place, and they turned Bridgette round to look at herself in the mirror. She was transformed, a princess!

'Darling girl, you look a picture,' Marie said brokenly. Her eyes were so full of tears that she had difficulty in fastening the amber necklace that she was loaning Bridgette. She managed it in the end, and Bridgette saw that it lay just above the scoop of the neckline and that the deep amber stone was indeed the same colour as her eyes. She turned this way and that, and the gold filigree surrounding the stone twinkled in the light.

'Oh, Marie, thank you so much. It's so beautiful.'

'It matches the person who wears it then,' Marie said.

Bridgette turned and put her arms around Marie. 'Thank you, thank you for everything, but most of all thank you for giving me Xavier.'

Marie was too choked to speak and eventually she pushed Bridgette gently away. 'You will crush your gown,' she said brokenly. 'And really we must be on our way.' She glanced up at the clock. 'By now Guiseppe will be waiting in Rue Jacqueline. When he sees us pass he will come along to fetch you.'

'We know that, Maman,' Lisette said. 'Go on now, and stop fussing. I will look after Bridgette. It's what bridesmaids are supposed to do.'

With a last look around the room and a kiss

for each girl, Marie was at last prevailed upon to leave.

As they stood at the window and watched her and Maurice hurrying quickly down the road, Lisette grinned at Bridgette and said, 'Isn't Maman a mother hen?'

'She's lovely,' Bridgette said. 'She just wants to make sure that everything goes right.'

'I know, and it will,' Lisette assured her. 'And you look magnificent. I just want to say how glad I am that you are marrying Xavier; there is no one that I would rather see him marry than you. I have enjoyed having you as a sort of sister these past few years and I am looking forward to you joining the family properly.'

It was too much. Tears were raining down Bridgette's cheeks and she was unable to speak.

'Me and my big mouth, upsetting you when we have to go in a few minutes,' Lisette apologised.

Bridgette struggled to control herself as she heard the rumble of Guiseppe's trap on the cobbles, and then it came into view and the driver pulled up in front of the shop. Bridgette saw white ribbons were threaded into the pony's mane and tail, and decorated the trap, and Guiseppe himself was dressed in his Sunday finery.

His blue eyes twinkled as the girls emerged. 'My, my!' he said, but there was a wealth of meaning in those two words.

Then he lifted first Bridgette into the trap as gently as if he were handling fine porcelain, and she sat on the silken cushion he had ready, and then Lisette was beside her. With Guiseppe at the head of the pony they set off. It was a glorious spring morning and the sun shone brightly in the pale blue sky, gilding everything in its golden light.

The children of the town, who had been clustered around the shop doorway, followed behind the trap, shouting and cheering, and shoppers and shopkeepers alike stood to watch. Some men doffed their caps and berets, and others just waved their arms in the air, but all had smiles on their faces as they called out, '*Bonne Chance!*' or '*Félicitations!*' By the time Bridgette reached Notre Dame she was warmed through by their good wishes.

She was nervous, though, and as the pony and trap drew to a halt, she whispered to Lisette, 'My mouth is so dry, I really don't know if I will be able to say anything.'

'You only have to say, "I do",' Lisette said. 'Those are all the words Xavier wants to hear.'

'I know.'

'And you will be all right. It's just the thought of it,' Lisette assured her. 'Look, there's your father waiting for you on the steps.'

'Is that supposed to make me feel better?'

Lisette suppressed a smile. 'Come on, Bridgette. Xavier will probably be just as bad. You do want to marry him, don't you?'

'Of course I do.'

'Well, come on then,' Lisette said briskly. 'Let's get on with it.'

Bridgette didn't bother protesting any more, but went forward to meet Legrand. 'You look very well,' he said to her, almost grudgingly.

'Thank you,' Bridgette said, and they moved towards the church door. There was no time to say anything else. In the small porch Lisette had just finished rearranging the folds on Bridgette's dress when the strains of the wedding march could be heard.

The church was fuller than Bridgette had expected it to be, and filled with the happy cheerful faces of friends of her own and her parents, or of the Laurents, or neighbours who had watched her grow up. With Lisette falling into place behind her, she walked down the aisle slowly and on Legrand's arm, and while he had an expression on his face that Yvette said later would curdle milk, she smiled from side to side at all the well-wishers.

Bridgette saw Xavier, with Edmund, leave the pew they'd occupied at the front of the church to stand in front of the altar and she felt a tingle of excitement that began in her toes and spread all over her body. She could never remember feeling so happy, and she loved Xavier so much she ached. She kept her eyes fastened on him, the man she would soon promise to love and honour in sickness and in health, whether they were rich or whether they were poor until they were parted by death.

FIFTEEN

Within a few weeks of marriage, Bridgette knew just how lucky she was in having such a considerate husband. Their first night together set the pattern when Xavier spent time caressing and fondling her slowly and sensually. When he placed his lips on hers, she responded eagerly, and then he kissed her lingeringly, then let his tongue slip in and out of her mouth until yearning shafts of passion were shooting all through her so that she moaned aloud. Still he waited, and not until she was giving little yelps of pure desire did he enter her.

Later that first night, as she lay in Xavier's arms, her mother's words came back to her about the gentle and considerate husband who would wait for his bride to be ready. She couldn't help wondering if her mother had been talking from experience, but then how could she be? She knew her father was the sort to seek his own pleasure first and she doubted it had been different when he had been younger.

She wished her mother had such joy and happiness in her life, and the contentment of curling up with a young husband, as she was doing, and she wondered afresh what had induced her to marry a man like her father. She hated him with a passion and didn't care how wicked that made her. But she could do nothing to help her mother, or try to cement over the wide-open chasms in her marriage.

Suddenly the events of the day made her feel very drowsy and she cuddled against Xavier, closed her eyes and was soon fast asleep.

As one month slipped into another Bridgette found herself loving Xavier more and more. She knew what a marvellous father he would make and she longed to hold their child in her arms, but she was disappointed time after time, and she told herself to have patience.

Great-aunt Bernadette sickened and died at the end of January 1935. Gabrielle had wanted to go to the funeral, but Legrand wouldn't allow it. Bridgette felt so sorry for her mother when she told her this, because she knew how much she had loved her aunt, and she told her to stand up to her father.

Gabrielle shook her head sadly, though some days she reflected on the courage she once had that enabled her to creep out at night to meet Finn. However, fear for her daughter, as well as herself, had dogged her life and stripped her of any confidence she might have had and so she had allowed herself to be treated shamelessly by both her husband and his son. Her daughter would have a much better life, she knew, and was immensely glad, but for her it was already too late.

Warmth began to steal into the days of early spring and buds started to appear on the trees when Lisette and Edmund Gublain became engaged. The marriage was set for September 1935. After, Lisette would move into the house in Rue Charles Jonart that Edmund shared with his widowed mother.

Bridgette was delighted for them. She had got to know Edmund since she'd married Xavier and liked him a lot, but she truly loved Lisette, like a sister and she knew that she would miss her greatly.

'I will still see you everyday when I'm married because I'm continuing in the shop,' Lisette said, a few days before her wedding. 'At least until the babies come.'

'That's what I said,' Bridgette reminded her. 'And the babies seem as far away as ever.'

'It's early days,' Lisette consoled. 'I'm sure that it will happen soon.'

'That's what I tell myself,' Bridgette said.

However, things got decidedly harder for Bridgette when Lisette fell pregnant almost immediately after the wedding and, in June 1936, she gave birth to a little boy she called Jean-Paul. He was the most adorable child and Bridgette loved him almost as much as his mother did. She missed

Lisette, though, for since his birth she had given up work in the milliner's and Maurice had taken on a young boy as an apprentice to train up.

Jean-Paul was only a couple of months old when everyone was talking of the Olympic Games, which were being held in Berlin. Herr Hitler, Chancellor of Germany had refused to shake the hand of the black African-American athlete Jesse Owens, or decorate him with the four gold medals that he'd won.

'The man is mad,' Maurice said one night at the evening meal. 'Anyone can see that, and the German people are worse for voting him into such a position of power.'

'They were bound to think that he was good for the country,' Xavier said, 'because he did turn Germany round. It was in a dreadful mess before.'

'And whose fault was that?' Maurice burst out. 'They were the aggressors in that dreadful war that took so many young lives. Many of my friends did not come back and I can't forget that.'

Xavier knew how much his father had suffered when he fought in the war. 'I'm no lover of Germany, Papa,' he said gently, 'All I'm saying is, if your country is in a mess and someone comes along and gives you a bit of hope for the future, then you are going to vote for that person. It's human nature.'

'I don't think the Jews in Germany have much hope,' Bridgette put in. 'Not according to Aunt

Yvette, anyway. She said that Jews fleeing from Germany are streaming into Paris and the tales they tell of what is happening to those left behind are so shocking they are almost unbelievable.'

'Well, I'm sorry for them if the tales are true,' Maurice said. 'But I'm not that surprised. Funny race of people, the Germans. Personally, I think the only good German is a dead one.'

It was a shocking thing to say, especially from the peaceable Maurice, but no one said anything to him because in their heart of hearts they all felt something of the same.

In March 1938, Hitler marched into Austria and took over the country. He called it the Anschluss and most of the world looked on in surprise, mainly because the Austrian people hadn't seemed to mind that much.

'Maybe that's because he is Austrian by birth,' Bridgette said.

'Well, whatever he is, he has control of the two countries now,' Marie said.

'I think that this is the tip of the iceberg,' Maurice murmured.

'It may be,' Xavier admitted. 'And perhaps we shouldn't be all doom and gloom. Austria, by all accounts, welcomed Hitler in and so that's that, really.'

'I hope it is,' Marie said. 'Lisette can do without this worry with her expecting again so don't you start all this war talk when she's around.'

Bridgette had no wish to upset Lisette, but how she envied her being pregnant again. When, in early September 1938, Lisette gave birth to a little girl she called Leonie, Bridgette tried to be happy for her, but though she said the right words her heart felt as heavy as lead because her arms ached to hold her own child.

In late September, the paper reported that Hitler was intending invading Czechoslovakia unless he was given Sudetenland, where the majority of people spoke German.

'Why do they?' Bridgette asked.

'Because Sudetenland belonged to Germany until the war,' Xavier told her. 'Under the terms of the Versailles Treaty after the Armistice, it was taken off them.'

'So what can they do about it now, if it was all agreed at the time?'

Xavier shrugged. 'Give it back, I suppose. Anyway, according to the paper, Britain's Prime Minister, Chamberlain, is having a meeting with Hitler in Munich to discuss it, and our own Prime Minister, Daladier, is going too, and Stalin.'

'That's another one I wouldn't trust,' Maurice said. 'That Stalin.'

'Nor me either, Papa,' Xavier said. 'I think that he and Hitler are in the same mould, but if between them they can come up with a scheme to avert war, then it has got to be a good thing, however it's done.'

The Laurents' weren't the only household to

breathe a sigh of relief when they had heard that with, the gift of Sudetenland, Hitler was appeased. The threat of war had been lifted.

In late autumn, the Laurents heard news of a pogrom against the Jews that had begun in Munich. They read with horror of the people thrown on to the streets while houses and businesses were destroyed, and synagogues set alight, till the sky was blood red with flames and the pavements like carpets of crystal with shattered glass. The violence quickly spread to other towns and villages until it was estimated that 1,300 synagogues had been burned to the ground and many people left dead or badly injured. Sinisterly 30,000 had simply disappeared.

The savagery and brutality of it shocked everyone. 'What was it all for anyway?' Bridgette asked as they sat eating dinner that night. 'What had they done?'

'They had done nothing,' Xavier said. 'It seems a Polish Jew shot a German official in Paris because he was angry at the way his family had been treated in Poland. This was Germany's idea of revenge.'

'Against innocent people?'

'Look,' Xavier said, 'this is how I see all this. After the Armistice and the terrible loss of life in the Great War, everyone wanted to make Germany pay. Land was confiscated and given to other countries Germany had violated and they had to pay back so much compensation that the country was sinking under the debts it owed. Then, along comes a little Austrian who feeds the German people's resentment and convinces them that it is somehow all the Jews' fault.'

'But why?' Marie said.

'They wanted to hear it.' Xavier said. 'They wanted someone to blame.'

'I think you have hit the nail on the head there,' Maurice said. 'And when they have finished with the Jews, who d'you think they'll blame then?'

'The countries that defeated them in the last war?' Xavier answered quietly.

'You have it exactly.'

'You mean France?' Marie said. 'We'll have to suffer it all again.'

'France, most certainly,' Maurice said. 'In fact most of Europe.'

'And,' Xavier said, 'I don't believe such a man as Hitler will be easily appeased, whatever paper he signed.'

Xavier was soon proved right. Despite Hitler's assurance, he invaded Czechoslovakia in March 1939. In doing so, Germany had broken the terms of the Munich agreement and the threat of war in Europe moved closer.

A few weeks later, Xavier said to Bridgette, 'I think that war with Germany is almost inevitable now. Italy probably will be dragged into it too, with Mussolini in charge, and Spain, now that Franco has won the civil war. At the moment, France is surrounded by potential enemies.'

300

'I know,' said Bridgette, and her voice was little above a whisper.

'And so, I must fight for France.'

'Oh, Xavier . . .'

'Every man will be needed, Bridgette,' Xavier said. 'Anyway, there will be no choice because I'll be called up. This is just to prepare you for what will happen. Edmund feels the same.'

'But Edmund has a family.'

'And he will not be the only one,' Xavier replied.

They both received their call-up papers as Germany cast its eyes towards Poland. Britain had promised to protect and support Poland, and Xavier knew once the German tanks rolled into Poland's streets, France, and all the countries surrounding her, would be plunged into another major war, and they would have to fight to try and stop the monster creeping across Europe.

By the time Britain declared war on Germany on 3 September 1939, Xavier and Edmund were at a training camp. Though Xavier wrote every week to both Bridgette and his parents, he could tell them little, certainly not where he was or what he was doing, except in the most general terms. As the autumn rolled on, Bridgette couldn't tell him either about the Allied soldiers, mainly British, who were coming ashore from ports all across Northern France to help the French Army in their fight against the German aggressors.

'You will see a difference now, mark my words,'

Maurice announced one night as they sat around the fireside. 'Trouble is, those Germans have not hit anything that you could really term resistance. I mean, they goose-stepped unopposed into both Austria and Czechoslovakia.'

'The Poles fought,' Bridgette reminded him.

'Yes they did,' Maurice conceded. 'And they could have won. What is facing us now could have been decided then and there if the Red Army had helped them. That's what I mean about Stalin. He held his armies back until the Poles admitted defeat. This time it will be different. You will find Hitler's soldiers running back to Germany with their tails between their legs.'

Bridgette hoped he was right. Maurice also had immense faith in the Maginot Line.

'What is it, exactly?' Marie asked one evening.

'Five hundred steel-reinforced, heavily guarded forts erected on a hillside, that's what,' Maurice said. 'You would be too young to remember, Bridgette, but France was left in a terrible state after the last war. There was so much bloodshed and we lost so many young fit men. But good farmland was churned up too, and we also lost so many buildings – homes, whole towns and villages and farms destroyed – that it was thought that we needed protection in case there was ever to be another war.'

'After such tragedy,' Marie said, 'and so much grieving all over France, no one imagined that it might happen again.'

'Well, it has,' Maurice said emphatically. 'So isn't it good that people had the hindsight to build this Maginot Line to protect us?'

'And you are certain it will?'

'Oh yes,' said Maurice confidently. 'It stretches from the Swiss border to the Belgium one, not all the way to the coast because it doesn't need to do that. The Ardennes forest is impassable.'

Bridgette felt herself relax. France would be safe from invasion. The French Army and its Allies would easily repulse any German offensive and the war would soon be over.

The men were coming home. It was mid-November and Bridgette, Lisette and Marie were in a fever of excitement. Their excitement, though, was tinged with apprehension because they all knew that the training was finished and when the leave was over, Xavier and Edmund would be making for the battlefields.

Bridgette tried hard not to let these thoughts spoil the few days that they had together. She wasn't totally successful, though, because they would flit unbidden across her mind and she would feel a hollow emptiness in the pit of her stomach. Xavier would see her face change, but he knew what was wrong. Their lovemaking those few days had a deeper and more ardent quality about it.

Bridgette had already decided that however she felt, when the time came for Xavier to leave she would not make things harder for him by weeping all over him and begging him not to go. So that morning, when he swung his kitbag on to his shoulders, though she felt tears tingling behind her eyes she held them back as Xavier drew her into his arms and kissed her goodbye.

With the men gone, the women grew closer, though they began to wonder after a few weeks if France was at war at all. Merchant ships carrying vital foodstuffs were sunk, and so things were in short supply, in the shops, but that was all. Christmas was very meagre, but they managed. The men's letters spoke of boredom and activities to fill their off-duty hours, and the only thing they complained of was the cold, which was intense at night. They were all looking forward to the spring.

Worry for Xavier was constantly in Bridgette's mind, despite his claims that there was nothing for her to fret over, so at first when she didn't get her monthly bleed, she put it down to her emotional state. It was when she started to feel nauseous in the morning that she realised she might be expecting a baby.

Marie had been aware that there had been no linen pads disappearing from the chest for some time and she had dared to hope herself, because she knew that a child was the one thing that Bridgette and Xavier wanted. When Bridgette confided in her, she put her arms around her in delight.

'It had to be now,' Bridgette grumbled. 'With

the country at war and the child's father not even around.'

'Huh,' said Marie, with a chuckle. 'The one thing I have learned about babies over the years is that they seldom come at an opportune time. You take yourself off to see the doctor and make sure, and then write and tell Xavier. I know my son and, whether he is here or not, he will be delighted at the thought of becoming a father.'

And Xavier was beside himself with joy. His concern was all for Bridgette. She had to take care of herself, eat well and healthily, and give up the work in the shop because she needed plenty of rest.

He wrote in the same vein to his mother, but when Marie asked Bridgette if she wanted to stop working in the shop she said, 'No, I don't. What on earth would I do with myself all day? The baby isn't due until August and anyway, the work is not arduous, especially as trade has dropped off considerably of late.'

Marie was only too aware of that. The downturn had begun just after the official declaration of war, although they had had a little upsurge just before Christmas. It affected Maurice even more. Women must have also decided that a hat in wartime was too frivolous a purchase, and he had such little trade that he had let the boy go that he had taken on to train. Most of his work now was revamping old hats to give them a new lease of life. This, of course, did not pay well, and Marie was seriously concerned how much longer they could continue in business.

Finding decent food to feed anyone, quite apart from a pregnant woman, was difficult too because of the shortages. You ate what they had in and made the best of it, or did without. Bridgette didn't burden Xavier with those concerns, though, and just emphasised how much she was looking forward to the birth of the baby.

Rumours about the progress of the war were flying as spring approached. In the end, Maurice went out and bought a wireless. As the warmer days took hold, the dress shop had had a little surge again as women bought pretty underwear and lighter dresses. Maurice had even sold a few new hats as Easter approached.

Just over a fortnight after Easter, on a Thursday evening, the Laurents learned of the invasion of Denmark and Norway. Lisette had come over, as she did some evenings, her mother-in-law being only too happy to listen out for the children. The four adults, gathered around the wireless, looked at each other fearfully.

'Norway had been warned by the British,' Maurice grumbled. 'Think they might have put up more of a fight. I mean, not to mine the fiords was madness. There were British warships in the area, according to what they said on the wireless, and they would have gone to their aid.'

'I think,' Marie said, 'neither Denmark nor

Norway was prepared for the might and precision of the German armies. It makes you wonder, is any country prepared for it?'

The question hung in the air for a few moments and then Lisette said, 'I wonder what Hitler's next move will be.'

'Yes,' Maurice replied. 'Praise God that we have the Maginot Line.'

About four weeks later Hitler struck again. The attacks were before dawn on Friday 10 May, and the stunned French people read in their newspapers in disbelief of a German offensive that had left their country wide open. The German armies had ignored the Maginot Line and instead one company had seized first Eben-Emael, the underground fort in Belgium. It was said to be impregnable, but the Germans got around that by landing 400 para-troopers on top of it. The fort was there to protect three strategic bridges, the main defence of Belgium and Holland.

Despite a spirited response by the surprised Allies, the fort was in German hands in twenty-four hours, allowing German soldiers, tanks and other military vehicles free access into the Low Countries. Luxembourg, with no defences to speak of, surrendered and the government fled to London.

Another sizable company of German soldiers also ploughed their way through the Ardennes forest. The French army were fighting for their lives, the broadcaster said, although they had barely sufficient resources.

'You know why, don't you?' Maurice said as he snapped off the wireless almost angrily. 'They hadn't expected any attack through that. We were told that it was a natural barrier and we believed them.'

'Maybe it was, once,' Bridgette said. 'But modern tanks might have been able to cope with it better.'

'You have it, my dear,' Maurice said. 'We cannot hope to win a war based on tactics from a war fought twenty years ago.' He shook his head sadly. 'France has made a grave mistake and that mistake could be very costly.'

Four days later, there was a massive raid on Rotterdam. According to the man on the wireless, who sounded totally stunned, it lasted for two and a half hours and it was estimated that almost 1,000 people had been killed, many many thousands more injured and 50,000 were homeless. The reporter said that Allies, moving in to help, were hampered by the streams of people trying to leave the city, and both they and the troops had been constantly strafed by machine-gun fire from the ever-circling Stukas.

That same evening, still coming to terms with the appalling loss of life in Holland, the Laurents learned that the Germans had broken through the French defences. The invaders, who had ridden rough-shod over so many countries, were now going to march through France. In fact it was no

308

surprise, because the family, like many, had heard the gunfire growing closer and closer and the relentless drone of planes overhead.

'They'll never hold them,' Maurice said with pursed lips. 'They'll be in Paris before we know it.'

Out of the corner of her eye, Bridgette caught sight of Marie as she glared at her husband and shook her head sharply.

'Don't try to shield me, Marie,' Bridgette said. 'This is absolutely dreadful news, but I really need to know everything. We are all involved. I'm sure Lisette would agree.'

'I would,' Lisette said. 'In fact, I would go further and say that now these savages are in our country, I will not come here often in the evening. My mother-in-law will be too nervous and I should hesitate to leave the children anyway. I think we know what cruelty the Germans are capable of.'

'Ah, yes, my dear,' Marie said. 'I'm sure you're right.'

'In fact,' Lisette said. 'I will do as Edmund suggested long ago and buy my own wireless.'

'I get a cold dead feeling inside me every time I think of Xavier and Edmund out there,' said Bridgette.

'That's perfectly natural, my dear,' Maurice said. 'I am worried too about both men. But I take heart in the fact that if anything happened to them, we would be informed by the military.'

'I know that that is what should happen,' Bridgette replied. 'I just think that this isn't a fight on some tidy battlefield, but spread out across various areas. They are under attack from soldiers on the ground, bombs and machine-gun bullets from the air.' Her voice was becoming dangerously high. 'Have they the least idea how many soldiers are stretched out by the roadside outside Rotterdam, shot down as they tried to help the fleeing people?'

No one spoke, for there was nothing to say.

No one was surprised either when the Dutch Commander-in-Chief, Queen Wilhelmina, surrendered the next day and she and her government flew to England.

When Bridgette visited her mother, they spoke of the terrible things happening all around them.

'The hardest thing in the world is waiting to hear from a loved one, as you are,' Gabrielle said. 'Throughout history that's what women seem to have done.'

'You can't possibly know how the longing to hear from Xavier almost overwhelms me at times,' Bridgette said.

Gabrielle knew only too well, for she had experienced those feelings herself, but she blinked the tears from her eyes and swallowed deeply before saying, 'I can imagine, Bridgette and your unhappiness is almost tangible. Try not to worry too much. You have the child to think of.'

'I know, Maman,' Bridgette said fervently. 'And though I long for the baby to be born, I know it will be another to fret about.'

'Ah, yes,' Gabrielle said. 'From the minute a child is born, it takes away a piece of your heart. I had a letter from Yvette today and they are sending their sons out of Paris to a cousin of Henri's in the countryside.'

'Why?'

'Yvette is afraid of Raoul being sent to a labour camp, and Gerard in his turn. She feels they will be safer there for now.'

Bridgette shook her head helplessly. 'No one knows what to do for the best these days. All we know is that the enemy is at the gate. I fear the country I know and love is going to be destroyed before my eyes.'

SIXTEEN

People from the coastal towns and villages began arriving in St-Omer, driven out by the advance of the German armies. They told of meeting bedraggled lines of Allies marching towards the coast and the roads strewn with discarded vehicles of every description and even some large guns.

There was no official news on the wireless other than that odd message on BBC World Service almost a couple of weeks before. Bridgette translated it and said it was from the Admiralty requesting all owners of self-propelled pleasure craft between thirty and a hundred foot in length to send specifications to the Admiralty within fourteen days. At the time it had made no sense.

A couple of weeks on, Maurice was sure that Allied soldiers were in retreat, disabling equipment and vehicles en route.

'But where could they retreat to?' Bridgette said. 'There are only the beaches.'

'And no naval ships could get near them there,'

Maurice said. 'That's what they wanted those small boats for – to try to lift the soldiers off before the Germans curl round and encircle them. Either way, I fear it is too late now for France. Our battle is already lost.'

'What d'you think they will do to any soldiers they capture?' Bridgette said. 'Will they take them all back to Germany as prisoners of war?'

Maurice couldn't meet Bridgette's eyes as he mumbled, 'Aye, they may well do that.'

Marie knew Maurice didn't believe that for an instant, and neither did she. She guessed that many on the beaches would never leave them alive, and Xavier and Edmund could easily be two of them. She could say none of this; Bridgette was agitated enough.

'Don't take on so,' she pleaded with Bridgette. 'Think of the baby.'

'I am thinking of the baby,' Bridgette said almost harshly. 'And of the baby's father, who I might never see again.'

On 3 June there was the roar of many German planes in the air. The noise and sight of them struck fear into the townspeople, yet St-Omer was not their target and they passed over towards Paris. They heard the noise of the ensuing Blitz and trembled in fear for the people there, especially Yvette and Henri. Bridgette realised how sensible they had been to send their sons away.

They heard on the wireless of the people

streaming out of Paris, fleeing south, pursued and strafed mercilessly by the German Stukas until, it was said, the roads were lined with bodies and ran with blood. Bridgette studied the grainy newsprint pictures in the paper and saw they were bodies of the old, of women and children, and of dogs and cats, obviously family pets, and there were dead donkeys still shackled to their carts.

She was glad when they heard that Yvette and Henri, who took shelter in a cellar, were unhurt, but she wept over the pictures of people who hadn't been so lucky. She realised with sick horror that a nation that could attack innocent civilians in that way would have no mercy for the trapped Allies on the beaches.

However, a few days later she heard Winston Churchill talking on the BBC World Service about Operation Dynamo, which was what they called the evacuation from the Dunkirk beaches, using small boats to ferry the men to the naval ships waiting in deeper water. She also heard that well over 300,000 Allied troops had been rescued, and that included over 140,000 French troops, and she prayed that Xavier was one of those.

For France, however, the war was over. The President resigned and the rest of the French Government fled to Bordeaux on 11 June, and Philippe Pétain was asked to form a new government. On 16 June Italy declared war on France, attacking from the south through the Riviera, and the following day Pétain applied for an armistice

314

with Germany. A furious General de Gaulle left Bordeaux for Britain.

While they were still digesting this distressing news, Lisette brought a letter she'd received from Edmund, written from a military hospital in Britain. He had been one of the 140,000 French men lifted from the beaches at Dunkirk and had been injured, which was why he hadn't written sooner. However, he told them, Xavier had been killed as they stood on the makeshift pier waiting for one of the smaller boats to carry them out to the troop ships.

Bridgette received the news in horrified silence. She had known, as the news worsened, that it was possible that Xavier hadn't made it to safety, but she had clung to the tiniest glimmer of hope, telling herself that she would have been informed if anything had happened to him. Now that hope was gone, and she gave a cry like a wounded animal, doubling over as the acute pain in her stomach matched the one in her heart, which she felt had shattered into a million pieces.

She continued to shout and scream and thrash out at Marie and Maurice, who were in tears themselves, and trying to hold her. Lisette took one look at her distressed friend and ran for the doctor. Before he arrived, Bridgette felt the stickiness between her legs. She looked down with horror and saw blood dripping onto the floor and pooling around her feet. Marie saw it at the same time and acted with speed. She had Bridgette in bed in minutes, packed around with towels.

The sight of the blood and what it might mean had stopped Bridgette's screams, but sent her into shock. She trembled all over and the desolation in her eyes, standing out in her white face, brought tears to Marie's. But she brushed them away impatiently, sat by Bridgette's side and held her hand tight.

'You'll be all right,' she told her. 'The doctor will be here shortly.'

He was just in time to deliver Bridgette's baby. It was a little girl, small, beautiful and perfect, and quite dead.

Bridgette couldn't believe it. She had known it was too early for her to give birth, but for a perfect baby to be stillborn . . . People were speaking to her, holding her, but she was unaware of them. There was room in her mind for one thing and one thing only, and that was hatred of the Germans who had taken first her beloved husband and then her precious baby. Now she would have no part of Xavier and she knew if she lived to be a hundred she would never forgive them.

The next morning, when Bridgette came to from a drug-induced sleep, it was too much effort to open her eyes. She lay in the darkened room and knew that what she wanted more than anything was to be able to float away from this harsh and cruel world and be with her beloved Xavier again.

She remembered the golden future they had once mapped out, which now lay like dust beneath her feet, and she gave a small gasp as a sudden pang of loss pierced her heart like a shard of glass. Marie, dozing in a chair, was roused enough to open her own saddened, rheumy eyes and she leaned forward and said gently, 'Bridgette?'

Bridgette heard, but when she tried to open her eyes they were too heavy. The watching Marie had seen the fluttering movements behind the lids, however, and she stroked her face so very gently.

'I know how you are feeling, my love,' she almost whispered. 'I am sorrow-laden myself.'

At her words, tears seeped from beneath Bridgette's closed lashes and then slowly she peeled her lids back. Marie wanted to recoil from the anguish in those beautiful, amber eyes, which she fastened on her as she said, 'What am I to do, Marie? How am I to bear such sorrow?'

'By taking each day as it comes,' Marie said. 'It is the only way.'

Bridgette shook her head. 'I don't think I can.'

Marie took hold of Bridgette's hands in her own and said earnestly, 'You will because there is no alternative. And you will not be alone in your sadness. Maurice and I have lost a much-loved son, and Lisette, the brother she has always adored. And that is not to mention the loss of the child, who could have been consolation for us in our bleaker moments.'

'I can't tell you how much I loved Xavier,' Bridgette cried. 'There will never be another like him.'

'And you will never forget him,' Marie said. 'He will lodge forever in your heart.'

Bridgette closed her overflowing eyes and sighed heavily. Deep pain filled every part of her until it seemed to be seeping out of her very pores. She couldn't see the point of living, knowing there would never be anyone special in her life ever again and she would never hold her own child in her arms. The future stretching out before her seemed sterile and of no purpose, and suddenly over-whelmed by everything, she turned her head to the pillow and cried as if her heart was broken, and Marie cried with her.

Eventually Bridgette left her bed and began to take up the threads of life again, but she was a shadow of her former self.

'She is standing there doing and saying all the right things,' Marie said to Maurice and Lisette, 'but it is as if the essence of her has gone.'

Lisette thought her mother had put it well. Bridgette now carried an aura of sadness around with her. In fact, the only thing she became impassioned about were the Germans occupying the town, and she didn't care who knew of her hatred of them, for all Marie and Maurice begged to be more circumspect. She had no fear of them because she felt that she had nothing more to lose.

Throughout that golden summer, their insidious presence was everywhere. Jackboots ringing on the cobbled streets, the black and menacing swastikas fluttering from every public building in the town, and arrogant Gestapo officers stopping people at whim. They were hated and feared, along with the SS officers, and with reason. They were known to be brutal and had immense power.

The occupying German soldiers liked to flirt with the girls and young women of the town. This made Bridgette's skin crawl and she was disgusted by those who played along with their oppressors, even going so far as to fawn around them. She could barely keep the contempt from her voice if she was forced to speak, but usually they were amused by her response and that angered her still further.

From early summer, the French expected Hitler's armies to invade Britain, for they had amassed a fair armada of vessels to cross the Channel: barges, cargo ships, motorboats and even tugs.

'And when that happens,' Maurice said, 'Britain will fall under Nazi dominance as well. How can one small country like that hold out when other, bigger powers have fallen?'

However, by the autumn, nothing had happened and the rumour was that for the invasion to be a success, the Luftwaffe had to disable the Royal Air Force and it was reported that many on the coast had witnessed dogfights between the two forces, but the RAF seemed as strong as ever and so the invasion plans had been put on hold.

It was the only cheering news. Life for most

French people was hard under Nazi rule. Food was getting even scarcer in the shops now that much was shipped back to Germany, and the towns also often had to provide food for occupying officers. One cold autumn day, Bridgette had gone into St-Omer with a basket and a few francs in her purse to queue for anything she saw that they could use for a meal.

However, when she saw the lines of people being herded towards the railway station, urged on none too gently with the butts of the guns the Germans guards carried, she was intrigued. 'Where are they taking them?' she asked a passer-by.

He gave a typical Gallic shrug. 'They are Jews. Who knows where they go? Germany, I suppose.'

Some of the trudging people were neighbours Bridgette recognised. A few had owned businesses in the town, some women had babies in their arms and others children no older than Jean-Paul and Leonie. Some of the babies were wailing, children sniffling and the elderly being helped along by younger relatives. In horrified fascination Bridgette followed them to the station, where she saw them being packed into windowless cattle trucks. So many of them pushed one against the other.

The people were crying in earnest now, shouting and protesting, but some were whimpering in an abject fear that was so profound it could almost be smelled. How long did it take to get to Germany, or wherever it was they were making for, and how would all those people breathe, Bridgette wondered. One elderly Jew seemed to have similar thoughts and as he approached the trucks he made a dash for it, running back the way he had come, pushing past the people. The guard by the train did not hesitate: a shot rang out and the old man folded onto the cobbles.

A gasp of shock rippled through those watching and Bridgette espied an old woman struggling to leave the truck, shrieking and screaming. She guessed the old man was her husband. She was being restrained by a young man who obviously didn't want her to face the same fate. Then the guard, seeing the commotion, hit her on the side of the head with the butt of his rifle. The old woman sagged forward, her head spurting blood, but the press of people was such that she didn't fall.

Bridgette turned her head away in disgust, but she was incensed at the injustice of it. She didn't blame the old man for being so panic-ridden – the thought of being incarcerated in one of those trucks filled her with horror – but there was no need to kill him so mercilessly and then abuse his wife. The other guards pushing the people on had no shame or thought for the man either, for one of them callously kicked him into the gutter and the shuffling people averted their eyes from the crumpled heap on the ground.

'It is happening in France now like it has happened in other occupied countries,' Marie said when Bridgette told them what she had witnessed.

'It's monstrous to treat people like that,' Bridgette said, still incensed. 'I didn't even know some of the people they were leading away were Jews.'

'No,' Marie said sadly. 'And some of them don't think of themselves as Jews either.'

'And we all stood there, every one of us, and no one said a word about it,' Bridgette said. 'I wanted to, maybe others did too, but I was afraid. What sort of a coward does that make me?'

'You did the right thing,' Marie said. 'You couldn't have stopped it.'

'I don't know,' Bridgette said. 'Maybe if I had spoken out, others might have got the courage to do the same.'

Marie grasped Bridgette's hands. 'It would have changed nothing,' she said. 'Listen to me. We are living through very dangerous times and we cannot stop anything these monsters want to do.'

Bridgette sighed. 'Oh God, Marie, what a sad, sad world we are living in.'

In mid-December, Bridgette again went into the town to try to get some food for the festive season, and if possible a toy of some sort for Jean-Paul and Leonie, but there was so few things in the shops that she was getting quite desperate. She knew she would have to go to the bakery and take the flour her mother always pressed on her. 'We have plenty,' she would say.

She was right, they had, and that was because Robert would make the best bread and cakes for

322

the German officers. It maddened her that the best of everything went to people like that when half the town was starving. But she couldn't refuse the flour, not when she had seen the children crying with hunger.

Suddenly a voice spoke in her ear. 'The news is that you are no lover of the invaders of our country.'

Bridgette turned slowly and looked at the smallish man beside her. He had quite a sallow complexion, black hair, a small black moustache and deep dark brown eyes. 'Who are you?' she asked.

'I am known as Charles.'

'Charles who?'

'Just Charles,' the man said, and then: 'You have not answered my question.'

'No, I am no lover of the butchering Germans,' Bridgette said vehemently. 'I have made no secret of it. My husband died on the beach at Dunkirk and news of his death caused me to miscarry our baby and so I hate them all with a passion.'

'So you will help us?'

'Who are you talking about?'

'Those who oppose the oppressor.'

'Doing what?'

'Making life difficult for the Germans in our town,' Charles said. 'There are groups set up, but they are fragmented at the moment and we need more organisation. Communication is the key and yet we dare not use the telephone. We need a messenger. Could you be that messenger?'

Bridgette felt excitement burn inside her. The thought of hitting back at the Germans raping and pillaging her country filled her with exhilaration. This would be a blow for Xavier and her baby. 'Yes, I could do that.'

'It is very valuable work.' Charles said. 'And we have found that girls have less trouble going about the town than men or boys.'

Bridgette had to agree that that was true. 'The soldiers try to flirt and make suggestions some-times,' she said with scorn. 'They are despicable.'

'We all know that,' Charles said. 'But to win a fight like this we have to be clever. Play along with them and never show them the disdain you have for them. You think you can do that?'

'Of course I can,' Bridgette said. 'For my husband and baby, and for love of France I can do anything, but I live with my in-laws and they are no longer young. I cannot put them in danger without first asking them if they wish me to do this.'

Charles nodded. 'Meet me tomorrow,' he said, 'same time and same place, and give me your answer.'

Bridgette told Marie and Maurice that night as they sat around the table and they listened without interrupting.

When she had finished, she said, 'I will quite understand if you do not wish me to be involved in this. It could be dangerous – for you, I mean, as well as me.'

'If you are prepared to take the risk, then so am I,' said Maurice.

'And I,' said Marie. 'But one thing I must say. Lisette must not be told because she has enough on her plate with the children and now Edmund's sick mother.'

Bridgette nodded. 'The fewer people that know, the better,' she said. 'I shall not tell my mother either. She will only worry.'

'We will do plenty of that too,' Marie said.

'I will do more than worry,' Maurice said. 'I will also make you a beret with a secret pocket to carry those messages and so skilful will this beret be that they will have to take it apart totally to find the hidden compartment.'

'Oh, Maurice,' Bridgette cried delighted, 'how lucky I am having in-laws like you and Marie.'

Bridgette never knew when she might be asked to do something for the Resistance. She never saw anyone. Instead, a note or letter would be slid underneath the shop door with details of where she was to take it and who she was to give it to. 'It is better that you know nothing,' Maurice said one evening when she queried this. 'What you don't know you can't tell.'

'But I wouldn't tell anyway,' Bridgette said. 'Surely you know that, Maurice?'

'I know that sometimes the Gestapo have ways of making someone talk,' Maurice said. 'I hope and pray that you shall never be put to that test.'

Bridgette, though, felt totally confident as she made her way across the town, because she knew that she wasn't suspected at all. Any that saw her now would imagine she was a great friend of the German solidiers, for she would flirt with them and tease them and they wouldn't even imagine that such a girl might have important letters or documents hidden in the beret that she wore at a rakish angle. She had some barbed remarks about her behaviour by some in the town though, and even Lisette had expressed surprise, but Bridgette was unable to say a word in her defence.

She returned home from shopping one day in mid-March, to find German officers in the shop, and she wondered if they had found out about her after all. Marie saw the trepidation on her face and said quickly, 'Ah, Bridgette. There you are at last. Take the shopping upstairs, will you, and then perhaps you can make coffee for our customers?'

Customers, Bridgette thought, and so it couldn't be anything to do with her activities. And she had been asked to make coffee for them. She would have preferred making it with ground glass, or at the very least spit in their cups, but she knew she could do neither of those things.

Later, Marie said, 'They just came in to buy clothes and hats for their wives and daughters back in Germany. They want them in time for Easter.'

'And you served them as if they were valued

customers?' Bridgette said, as if she couldn't believe it.

'Bridgette, all customers are valued just at the moment,' Marie said. 'Germans are virtually the only ones with money to spend today. I know that you haven't taken wages for some time, but even without that, we are living on our savings and they are running out fast, especially since we bought the coal for last winter. We cannot afford to turn away business. How will it help if we all starve to death?'

Bridgette knew that Marie spoke sense. 'I'm sorry,' she said, suitably chastened. 'I spoke out of turn. You could hardly refuse to make things for the German officers, anyway.'

She wondered if she should look for a job, for there was not enough work for both her and Marie in the shop. She knew she should help her mother in the bakery shop, for she looked positively ill at times, but if she helped her, she would not be paid, and at that moment she needed a wage each week.

There was plenty of work about because so many working men had answered France's call to arms and were now incarcerated in POW camps in and around Germany. The only problem with factory work was that most of them were now making war-related goods. Bridgette felt now that that was helping the Germans win the war.

She knew she had to do something. The dress shop had a flurry of orders from many of the German officers as Easter grew nearer, but these would probably dry up again when Easter was over. So, not wishing to be a burden on the Laurents, she took a part-time job in a café bar in the town.

Before April was over, Edmund's mother, who had been ailing for some weeks, took a turn for the worst and was dead before the doctor arrived. After the old lady was buried, Marie said that Lisette wanted to move back in with her parents until the war was over.

Bridgette was surprised. 'Don't you want to stay where you are,' she asked Lisette, 'so Edmund will have a home to come back to?'

'And when will that be?' Lisette said. 'I haven't even any idea where he is.'

'I wouldn't worry too much until you have reason,' Bridgette said. 'Edmund might even be in the Free French army under General de Gaulle.'

'How on earth do you know about that?'

'Your father can get the BBC World Service on the wireless,' Bridgette said, 'and I translate it.'

'Aren't you forbidden to listen to it?'

'Of course, but no one takes any notice of that,' Bridgette said. 'And you get to hear proper news about this awful war. Sometimes de Gaulle speaks too, urging France to stand firm, and seems convinced that Germany will be defeated in the end.'

'Do you think that?'

'I'd like to think it,' Bridgette said. 'Who knows, though, really?'

'You are good for me, Bridgette,' Lisette said.

'You stop me feeling sorry for myself. You don't mind me coming to live back here, do you?'

'No, why should I?' Bridgette said. 'It will be like old times, with the added bonus of the children to make us smile.'

On 7 December 1941 the Japanese bombed Pearl Harbor and America was in the war. This put the damper on the whole Laurent family that Christmas. Altogether it was a poor Christmas. The children had no presents to open and it was hard to raise anyone's spirits, although they tried for the children's sake.

It would have helped if they had anything in the way of festive food, but there was none of that either. In fact, studying the children that day, Bridgette thought them listless. Their faces were thin and white, and she knew that they were neither getting enough food, nor the right kind of it. Yet she regularly got up from the table still hungry so that the children should eat their fill.

Lisette had noticed this too. The day after Boxing Day, she left the house sometime that afternoon without telling a soul where she was going. When she returned some time later she had savoury sausages, crusty bread, butter and cheese in her shopping bag. Marie looked at the delights on the table with stupefaction.

'I used the last of my savings,' Lisette said. 'I will be able to replenish them for I have taken a job in Dupont's factory, near the tile factory where Xavier worked. The wages are good and they also give you tickets to exchange for certain basic foodstuff in the shops.'

She looked at Bridgette. 'I will be making shell cases. I do understand how you feel about jobs like this, but my first priority has to be getting enough money to feed and clothe the children.' Then she looked at her mother. 'Will you take care of Leonie through the day and take Jean-Paul to and from school?'

'You don't really have to ask that question,' Marie said. 'We will help you all we can.'

'And I don't work full time, don't forget,' Bridgette said. 'I can easily take a hand with the children.'

'And you won't mind that?' Lisette said. 'After all, I'm helping the enemy.'

'All you are doing is caring for your children the best way you know,' said Bridgette. 'And really, that is all that matters. I know my stance might be very different if I'd had a baby to consider.'

'So you're not offended?'

'No. Not at all,' Bridgette told Lisette sincerely.

'I'll tell you what offends me,' Marie said, getting to her feet and scooping the shopping into her arms. 'And that is good food going to waste. Let us make a feast today to celebrate Lisette's good fortune in getting a job.'

SEVENTEEN

With Lisette's money added to the family pot, there was more food in the house but little coal to be had by anyone in those cold bleak days of late 1941 and early 1942. It was sometimes hard to keep warm and find warm clothes, especially for the growing children. Knowing this, Yvette sent Lisette a big parcel of clothes that her boys had grown out of, to adapt for Jean-Paul and Leonie. Bridgette told her mother all about it the next time she called.

'Aunt Yvette is just as kind as she ever was,' she said. 'She has sent lovely jumpers that we can unravel to knit up again.'

'I didn't know you could knit,' Gabrielle said.

'I couldn't,' Bridgette admitted. 'Marie taught me.' She smiled as she went on. 'She told me knitting is a very French activity, that it is reputed that Parisians sat knitting while Madame Guillotine did her work during the Revolution. They never told us that in our history lessons. Anyway, it all saves money, and that is important just at the moment with food the price it is.'

She sighed. 'You know, despite the hours Lisette works at the factory, and the money I bring in too, there is only just enough food. I still get up from the table some days nowhere near full, but it is the same for everyone. In fact, Maman, you are the only one that never talks of any deprivation.'

'That is because it doesn't affect us,' Gabrielle said, adding bitterly, 'your father's hand in glove with the German Command. Oh, I am not talking about the best cakes and bread that go their way. Maybe he had to do that – he told me he did, anyway. But it's other things now.'

'What sort of things?'

'Well, German officers are always here,' Gabrielle said. 'They see we go without nothing. In the evening they bring German beer and whisky, and your father produces wine. He and Georges play cards with them and they drink together like they are the best of friends. You will never see Georges being sent away to a labour camp, more's the pity. But the worst thing is that they betray their own people.'

'Surely not?' Bridgette exclaimed. 'Bad as they are, I'd never have thought of any Frenchman betraying his own.'

'I didn't want to believe it either,' Gabrielle said with a sigh. 'But I had suspected them, and one night I listened outside the door and heard Robert tell them of the Pasquiers harbouring a Jewish family.'

'He told them that?' Bridgette said with distaste.

She remembered hearing of the Pasquiers' house being raided in the early hours of the morning and the family dragged away, even the almost blind and arthritic grandmother. Then the poor, bewildered and frightened Jews had been pulled from their hiding place, a party of five, including two young children.

'Remember the whole Pasquier family were shot the next day as a warning to the rest of the town?' Gabrielle said.

Bridgette nodded. 'I remember. Did you hear what happened to the Jewish people?'

Gabrielle shook her head helplessly. 'Does anyone ever hear what happens to Jews today? They might have been transported to Germany or else disposed of some other way. No one seems to care. The officers talk about them as if they are some sub-human class of people, and Robert and Georges are just the same. They have told on other people too. Georges creeps about and spies, and they don't even care if the information they give the Germans is accurate. The lad they had for cutting telephone wires, for example, had nothing to do with it. Recently, Georges told the Gestapo the names of two young men he said had set fire to a fuel dump, and they were both shot.'

Bridgette knew about that, just as she knew those men hadn't been involved at all. 'How do they live with themselves?' she burst out.

Gabrielle sounded desperate: 'I can't understand either of them. Yvette is worried that Raoul might become embroiled in some of these subversive activities. And if he does she knows that Gerard will follow suit.'

'The Resistance, you mean?'

'What else?'

'Do you really think them subversive?' Bridgette asked. 'Isn't it justified to hamper the aggressor who has taken over your country? We can't all just roll over.'

Hearing the way Bridgette spoke and witnessing the fire in her eyes, Gabrielle whispered fearfully. 'You're not mixed up in it too, are you?'

'Maman, you know better than that,' Bridgette said. 'If I was, I could hardly tell you.'

But Gabrielle knew her daughter, and when Bridgette left that day she trembled in fear for her. If Robert or Georges had a hint of what she was doing, they wouldn't try to save her, but take great glee in dripping that information into the ear of a Gestapo officer. If that happened and they stood Bridgette up against a wall and shot her, Gabrielle knew her reason for living would be gone. However, she promised herself, before she took her own life she would endeavour to take at least Robert with her, even if she had to wait until he was asleep before she stabbed him through the heart.

One balmy, sultry evening in mid-July 1942 Bridgette found Charles waiting for her as she left work. She hadn't seen him for some time, nor had she had messages to deliver for a fair few weeks. However, she knew better than to greet him because she didn't know who might be watching, especially as most of the customers in the café bar were Germans.

He let her pass, and only fell into step beside her when they were well clear of the bar. Even then, their words were muted for there were many people out in the streets that fine evening.

'De Gaulle has set up a new organisation in London,' Charles said. 'He has sent in agents and they have been in communication with Resistance groups all over this area. He said we should all join together, even with the communists, so that our attacks could be more effective.'

'Makes sense,' Bridgette murmured.

'Yes,' Charles said. 'But to do more damage we need explosives and guns. They are sending a planeload over tomorrow night.'

'Where will it land?' Bridgette asked. The airfield at the other side of town was in German hands.

'That is not your concern,' Charles said. 'There will be a truck waiting for you in a small road off St Marin du Laert behind the *jardin public* at midnight. We need as many people as we can get. Can you be there? Can you get out without being seen?'

The Laurents were always in bed by about half-past ten, and even though Bridgette shared a bedroom with Lisette she didn't think it would be a problem sneaking out without her knowing, for

Lisette was often worn out with the work in the factory. Sometimes she would seek her bed not long after the children and be heavily asleep when Bridgette went up.

'That shouldn't be much of a problem,' Bridgette said.

'Wear dark clothes and black your face,' Charles said. 'And move carefully through the streets. Remember there is a curfew from ten o'clock.'

'I'll remember,' Bridgette promised. 'And I will be there.'

'Good enough.' Charles melted into the shadows as Laurents' house came into view.

Bridgette was filled with exhilaration at the thought of the delivery of explosives. When they had those, they would really show the Germans what they were made of, she thought. She had to hide her excitement from the family and didn't fully succeed because they all remarked on the good spirits she was in.

Before Lisette went to bed the following night, she went through Xavier's things, which were packed up in boxes in the wardrobe. She found a pair of trousers that she knew would do for her with the legs rolled up and a belt around her waist, and a dark jumper, and she left them ready so that she could slip them on quickly when the time came.

The following night, Bridgette dressed silently in Xavier's clothes. She crept downstairs, pulled her beret over her head to cover her hair and then stopped at the coal shed to blacken her face before slipping through the gate and out into the streets.

It was very quiet, the only voices guttural German ones, and the only other sound the tramp of patrolling soldiers' feet. Bridgette took care that she was neither seen nor heard as she sped through the darkened streets. Once she reached the *jardin public* she kept to the shadow of the trees till she reached the other side. Charles was waiting for her. He put his finger to his lips and they made their way to the truck in silence. There were five men besides Charles and the driver. Bridgette was the only woman. Though a few were familiar to her, she wasn't told their names and they weren't told hers, and as soon as they were all aboard, the truck moved off.

They travelled for about half an hour before stopping. Two men met them. They had been using torches to signal to the plane circling just above them that it was safe to land. Bridgette watched as it made its descent and rolled bumpily across the grassy field. Speed was then essential, but so was care, with the explosives, but soon all were unloaded from the plane. As it took off again the Resistance group began stowing the ammunition in the truck.

Bridgette didn't ask where they were going to store it all. In this organisation, suspicion would rest on anyone considered too inquisitive, and no questions would be answered anyway.

She was tired once she reached the Laurents'

house and ready to seek her bed, but remembered to wipe her face around with a flannel and hide the clothes she took off in the wardrobe before she climbed into bed and fell into an exhausted sleep.

The next morning she had trouble opening her eyes, but when she did, it was to find Lisette already up and getting ready to go to work.

Seeing that Bridgette was awake Lisette said, 'Where did you go last night?'

Bridgette, completely nonplussed, played for time. 'What do you mean?' she asked. 'Nowhere.'

'Don't give me that,' Lisette said. 'You crept out of here last night at a quarter to twelve; I lit the lamp and looked at the clock after you left. The only thing I do know is that, dressed as you were, I wouldn't have said it was a romantic liaison you were making for, so what was it all about?'

'Lisette, it really is better if you know nothing.'

Lisette shrugged. 'Maybe. But I do know. At least, I know you crept out last night. That is such an odd thing to do, isn't it? And so it's not un-reasonable to ask where you went.'

'It's unreasonable in occupied France,' Bridgette said quietly.

Lisette looked at Bridgette with eyes full of astonishment but also trepidation. 'Are you part of the Resistance movement?' she asked, almost disbelievingly.

'Look, Lisette, I shouldn't really speak of it.'

'You don't have to,' Lisette said. 'I can read it

338

all over your face. And if you want to know, I think that it is terrific and if I hadn't the children to think about, I would do the same. So what have you done so far and what were you doing last night?'

'I shouldn't be telling you any of this,' Bridgette said. 'Anyway, I have done little but deliver messages.'

'Do Maman and Papa know what you are involved in?'

'Of course,' Bridgette said. 'I live in their house. However I feel about things, I would do nothing that might bring risk to them without asking their permission.'

'Well, they obviously gave it.'

'Oh, yes,' Bridgette said. 'In fact, your father made me a special beret with a secret compartment in it.'

'Good for him,' Lisette said. 'But I bet they didn't know about last night. So what was all that about? You weren't delivering messages at that time of night.'

Bridgette sighed as she swung her legs out of the bed. 'No, I wasn't. And really you mustn't breathe a word of what I am going to tell you.'

'I'm surprised you even have to ask,' Lisette said.

Bridgette told her all about the ammunition brought in by plane.

'Was that the reason for the elaborate disguise?' Lisette asked.

Bridgette nodded. 'We had to wear dark clothes. I even blacked my face.'

'Yeah, I can see that.'

'What d'you mean?'

'You missed a bit,' Lisette said with a smile as she tossed Bridgette a handkerchief. 'You have a sooty smudge by the side of your nose. If I were you, I would remove it before the children catch sight of it.'

It was better that Lisette and her parents knew about her involvement, Bridgette thought, as the summer and autumn gave way to the icy blasts of winter. She was becoming increasingly involved in more active work. They never asked her anything, though, and she told them very little, for it was safer that way.

They did worry, because they knew what her fate would be if she was caught. 'Shooting would be the very least of it,' Marie said to Maurice one night as they lay in bed. 'I couldn't bear to think of Bridgette being tortured. The screams of the poor people the Gestapo hold in that place can sometimes be heard all over the town, and they strike fear into the most stout-hearted.'

There was nothing Maurice could say that would comfort his wife. She knew as well as he what fate lay in store for Bridgette and she had accepted that risk to avenge the death of Xavier and the baby she had so longed for.

Bridgette, though, never felt even the slightest bit afraid, whatever operation she was asked to do. Charles said she had nerves of steel, but she knew that those nerves were strengthened by bands of hatred. These bands were tightened when she helped set fire to fuel dumps, or disabled military vehicles, tampered with railway signalling, or shinned up a telegraph pole to cut the wires.

She was taught to lay charges, mainly on railway tracks for the stations were too well guarded. Bridges to were strongly defended and it was extremely risky setting any sort of explosive charge there. But one icy night just before Christmas they managed to destroy a strategically important bridge by killing the sentries posted there first.

After each operation, the Resistance cell would go to ground and lie low. The response from the outraged Germans was swift as they took townspeople in reprisal. They rounded up members of the Communist Party first, but soon any man would do to stand against a wall and shoot. This frightened and intimidated people, as it was meant to, for every boy and man was at risk.

It did bother Bridgette that these usually innocent men should pay the price for Resistance acts of sabotage, but Charles was angry with her when she said this.

'What did you think the Germans would do when we are trying our damnedest to disrupt things for them? Did you think they would have a welcoming committee set out for us and shake us warmly by the hand?'

'No, but—'

'No buts, Bridgette,' Charles snapped. 'We are at war and we either lie down and let the Germans walk all over us, or we fight. Face facts. Innocent people will get killed because that is how it is. Now are you with us, or against us?'

'You don't need me to answer that, surely?'

'Good girl,' Charles said approvingly. 'We are having another supply of explosives flown in just after Christmas. This time they have given us a list of key places they want the charges laid. Are you up for that?'

'Of course I am,' Bridgette said. 'I am not giving up now.'

At the end of January 1943, the Resistance nearly annihilated a whole company of soldiers one night travelling into the town by road. Bridgette had been hidden behind the trees lining the road that dusky evening as the soldiers approached, having helped lay the line of charges earlier.

When she was given the word she pushed down the plunger. Truck after truck full of soldiers exploded. Bridgette could see little through the swirling black smoke, but she could hear the screams and cries of the soldiers and hear the cracking of the flames. She felt only exhilaration that she had killed so many of them.

Charles pulled her away. Not all the men had been killed, and through the smoke he had seen survivors climbing the bank towards them, guns in hand. It had been the first time the Resistance cell had been in danger of being caught, but they all got away safely.

When Bridgette was dropped outside the park, she made her way home as swiftly as possible, though mindful of patrols. She slipped inside the door with her heart pounding. She was dreadfully tired and sought her bed straightaway, but once there she lay wide-eyed and went over and over the scenes from that evening's work in her head. She wondered what the German response would be.

They had once issued a directive that fifty Communists or de Gaullists should be killed for every German, and over the following days ninety prisoners were taken, many from St-Omer.

From the windows of the bar, Bridgette watched the men they had chosen march away, and she also saw the weeping women and the screaming children. Despite Charles's words she felt both sorry for her fellow townspeople and also responsible for much of their grief.

In February 1943, in Buncrana, Biddy Sullivan's funeral was held. When Christy Byrne was told this he fell to remembering what he knew about the mother of his best friend. She had never been what he would call an easy woman, and everyone knew of her violent temper. Of all her children, she had only ever had time for Nuala.

Tom, on one of his many visits to Christy, had said that was why Biddy had been so incensed when Nuala had married a Protestant in 1921.

'She had built her up so much, you see, so she had further to fall,' he said. 'Nuala was no angel. She was human being, just like anyone else, but her only crime was falling in love with a man of a different religion.'

'But didn't your father die of shock when he got the letter telling him that?' Christy asked.

'Christy, my father was on borrowed time,' Tom said. 'His heart was very bad. He had had one warning attack and the doctor had told him to take life easier but he had taken no heed of it. I should imagine that, though he would undoubtedly have been shocked at Nuala's news, his heart wouldn't have given out if it had been fine and healthy in the first place. There was no need to blame Nuala and, like Mammy did with Aggie, forbid her name to be spoken and not allow us any contact with her, and we shouldn't have allowed it to happen either.'

It been harsh, everyone said so, but few said it to Biddy herself. And when Joe went to America, not long after his father's death, the only one Biddy Sullivan had to vent her spleen on was Tom. Most of the townsfolk didn't know how he put up with his mother and nearly everyone agreed that he deserved a medal. Christy thought the same, because when Tom popped along to see him sometimes his manner and demeanour reminded him of a whipped dog.

He was certain that the way Tom's mother behaved was the real reason that Tom had never married. When asked he always said that he wasn't the marrying kind, but Finn had never been able to understand that at all. He always said he had it made, as far as women were concerned, for he was a fine handsome man, kindly and considerate, and added to that he was set to inherit the farm. 'You should see the girls lusting after him at Mass, Christy,' he would say. 'And their mammies encouraging them. Tom must go round with blinkers on, for he never even sees them.'

But how could he have married, Christy often thought. What woman could he take back to that farmhouse with his mother acting the way she did? What sort of person would stand it? He recalled what Tom had told him about the way she had been with Nuala's daughter, Molly, when she had brought her back from England after Nuala and her husband had been killed in a car accident.

Christy had been sorry to hear that Nuala had died. She had been a pretty wee thing, and so friendly too. She and Finn had been the best of friends and Christy had heard she had been so upset when she'd heard of Finn's death.

Christy had seen for himself the young girl, Molly, who looked the image of Nuala, when his father had taken him on a rare trip into Buncrana and he had caught sight of her. There had been a wee boy too, Tom had told him, but he had been left in Birmingham, England in the care of his grandfather, and Biddy Sullivan had led the orphaned Molly one hell of a life. 'It was like she had Nuala back and she punished Molly for what Nuala had done,' Tom said.

Christy wasn't at all surprised that Molly had taken off to find her brother and grandfather when war was barely begun. But Biddy had got her come-uppance, for a stroke had felled her in the end and eventually took away her speech too.

And now she was six foot under and could not do any more harm. Christy had come to a decision and he had something to tell Tom the next time he saw him. He hadn't long to wait, for Tom paid him a visit the day after Biddy's funeral.

'I'm sorry about your mother, Tom,' Christy said, because it was expected.

Tom smiled ruefully. 'No you're not, Christy. And, God forgive me, I'm not sorry she's dead either. If I am honest, I'm relieved.'

'Well, no one would wonder at that,' Christy said. 'Did it go off all right?'

'So-so,' Tom said. 'There were only a handful of people there. As Joe's wife, Gloria, said, what a wasted life she had.

'It was of her own making,' Christy said. 'And now there is nothing to stop you going to see Molly and her brother in England.'

'Spring's a busy time on a farm,' Tom said. 'We have two calves ready to drop and Joe would be glad if I hung round for a while. I will write to Molly and explain. She lived on the farm for long enough to understand these things.'

'Yes,' Christy said and then he was silent,

thinking of what he was about to say to Tom, a secret that he had kept for years.

But Tom, watching him, knew that he was worrying about something and he said, 'Come on! Out with it, Christy? Tell me whatever it is you are fretting over.'

'I said I would never tell,' Christy said. 'And I wouldn't have either while your mother was alive. She was the sort to cause trouble.'

'She was indeed,' Tom agreed. 'So what have you done, Christy? Killed your granny and buried her on the farm somewhere?'

'No, nothing like that,' Christy said with a grin. 'This is about Finn.'

Whatever Tom expected Christy to say it wasn't that. Finn had been dead twenty-seven years. 'Go on,' he said.

'Well, it was just that Finn got married.'

'What!' Tom exclaimed. 'He couldn't have. We would have been informed.'

'Tom,' Christy said, 'I was his witness. The girl's name was Gabrielle Jobert and she was the daughter of the baker in St-Omer, the town we were billeted near. We were all ready for the off, moving out that morning, and old man Jobert comes up to the camp screaming that his daughter has been taken down and she had named Finn as father of the child she was carrying.'

'Christ,' breathed Tom. 'What did he do?'

'What could he do but marry her? A Catholic priest attached to our battalion did the honours.'

'We heard nothing, though,' Tom said. 'Honest to God, Christy. This has knocked me for six.'

'I don't think news of the marriage had filtered through to the authorities,' Christy said. 'We were on the march as soon as the marriage service was over and heading south, only staying a day or couple of days at each place till we reached the Somme.'

'But why didn't Finn write and tell us?'

'Because he was under age,' Christy said. 'At the time of his marriage Finn wasn't quite twenty so he gave the priest a false date of birth to protect Gabrielle. He was never sure whether that meant that the marriage was legal or not.'

'If Mammy had known she'd have made trouble all right,' Tom said. 'She'd have ended up having the marriage annulled or something.'

Christy nodded. 'That's what Finn was afraid of. France is a Catholic country and they have the same view of unmarried mothers there as they do over here. That's why he lied in the first place. I wrote to Gabrielle too and explained, because she had been so frightened and upset at the time of the wedding, and I might say quite badly beaten up by her brute of a father. I knew she was probably not aware what Finn had done and I didn't want her to write to your parents.'

'Oh, that would really have set the cat among the pigeons,' Tom said. 'I mean you are sure, I suppose, that the child was Finn's?'

'Absolutely,' Christy said. 'Gabrielle was a

348

respectable girl who loved Finn dearly.' He shrugged. 'They got carried away. It happens. Anyway, before we went into battle Finn left details of all this with the priest who married him and said if anything happened to him he was to send this news to his parents, but the priest was blown up before he was able to deal with it and all the letters, papers and everything blown to kingdom come with him, I should think.'

'It's amazing really,' Tom said. 'He used to boast to us of his sexual exploits. Bound to get his fingers burned one way and another. How did he die, Christy? I have wanted to ask you that for years but wouldn't risk upsetting you.'

'It won't upset me any more,' Christy said. 'Finn died impaled on a German bayonet. I was with him to the end and removed his dog tag as he asked me to. Later, when I was carried in unconscious from the field, they found Finn's tag and mine around my neck and just sent off the relevant telegrams. Twenty-one thousand Allies were killed in the first half-hour of that battle. Imagine the bodies littering the battlefield at the end of that first bloody day? I think they were glad to get the telegrams off to any they could as soon as possible, and I wasn't able to put them right about Gabrielle, but I wrote to her as soon as I was able.'

'Of course, the poor girl wouldn't know until then.'

'No,' Christy said. 'Must have been awful for her, not knowing anything. As it was, the shock of the letter caused her to go into labour and she gave birth to a little girl she called Bridgette, after your mother.'

'Oh God,' said Tom. 'I bet she doesn't know what my mother was really like if she called a child after her. Do you know where she is now?'

Christy shook his head. 'She could be anywhere, but wherever she is she is likely married, because she was a looker, and she had a lovely personality too. To be honest, I could see why Finn was smitten. I fancied her myself, but the only one she had eyes for was Finn.'

'Even if she is still in the same town,' Tom said, 'as you say, she might be married and probably has many more children. Maybe none of them knows about Bridgette's real father. It could cause a lot of upset and trouble if we tried finding out any more about this child – or young woman, as she will be now – even if she is Finn's daughter. Anyway, France at the moment is an occupied country, but even if it wasn't I think we should leave well alone.'

'So do I,' Christy said. 'But I just thought you ought to know.'

'Yes,' said Tom. 'Thank you, Christy. You were a good friend to my young brother. I don't think I will tell Joe and Gloria about this, because there is little point.'

'No,' Christy agreed. 'We'll likely never hear from Gabrielle ever again.'

EIGHTEEN

The Resistance continued in their sabotage work through the spring and early summer of 1943. Then one day Charles met Bridgette from work and told her that the rumour was there were going to be bombing raids soon.

'Here? In St-Omer?'

'Well, I would say that most will be concentrated on Eperlecques Forest.'

'Why should anyone bomb there?' Bridgette asked.

'The Germans have built an enormous concrete bunker there. I've seen it through field glasses. No one would get near. That's why the bombing will be from the air. Anyway, our bombs are not powerful enough to raise more than a dent in it, they say.'

'Why do they want to bomb it anyway?' Bridgette asked. 'What's it for?'

'That I can't answer,' Charles said. 'But you can bet that if Hitler is involved, whatever the purpose of that huge monstrosity, it will not benefit France.

And you should see the poor prisoners who have built the thing in the first place and now work in it.'

'Well, they will have had no choice in that.'

'None of us has any choice,' Charles said grimly. 'Not when our country is controlled by Germany.'

On the night of 27 August Bridgette heard the drone and rumble of many planes and went to the window to look.

After a few minutes Lisette joined her. 'Oh, don't they look menacing?' she exclaimed.

'These are probably the first of the Allied raids I was warned about,' Bridgette said. 'And if that is the case, they will be bombing the construction built in Eperlecques Forest.'

'What's it for?'

'I don't know,' Bridgette answered as the blast of the first explosion shook the house. 'But I would say the Allies have a good idea.'

'I think you're right there,' Lisette said as the noise of another massive explosion rent the air.

However, despite the bombing raid in August and another in early September, the mood in France was more buoyant after the BBC gave the news of several German defeats. It seemed that for the first time the war was not going all Hitler's way. And then on 8 September, two days after Leonie had joined her brother at school, Italy surrendered.

'Told you,' Maurice said. 'No good at fighting, the Italians. Mussolini dragged them in. Their hearts weren't in it.'

It was good news just the same, Bridgette thought. Was it possible that they might actually win this war after all? That would be almost unbelievable.

The winter set in early that year and it was a cold one. Bridgette had been worried about her mother for some time, for she had had a severe cold and her cough lingered. Legrand had told her to stay out of the shop because he didn't want her spluttering and coughing over the bread and cakes, and he engaged a girl to serve.

'That's all well and good,' Bridgette said, 'and more than time you had a rest, but you really need to see a doctor.'

'You know that your father won't pay for the services of a doctor when all I have is a chest cold,' Gabrielle said. 'What can a doctor do for me anyway?'

'Well, if you were to call him in, maybe you would find out,' Bridgette pointed out.

'I'll be all right in a day or two,' Gabrielle assured her. 'Don't fuss. I can't bear it.'

But Bridgette had been very worried about her though and therefore she was not totally surprised when Legrand called at the Laurents' house just a couple of days later. Bridgette was getting ready to go to work for the afternoon and evening shift and she asked her father inside grudgingly.

'Your mother is ailing,' he said. 'She has need of you.'

'What's wrong with her?' Bridgette demanded. 'You have had the doctor out?'

'Yes,' Legrand said. 'Your mother has TB. The doctor said she could go to hospital, for all they are so full, but she won't hear of it. She wants you.'

TB. The dreaded disease. Whole families had been wiped out with TB and Bridgette's concerned eyes met those of Marie. Marie saw how agitated and upset Bridgette was and couldn't wonder at it.

'I must go and see to Maman,' Bridgette said. 'But I am due at work.'

'I will go and explain your absence, don't worry,' Marie said. 'You go to your mother and pop back when you can and tell us how she is.'

'You can be sure of that,' Bridgette said, and she kissed Marie on both cheeks before lifting her coat and beret from the hook behind the door.

From the first moment that Bridgette saw her frail and pale-faced mother sitting in her bed, she knew that she was looking at a dying woman and her heart sank.

She betrayed none of her fears, though. She smiled at her mother and said as cheerfully as she could, 'Well, what have you been up to? Glad to see that you are being a good girl now and behaving yourself.'

Gabrielle replied in like manner: 'You know I always do as I'm told.'

'Huh,' Bridgette said. 'Of course you do.'

354

Gabrielle had a spasm of coughing then and neither mentioned that the handkerchief she put to her mouth was blood-spattered or that Gabrielle tried to hide it in her fist. When she had recovered she looked at Bridgette directly, all banter gone from her as she said, 'I don't want to go to hospital.'

'Then you won't have to,' Bridgette assured her.

'But I am afraid for you,' Gabrielle said. 'Maybe I'm being selfish. This is infectious, Bridgette.'

'I know that, and I also know that I have the constitution of an ox. And as for being selfish, you wouldn't even know where to begin,' Bridgette said. She knew there was only one thing to be done and the decision had been made as soon as she had seen how sick her mother was. 'When I have made you comfortable I will go back to the Laurents', pack up my things and come and stay here with you.'

Tears of gratitude stood out in Gabrielle's eyes and Bridgette put her arms around her. 'You looked after me when I needed it,' she said. 'Now it's my turn.'

The Laurents could see as well as Bridgette where her duty lay. However, mindful of the reason Bridgette had come to them in the first place, Maurice went out and bought a large bolt and fixed it on the inside of Bridgette's old bedroom door. She felt so much safer with that in place. She knew too that her days in the Resistance were over, for she could never put her terminally sick mother in any sort of risk.

Even Charles could see, albeit reluctantly, that Bridgette had to curtail her Resistance work, but even if it hadn't been for Gabrielle being so ill, he knew it would be far too dangerous for Bridgette to do anything for the cell while sharing a house with Robert Legrand and his son.

The fear of infection also meant Legrand was now sharing a bedroom with Georges and would only come as far as Gabrielle's bedroom door, and Georges never came near at all. This suited Bridgette just fine. She had wondered how she would cope living with them again, but they spent so little time in the place it wasn't much of a problem.

She had also dreaded sitting around the table with them, but that didn't happen either, because though she cooked for them, she ate her meals with her mother, and Gabrielle seldom left her bed, never mind the bedroom. The German officers didn't come either now that there was serious illness in the house. She supposed her father and Georges met them somewhere else, because there was still no shortage of food in the house or coal in the cellar.

Bridgette seldom left her mother but she never minded this, she valued it as a special time in both their lives. They had few visitors but the doctor and the priest as people were frightened of catching TB. Marie Laurent came to see her friend, though, with Lisette, and Gabrielle was always glad to see them.

Christmas passed quietly. Around that time the people of St-Omer couldn't help but be aware that the Germans were working on another building of some size very close to the town, on the site of Wizerness quarry, which had been disused for some years. Many saw the lines of gaunt and shackled prisoner offloaded at the huge site, and while they said some were French, the majority were Soviet and Polish prisoners.

'And you say men and woman too?' Gabrielle asked, as Bridgette brought in a tray with their breakfast on.

'That's what a couple of the men were saying after Mass,' Bridgette said, as she helped her mother sit up in the bed 'They watched it all through field glasses and said the prisoners looked half starved and some could barely walk.'

'But what are these places for?'

'I don't know, Maman. But I know this much: whatever they are doing in these places is probably not good news for the rest of us.' She placed the tray across her mother's knees as she spoke. 'And now let us eat this while it's hot. You need to keep your strength up in this weather because, for all it's almost February, it's just as chilly as it ever was.'

The following day there was another air raid, which seemed again to be targeting Eperlecques Forest. This was followed by another five days later, and another five days after that. In March

357

there were also raids much closer to the town, so close that the windows in the bakery sometimes rattled. Bridgette realised the new construction was being bombed, and these attacks went on through March and into April.

It was hard not to be unnerved when the throbbing drone of many planes could be heard overhead, followed by ear-splitting explosions but she tried to speak reassuringly to her mother.

In mid-April as she was returning home with the shopping, Bridgette was alarmed to see Charles appear from a shop doorway and fall into step beside her.

'What do you want?' she said. 'I told you I can do no more.'

'I need a favour.'

'I can't help you. You know how I'm placed.'

'There isn't anyone else I can ask.'

'There must be.'

'D'you think I'd be here if there was?'

'Charles, stop this,' Bridgette said heatedly. 'It isn't fair to ask me, really it isn't. My mother has only weeks to live.'

'The person I am talking about might have only hours,' Charles said grimly. 'He's a British agent. We were getting him out, but the escape route has been rumbled. Worse than that, someone has talked and so the Nazis know that he's here. At least, they know he landed in this area. You could hide him until we could find a safe route out.'

'Are you mad?'

'I don't think so,' Charles said. 'If they start house-to-house searches, they will find this British man and when they have finished torturing him, he will be glad to die, and so will the people who are harbouring him at the moment.'

'I know that. So why should I take him into my house and risk that?'

'Because your house will not be searched.'

'How can you be so sure?'

'Because your father and brother are collaborators and informers.'

'You know that?' Bridgette breathed.

'I make it my business to know,' Charles said. 'And when the war is over, they will pay, as all traitors will pay.'

Bridgette shivered from the look of sheer hatred in Charles dark eyes. 'Don't glare at me that way, I'll not try to stop you,' she said. 'I would rather help you. I would like that pair to get their just deserts.'

'Ah yes, but that is for later,' Charles said. 'The bakery is about the safest house in the town. Your father and brother as thick as thieves with the German officers, and your mother terminally ill with TB.'

'But that is why—'

Charles reached out and grasped Bridgette's arm. 'Ask your mother before she dies, does she want to do this noble thing? Many lives will be saved if she does, and not just the British man's. The Germans have obscene ways of making a person talk and this could break the Resistance cell wide open. And it will only be for a week or maybe two until we can get another route organised.'

'Charles—'

'Ask her,' Charles said. 'Surely you owe her that. I will meet you here, same time tomorrow, for your answer.'

He was gone before Bridgette could say another word. She couldn't do it. Anyone could see that. Charles was a fanatic. Nagging at her, however, was the fate of them all if she refused, and she knew the guilt that she had condemned them all to death would lodge on her conscience for ever.

Gabrielle knew every beat of Bridgette's heart and so was well aware that something was bothering her. 'Let me help you while I am able?' she said later that day. 'Tell me what you are fretting over and remember when a person is dying, nothing is too bad to hear. Your whole perspective changes.'

Gabrielle knew her mother was right and so with a sigh she sat on the bed and told her everything about her involvement with the Resistance. It was what Gabrielle had feared and yet she was so proud of her brave daughter.

Bridgette held her mother's eyes as she went on, 'I told Charles that I could no longer be in the Resistance when I came to look after you. He fully understood and then today I met him again and he asked me to hide a British agent. The Germans found out about the escape route to get him home, and Charles asked if I would hide him until they can make other arrangements.'

'Do they know that he is here?' Gabrielle asked.

'Well, they know that he is in this general area.' Bridgette said. 'And I quite understand, and so will Charles, if you feel that you can't do this.'

Gabrielle knew what she wanted to say, and that was to bring the agent here immediately. For her it wouldn't matter if it were discovered what they had done – a dying woman views risk in a totally different way – but it was dangerous for her daughter.

'What if he should be found?' she asked. 'What would they do to you?'

Bridgette shivered. 'You don't want to know.'

'Well, won't they turn the town upside down to find him? If they search everyone's house, there is nowhere for him to hide here.'

'Charles doesn't think they would ever search the bakery,' Bridgette said. 'They know about my father and Georges's involvement with the Germans, and think that they are the last people they would expect to harbour an enemy agent.'

'Yes, I see that.' Gabrielle nodded. 'And if they're right, and if this British man is willing to risk TB, then he can bide here in comparative safety until the Resistance can get him out.'

'You do know what you are saying, Maman.'

'Of course I do,' Gabrielle said. 'Tell this Charles that the man can come here for now.'

When Bridgette told Charles this the following day, he was noticeably relieved. 'He is risking catching TB,' Bridgette said.

'Yes, as you do every day,' Charles commented drily. 'Speed is essential. The Germans have already searched all the farmhouses around the area where he landed. Next I believe they will start on the town. His name is James Carmichael and I will deliver him to your house this evening, just as soon as we make certain where your father and Georges are.'

'Come through the bakery,' Bridgette said. 'I will be waiting for your knock.'

'It will be after curfew when the streets are dark.'

'It doesn't matter what time it is,' Bridgette said. 'I will be waiting.'

She was waiting, and opened the door immediately. Charles didn't go in with the Englishman and neither did any of them speak. However, with the door closed Bridgette whispered, 'I will not risk putting the light on, but if you follow behind me then you should be all right.'

The man didn't answer but did as Bridgette advised. It was only when they reached the relative safety of Gabrielle's room that Bridgette had a good look at the man and she liked what she saw. James Carmichael had an open, honest face. His deep brown eyes matched his hair, and his mouth looked almost gentle. Looking at him, she knew instinctively that he was a man to be trusted.

The man, on the other hand, was stunned at the whole set-up. When the escape plan had fallen through, everyone had been flummoxed as to where to hide him, especially when the Gestapo were so quickly on his tail. It was the sallow man known as Charles that said that he might know of somewhere. And here he was, in the bedroom of a dying woman tended by her daughter, who he thought one of the most stunning women he had ever seen.

Charles had filled him in on the details. 'Bridgette is a very courageous girl,' he told Carmichael. 'She used to be a member of the Resistance herself before her mother's illness, and the two of them will be fully supportive of you.'

'What of her father?'

'Both her father and brother are Nazi sympathisers,' Charles had said. 'The chances are that their house won't be searched because they are so pro-German, but there is no guarantee. Don't forget the risk they are running hiding you in the house, which is at least as great as yours.'

'Yes,' the man said. 'I know that, and I know that you are doing your level best to help me.'

'No matter,' Charles said with a shrug. 'Many are short tempered these days. Maybe I am one of them.'

Charles's words came back to James Carmichael as he gazed around the room. He approached Gabrielle in the bed and in his basic and faltering French began to tell her and Bridgette, standing beside her, how grateful he was to them both.

Gabrielle smiled as she said in English, 'You can talk in your native tongue, if it is easier for you. Both my daughter and I understand and speak it.'

'My French is not a tenth as good as your English,' the man said, 'for all they gave me a crash course before they dropped me over here.'

'Ah,' said Bridgette with a smile. 'But you see we learned to speak English from childhood, Mr Carmichael.'

'Oh, please call me James,' the man said extending his hand. 'Charles told me your name is Bridgette.

'That's right. And this is my mother, Gabrielle.'

'I am so pleased to meet you both,' James said. 'And so incredibly grateful that you have agreed to hide me at great risk to yourselves, especially,' he said to Gabrielle, 'as I understand your husband is a Nazi sympathiser.'

'He is, to my great shame,' Gabrielle said. 'And my stepson too. But there is no need to worry, my husband is so afraid of my illness that he never comes further than the threshold. He shares a room now with my stepson, who never comes near me at all. However, they are very friendly with the German officers, often feeding them information about their own neighbours, customers, many of them, at the bakery. It is a despicable thing to do, and we both hope he pays for it when the war is over, but just for now it makes this house one of the safest in the town.'

'Despite all that, it is a grave risk you are both running,' James said. 'What if he does find out I'm here?'

'The only time you have to talk very quietly or

not at all is when my father or brother are on this floor and might overhear you,' Bridgette said. 'The bakery is too far away, and he and Georges go out every evening, so it is moderately safe if we are all careful.'

'If you don't mind, I feel very tired all of a sudden,' Gabrielle said. Bridgette could see the lines of fatigue etched on her mother's face and realised that the unusual animation that she had shown in front of James had exhausted her. She guessed that she might suffer for it the next day too.

Gabrielle had neither the will nor the breath to speak further. Bridgette could hear the rattle of her chest and the sound of her laboured breathing as she clutched at the air and she signed for James to follow her from the room and into her own along the corridor. 'What of your father?' James said.

'He's not in yet,' Bridgette replied. 'Believe me you will know when Georges and my father are home. In fact, even before they reach home you will probably hear them coming along the street. Sorry about the boxes,' she said, lifting them up off the bed so that they could sit down. 'They are full of clothes that might fit you. I asked my father-in-law to bring them down for me. He brought the bedroll he used in the Great War too so you haven't got to lie on the floor.' She caught sight of James's face and said, 'it is all right. He came at dusk and made sure that no one saw him bring the things in.'

'It's not that,' James said. 'Well, not that entirely. I was just under the impression that the fewer people know about me the better.'

'And so it is,' Bridgette said. 'But the Laurents had to know. I was living with them when I began with the Resistance, you see, and so I had to ask them if they minded. Sometimes the families of Resistance fighters are punished too. Anyway, my mother- and sister-in-law like to visit Maman and would think it very odd if I said they couldn't come – and how else would I get hold of Xavier's clothes.'

'Xavier? Is that the name of your husband?'

'Yes,' Bridgette answered quietly.

'But won't he want any of these things? James asked, pulling some out of one of the boxes.

'I don't think so,' Bridgette said quietly. 'His was one of the bodies left on the beaches of Dunkirk.'

'Oh, Bridgette, I am sorry.'

Bridgette shrugged. 'I hoped some of them might fit you.'

'And you won't mind me wearing them.'

'Why should I?'

'You might find it upsetting.'

Bridgette shook her head. 'The fact that Xavier died is upsetting,' she said. 'The fact that I haven't even a grave to tend is upsetting.' She looked at James. 'Are you married?'

James nodded. 'I was. I married a lovely girl, Sarah, in 1937. She wanted a family straightaway,

366

but I saw the writing on the wall in 1938 and wanted to wait a while. Anyway, when war was declared and I joined up she went to live with my parents.'

'Where was that?'

'A place called Sutton Coldfield, which is just outside Birmingham in England,' James said. 'Although Birmingham was hammered, Sutton Coldfield was virtually free of bombing raids, but Sarah wanted to do her bit.' He smiled sadly and said, 'She wrote and told me what she intended because she heard that the Jewellery Quarter, which is very near the centre of Birmingham, had converted to making radar parts and as she had always been good with her hands, she wanted to try for a job there.'

He paused and then went on, 'I wasn't pleased at first, but she said she had nothing to do all day, and radar parts were needed, and then reminded me that I was doing my bit so wasn't it unreasonable of me to try and prevent her from doing the same.' He stopped and smiled at little sadly. 'She was right. All over Britain, girls and women are doing the jobs that men used to do, even driving buses and trucks and dirty work in factories.'

'What happened to your wife, James?'

'She was caught in a raid on her way home one autumn night in 1940 and the public shelter she was taken to took a direct hit,' James said. 'My parents wrote and told me. Killed outright, they said.'

'So you had no family then?'

James shook his head. 'Have you any children?'

'No,' Bridgette said, 'I was pregnant with my first baby when news came of Xavier's death and I miscarried the child.'

'Oh my dear girl,' James said, and the genuine sympathy in his voice caused the tears to prickle in Bridgette's eyes.

'Don't,' she said. 'Now look what you have started, and I can hear my father and Georges carousing their way home. So you must be quiet. My room is better for you to stay in because it has a powerful bolt on the door that I fix in place every night. It will probably feel strange for me though, for I've never slept in a room with a man since my husband.'

James grinned at her. 'Sleep is all I'm after,' he whispered. 'And I will turn my back when you wish to get undressed.'

A few minutes later they lay side by side, Bridgette in the bed and James on the bedroll on the floor. She heard her father and Georges stumbling about as they did most nights but James slept on oblivious to it all. Sleep eluded Bridgette, though, as she went over the events of that evening. She was glad that she had eventually agreed to hide James, though she hoped soon that they would be able to ship him safely back home, and she eventually went to sleep with that thought running round her head.

NINETEEN

Bridgette woke the next morning before the alarm
went off, as she did most mornings, and she shut
it off before it should wake the man still slumbering
beside her bed. Since she'd returned home, she had
slept much easier in her bed with the bolt in place
each night, though she doubted that even Georges
would dare to enter her room now. When she had
arrived at the house to nurse her mother, she
had told him about the large bolt immediately.

'I don't have to say why,' she'd said, looking
fixedly at him. 'You try violating me again and I
will go straight to the police. There are laws about
that sort of thing, you know.'

'I never touched you.'

'No, of course you didn't,' Bridgette said sarcastically. 'You must love a little fantasy in your life.'

'I wouldn't touch you with a barge pole,'
Georges said disparagingly.

'Good,' Bridgette said. 'Keep it that way and it
will suit us both.'

Georges had given Bridgette a wide berth after that, but she still took no chances and would be doubly careful while James was there. From the door she surveyed the room. James had tucked himself at the side of her bed from which he couldn't be seen from the doorway, A person would have to go into the room to see the bed made up on the floor. Fully satisfied with that, Bridgette closed the door and went down to make breakfast for them all.

When her father and Georges had eaten their fill and had gone down to the bakery, and the girl had arrived to open the shop, she made breakfast for her mother, James and herself and went in to tell him the coast was clear. James had tucked the bedroll and blankets neatly under her bed and the clothes he had been wearing the day before he had left on the chair beside the bed. He was wearing a shirt and trousers that had once belonged to Xavier.

Despite what she had said, Bridgette found that quite a shock. For a brief second she remembered Xavier wearing those same clothes. It was before war ripped their lives apart and they had both been in the town together. He had his arm around her and she suddenly remembered the feel of that arm and the light kiss as their lips touched.

James saw her face and said softly, 'I'm sorry. I changed because I have been wearing the same clothes for over a week, but I see how it has distressed you and I will change back immediately.'

'No,' Bridgette said firmly. 'No, it's me just being

silly. Xavier would laugh at my foolishness. Of course you must wear his clothes. It is the most sensible thing to do. Leave your other things where they are and I will deal with them later. Now that my father and Georges are in the bakery, let's go and have breakfast with my mother.'

As they were eating breakfast, Bridgette asked James what he had been trying to find out. 'Though I don't suppose that you can tell us that,' she added.

'I shouldn't tell you, it's true, but as I am accepting your hospitality I feel it only fair,' James said. 'My brief was to check out the missile bases. Do you know of them?'

'Missile bases?' Bridgette repeated.

'That's what the Intelligence boys think they are,' James said. 'One is in an area called Watten, in the middle of the forest.'

'Eperlecques Forest?'

'That's the one,' James said. 'It's a gigantic concrete structure, a truly massive thing. The Allies have been bombing it relentlessly and it is damaged, no doubt about that, but some areas of it still seemed usable. I went first at night and though I couldn't get close there was evidence that people had been at work there. Charles told me he had seen them, and the next day he took me to a place overlooking the site and I could see them myself through field glasses. I communicated what I had discovered to London.'

'What about the one nearer here, which people are beginning to call La Coupole?' Bridgette asked.

371

'That was spotted being built, from a reconnaissance plane last November. It was easier to see from the air then than it is now. Most of it appears to be underground and there is just a giant mushroom over, which is effectively hidden by the foliage of the trees at this time of the year.'

'There was a chalk quarry there before,' Gabrielle said.

'They knew that,' said James. 'It explained why it is so easy to dig down deeper. I think that very powerful bombs will be needed to penetrate La Coupole. They were working on that when I left.'

'Don't,' Bridgette said. 'We live very close, and the bombing has already been scary enough.'

'I know,' James said. 'It must be really frightening, especially as you can't take shelter in a cellar or anything, but we must knock out these sites, because they think the Germans are developing pilotless planes with war heads in the nose, and even rockets built the same way. If they're right – and they usually are about things like this – then these places are where they will be manufactured, and they might later be using them as launching pads too. What about a few of those landing on British cities that have already taken a pounding? You have no idea what some of them have already gone through.'

'I did know about the bombings,' Bridgette said. 'We would listen in to the BBC on the wireless. And you're right: they surely have gone through enough already. And had you finished what you had came here to do?'

'Oh, yes,' James said. 'My mission was finished but the route to get me out collapsed. The network was infiltrated in some way and some people were lifted. One or more broke under questioning.'

'No one knows how they would withstand torture until it's put to the test,' Bridgette said. 'And it's even worse, I think, when your loved ones are punished along with you. That was one of the reasons I gave up the work when I knew I would be caring for Maman.' She turned as she spoke and saw that her mother had fallen asleep, even propped up as she was.

'When did she go to sleep?' she asked James.

'I don't know,' James admitted. 'I only just noticed it myself.'

'She has hardly touched her breakfast,' Bridgette said, as she removed the tray. 'But then she eats very little. Will you help me lift her down the bed so that she will be more comfortable?'

'I'll do that with pleasure.'

It was as they bent to the task that their eyes met and Bridgette was totally amazed at the jolt that ran through her body. Since Xavier had died, she had never ever thought of any other man in that way, and nor had she wanted to for she knew that no one could take his place. She was annoyed with herself that she had allowed this unknown Englishman to unlock feelings she thought dead and buried.

She saw that his eyes too were slightly puzzled, but neither spoke of it. They lifted Gabrielle down the bed and Bridgette arranged the pillows without another word being spoken.

To break the silence, before it should become too awkward, she said, 'Tell me about yourself, James.'

'What do you wish to know?'

'Oh, where you come from, your family. The usual stuff.'

'I am a very ordinary chap,' James said. 'As I said, I lived in a place called Sutton Coldfield. It's a royal town, given to the people of Sutton by Henry the Eighth. We lived near a large park, so large that there are five sizeable lakes in it and streams running all through the park to feed those lakes. When I look back it seems like every fine day all the kids from the area would be in that park, and what adventures we had there. I used to sometimes be mad if Mum made me take Dolly, my little sister, with me. I remember I seemed to spend a lot of time pushing her on the swings.'

Bridgette saw the smile playing around his mouth and she asked, 'Have you any other brothers or sisters?'

'Oh yes,' James said. His eyes suddenly clouded over and he said, 'I had a younger brother, Dan, as well. He was killed in action in the summer of '41, along with Dolly's fiancé.'

'Oh, James!' Bridgette cried. 'You must have barely got over the loss of your wife. Were you close to your brother?'

374

James nodded. 'As the Yanks would say, we were real buddies. We were all very cut up about his death and that of Dolly's fiancé, Stuart, too. He was a fine man and got on well with us all. I volunteered to undertake this sort of work the following year because, to be honest, for a long time I didn't care whether I lived or died. I felt as if I had lost so much – first Sarah and then Dan and Stuart.'

'I took up Resistance work for the same reason,' Bridgette said. 'To avenge the deaths of my husband and baby.'

'And has it helped you feel better?'

Bridgette nodded. 'When I kill Germans it does. That's strange in a way because all my life I have disliked violence or even unpleasantness.'

'Was there a reason for that?'

Bridgette hesitated. She didn't know James well enough to tell him just how awful her earlier life had been, and so she contented herself with saying, 'Well, I never really saw eye to eye with my father, and Georges is my half-brother, and we have never got on either. However, I have a lovely aunt in Paris, Yvette. She is Maman's sister but I haven't told her how sick Maman is,' Bridgette said. 'I will do so, though, as soon as they get something organised for you.'

'Let's hope that it's sooner rather than later then,' James said.

'I hope that to,' Bridgette said. 'Until then, we will just have to cope.'

*   *   *

Later that day Bridgette said to James, 'Marie and her daughter will be here tomorrow. They come every Saturday afternoon, because Lisette is not at work and Marie shuts the shop up. There are very few customers these days. In fact, any trade comes mainly from the Germans.'

'Why is that?'

'There's no money about,' Bridgette said. 'A lot of the food is sent to Germany, so what little is left is expensive. When I lived with the Laurents I helped in the shop and also worked in a bar, and before Lisette got the job in the factory we were always hungry. Few of these shortages affect us here, though, for anything we are running out of is replaced by my father's German friends just as soon as he tells them about it. It bothers me, but what can I do? And I suppose it is better for my mother to have the best food available for all I nearly choke on it sometimes when I know how sparsely most people are living.'

'In the short time I have been here I have seen the suffering of the French people,' James said. 'I felt sorry for all of you, and all the other countries under Nazi control.'

'It's not for ever,' Bridgette said. 'I must say I am surprised at Britain. I thought you would sink as well, one more notch to Hitler's belt.'

James smiled. 'To hear the Americans, it was their intervention that saved us.'

'Does that annoy you?'

'No,' James said. 'It's just their way. Most British

people are brought up to think that it is extreme bad manners for a person to blow their own trumpet.'

'Blow their own trumpet?' Bridgette repeated questioningly.

'It means boasting, bragging about what you can do,' James said in explanation. 'And let's face it, their involvement didn't do us any harm.'

'Are you always so easy-going?'

'I suppose,' James said. 'I don't see the point of getting worked up over little things.'

Bridgette sighed and said, 'I find that attitude very restful.'

He smiled. 'I'm glad of that.'

Once again there was that tug in her stomach and she busied herself doing things for her mother so that he wouldn't see how that smile had affected her.

That same day, storm troopers began searching the town for James and had reached their street by the afternoon. Bridgette, watching through her mother's bedroom window, felt as if her heart was in her mouth and, as they drew nearer, her spine began to tingle. She saw the brutal way they dealt with any who protested: they were thrown un-ceremoniously out onto the cobbled streets, and she heard the shattering of glass and the splintering of wood, and heard the cries and sobs of the distressed people.

Then, Bridgette felt as if her heart had stopped

beating altogether for they had reached the bakery and she heard the bell tinkle as they entered the shop. Gabrielle read the naked fear in her daughter's eyes for both of them knew there was nowhere in the house or shop where James wouldn't be found.

James too was distraught, and not for himself alone, but also for Bridgette. He knew that her mother might be spared, not only because of her illness but because it was such an infectious illness, but they would take Bridgette. As the soldiers' boots were heard pounding up the stairs he slid under the bed, even knowing it was futile. Bridgette decided that she would not cower in her mother's room and went out to meet them with her head held high to see her father coming out of the bedroom he shared with Georges, roused from his slumber by the commotion.

'What is this?' he demanded of a German officer pushing past the troopers lining the stairs. 'I thought we had an agreement.'

'I'm sorry,' Bridgette heard the officer say to her father. 'There has been a mistake,' and he gave a curt order to the storm troopers, who turned and went back down the stairs.

Bridgette let out the breath she hadn't even been aware that she had been holding and felt almost light-headed with relief. Without a word to Legrand she went back to her mother.

'Charles was right. This house is not to be searched, and while I am more than glad about that,

378

my worry now is that that might appear odd to our neighbours.'

'They'll know why,' Gabrielle said. 'Don't worry, Legrand has marked his card very well.'

Bridgette hoped they were right because the whole thing had shaken her up more than she thought it would.

Marie, when she came the following day, agreed with Gabrielle that the townsfolk would know why the bakery had been spared a search. 'You should be grateful anyway,' she said. 'At our house they ruined bales of cloth, and took two pictures from the wall and smashed them to pieces with their boots.'

'Did you say anything?'

Marie shook her head. 'My energies were taken up trying to stop Maurice saying anything,' she said. 'I've heard since from men who did that, and after the soldiers had beaten them up, they trashed the place. As it was, it took me hours to clear up after they had all gone.'

Marie and Lisette were obviously interested in James Carmichael, though he had been a little nervous about meeting them, or anyone really, because Charles had impressed upon him the need for secrecy. However, he trusted Bridgette's judgement and found he liked both women and he relaxed a little, especially when Bridgette told him that Lisette's husband, Edmund, survived Dunkirk and was one of those rescued from the beaches and had been taken to Britain.

'Does she know where he is now?' he asked.

Bridgette shook her head. 'Nothing definite, though Lisette feels certain that he would have joined the Free French army under de Gaulle.'

'She's probably right,' James said. 'A good few Frenchmen did that.'

Bridgette translated this to Lisette and her mother as she translated anything they said to James, and when they had gone home later that day, James asked if Bridgette would teach him to speak better French.

'To be able to understand what people say would be a great advantage. I watched you today and you must be worn out.'

'Not really,' Bridgette said. 'Though it might be a good idea for you to learn anyway. Of course we don't know how long you are going to be here and you might be moved on before we have got very far, but we can make a start at least.'

The next day, as Bridgette approached the cathedral before Mass, she was accosted by Madame Pretin. Bridgette hadn't a great liking for the woman, who she thought must love grumbling and complaining as she did so much of it.

That morning she fixed her gimlet eyes upon Bridgette and they glittered with malice as she said, 'What I want to know – what many want to know – is the reason why your house wasn't searched the day before yesterday like everyone else's in the town?'

Bridgette looked at the knot of women standing a little way from them and thought that Madame Pretin had put into words what they were thinking. They might have all being discussing it before she arrived.

She lifted her head a little higher and said stiffly, 'I have no say in what the Germans do. Maybe they didn't search our house because Maman is so ill and they knew they would find nothing anyway.'

'You're hand in glove with them, that's the truth.'

'I am hand in glove with no German.'

'So you say,' one woman spat out. 'But I remember the way you behaved with them stationed in the town and that was only a little while ago.'

Bridgette knew that was the time she pretended to like and even at times flirt with the German soldiers so that she could get across the town unmolested by them with the vital messages she had hidden in her beret. She couldn't say this, though, but what she did say was, 'I really don't know what you are talking about.'

'Oh yes you do,' the older woman said. 'I was not the only one to notice.'

Bridgette's eyes flashed with sudden anger and she snapped out, 'I am surprised that one person notices with such interest the actions of another. My life is too busy to do that. Maybe you should think of doing more with your own life and keeping your nose out of other's business. In fact,' she said

381

to the other women watching the exchange, 'maybe you should all do the same.'

She walked away before Madame Pretin or any of them could make a reply and all through Mass she could almost feel their affronted eyes boring into her back. As Mass finished she was out of the door in an instant and hurried home without stopping to speak to anyone, though she had seen Marie and Lisette in the congregation.

She regretted losing her temper. Despite what her mother and Marie had said, she knew many of the congregation would be unaware of her father's relationship with the German officers in the town. It was not something he broadcasted. And so, people being people, would probably assume her house had been spared because of favours given and this would be compounded by the way she had reacted. She should have held her tongue, though she feared the damage was done now.

Life at the bakery with James in residence assumed something of a pattern over the next few days, although they never took chances or dropped their guard. And yet, despite the danger, Bridgette realised that she liked having James around. He was a good, kind man and she loved him for the way he was with her mother. He would do anything for her, however distasteful, without the slightest hesitation, and he would entertain her when Bridgette was busy. If Legrand and Georges were away in the bakery and there was no danger of hearing the timbre of his voice he would talk to her or they would play cards together.

Each day, Bridgette made an early lunch for everyone and when she had eaten hers, she went downstairs to relieve the girl in the shop so that she could have a lunch break too. She had told James that if her father was going to look in on Gabrielle, he usually did it on his way to bed after the midday meal and so James went into Bridgette's room where he hid under the bed until Bridgette came to fetch him. Then she'd take him into her mother's room because it was further away from the two snoring men than her own was, and she would give him his French lesson.

James was making excellent progress, as he proved the next time the Marie and Lisette came. He found that he could understand a lot of what they said, although he was still wary of talking in French, certain that he would make a fool of himself. Bridgette was really pleased for him, though she knew when James eventually left them she would miss him enormously.

After the encounter with Madame Pretin, Bridgette didn't risk going back to the cathedral to Mass on Sunday mornings, using the excuse to the priest and to Marie and Lisette, that she didn't like leaving her mother so long. Even the priest accepted that because he knew that Gabrielle was very ill, though Marie and Lisette both offered to sit with her mother so Bridgette could attend Mass if she wanted to.

She thanked them, but never took the offer up and instead attended the Mass that the priest said for her mother in the house on Wednesday. James stayed in Bridgette's room when the priest was there and he was just as careful whenever Legrand and Georges were around, particularly when they were not down in the bakery, but he only really breathed easier when they were out of the house altogether, and he knew that Bridgette felt the same way.

As Gabrielle's morphine was increased to deal with the pain she often felt dizzy and disoriented in the evening and too tired to want company. So Bridgette and James too would make her comfortable and check she had everything to hand before leaving her until the morning. And then, as her father and Georges would almost definitely have left the house, Bridgette usually went to the kitchen to wash the dishes and James would follow her.

She knew that James needed to make his way back to Britain, and as quickly as possible, and she had imagined that he would be with her for a week or ten days at the most, but one week followed another and when he had been there four weeks, she'd still had had no word from anyone.

'It's the not knowing anything that gets you in the end,' Bridgette said as she plunged her hands into the soap suds that night. 'I did think I would have heard about some system of getting you home by now.'

'So did I,' James said, picking up a drying cloth. 'Why don't you contact Charles and ask him?'

'Because I can't,' Bridgette said. 'I know nothing about Charles, but his first name. If I was lifted, whatever they did to me I could tell them nothing more than the name he gave me, and that might be false for all I know. He always contacts me. And,' she added, 'I thought that he would be as anxious as we are to get you home.'

'I know, and I worry about it for your sakes.'

'I worry about it for all our sakes,' Bridgette said with a sigh. 'But there is nothing that we can do about it, is there? We must, like you English say, "grin and bear it", and at least the Germans have given up looking for you in this town anyway. They must think you have outfoxed them and are home and dry now.'

'I wish I was,' James said. 'Yet I will never forget this bakery and the courage you had to hide me in the first place, and the kindess you have shown while I have been here.'

Bridgette turned to look at James and saw his eyes were alight with emotion and when he suddenly said, 'Dry your hands,' she did so hurriedly. Then James enfolded them with his own and his eyes held hers as he said, 'If anything happened to you, I don't think I could bear it. This is neither the time nor the place, and yet I must tell you that I think I have fallen in love with you.'

Bridgette's heart quickened. 'Oh, James,' she

said. 'Please don't be cross at what I am about to say. These are not natural times and we are not living normal lives and are under extreme pressure. In such an atmosphere emotions probably get intensified.'

James withdrew his hands and said, 'I don't expect you to think of me in the same light, Bridgette. I know that I have sprung it on you. I just needed to tell you that at the moment I am eaten up inside for you. I don't know whether that is natural or normal, but at the moment that's how I feel.'

'And now, I must be as honest as you,' Bridgette said. 'You have engendered feelings in me that I thought were left with my husband's body on the beaches of Dunkirk.'

'You mean . . . ?'

'I mean I love you too, James. And yet I don't know whether it's the strange and confined way we are living that has caused us to become so close so soon.'

'What does your heart say?'

'My heart quickens every time you are near,' Bridgette admitted. 'But hearts are not always reliable indicators of sustainable love. I have tried to deny the way I feel about you, and the fact that we have now admitted our feelings changes nothing. If anything, I will worry even more about your safety.'

'And I yours,' James said. 'We know that our future is uncertain. Any moment we could make a mistake, get careless and it would be over for both of us. In the meantime, can we not be a comfort to one another?'

Comfort, Bridgette thought. How good that word sounded.

James held out his arms. 'Come,' he said gently, and Bridgette went into them as if he had done it every day of her life. James's arms enfolded her and it felt so right she sighed with contentment. Arm in arm they walked through to the living room and sat together on the sofa, and when James's lips met hers she felt the beat of her heart increase.

It was the very start of a bittersweet romance, and as each day passed Bridgette wanted more. Another week went by and she knew that she would ask James to share her bed that night. Now, accepting how she felt about him, it was a torment to have him lie beside her bed the way he did, so close and yet not close enough. She was surprised at herself for even considering having sex with a man when there wasn't even any sort of understanding between them, as there could never be in the circumstances.

She suddenly didn't care how society would view their liaison, or even the Church, which she knew would regard what she intended to do as a grave and mortal sin. She yearned for James to make love to her and then to sleep in his arms all the night long.

However, when later that night she said this to

James as she flung back the sheets, he shook his head.

'It's not that I wouldn't love to,' he said. 'But we couldn't risk you falling pregnant.'

'I am almost infertile,' Bridgette said. 'I was married to Xavier for years with no sign.'

'Even so.'

'Please, James?'

'Don't do this to me,' James pleaded. 'I am only flesh and blood like everyone else. It's because I love you so much that I don't want to do this to you.'

Bridgette dampened down her ardour. She knew deep down that James was right but still she grumbled, 'Why have you to be so wise and worthy?'

James gave a chuckle. 'Because one of us has to be,' he said, getting to his feet and giving Bridgette a chaste kiss on the cheek. 'Now lie down like a good girl. The men come in at this time of night, as a rule, and it would never do for them to hear us talking.'

Bridgette stayed silent, knowing James spoke sense, but she was too churned up to sleep for a long, long time.

TWENTY

When Bridgette saw Charles in town a few days later, her mind was teeming with questions but she knew she had to wait until they were in a much more private place. Suddenly Charles ducked into an alleyway and Bridgette, with a surreptitious look behind her, followed him.

Before she was able to utter a word, Charles, never a man to waste time on pleasantries said, 'We have trouble getting your Englishman out.'

'Why?' Bridgette said. 'He's been with us now over four weeks.'

'I know,' Charles said. 'We were arranging an escape route for him. But two weeks ago we heard something that made us stop. It's too late now and he must stay where he is for the moment.'

'How big a moment?'

'How the hell should I know?' Charles said. 'Anyway, what's scheduled to happen in the next week or month is bigger than both of us and

Carmichael too. We have had news that the Allies are massing on the other side of the Channel.'

Bridgette stared at him. 'Invasion?'

'What else could it be?'

'Oh God,' she breathed. 'Another Dunkirk?'

Charles shrugged. 'Maybe, maybe not. But you can see that with all that activity on the British side it would be far too dangerous to try to move Carmichael anywhere just now.'

'And you have no idea when this invasion will take place?'

'They're not going to let that information slip out, are they?' Charles said. 'And then have a welcoming committee waiting on this side. All we have to do is sit tight and hope the right side wins. Anything the Resistance can do to help that along a little we are ready and willing for.

'Charles—'

'There's nothing more to say, Bridgette,' Charles said. 'You're doing a grand job just at the moment. Just keep on with it a little longer.'

'Have I any choice?' was on the tip of Bridgette's tongue, but she never said the words for Charles had left the alley and was heading towards the town. She knew better than to follow him and draw attention to herself.

Later, as they sat together in Gabrielle's room, she told her mother and James what Charles had said.

'So, we're in for a long wait perhaps?' James said.

'Maybe,' Bridgette said. 'I have been thinking

about it since, though, and I would have thought it always better to invade in the spring or early summer.'

'I would too,' James said. 'I have a feeling that this isn't the relatively small Expeditionary Force they sent last time; this is make-or-break time.'

Bridgette felt icy fingers of fear trickle down her spine and when she shivered, James put his arm around her automatically.

Gabrielle's eyes opened wider. So that's how it was between them, she thought. She had seen a difference in Bridgette over the past couple of days. She had sort of bloomed with happiness and this now was the reason.

Left alone in her bed later that night she thought it a very silly time to fall in love but then love was no respecter of time, place or suitability. Look at her and Finn all those years before. Funny, he had often come to her mind just lately.

She wondered if there really was an afterlife. She had scandalised the priest the last time he had called, by expressing doubt. She hoped they were right because then she would see her beloved Finn again and her dear mother. She would know soon enough and she feared for James and Bridgette, for the tentative journey they were undertaking together. There was no way that things could ever run smoothly for them and her heart bled for her poor daughter and the heartbreak she was storing up for herself.

*   *   *

Marie and Lisette came the following Saturday afternoon and told them all about the almost expectant mood in the town.

'And the Germans are really jumpy,' Lisette said. 'It's as if they know that the writing is on the wall.'

'They're windy, all right,' Marie said. 'They gathered together all the remaining Jews in the town the other day and shipped them out in the cattle trucks they seemed to have reserved for them, and many of the Communists disappeared as well, people say.

'And I'll tell you who else is worried.' Bridgette said. 'Georges and my father. Let's hope they have reason.'

'Well, invasion is on everyone's lips just now,' Marie said.

James had followed the conversation, but replied in English, 'It can't come soon enough for me. And when it does, I will leave here as soon as I can.'

'James, you can't.'

'Of course I can,' James said. 'It wouldn't be right for me to sit here in comparative safety when I could be helping. I was, after all, a trained soldier before I volunteered to be dropped into France. I was brought here in the middle of April and now it's June and I have done nothing in all that time but hide away. I want to be part of any planned invasion.'

Bridgette knew James's mind was made up. Marie and Lisette only got a smattering of what James had said, but they understood his meaning, and Marie also noticed the way James's eyes locked with Bridgette, and the stricken look on her face when he told her of his intentions. She knew with certainty that there was something between them and that they were aware of it too. She wasn't upset that Bridgette might have found herself someone else – she was still a young woman with needs of her own – but she thought it was bad enough to lose one man to war, without going through all that worry and possible heartache again.

Three days later, the programme on the wireless that they had been listening to on the BBC was interrupted by an announcement from Reuters News Agency.

'The official communiqué states that under the command of General Eisenhower, Allied naval forces began landing Allied armies this morning on the northern coast of France.'

James switched off the wireless and in the ensuing silence they could hear the sound of distant gunfire, the drone of planes in the air and they knew that war had been brought to France for the second time and this time the Allies had to succeed.

Although the sound of conflict was all around, essentially nothing had changed for the people of St-Omer. Then just a week after the invasion, which was being called D-Day, a German pilotless plane carrying a bomb in its nose landed in Kent. Though the newscaster said it had caused little damage and no loss of life, James was still flabbergasted. He'd felt sure that the bombing which had continued throughout May, had put the two constructions – Le Blockhaus and La Coupole – out of action.

The Allied bombing of both sites began again. The sirens screamed out in St-Omer once more, and though the people took shelter, some houses near to La Coupole were damaged or demolished altogether. Dispossessed and homeless people wandered into the town with all they had been able to retrieve from their damaged homes carried in any receptacle they could find. Bridgette had caught sight of a few of them as she was out shopping, and the despair and desperation on their faces tore at her heart strings. And yet the bombing had to continue because those harbingers of death were still being launched across the Channel.

It was Charles who told Bridgette why the rockets were still being launched. The Germans were using launchers hidden in the trees, well away from the two constructions sites in the forest.

The Resistance had located them and communicated the information to London, and most had been rendered unusable by Allied bombing.

'So why are they still able to target London in particular?' James said when Bridgette told him this.

'Well,' Bridgette said, 'Charles doesn't know, but people who have studied the direction they are coming from think they are being launched from various mobile sites across Europe.'

'Oh well, that's that then,' James said morosely. 'Unless someone can tell us where they are it will have to wait until we have overrun the countries concerned to stop them. I feel as if I came here for nothing. And now I seem to be playing a waiting game.'

'For all of us now, it's a waiting game,' Bridgette said. 'My mother is waiting too and I want to make that as easy as I can for her, but I have given her the last of her tablets. Will you sit with her while I go for the doctor? I think she wants her medication increased.'

'Of course,' James said. He took up position by Gabrielle's bed and held her hand.

She was feeling woozy, but when she felt his hand holding hers, she opened heavy eyes and smiled at him and said, 'I was dreaming.'

The words were indistinct, but James was able to understand them and he said. 'I hope they were nice dreams.'

'I was dreaming about letters,' Gabrielle said, and James knew that she was battling to keep the slur out of her voice. 'Everyone loves getting letters,' she continued and a smile played around her mouth for a moment before she went on, 'I had some wonderful letters from Bridgette's father.'

'Did you?' James said in surprise. Somehow wonderful letters and Legrand didn't go hand in hand. 'When was this?'

'In the Great War.'

James decided that Gabrielle was rambling, for Bridgette had told her that her father hadn't served in the war. He didn't know whether to say anything or not, but Gabrielle caught the doubt in his eyes. 'You don't believe me,' she said.

'It's not that,' James said. 'It's just that I understood your husband wasn't in the forces in the Great War.'

'Not this husband, no,' Gabrielle said. 'I am talking of Bridgette's father.'

'So, Legrand is not her father?'

'No.'

'Does she know?'

Gabrielle shook her head slowly.

'But you must tell her,' James said. 'She has a right to know.'

'I will tell her,' Gabrielle said. 'But you mustn't say a word to her about this. Promise me?'

'I wouldn't,' James assured her. 'It's your story to tell, but she should hear it from someone and that someone should preferably be you.'

'I will tell her,' Gabrielle promised. 'When I think the time is right.'

James hoped that she wouldn't leave it too long, but he could say nothing just them because he heard Bridgette coming in the door. She had obviously brought the doctor back with her because she was talking to him and it was time for him to disappear.

He found himself watching Bridgette the rest of

the day, wondering who her father really was. That was, of course, if Gabrielle had been telling him the truth and it wasn't some figment of her imagination. If it should be true, though, he knew Bridgette would be pleased. When they were alone that evening he longed to tell her what Gabrielle had told him, but he had given his word to a dying woman and couldn't go back on it.

Bridgette was aware that he had something on his mind, but she presumed that it was to do with the invasion and she didn't want to talk about it that night. The doctor had told her that day that her mother could have as little as two weeks to live. That was enough for her to come to terms with and she also had the worry of breaking the news to her aunt Yvette, who the doctor said should be contacted immediately.

The next afternoon Bridgette came back from shopping full of excitement to find James standing looking out the window in her mother's bedroom. 'Get away from the window,' she said. 'You'll be spotted.'

James didn't move away, though he turned to face her. 'Hardly,' he said. 'The streets are full of people, but they all look too agitated about something to notice me looking down on them. What's going on?'

'You can't see it from here, but there are plumes of smoke rising up from the Gestapo Headquarters and someone was telling me they have cleared the cells of prisoners and packed them off on trains.'

'Destroying the evidence,' James said. 'The Allies must be drawing close now. There's Charles, look.'

Bridgette nodded. 'I was talking to him,' she said. 'He thinks the Gestapo will pull out next. That's what he is waiting for. Loads of people want to storm the building when they're gone and check the place is really empty.'

'Well, I would imagine many went in there and never came out,' James said. 'I doubt they'll find any live prisoners, though there maybe some dead ones.'

'It was a terrible building,' Bridgette said. 'I hated even passing it. Won't it be wonderful if they all leave?'

And it was wonderful when, just an hour or so later, the hated Gestapo piled into their military vehicles and sped away. The waiting crowds on the pavements watched them go silently. Later, however, when the soldiers marched down the streets, many booed or spat or shouted after them. And while Bridgette was watching this marvellous spectacle, and explaining to her mother what was happening, James disappeared.

Seeing her preoccupation, he knew it was his chance to speak to Charles and see if there was any chance of meeting up, if not with his own unit, then some other British one. He slipped quietly from the room and down the stairs. Here he was cautious, because even now he didn't want Bridgette involved, but he heard the voices of Legrand and Georges in the bakery, where they had returned to after their afternoon nap, and so he went out the back door that opened onto the yard and into the street that way.

Georges and Legrand were unaware of the exodus happening in their small town at first, though they knew the Germans were worried and had been for days. They had both been nervous when they had heard about the invasion, but certain that the Allies would be repulsed by the Germans, as they had been before.

However, as the days passed, and they heard of the scale of the whole operation it did concern them, as did the attitude of the German officers, who seemed to forget the help that Legrand had been to them over the years. Suddenly, they wanted little to do with him and the steady supply of food and coal dried up.

However, they had given him no hint that they were pulling out of the town. Even the girl in the shop was not aware of it straightaway, though she did think there were more people on the streets than normal, and in the end she stopped a man who was hurrying past.

'What is it?'

'It's over, that's what it is,' said the man. 'The Gestapo have gone already, and now the soldiers are following.'

The girl could scarcely believe it, though she didn't doubt the man, and she went into the bakery, a thing she very seldom did, to tell them all about it.

Bridgette, still at the window, was relating all that was happening outside to her mother, and when she noticed James's absence she'd assumed he had gone to the bathroom. But suddenly there he was in the street below, gesticulating to Charles, who was on the other side of the road. Charles spotted him almost immediately and crossed over to him, and they were soon lost to view. Bridgette guessed that Charles would have taken James to some alleyway for discretion.

Barely had they disappeared than she saw her father and Georges and the girl from the shop emerge from a side street, looking totally bemused at what was happening. No one took any notice of them. The mind of most of the townsfolk, and certainly those on the streets, was set on one thing. Barely had the last soldier left before the people set off for the Gestapo headquarters, the building that had been such an object of terror to so many.

Bridgette knew the Allies would soon be in her town. That was a heady thought and one she had waited long years for, but then James would be able to leave. She had no right even to try to stop him, although she knew that when he was gone, he would leave a gaping hole in her heart. That hole would widen when eventually her mother lost her tenuous grip on life. She would be totally alone, and she felt desolation fold around her like a cloak,

When James returned, Bridgette knew by his face that something had been decided. She heard her father and Georges come into the house, complaining and grumbling about what they had witnessed, and James had to stay hidden. She did what she could with the meagre fare that was left in the cupboard and set it before the two of them.

Legrand seldom spoke to her but that day he said, 'Did you see what those louts have done to the Gestapo headquarters?'

'I didn't see it,' Bridgette said. 'But I heard it.'

'Wanton vandalism that's all it was,' Legrand said angrily. 'In the end someone set fire to it. I just hope that the police get the people responsible.'

Bridgette laughed. 'I doubt they will. They'll have to arrest more than half of the town, and you might find the police reluctant even to try. They might think the place is best razed to the ground in memory of the people who died there.'

'They should have no opinion about it,' Legrand said. 'They are there to uphold the law.'

'Are they?' Bridgette said sarcastically. 'Well, there hasn't been much law the last few years, just violence and brutality, and I'm glad that's over at last. And here's another problem for you. The girl in the shop won't be working here any more. Her brother came to fetch her before you came in and said her family don't want her working for people like us any more, and I had to close up early.

'What did he mean, "people like us"?' Legrand asked.

'Oh, Papa work it out,' Bridgette said impatiently.

401

'It's not hard. With the mood the townspeople are in, now is not a good time to associate in any way with people who counted the Germans as friends. This used to be the best bakers in the town and now people are no longer beating a path to our door, are they? You might find after today even more people will be buying their bread elsewhere.'

Legrand leaped to his feet and made a grab for Bridgette, but she twisted from his grasp. As he raised his hand as if to strike her, she grabbed a pan from the stove. 'You lay a hand on me, either of you,' she yelled, 'and you will get the same back. I'm warning you.'

Legrand was astounded, but he lowered his arm as he ground out, 'One of these days, my girl—'

'Don't threaten me,' Bridgette said. 'Just you get about your business and let me get about mine.'

Legrand glared at her but she met his eyes, and he was the one who turned away first.

That night Bridgette thought it took an age for her father and Georges to go out because she was in an agony of suspense to know what had been decided between James and Charles. She busied herself getting her mother settled for the night, and as soon as she could, she grabbed James's hand and took him into her room. Then with the door closed and bolted she said, 'All right, now tell me everything.'

'Charles has it all worked out,' James told Bridgette. 'He says the American troops are in front of the British, but we can reach the British lines virtually unmolested if we go through the Eperlecques Forest.'

'But that's where that Blockhaus place was that the Allies have tried to bomb,' Bridgette cried. 'The forest will be crawling with Germans.'

'Charles says it isn't,' James said. 'It used to be heavily guarded, but much of it is abandoned now. The forest is where the Resistance have been working for some time. That's how they were able to let the Allies know where the mobile launch pads were hidden. Charles knows the forest like the back of his hand, he says, and all the safest routes through it.'

'And he will go with you?'

'All the way,' James said.

Bridgette felt fear for James running through her, but she knew the die was cast now.

'I love you very much, Bridgette,' James said. 'Please believe that. But this is something I must do. I owe it to my comrades and I would feel less of a man if I didn't at least try to rejoin some army unit to continue the fight to liberate Europe. Can you understand a little of that?'

Bridgette nodded. 'I understand all of it,' she said. 'But that will not ease the heartache.' Her eyes were shiny with unshed tears, but her voice was steady as she said, 'When do you intend to go?'

'Tomorrow morning early.'

Bridgette gave a small gasp. 'So soon?'

'There is surely no point in putting off the inevitable.'

'I suppose not,' Bridgette conceded. 'This then will be our last night together.'

'Till we meet again at the other side of this damned war.'

Bridgette said nothing. She knew when James walked out of her life the following day she would never see him again. Maybe he felt the same because that last night their passion rose higher and higher, until Bridgette was breathless with longing. And this time, when Bridgette threw the covers back, James didn't hesitate, and he slipped in beside her. Bridgette had not lain with a man since Xavier had walked away to war and yet she knew that she was more than ready.

But James seemed in no hurry as he stroked, caressed and kissed her to bring her to the peak of arousal. Then suddenly he broke off from a kiss that Bridgette was almost drowning in.

'What is it?' Bridgette cried. 'You cannot stop now. You leave tomorrow and this is perhaps all that either of us will ever have, one night together. You cannot deny me that, James.'

No, he couldn't. He was so aroused himself that he ached with longing for Bridgette, who lay so sensuously on the bed with her lips slightly open and her body so ripe and ready that she trembled all over. He couldn't wait any longer and with a sigh he entered Bridgette and heard her groan in pleasure and satisfaction.

*   *   *

She had half expected to feel ashamed of herself the next day, but she didn't. She woke very early, still enfolded in her lover's arms. She tried to ease herself gently from his embrace to lean across him to turn off the alarm but as she did so, suddenly James's eyes opened, his arms tightened around her and he nuzzied at her neck, saying as he did so, 'Don't get up yet.'

'I must, James,' Bridgette said firmly. 'Anyway, won't Charles be waiting for you?'

James sighed as he checked the time. 'Yes,' he said resignedly as he swung his legs out of bed and began to dress. 'I'd best get packed up and ready to go.'

'Take those spare clothes I washed for you,' Bridgette said. 'You don't know how long it will be until you reach the British Forces. I have some bread for you already wrapped in muslin. There is nothing else now the parcels of food from the German officers have stopped.'

'I wouldn't take it off you anyway,' James said. 'I'm just grateful for the bread. D'you think that Gabrielle will be awake yet? I would like to say goodbye before I leave.'

'Probably. She sleeps fitfully at the moment,' Bridgette said. 'I'll check she is all right and that the coast is clear, and you can bid her farewell while the other two are eating breakfast, such as it is.'

Gabrielle was awake and James sat carefully on her bed and told her he was leaving that morning.

'I will miss you,' she said. 'But that is nothing to the way that Bridgette will feel. I remember feeling such helplessness when Finn marched away.'

'Finn? Was that the name of Bridgette's father?'

Gabrielle nodded. 'He was so young, and so full of life, – as they all were, of course. War to end all wars, that was supposed to be, so when Bridgette married Xavier I thought the future was set for the pair of them. I never dreamed that another war would take him away. But it did. She suffered that anguish once and now she must go through it again. I wish I could spare her that.'

James shook his head. 'There is nothing you can do about that, but one thing you can and must do is tell her about her real father before it is too late.'

'You are right, James,' Gabrielle said. 'She has a right to know and I promise you that I will do that as soon as you are gone.'

With the imminent departure of James, and her mother getting worse daily, Bridgette was in no mood for truculent Georges, who moved the bread disparagingly around his plate as he and his father sat at the table later.

'What's this?'

'I think it's quite apparent what it is,' Bridgette said. 'Most people call it bread.'

'Is that all we're having?'

'That's all there was in the cupboard,' Bridgette said. 'And I was given no money to buy anything else.'

She was suddenly irritated, because most of France had got used to going without sometimes even basic necessities. Her father and Georges, however, had never had to stint themselves until now, and they didn't like it.

'What do you want me to do?' she snapped. 'Magic food to put on the table?' She turned to look straight at her father and said, 'Give me a decent amount of money today and I will see what I can find.'

'I'm not made of money, you know,' Legrand growled. 'You said yourself the shop isn't doing so well these days.'

And set to do worse, Bridgette might have said, and yet you still have money for drink each night. She didn't say this however, because she didn't want to start an argument. She wanted them both out of the way as quickly as possible, so that she could say a proper farewell to James. So instead she said emphatically, 'Then you'll have to make do with bread, like most people in France have been doing for over four years.'

It was hard to linger too long over a cup of coffee and dry bread, and soon Legrand returned to the bakery and Georges to open the shop a little later. Bridgette took James into her room, where she shut the door firmly and shot the bolt before going onto his open arms with a sigh of contentment.

'I will get word to you as soon as I can,' James promised after kissing her long and hard.

'I know.'

'And you must contact your aunt now.'

'It's too late,' Bridgette said. 'The BBC say that the Free French and the Americans are advancing on Paris.'

'She still needs to know how ill Gabrielle is,' James insisted. 'You can't leave it until she is no more to tell her.'

Bridgette knew she couldn't, but she knew how upset and shocked her aunt would be, because in her letters she had given no indication that her mother was so ill in case her aunt should take it into her head and come to see for herself.

'I will send a telegram,' Bridgette promised James. 'But I will say that I fully understand if she is unable to come.'

'If things had gone to plan, Yvette could have come sooner,' James said.

'And I might never have realised that I love you,' Bridgette said. 'Whatever happens to us in the future, I couldn't ever regret that.'

'Nor I,' said James. 'Though I wish that we had met in peacetime.'

'We probably never would have met at all in peacetime.'

'That's true,' James said. 'And people have to deal with circumstances they have no control over the best way they can.'

'Yes,' Bridgette said sadly. 'And I know you must go. Charles will be waiting. Will you kiss me once more?'

'Gladly, my darling,' James said, and he gathered her into his arms.

She kissed him with all the passion in her, for she knew it would have to last her a long, long time, possibly her lifetime. She wasn't at all sure that she wasn't kissing James goodbye for ever.

TWENTY-ONE

Bridget sent the telegram to her aunt as she had promised James she would. When she returned Gabrielle said, 'Well, at least she knows now, even if she can't get to see me. It would be madness to put her life in danger for a woman who is dying anyway. And now sit down, my dear child, for I have something to tell you.'

'Are you not tired, Maman?' Bridgette asked, sitting on the chair beside the bed.

'A little,' Gabrielle admitted. 'But soon I shall have all the rest I need and meanwhile there are things I should have told you years ago, but Robert forbade me to, and in those days I did what he said.'

'I know you did, and with reason,' Bridgette said.

'In this I should have defied him,' Gabrielle maintained. 'You needed to know that he is not your father.'

Bridgette jumped on the bed. 'What did you say?'

Gabrielle smiled gently, 'You heard me the first time. Robert Legrand is not your father. You have none of that man's blood running through your veins.'

'Oh, thank God,' Bridgette said fervently. 'Thank God.' She turned to her mother, her eyes shining. 'You couldn't have told me anything that would please me more. But who is my real father?'

In answer, Gabrielle said, 'Bridgette, will you go across to my wardrobe? It has an artificial floor and under it you will see a box. Can you lift it up and bring it to me?'

Bridgette had not known of the wardrobe's artificial floor, or the box beneath it, and so she was greatly intrigued.

'Your father was an Irishman called Finn Sullivan, a soldier in the British Army,' Gabrielle told her, when she had the box beside her. 'He was killed on the first day of the Battle of the Somme in 1916.'

'So I am illegitimate?'

'No, you're not,' Gabrielle said. 'Finn and I were married at the camp. They were moving out when it was discovered I was expecting you.' She rooted around in the box and handed Bridgette a ring. 'That is the ring my mother gave me to use as a wedding ring until we could get a proper one. It's yours now. And here is something else that you can have, my only present from Finn,' and she gave Bridgette a package.

Inside it, wrapped in tissue paper, was a silver

locket with a curl of hair inside, and the locket was inscribed: 'F loves G, Christmas 1915'.

'Maman, it's beautiful,' Bridgette said.

'Yes,' Gabrielle sighed wistfully. 'I promised him that I would wear it always near my heart and I did until I married Robert. Then I hid it away. That false floor in the wardrobe, which my mother showed me when I was a girl, was very useful to hide things from Robert. These, for example,' and she withdrew a bundle of letters tied with a pink ribbon. 'This is every letter Finn sent me. When you read them you will see the type of man he was. I loved him so very much and that is why just the once we forgot ourselves. You're not ashamed of me for that, are you?'

Bridgette thought of the rapturous sex she had enjoyed with James just the night before and she said, 'Of course I'm not. I know only too well how feelings can overcome two people who love each other so much. One thing puzzles me, though.'

'What's that?'

'You said you married my father,' Bridgette said. 'And that he was an Irishman. Has he any family and, if so, why have they never written to us?'

'To explain that you had better read these,' Gabrielle said. She handed Bridgette the two letters she had received from Christy, and Bridgette scanned them both quickly. 'Christy was Finn's best friend,' Gabrielle explained. 'And he lost a leg in the same place and on the same day that Finn was killed. He was ill and wasn't able to contact me straightaway. Until I got Christy's first letter, I had no idea whether Finn was dead or alive. His family were informed of his death, as next of kin. News of our marriage obviously hadn't reached the army records.'

'I can quite see how it might be like that in a war situation,' Bridgette said.

'So can I,' Gabrielle agreed. 'At the time, though, I was distraught. In fact, the news of Finn's death caused me to go into labour. But I loved you so much from the first moment I saw you, and the more because you were a part of Finn, the only part that I would ever have. Having you to care for helped me bear his loss.'

'I know that feeling so well,' Bridgette said. 'Even now I regret that I lost Xavier's baby. But, according to the other letter from this Christy, my father was under age to marry you and so his date of birth on the marriage lines is false.'

'Yes.' Gabrielle said. 'Neither of us knew if that made the marriage legal or not.'

'I don't know either,' Bridgette admitted. 'It's not something I have ever thought about, but I can quite see why neither of you said anything, particularly as you were living with Grandfather Jobert at the time.'

Gabrielle nodded. 'We dared not contact the people in Ireland either,' she continued. 'There was a war on at the time, anyway, but even afterwards.' She looked at Bridgette. 'The false entry on the marriage certificate was done for my sake, to give me the respectability of marriage. If that false entry made the marriage null and void and any got to know about it, can you imagine how hard our lives would have been, Bridgette? And I am not trying to pretend that, as it was, we had a bed of roses, anyway.'

Bridgette nodded. 'I would have been known as a bastard all through my growing up, and you a fallen woman. I fully understand the secrecy.'

'Robert Legrand might not have been so keen to marry me either,' Gabrielle said. 'Mind you, that would be no bad thing.'

'Why did you marry him?' Bridgette asked. 'I often wondered, even when I thought he was my father.'

'Your grandfather forced me into it,' Gabrielle said. 'He said that if I didn't marry Robert he would put us both on the street. I had you to care for, and no money, and so I had no alternative.'

'That's despicable,' Bridgette said, 'Why didn't my grandfather like me?

Gabrielle didn't insult Bridgette's intelligence by claiming he did. She deserved total honesty. 'I think it was because I had brought shame on the house and you were the evidence of that, though you might have had an easier time if you had been a boy. He craved sons and had none and so he was relying on grandsons.'

'And that's why he disinherited me in the will,' Bridgette said. 'I think he was a nasty piece of work. I don't want to think or talk about him any more. Will you tell me all you know about my real father instead?'

'I will gladly,' Gabrielle said. And she told Bridgette all she knew about Finn's birth on a farm in Ireland and his family. However, when she heard about his eldest sister, Aggie, who had disappeared when he had been a small boy and she just fifteen years old Bridgette was as affected as Gabrielle had been when she had first heard it.

'Did they never find out what had happened to her?'

'No. It was if she had disappeared into thin air, Finn said. He said he was very upset at the time, because she was ten when he had been born and she had been like a mother to him.'

She looked at Bridgette levelly then, before saying, 'After I am gone, maybe you could see them for yourself. They are your family. My father kept my marriage lines, but when he died I went through his papers and retrieved that and your birth certificate. They are both in the box and I shouldn't think that a false entry on my marriage certificate matters after all this time.'

Bridgette shook her head. 'These people are strangers to me, Maman,' she said. 'It was you who should have sought them out.'

'It wasn't possible for me' Gabrielle said. 'But my time here is nearly done. Hopefully I'll go to a better place, but it's you that I worry about. I don't want you alone.'

'What if James comes back?'

Gabrielle was silent for a minute and then she said quietly, 'Don't be cross with me, Bridgette. I truly have no wish to hurt you, and I'm sure James meant every word he said at the time, but if he survives the war there might be a hundred and one reasons why he cannot return for you.'

Bridgette couldn't be cross with her mother because she had thought the very same thing, so what she did say was, 'You needn't worry about me, you know. I am a big girl now and don't need looking after. Please tell me where you met my father.'

'I met him here in the town,' Gabrielle said. 'He was batman to one of the officers in the British Headquarters and that officer had a fancy for my father's bread and cakes and he used to send Finn for them. From the moment I first saw him there was some sort of pull between us.'

'Ah, Maman! It's so romantic.'

Gabrielle smiled wistfully. 'I thought so too.' She went on to tell Bridgette of their walks in the park on Sunday afternoons, which had to be curtailed when the weather grew colder. And how Finn had eventually found the deserted farmhouse and the way she would climb down the tree outside her bedroom window into Finn's waiting arms.

Bridgette's eyes opened wider as she said, 'There is no tree outside that room, there's just a stump in the yard.'

'My father had it cut down when he found out

how I had been sneaking out of the house,' Gabrielle said. 'And had those bars fitted to the windows.'

'I often wondered about those,' Bridgette said. 'Oh, Maman, thank you for telling me all this, but do you want to stop now? I don't want to tire you out.'

'It's pleasant remembering,' Gabrielle said, lying back on the pillows. She told Bridgette of her courtship and Bridgette watched her dreamy eyes, which still had the love light shining in them as she recalled her precious time with Finn. She knew her mother had loved Finn Sullivan deeply and as she prepared her for bed a little later she felt sadness that her life had been so harsh.

Early the next day, before the shop was open, there was a knock on the door and, on opening it, Bridgette found a telegraph boy outside. With her heart in her mouth she ripped open the telegram with fingers that trembled.

And then her face was flushed with joy. 'No answer,' she said to the boy, who stood waiting, and she shut the door on him. Ignoring the men in the bakery, she ran straight up to her mother.

'Aunt Yvette is coming this afternoon,' she cried. 'Uncle Henri is driving down.'

'Why?'

'It's only a telegram,' Bridgette said. 'There are no details. I'm sure she will tell us all when she gets here, but isn't it wonderful news?'

'It is, Bridgette,' Gabrielle said. 'It's better than I ever dreamed of.'

'I had better go and warn that man and his snivelling son that we are expecting visitors,' Bridgette said, and added sarcastically, 'that will brighten his day for him.'

Gabrielle gave a wry laugh. 'Yes, I'm sure it will.'

Since her mother had told her that Legrand wasn't her father, Bridgette had wanted to fling that knowledge into his face, but she knew how vindictive and nasty he could become, and Gabrielle's health was too precarious to risk any sort of upset.

In the meantime, she begrudged anything she did for either of them. Ask as she might, she couldn't get money from Legrand for food and, anxious for her mother, she had been drawing from her savings each week so that she could buy something wholesome. She resented every morsel of food that Legrand and Georges put in their mouths, and she knew that if she hadn't her mother to consider, she would have let them go hungry.

She set out after dinner that warm sunny day to buy something decent to make a meal for her uncle and aunt. However, she hadn't gone far when she came upon a cluster of people speaking agitatedly.

'What is it?' she asked

A man turned to her and said, 'A man's body found in Eperlecques Forest.'

Bridgette's heart was pounding as she repeated, 'A man's body?'

'Yes,' the man replied. 'An ambulance has been summoned to bring him in.'

'So he isn't dead then?' Bridgette said, hope rising in her.

'The man who found him couldn't be sure,' another told her.

'Was there only the one body?'

'As far as I know,' the first man said and added, 'Isn't one enough for you?' A woman beside her remarked, 'Are you all right, my dear? You've suddenly gone as white as a sheet.'

Despite the fact that she knew her aunt and uncle would probably be at home and waiting for her, Bridgette couldn't move until the ambulance returned. There was another man in the ambulance whom Bridgette recognised from her Resistance days. It was he who told her that it had been Charles's body they had brought back, that he had been killed by Nazi snipers in the wood.

'I thought he was dead from the first, when we came upon him, though in the dimness I couldn't be absolutely sure,' the man told Bridgette. 'Gaston went off to summon an ambulance and then I tracked down those murdering German bastards and dealt with them.'

'But there was only one body?'

'Only one body we found,' the man corrected. 'Was there someone with him?'

Bridgette nodded and because there was no

longer any point in secrecy she said, 'He was the secret agent dropped some time ago that I had been hiding. He was trying to reach British Lines. Charles said he would take him through the forest, that he knew the safer routes.'

The man nodded. 'Le Blockhaus has been virtually abandoned and most prisoners that survived transported back to Germany. Charles was probably trying to take the man through parts of the forest that have been fairly quiet of late. There is always a danger, though, that you will be spotted by a group of Germans patrolling the woods, like those today. The man you spoke of is probably already dead.'

'There is no possibility that he could have made it?' Bridgette asked desperately.

The man shook his head. 'Not a chance. For one thing, the woods are swarming with German soldiers just now, alerted by gunfire, I suppose, and if he is there they would be sure to find him. But even if he survived that, he'd never get through the forest on his own. The fact that we didn't come upon his body signifies nothing. It was dense woodland where we found Charles and we didn't know that there had been anyone with him, so we didn't look for anyone else. There had certainly been plenty of shots fired, and there are lots of places in those woods for a body to lie undiscovered. I'm afraid the agent's body is probably still lying there. And now I must go and see Charles's family and tell them the news.'

Devastated, Bridgette watched him go, his shoulders hunched as if to protect himself from the words he had to say, and she felt her heart plummet. The man she loved, whom she had given her heart to, was no more, though his body hadn't been recovered and might never be. She felt despair flow all through her.

Though she was saddened at the loss of Charles, who had worked so hard to impede and harass the Germans at every opportunity, James's death filled her with anguish too deep to even cry out against, though she gasped aloud. People turned to look at her, but they were blurred and fuzzy and seemed a long way off and, though she could see their lips forming words, she couldn't hear what they said. There was a roaring in her ears and she saw the pavement coming up to meet her, seconds before blackness settled all around her as she fell to the ground.

When Bridgette came to, she was lying in her own bed. Sitting beside her on a chair was her Aunt Yvette. 'What happened?' she said, but even as she spoke the words she knew what had happened and the realisation that she would never ever see James Carmichael again swept over her.

Yvette told her that their car had been brought to a halt by a crowd of people thronging the pavement and the street. 'We got out to see what had caused the commotion,' she said, 'and what a shock we both got to see you lying there in a heap on the ground. The people told us a doctor had been summoned, and Henri told them to direct him to the bakery. He scooped you up, put you in the back seat of the car and brought you home.'

'And has the doctor been?'

'Yes,' Yvette said. 'He could shed no light on why you had fainted. He did say that you were very thin, but he said lots in the town are suffering from malnutrition at the moment.'

In fact, Yvette had been in the room while the doctor examined Bridgette, as Gabrielle had expressly asked her to be, and she had been totally stunned by Bridgette's appearance. She was more than thin, her ribs stuck right out, the skin stretched tight across them, her shoulder blades were scrawny and her arms and legs positively skinny. Yvette had lost weight herself, most people in France had, but she looked nothing like as thin as Bridgette.

Yvette had thought she had looked a fright because, with the Parisian costume houses closed or converted to making military uniforms, and rationing and restrictions on clothes, style had to go out of the window. The lemon summer suit she wore was more than three years old but it was well cut, and though her legs were bare when once she would have worn fine silk stockings, her sandals showed off her slender feet. She'd had her old navy-blue hat revamped and adorned with a few feathers.

To Bridgette, though, she looked magnificent and

she said so. Her own dresses were threadbare and bedraggled, and had had the goodness and colour washed out of them, and her shoes were worn down nearly to the uppers.

'Oh, this is just some old thing,' Yvette said. 'Most of my things are old now. You can get nothing decent at all, even in Paris, these days. But never mind about that. You are far too thin, Bridgette, and need a bit of feeding up, I feel. Was it just hunger that made you faint? The doctor said it could have been caused by some sort of shock.'

'The doctor was right. I have had a shock,' Bridgette said, drawing back the bedcovers. 'But I must see if Maman is all right.'

'She's fine,' Yvette said pushing her niece back on the bed. 'Except that she is terribly worried about you. Henri is sitting with her now.'

'Henri?'

'Yes, and don't look so surprised,' Yvette said. 'He is very good at things like this and if he can't cope he'll call us. What's upsetting your mother at the moment is your collapse and the reason for it.'

'As I said, I had a shock,' Bridgette said.

'D'you want to tell me about it?' Yvette asked gently.

'I may as well.' Bridgette said. 'I don't suppose it matters now.'

She told her aunt first about joining the Resistance after Xavier's death. She thought Yvette might be shocked at that but she wasn't.

'How could I be?' Yvette said when Bridgette queried this. 'My boys did the same thing. Not at first, though Henri and I both knew that they were restless on the farm. We had thought to protect them, but there was nowhere in France to ensure their safety. One day, the soldiers came to the farm to round up the men for the labour camps in Germany. Raoul and Gerard had been given jobs around the farmhouse that day and they hid in the hayloft until the soldiers left, taking with them Henri's cousin's husband and two sons. We went on a visit when we hadn't heard from the boys for some time and were told they had packed their bags the very next day and set off to find what they termed the Freedom Fighters.'

'I'm sorry. You must be worried.'

'Every day,' Yvette said. 'Liberation cannot come too soon for me, but now you go on with your story.'

And so Bridgette told her aunt about her time in the Resistance, right up the point when she hid the secret agent, James Carmichael. She even told her that their fondness for each other had grown into love. In fact she explained everything, except the details of their last night.

'And then today,' she said, 'I heard something that I hoped never to hear. She told her aunt what had transpired, not even aware when she began to cry.

Yvette felt her own eyes prickling at the wretchedness in Bridgette's face as she said, 'I feel as if I am some sort of jinx. I have loved two men in my life, Xavier Laurent and then James Carmichael, and now both of them are dead and gone.'

'Oh my love,' Yvette cried as she held her niece close. 'That isn't anything to do with you. It's this dreadful war.'

'Well, I'll not risk it again,' Bridgette said fiercely. 'This heartbreak isn't worth it.'

The following day, once Bridgette was properly on her feet again, she asked why Henri had driven from Paris in the black Citroën he had parked outside the bakery.

'Well, the trains are not the safest route in or out of Paris at the moment,' Yvette said. 'The FFI keep blowing up the lines. It's done to harass the Germans, but of course it affects everybody else as well.'

'Who are the FFI?'

'Resistance groups from in and around Paris under the one banner "*Forces Françaises de l'Intérieur*"', Henri told her. 'They are said to be more effective joined together in one mass.'

'I can see that,' Bridgette said. 'And to be honest I have done my share of blowing up railway lines, but isn't petrol for cars hard to get hold of?'

'Dreadfully hard,' Henri said. 'Though if you have the money, they sell it on the black market.'

'Is that where you bought the petrol to get here?'

'In Paris I didn't have to,' Henri said. 'I have

425

contacts. But how we will get home is another matter. And,' he added, 'not one that you have to fret about. I think you have got more than enough to worry over as it is.'

Henri was right because although the arrival of her sister had perked Gabrielle up initially, it was a false high that exhausted her and she went steadily downhill from that moment.

'Does Robert not come in to see her?' Henri asked. 'He seemed not the least concerned when I told him how her condition had worsened.'

'You shouldn't be surprised,' Bridgette commented wryly. 'There are only two people that Robert Legrand cares about. One is himself and the other his son. He seldom looks in on Maman and he never comes into the room. He is afraid to.'

'Are you not afraid?'

'I take basic precautions,' Bridgette said. 'I keep her towels and flannels and plates and cups separate, but I don't think about the risk. Maman needed care and I promised to provide it.'

'Well, while we are here we shall help you,' Henri said. 'And there is no more dipping into your savings. Any food needed I will buy.'

Bridgette felt the weight eased from between her shoulder blades and she was glad to leave that problem in Henri's capable hands.

Yvette and Henri had been at the bakery two weeks by the beginning of August, when Gabrielle had been given the Last Rites.

The next day cheering could be heard in the distance. They were all in the bedroom and Henri crossed to the window and looked out to see people running down the street.

'I think the Allies are here at last,' he said.

Gabrielle opened her weary eyes, her lips twisted into a smile, and she said in the husky whisper she had developed, 'Good news!'

'The best news in the world,' Henri said, and Bridgette could have echoed that sentiment. In the streets below it was like carnival time. The smiling, marching American soldiers were welcomed and encouraged by the waving, cheering crowds. The noise was almost deafening, and Bridgette saw women lifting their babies to see those who had set them free from Germanic tyranny and children dodging about for the sweets some of the soldiers threw.

Gabrielle began to cough and Bridgette turned from the window and lifted her quickly in case she choked. Suddenly blood spurted from her mouth in a scarlet stream. Bridgette had a sense somehow that this was the end.

'Fetch the doctor,' she called to Henri, though she knew in her heart of hearts that the doctor could do nothing now.

Yvette swallowed her distaste and helped her hold Gabrielle up in the bed to prevent her choking to death on the blood that was still pumping from her.

'And you'd better tell Legrand as you pass,' Bridgette added. Henri nodded as he went out.

By the time the doctor came, the haemorrhage was over, the soiled bedding had been removed, and Gabrielle lay propped up on fresh pillows, every breath coming like a tortured gasp in her throat. Bridgette left the doctor examining her mother and crossed to the window to join Henri and Yvette, not wanting to be anywhere near Legrand, who had taken his usual stance in the doorway.

As the doctor finished, Bridgette turned from the joyful gaiety on the streets and she didn't need to see the doctor's grave voice or hear his words. She took her place by her mother's side and lifted up her blue-veined hand, knowing that it was the last thing she would ever do for her.

Suddenly Gabrielle opened her eyes. Bridgette saw that they were glazed with pain, and she felt her stomach contract in sympathy for her mother's suffering. 'Lie easy, Maman,' she said.

Gabrielle was agitated, as if she had something to say, and Bridgette leaned forward because she could hardly hear the words: 'Go and find your father's family.'

Bridgette, thinking it would ease her, said, 'I will, Maman.'

Gabrielle's hand tightened slightly in Bridgette's as she said, 'Promise me, Bridgette.'

Bridgette didn't want to promise, but how could she deny her mother anything when she was so close to death? She had thought she had prepared herself for this moment when they would say goodbye. She had known from the first she wouldn't recover, but she found at the point of death none of that helped. 'I promise, Maman,' she said.

She heard Gabrielle's sigh of relief, and then she suddenly went limp. The rasping breathing was stopped and the room was suddenly incredibly still.

The doctor moved to the other side of the bed and said gently, 'She's gone, Bridgette.'

'I know,' Bridgette said and she laid her mother's hand across her chest and got to her feet.

'What did she want?' Yvette said, for none had been able to hear the whispered conversation between Bridgette and her mother.

'Nothing of any consequence,' Bridgette said.

Afterwards, she knew why she hadn't told her aunt the truth, and that was because she didn't know what she was going to do about the deathbed promise she had given to her mother. It was a promise that she definitely didn't want to keep.

TWENTY-TWO

Yvette and Henri assumed that Bridgette would return with them to live in Paris permanently after the funeral, but when they first mentioned it she wasn't sure she wanted to go. The Laurents were good dear friends, and her mother would also be buried here. She had lived in St-Omer all her life and knew most of the town through serving in the bakery and later in the ladies' outfitters, and also attending Mass. She knew not a soul in Paris apart from Yvette and Henri, and because Legrand had cut off all contact she didn't really know them that well.

And yet once Yvette and Henri returned, what would happen to her if she stayed? Legrand would not let her stay in the bakery and, indeed, she didn't want to stay with him and Georges neither of whom could she trust one inch. So she would have to find somewhere to live and some way of supporting herself.

She wished she didn't have to make a decision

so quickly, although she knew that Henri had a business to attend to, but she was so saddened she felt hollow and empty inside. Yvette understood this; she was missing her sister dreadfully, for all they seldom saw each other.

'When you lose someone – or in your case two people – who were dear to you,' she said gently, 'it's comforting to cling to the familiar, but I can see no future for you here. Come back with Henri and me, at least for a while, to get stronger emotionally, take stock and decide what you want to do with your life. You have looked after your mother so well, you must feel drained of all strength. Let us look after you for a change.'

Yvette's words were like balm on Bridgette's broken and bruised heart, and the thought of someone looking after her for a time was comforting. It needn't be for ever, but for now she sensed that it was the wisest decision and she nodded.

'You are as lovely and kind as I always remember you,' she told her aunt in a voice husky with unshed tears, 'and I will return with you to Paris.'

Yvette breathed a sigh of relief. She knew that Henri would feel the same because they had worried about leaving Bridgette behind in St-Omer when they went back to Paris.

Gabrielle's funeral, on a beautiful morning three days later, was well attended, but Bridgette couldn't help feeling that it might have been better if just some of the people thronging the church had come to spend a little time with her mother before she died. She was so sorrow-laden she barely noticed Madame Pretin and her cronies gathered around her, all glaring.

Yvette noticed, though, and was determined to ask her niece about it at the first opportunity, but she would have to tread carefully for they had already had a difference of opinion about the mourners to be asked back to the house. Bridgette refused to invite any but the Laurents.

'But they will expect—'

'Well then, they will be disappointed,' Bridgette snapped back. 'How many times do you think Maman was disappointed that no neighbour but Marie and Lisette came to visit?'

'TB is a frightening illness.'

'Fear of that, or anything else, would not keep me from the bedside of a sick friend,' Bridgette said fiercely. 'They're not coming and that's that.'

'It isn't worth upsetting Bridgette over this,' Henri told Yvette. 'I mean,' he added, as Yvette continued to chew her bottom lip in an agitated manner, 'she hasn't even got to live with these people afterwards now she has decided to go travel to Paris with us when we leave.'

And so it was a sad little party that gathered in the living room of the bakery later. Bridgette's sorrowful mood affected the whole atmosphere. Legrand and Georges were worse than useless and kept complaining at the scarcity of drink offered, and Yvette herself was filled with melancholy and already missing her sister.

Marie, Maurice and Lisette didn't stay very long, and barely had the door closed on them when Bridgette turned to Legrand and said, 'I heard you complain about the lack of drink more than once, but I didn't see you put your hand in your pocket at all. If it hadn't been for Henri's generosity it would have been a poor send-off for Maman.'

'I haven't any money,' Legrand said. 'You know how we are placed.'

'Yes, I know,' Bridgette sneered. 'I also know why. You are not the only baker in town, but if you were, there are plenty who would walk to the next, rather than buy bread from you.'

Bridgette was right, and Legrand knew it. There were few people seemingly wanting his bread and cakes now. He and Georges were increasingly not made welcome in the bars in the town either. That maddened him because, before liberation, they had been more than willing to take his money off him. However, he wasn't going to admit that.

'You should keep a civil tongue in your head and show me some respect,' he said.

'How could I respect a Nazi lover?' Bridgette spat out. 'Anyway, you have no jurisdiction over me because you are not my real father. And Maman made me one of the happiest people in the world when she gave me that news because I have none of your blood running through my veins.'

'Why you . . .'

Legrand made a lunge towards Bridgette, his arm raised, but Henri stepped between the two of them, his eyes flashing with temper. 'I shouldn't do that if I were you,' he said, and though he spoke calmly enough, his words were like steel.

Henri was a well-set-up man, while much of Legrand's bulk had run to fat. He also spoke with an air of authority.

Legrand lowered his arm and growled, 'I'm going out. Coming, Georges?'

When the door closed behind Legrand and his son, Yvette squeezed Bridgette's hand and said, 'I'm glad that Gabrielle told you about your father at last. I wanted to tell you years ago.'

'She was too afraid of Legrand to go against anything he said,' Bridgette said. 'She explained all that. It was better than Christmas, though, when she told me that I was not related to him.'

'Was it right what you said about him?' Henri asked Bridgette. 'Was he a Nazi sympathiser?'

'He was worse than that,' Bridgette said. 'He also informed against his own people. And Georges was just as bad. The Resistance knew all about them.'

'And those women today in the church, who looked as though they hated you – where do they come in?'

'You noticed too?' Yvette said.

'Oh yes,' said Henri, 'I noticed. Well, Bridgette?'

Bridgette sighed and said, 'It was because Legrand was so well in with the Germans that I

434

was asked to hide the British agent. They thought it unlikely that this house would be searched although the storm troopers were searching every other house. It was noted, of course, that ours wasn't, and the following Sunday, Madame Pretin was waiting for me before Mass, together with her cronies, who are nearly as bad as she is, and she said that our house hadn't been searched because I had been doing favours for the Germans. God,' she said, and gave a shiver, 'I would rather have dealings with a sabre-toothed tiger than have any sort of a relationship with a German. Some believed it too – I could see in their eyes – but I couldn't tell them the truth, so I stopped going to church, using Maman's illness as an excuse. I suppose I thought that they'd get over it.'

'Madame Pretin never gets over anything,' Yvette said. 'I remember her well. I pointed her out to you, Henri.'

'Yes, and I have met her sort before,' Henri said grimly. He turned to Bridgette. 'Is there any who could verify your time in the Resistance?'

'Not now,' Bridgette said sadly. 'You see, because of security you only deal with one, or perhaps two people. I knew only one man, Charles, whose body was found in the wood the day you arrived. That might not even be his real name.'

'Then, my dear Bridgette,' Henri said gravely, 'I fear your life is in great danger and the sooner we leave here and go back to Paris, the better I will like it.'

Bridgette stared at him. 'What on earth are you talking about?'

'Listen to me,' Henri said earnestly. 'Most of the Allies have moved on now, and the euphoria that this town is free again is dying down. Shortly this will turn to anger and they will be looking to blame and punish those who were friends in one way and another to the Germans.'

'But I wasn't, I didn't,' Bridgette protested.

'Can you prove that?'

'Well, no, but—'

'Bridgette, those women staring at you today in the church mean business; they mean to harm you,' Henri said. 'You could almost feel their malevolence against you.'

'Don't you think that you are being a little dramatic?'

Henri shrugged. 'Maybe I am,' he said. 'But you haven't been out in the streets just lately as I have, sorting out the shopping for us all, and over the last few days the mood amongst the people has changed. You can almost feel it, and now they seem set on revenge against those they will see as the traitors of France.'

'I am no traitor.'

'That might not be the way that they look at it,' Henri said. 'You lived in the same house as two known informers. That alone might taint you.'

'But it's so silly.'

'It's not silly, Bridgette,' Henri said. 'It's frightening. People like that woman that we saw today

436

in church thrive on inciting others. Never under-estimate people like that. Up until now, you had been protected a little by the fact that your mother was so ill, but today we buried her and so any protection you had is now gone.'

'I can scarcely credit this,' Bridgette said, shaking her head. But she knew that Henri, never given to flights of fancy, was really concerned. 'All right,' she said. 'What d'you want me to do?'

Bridgette could see Henri gave a sigh of relief. 'Pack up all your clothes,' he said, 'and anything else you want to take with you. I want to leave tomorrow and as early as possible.'

'So soon?'

'The earlier the better. I am off now to beg, borrow or steal enough petrol to get us back to Paris.'

When he had had gone, Bridgette said to Yvette, 'Henri is not one to dither, is he? He makes a decision and that's it.'

'Yes,' Yvette said. 'But he usually is right about these things, and you were coming back with us anyway. You're just making the journey a little earlier than expected.'

'Mmm, I suppose,' said Bridgette. 'And I had better start packing up my things because I want to pop along and see the Laurents before I leave. They have been good friends of mine and I know that I will miss them sorely.'

Marie and Lisette commiserated with Bridgette over the loss of her mother. She had never really

437

had the chance before to tell them about James, but she told them that night and they were all full of sympathy and support. They were very upset too when Bridgette told them that she was leaving early the next morning, but even more concerned when she said why Henri thought the haste so necessary.

'Couldn't we verify the fact that you were a member of the Resistance?' Lisette said. 'I mean, we all knew. Papa even made you a special beret.'

'You might not be believed,' Bridgette said. 'They know what friends we all were and, as well as that, I was married to Xavier so part of the family. If they didn't believe what you said then you could become targets as well.' She shook her head, 'I couldn't take that risk, and it might even affect the children,'

'Do you think so?'

'I don't know,' Bridgette said. 'I can't be sure of anything. It's just that Henri seems to think that vindictive people are dangerous and Madame Pretin is about as vindictive as it is possible to be.'

'Well, I agree with him there at any rate,' Lisette said. 'She's a horrible person.

'And if you speak for me, you will have to live in the town afterwards and cope with Madame Pretin and her ilk. I am leaving, getting away.'

'But you wouldn't have to go if we told people how it really was. That's what we're saying,' Marie said.

'But Henri seems to think that I might be in

danger in any case because I am related, or at least they assume I am related, to Legrand, and living in the same house as a known collaborator is not a healthy thing to do. It is really better that I go away for a while and that you don't get involved.'

'It's just so sad when you've done nothing wrong at all,' Lisette said. 'We will all miss you so much.'

'I will miss you too,' Bridgette said. 'But it may not be for ever.'

'The children will be sorry that they were asleep and weren't able to see you to say their goodbyes,' Marie said.

Bridgette was sorry not to see the children too. She hadn't seen them for weeks because of her mother's illness, and when she stopped going to Mass on Sundays she didn't see them there either. 'Just give them my love in the morning,' she told Lisette.

'They will probably be much changed the next time that you see them,' Lisette said. 'And there must be a next time. You must come back and see us when everything has calmed down and the world is a more stable place.' And then she added plaintively, 'This can't be the end of everything.'

'Of course it can't,' Bridgette cried. 'I will certainly come back.'

When she bid her dear friends goodbye, they were all crying – even Maurice's eyes were glistening – and Bridgette had to compose herself and wipe her eyes before she went into the bakery.

*   *   *

The next morning she left the bakery with very mixed emotions. Legrand and Georges were still in bed. In the general way of things they would usually be up by then, but Legrand had said that he was closing the shop for three days as a mark of respect for Gabrielle.

Bridgette had snorted in disbelief when Henri told her that.

'He never showed my mother an ounce of respect when she was alive,' she said. 'And after the way he behaved at her funeral I cannot see that changing now she is dead. The real reason they will not be opening the shop is because he has such few customers now it's hardly worth starting the ovens up.'

'Have you left him a note to say where you have gone?' Yvette asked.

Bridgette shook her head. 'He'll know. Come on, Auntie, Henri is getting impatient.'

'You ready then?'

'Absolutely,' Bridgette said. 'My life has been packed neatly into two suitcases.'

'Ah, but a new life is just beginning,' Yvette said.

'You're right,' said Bridgette, and she left her home without a backward glance, closing the door behind her with a definite thud. She climbed into the car beside Yvette and they drove through the mainly deserted streets of the town and started their journey to Paris through the pearly dawn of a summer's day.

*　　*　　*

Within a few days of arriving in her aunt's house, Bridgette knew that she could never settle in Paris. It was no longer the lively city that her aunt had described in her letters. It was a grey, grim place that Henri had to approach cautiously, trying to avoid the fighting that got ever closer as they drew nearer to the city. Burning oil drums at the city's edge sent a pall of grey smoke into the summer air, and the acrid stench of it reached them even in the car, lodging in their throats and making their eyes water.

As Henri edged his way down the back roads, the gaping holes, piles of masonry and white splashes on the buildings were evidence to the battering the city had endured. Stern, black-booted soldiers were everywhere, the hated swastikas daubed on every building and fluttered from every flagpole, and any Parisians she did spy scurried along the city's streets with head lowered, their clothes drab and almost shabby.

'It is what I said to you when we arrived at the bakery,' Yvette explained to Bridgette. 'Many of the fashion houses closed up when the Germans moved in, and those that stayed open had to convert to making military uniforms.' She shrugged. 'And there are so many restrictions too on clothes they do make. They are allowed only so much material for each garment and there are few adornments allowed, so they have no lace or fancy buttons or seed pearls, and they are rationed too, and you have to save your coupons to buy anything at all. It's especially hard for mothers with growing children to keep them decently clad, and that's why I sent that parcel of clothes to Lisette.'

'She was terribly grateful,' Bridgette said.

Yvette smiled. 'She wrote and told me. I was just glad to be able to help, and Jean-Paul sent me a delightful picture.'

'We didn't worry much about our own clothes.' Bridgette said. 'As you can see from what I wear, I've had nothing new for years and what I have is faded and washed out. But certainly fashion wasn't to the forefront of our minds. It was far more a battle to keep food on the table; it must have mattered far more to many Parisians, though. Everyone knows that Paris was a fashion leader and had some of the most prestigious fashion houses in the world.'

Yvette nodded. 'And, of course, the fashion industry did employ so many people.'

'Yes of course,' Bridgette said. 'I never thought of that. The people that we passed in the street look so dispirited somehow.'

'They are,' Yvette said. 'We all are. And even if we had the fancy clothes there are few places to wear them. Many theatres and concert halls have closed and there have been restrictions everywhere, on drama, music, books . . . Jazz music is banned totally. The Germans are a race of barbarians.'

'The war will soon be over, I think,' Henri said,

'and then things will be back to normal. This, I'm sure, is the beginning of the end.'

'Oh, I do hope so,' Bridgette said fervently. 'That's all anyone wants now.'

And she did wish that. Paris had suffered mightily, and yet she felt even should peace reign again the city could never be home to her. As each day passed the sadness inside her grew as she mourned not only the loss of her mother and her lover, but also the only home she had ever known in St-Omer.

And then a letter came from Marie Laurent that meant that St-Omer too was closed to her. She opened it eagerly but as she read it she gave a cry of alarm.

'What is it?' Yvette cried, seeing her niece drop the letter with a cry.

Bridgette turned stricken eyes to Yvette. 'It is good we got out when we did. The vigilantes came that very night and took Legrand and Georges away and the women searched the house for me. Marie wasn't even aware of it until later but people who were there said that they seemed hellbent on revenge and weren't open to listening to any sort of reason.' She looked up at Henri and Yvette. 'The Laurents wanted to speak for me and refute the lies that I was a traitor and a Nazi lover, which Madame Pretin was dripping into the ears of any who'd listen, and tell them instead of my work in the Resistance. I told them not to take the risk of it rebounding on them and how right I was. Marie

443

says if I had been there I would probably have been tarred and feathered, as they did to others they accused of fraternising with the enemy.'

'Ugh, how horrible!' Yvette said.

'It's the mob mentality,' Henri said. 'And it's what I was afraid of. In situations like that, normal ordinary people can behave like a pack of baying wolves.'

'You're right,' Bridgette said. 'When they couldn't find me they set the bakery alight.'

Yvette gave a gasp of shock and Henri exclaimed, 'That really is a monstrous thing to do!'

'I agree,' Bridgette said. 'Marie says they made a good job of it too, for she said it very nearly burned to the ground. It's just a shell now. It has really shaken me up. If the Laurents had taken my side, they could have been next in the firing line.'

'What happened to Legrand and Georges?' Henri asked.

'They were both shot.'

'Shot?' Yvette repeated in horror.

'Shot along with other traitors, so Marie says,' Bridgette told her. 'But before you think it is just too barbaric, remember the type of people they were. They must have quite a few deaths on their consciences, so I'm sorry if it sounds hard, but I can't even feel the slightest bit sad that they are dead.'

'I'm not surprised,' Yvette said. 'But as you said, thank God you got away in time.'

* * *

444

A week after the arrival of the letter, violence spilled onto the streets of Paris. The news reports spoke of FFI ripping up paving slabs and using abandoned German vehicles and furniture to make barricades, until every road leading down to the Seine was blocked in this way. The ensuing battles went on for days. The noise was indescribable – the relentless whine and crack of rifle shot, and the tattoo of machine-gun fire – and then a few days into the conflict they heard the boom of what Henri told the women were probably twelve-pounders.

The air stank of a mixture of cordite, brick dust and gas. Few ventured out and, despite the warm dry weather, windows were kept tight shut. The Germans retreated to Notre-Dame and nearby houses, or the Senate Building in the Luxembourg Palace, and the battles with the holed-up Germans and the Resistance groups went on relentlessly, while the Free French and the Allies continued to fight their way into the city.

And then, after almost ten days of fighting, the rumour was that de Gaulle was returning to France. By the time he arrived, the commander of German forces Paris had signed a formal surrender and had been arrested.

'An historic day,' Henri said when the news was broken to the French people over the wireless. 'Friday 25 August, and it is all over for Paris. Now the rest of France will follow.'

The whole city turned out to welcome and cheer

445

de Gaulle riding in front of the victorious troops the following day. When the tricolour fluttered from the top of Notre-Dame and another enormous one was draped from the top nearly to the ground, Henri admitted later that it had brought tears to his eyes.

Bridgette knew that he wasn't the only one. She had seen many surreptitiously wipe their eyes, and when the bells of Notre-Dame pealed out for the first time in four years, there was a collective sigh from the crowds.

'As soon as I can I will try and make some enquiries about the boys,' Henri said to Yvette that evening.

'Thank you, Henri,' Yvette said and her eyes were shining. 'If Raoul and Gerard have survived, then my joy will be complete.'

Bridgette also hoped and prayed that Yvette's sons were alive, but she knew if they were and they returned home, then she would feel in the way. They had been apart for many years and needed to be together and learn to live as a family once more, and they didn't need an interloper in the house.

TWENTY-THREE

The months passed and Paris started to come alive again. Many of the people who had deserted the city returned, and the fashion houses reopened their doors. One evening in mid-December as they sat around the table eating the evening meal, Yvette suggested, now that rationing and restrictions were easing, she and Bridgette might buy some new clothes.

Bridgette, however, was harbouring a secret, for she had not a period since a month before her mother died. She had initially put this down to the upset of everything, but when she noticed that she had put on a little weight too, she had surveyed herself in the mirror the previous evening and had seen the round of her stomach. Heat rose up from her toes and spread throughout her body as she realised there might be another reason why she had had no periods.

She felt filled with such joy and excitement that her hands trembled as she struggled to get

447

undressed. She could scarcely believe that the one thing she had wanted in her life, that she had thought denied her, was happening. The child she was carrying would be part of James, the only part she would ever have, and she already loved that unborn baby, his seed, with all her heart.

She knew, though, that Yvette and Henri were unlikely to feel the same way as she did, and she couldn't help remembering that in this same city twenty-eight years before, her mother had admitted her pregnancy to her aunt Bernadette. She had told Bridgette that her aunt had been shocked and disappointed, and she couldn't get her back to St-Omer quick enough. But Bridgette knew however her aunt and uncle felt about her news, that option was no longer open.

One thing she couldn't do was allow them to buy clothes that shortly she wouldn't be able to fit into. There was no easy way to tell them about her pregnancy, she knew, and so she faced her aunt and uncle across the table and said, 'Thank you, Aunt Yvette. You have always been so kind and generous to me, but really there is no point in my buying clothes now, because you see . . . there is no way to break this to you gently, but I am afraid I am having a baby.'

To say Yvette was shocked would be an understatement. She stared at Bridgette as the seconds ticked by as if she couldn't believe her ears.

'You can't be,' she said. 'How did such a thing happen?'

'The child's father is James Carmichael,' Bridgette said. 'The secret agent that I hid.'

'You said you loved him,' Yvette said, 'but I had no idea it had become such an intimate relationship.'

Before Bridgette could answer, Henri said, 'Well, I am disappointed in you. You have shaken me to the core, Bridgette, and I don't mind admitting it.'

Bridgette really liked Henri and valued his good opinion, but still she swallowed deeply and went on, 'To tell you the truth, if it wasn't for the effect this will have on your lives, I would be delighted to be bearing this child. It is like a gift from James and the only thing I will ever have from him. I understand, though, that you are ashamed of me and if you wish me to leave here then I will.'

'And how would you support yourself when you have a child to see to?'

'The same as many others do, I suppose.'

'We don't want you to leave,' Henri said. 'Neither of us wants that.'

'No,' Yvette said. And she too was aware that it was a case of history repeating itself. At least Bridgette had been married. She was already known as Madame Laurent, so all they had to do to save face was to let people believe that Xavier had died later than he did.

Bridgette knew that she would have to agree to this to save her aunt and uncle from shame, but she vowed that when the child was born, she would tell

449

him or her who the real father was. There would be no secrets between them.

Soon, though, Yvette had something else to occupy her. Henri had been searching for news of their sons for months and had discovered, that even with his contacts, finding out details of any in a Resistance cell was more difficult than he thought. But then, just a couple of days after Bridgette's announcement, Henri had at last been able to contact both boys. Yvette hoped they would be able to come home for Christmas but the letter Raoul wrote put paid to that.

He said that both he and his brother were working with an organisation helping the homeless and destitute in central Europe and neither had the slightest intention of completing their education, which was curtailed because of the war. There was too much to do for them to leave at the moment, but he said they might have some time off the following spring.

Henri had had the boys' futures mapped out almost from the day they'd been born and he was totally stunned by what Raoul had written. Bridgette felt sorry for him because she knew Henri was still seeing the young men as the boys he had sent to safety at the beginning of the war, but they had experienced things he would have never wanted them to experience and rode alongside danger and so were bound to have changed.

Yvette understood this. She covered her husband's

hand with her own as she said, 'Their attitude to life has been changed by circumstances, my dear, and if we are not to lose them totally I'm afraid that we must accept it.'

'I know,' Henri said. 'I certainly don't want to write a censorious letter to them. Many many fathers, grieving for a son who hasn't made it, would change places with me today. Let's just be grateful that they have survived and are doing something useful.'

Yvette was unable to sleep for worrying about Bridgette and her predicament. For the first time she realised how hard it must have been for her, virtually alone in a house with a terminally ill mother and a man for many weeks – months, even – with no possibility of any sort of normal life. She had known in hiding the man she was taking a great risk, and surely that added an extra edge of heightened emotion to everything. Small wonder that they had been overcome by their feelings for one another. She felt bad that she had been so judgemental. She should have been more supportive, more understanding.

So with these thoughts tumbling about her head, she sought out Bridgette the next day and said, 'I'm sorry for the way I reacted when you told me about your pregnancy. I failed to see how it was for you both all that time, cooped up together.'

'You have no need to be sorry, Aunt Yvette.'

'Oh, I think I do,' Yvette said firmly.

'But how does Uncle Henri feel about it?' Bridgette asked.

'Oh, don't worry about Henri,' Yvette said. 'He will follow my lead in issues like this. I will explain it all to him, never fear. And now let us look forward to the birth, because after all, a new baby is still a new baby. The first thing to do is get you registered with the doctor and draw out a list of things we'll need to buy.'

Yvette was right, and Henri said that he had maybe been too hasty in condemning her, that she was not to worry about a thing, and all she had to do was look forward to the spring and the birth of her child.

It was all so different from the way her poor mother had been treated, Bridgette thought that night as she lay in bed. Gabrielle had spent the rest of her life paying for the sin of making love to the only man she ever loved, who the war had stolen away from her.

Bridgette knew what her mother meant when she had said that her heart was too hurt to truly love another after Finn Sullivan. Bridgette herself had loved and lost two wonderful men, but now she had a child, her child and James's, to love and cherish and watch grow up. With her hand curled protectively around her stomach she soon drifted off to sleep.

The war dragged on throughout the rest of the winter and the early spring. The Red Army, beating

452

the Germans back, came upon the first concentration camps in Poland. Then the Allies discovered and liberated Belsen-Bergen and Buchenwald.

Reporters on the wireless brought the appalling horror of what had been happening at these camps into people's living rooms. Sometimes, after such a report, Henri, Yvette and Bridgette would sit in silence, digesting the terrible brutal things done to innocent civilians who just happened to be Jews.

Yvette would have liked to have kept the gruesome details from Bridgette but she insisted on knowing. 'No one should be protected from this,' she told Yvette. 'Only by acknowledging that these awful things happened can we ensure that they will never happen again.'

'We knew, Parisians all knew,' Yvette said. 'I don't mean we knew about the butchery of the Jewish nation, but some Jews escaped to Paris before the war and I am ashamed to say that the tales they told us then were so shocking, so uncomfortable to hear, that we closed our ears to them. Well, I did anyway, and now I am so bitterly ashamed of myself.'

Bridgette knew what Yvette was saying though, and she also felt a sense of guilt. The words next to the gruesome newspaper pictures often danced in front of Bridgette's eyes because they would be filled with tears as they heard of prisoners stripped of their hair and their clothes and herded into gas chambers they believed were showers.

Henri came upon Bridgette weeping one day

453

with the paper showing the mounds of hundreds and hundreds of corpses, men, women and children, hastily buried, or in burned pyres. There was no sign of Yvette and so Henri put tentative arm around Bridgette.

'Try not to upset yourself too much. Remember you have a baby to consider.'

Bridgette nodded. She struggled for control and said, 'It's not just what's in the paper, or at least not totally that. I was remembering the Jews I saw at the station in St-Omer being herded into these airless, windowless railway trucks and probably *en route* to one of those hellholes. One old man panicked and tried to escape and they shot him. I felt so bad about that at the time, but now I think the old man was one of the lucky ones. At least he died quickly. But what made them do it, Uncle Henri?'

'I have no answers,' Henri said. 'Surely you would need a peculiar state of mind to want to inflict such suffering on another person, and the numbers killed are almost past belief.'

'Even the few survivors are often past saving,' Bridgette said.

'I know,' Henri said. 'It's a savage example of man's inhumanity to man.'

Shockingly, people became slightly inured to the news of the death camps. It wasn't that they cared less, just that there was only so much that they could take in. Most people's minds were fixed on

Germany's surrender, which everyone knew was only a matter of time.

Bridgette's mind was also on the birth of her baby. By now she was so heavy and cumbersome that doing anything was an effort. Eventually, her pains began one early morning towards the end of April. She woke Yvette, who immediately took charge, and sent Henri for the doctor and made up the bed for Bridgette.

The doctor examined Bridgette and said she would be a while yet and he would be back later. It went like that all day, with the doctor popping in and out, but Yvette never left her side. The last time the doctor came in it was coming on to evening and Bridgette was having the urge to push. He immediately asked for hot water to wash his hands so that he could examine her. 'You are doing very well,' he said, when he had finished. 'I can nearly see the head. Now I want you to push with all your might next time you get the urge.'

She did, and had a fleeting memory of the still-born baby girl she had lost all those years ago, and she redoubled her efforts, Yvette and the doctor encouraging her to push harder with each contraction.

Just as she felt she could do no more and the baby was too big to be born, another push took her unawares and suddenly newborn wails filled the room.

'Isn't that the sweetest sound in the world?' Yvette said, and she had tears in her eyes.

'Is it all right, Doctor?' Bridgette asked. 'And is it a boy or a girl?'

'You have a fine son, Bridgette,' the doctor said with a smile on his face. 'And he is absolutely perfect.'

Bridgette had thought she loved the baby before, but she wasn't prepared for the power of it that struck her with such force when the child was laid in her arms so that she gasped aloud. She kissed the soft skin on his forehead and he opened his milky blue eyes and tried to focus on her.

'Have you a name for him, Bridgette?' Yvette asked, for she would never discuss it before.

'Oh, yes,' Bridgette said. 'He will be called for my father and his father. This is Finbar James, but he will be called Finn, as his grandfather was.'

Just a few days after Finn's birth the Red Army had entered Berlin and there they found Hitler's body and that of his mistress, Eva Braun, hidden in an underground bunker. They had both committed suicide. Germany's surrender was a foregone conclusion. It became official on 7 May. The war in Europe was over and the next day was declared a national holiday. Bridgette was officially lying in, but she encouraged Yvette and Henri to go and enjoy the celebrations taking place all around Paris. They could clearly hear the cheering and shouting in the streets, and over it all the church bells chimed. Excitement and expectation were in the very air.

'Will you be all right on your own?' Yvette

asked anxiously as she hovered in the doorway of Bridgette's bedroom.

'Will you go?' Bridgette said in exasperation, for Yvette had been fussing all morning. 'I will be perfectly all right and I am not on my own. I have my little man for company.'

As soon as Yvette and Henri had left she peeled back the covers of the crib and lifted the baby out and held him close. She loved him so much it hurt, and she knew that she would willingly lay down her life for him. She was sorry that he would grow up without a father, but he didn't lack for love, and Yvette and Henri seemed to dote on him more with each passing day.

Bridgette knew that she would have to ask them to be his godparents although they were really too old for the task. It saddened her that she was so lacking in family and also so friendless, for she knew few people in Paris and felt very alone in the world.

She thought of the charge her mother had laid on her, minutes before she died, to find her father's people. She hadn't had any desire then to travel to a new country to see relatives who knew nothing about her. That had changed, though, since she'd given birth to Finn. He too would be related to them through her, and she wondered if she should deny him the right to get to know his family.

She tossed and turned over this dilemma and as the months passed the feeling in her grew stronger and stronger. Christmas, the second without her mother, she found very hard, and then in January of the following year Yvette suddenly said, 'Bridgette, is anything troubling you? You have not been yourself for weeks now.'

Bridgette looked at her aunt's concerned face and the slight frown puckering her brow and she knew that she deserved to be told the truth. 'Just before Maman died, she wanted to speak to me and I had to lean forward to hear her. Do you remember that?'

Yvette nodded and Bridgette went on, 'You asked me what she had said and I replied something like it was of no consequence. That wasn't absolutely true. Maman asked me something specific, which was that I should go and find my father's family in Ireland. In fact, she made me promise that I would.'

'You can't let a deathbed promise like that dictate your life,' Yvette said. 'Remember your mother was doped up most of the time.'

'I know that, and I also know that her mind was crystal clear when she asked me to do that,' Bridgette said. 'Until Finn was born, I had no inclination to do as Maman asked,' she said. 'But he is linked to them too, through me, and as I intend to tell him everything as soon as he is old enough, I think I owe it to him at least to try to contact them.'

'Do you know where they live?' Yvette asked

'Not really,' Bridgette said. 'But, anyway, I thought the best thing to do is write to my father's friend, Christy Byrne. Maman kept the couple of

458

letters he sent to her so I have his address. He will know the whole set-up and may advise me how to go about things.'

'I remember Gabrielle talking of a Christy Byrne,' Yvette said. 'And I saw the first letter he wrote to tell Gabrielle after Finn's death. Fancy her keeping it all these years.'

'She kept everything in that box I showed you, and she had that hidden in the wardrobe,' Bridgette said.

'That man Christy might be dead himself by now.'

'He might,' Bridgette agreed. 'And if he is then it is a sort of closure, but I think I will write anyway and see what happens.'

However, it was the March before Bridgette wrote telling Christy her name was Bridgette Laurent now, and she was the daughter of Gabrielle Jobert, who had married a British soldier called Finn Sullivan in 1916, and that she had been born in August of that same year.

She went on to say her mother had only told her about Finn Sullivan being her father as she lay terminally ill with TB and her dying wish was that she made contact with Finn's family. Bridgette explained that she was more especially anxious to do this now that she had a son of her own, whom she had called Finn, after his grandfather, and she asked Christy's advice on how best to introduce herself to the family.

*   *   *

Christy couldn't ever remember having a letter for years. In fact, the last letter he had received was from Bridgette's mother advising him to keep the marriage a secret from the family in case it was not legal. He believed Bridgette's letter to be a genuine one, though, and he remembered Finn before he died asking him to help Gabrielle and the child if he could. This was the first thing he had ever been asked to do and he felt Finn's daughter had a perfect right to meet her father's family, especially as she had given a promise to her dying mother. It was a human need to know who you were and where you came from.

He had kept the secret of Finn's marriage for years and only eventually confided in Tom. The others were probably unaware of her existence at all, so he thought Tom was the one Bridgette should contact first.

He didn't have Tom's actual address, though. Tom had surprised everyone when he said that he had decided to sell the farm. It had been a little overshadowed then, though, by the shocking news of Joe Sullivan's wife, Gloria, who had left him – and for an American, no less – and had sailed to the States leaving her child behind with his father. That had outraged nearly all women in the town and their indignation meant that the story had been kept alive for a long time. Tom's sale of the farm slipped well into second place as a topic of conversation.

Tom had told him that he had a flat in a place

460

called Boldmere. He said it wasn't a very big place and it was part of a market town called Sutton Coldfield, which was outside the city of Birmingham.

He supposed he was still there and so he sent a letter off to Bridgette telling her this and saying Tom's actual address could probably be got if she wrote to the McEvoys at the post office in Buncrana, for they had been great friends of the Sullivan family.

Christy's letter was a surprise to Bridgette. Her mother had told her that Finn had thought Tom a born farmer, so why had he left to live elsewhere and where were the others? In her mind's eye she had seen them all living in that squat whitewashed cottage in rural Ireland and she had nothing to put in its place though the need to go and meet them was stronger than ever.

She toyed with the idea of writing to the people in the post office in Buncrana to get Tom's address, but rejected it. She had written to Christy because he had met her mother and later communicated with her, but she balked at writing to complete strangers. They probably didn't know even of her existence, so why would they send Tom's address to her just because she asked them to?

The mention of Sutton Coldfield. had given her a bit of a jolt because James had told her that he came from there. She remembered the park that he had described. She would love to see it, she thought suddenly, to take his son there and show him where his father had spent much of his youth.

However, her priority had to be finding Finn's family first. Boldmere appeared to be a district of some sort and if Sutton Coldfield was only a small town then Boldmere was bound to be smaller still. It was very possibly only the size of St-Omer, where everybody knew everyone else. Surely in such a place it would be relatively easy to find out where Tom Sullivan lived.

She didn't tell her aunt and uncle that she had no actual address for Tom Sullivan because she knew how they would fuss. She just said that Christy Byrne had given her all the information she needed, but she agreed to stay in Paris for Finn's first birthday.

The following day Yvette and Henri got a letter from Raoul. Neither he nor Gerard had been able to have any leave in the spring so far and Yvette had been very disappointed, so Bridgette hoped Raoul's letter would give some indication of when he or his brother would be coming home for a break.

However, his letter did much more than that. Yvette's face flooded with joy as she read it. She turned to her niece and her husband and her eyes danced with happiness as she cried, 'He's engaged. Raoul's engaged. The girl, Monique, works for the same refuge project as Raoul and Gerard. The headquarters is going to be set up just outside Paris, and so the two of them will be working

462

there, not that far away at all. In fact,' she said, looking across the table to Henri, 'Raoul asks if they might stay here while they are looking around for a place of their own. They plan to marry in the autumn.'

Bridgette was so pleased for Raoul. Yet she knew that though her aunt and uncle would never say or intimate that she might be in the way when Raoul and his fiancée arrived, she would feel it just the same. Yvette and Henri would want time with their elder son and the girl he had chosen to share his life with, and Bridgette intended to make arrangements to leave Paris before they arrived.

TWENTY-FOUR

Bridgette found that she was a good traveller and not even the ferry crossing the turbulent water of the Channel had made her feel the slightest bit queasy, though Yvette had fussed about that. But then, Bridgette thought, smiling fondly, Yvette fussed about anything. Yet even though she was upset at Bridgette leaving them, she had gone out and bought two beautiful leather suitcases that she had filled with clothes for both her and Finn, and a matching shoulder bag for Bridgette to carry for Finn's immediate needs.

Henri, who assumed Bridgette had someone waiting for her at New Street Station in Birmingham and a family who knew about her arrival and were waiting to welcome her, could understand Bridgette's need to find out where she had come from, for her own sake and that of the child. He found out the times of the ferry and the train, booked her tickets, and insisted on driving her to Calais. He had also bought her a beautiful Silver Cross pushchair that folded up, which he said would make the journey easier for her, and she had been very touched by his and Yvette's thoughtfulness and generosity.

So here she was, in the afternoon of Saturday 4 May, with Finn in her arms and her luggage around her as the train pulled into New Street Station. Suddenly her heart sank and she wondered for a moment if she had done the right thing, especially when she didn't even know where they were going to sleep that night.

She had a little money. Henri had been very generous and had given her an allowance from the moment she had arrived from St-Omer, but she had spent very little of it, especially as Yvette insisted on buying so much for the baby. Even so, she knew the money she had wouldn't last if it took her a long time to find her family.

The train ground to a halt and Bridgette climbed out apprehensively. She lifted her cases out one by one, unfolded the pushchair and seated the compliant Finn into it before she could take stock of where she was. The station was thronged with people, more than she had ever seen in one place, many laughing and talking, children shouting.

Somewhere a woman was speaking through a loudspeaker, though Bridgette couldn't understand a word she said, and the same could be said of the news-vendor who was advertising his wares in a thin nasal whine. Porters, careering about the platform with trolleys piled high with luggage, were warning people to get out of the way, but it was like double Dutch to Bridgette. People didn't speak the same English as she did and sometimes it was hard to understand all that they said.

Over everything was the clattering of the trains with an occasional screech of the hooter as they thundered into the station to draw to a halt with squeals of brakes and hisses of steam. Even when they were stationary they continued panting puffs of grey smoke into the already soot-ladened air like a crazed beast who couldn't wait to be off again.

The shouts of Finn, tired of being ignored, broke into Bridgette's thoughts and she gathered up her courage, hung her bag on her shoulder, balanced the two suitcases on the hood of the puschair and followed the mass of people out of the station and into the street. A sour, acrid smell hit the back of her throat, so pungent she could even taste it on her tongue. The streets were teeming with people of all shapes and sizes. Most had serious expressions on their faces and determined strides, as if they were on a mission of some sort.

But, added to the press of people on the pavements, was the traffic on the roads: cars, buses, lorries and vans jostled with the carts and wagons pulled by huge horses with shaggy feet. And then, as Bridgette made her way to the taxi rank, a clanking swaying monster running on rails set into the ground came careering towards her, to turn the corner just in time.

'It's a tram,' one of the taxi drivers said. He

was leaning against the bonnet of his cab and had been watching Bridgette's nervousness with slight amusement. 'Ain't you never seen one before?'

Bridgette got the general gist of what he was saying and said, 'No, not like that.' Although she knew Paris had its share of traffic, she had seldom gone into the city centre. The taxi driver, though, had caught the hint of Bridgette's accent and he said, 'You Foreign?'

Bridgette nodded. 'I'm French.'

'Well, what you doing in Brum?'

'Brum?'

'Here,' the taxi driver said. 'Birmingham, or Brum or Brummagem – whatever you call it.'

'Oh,' Bridgette said, 'I have only recently found out that I have relatives here. Now the war is over I've come to seek them out.'

'Right,' the cabbie said, pulling himself upright, 'you'll be needing a taxi, no doubt. Where are you making for?'

'A place called Boldmere.'

'I know that well enough.' The taxi driver lifted up the suitcases. 'If you unstrap the little fellow I'll have this lot stowed away in no time.'

In minutes Bridgette was being driven through the city centre. 'You have a lot of bomb damage here,' she said, looking from one side of the street to the other as the taxi cruised along.

'New Street took a pounding all right,' the taxi driver said. 'The biggest raids of the war were in November 1940. If they had returned the next night Birmingham would have burned to the ground because three trunk water mains were bust on the Bristol Road. Not that we were told this at the time, like. Bad for morale and all that, but it's all come out later.'

'I thought Paris was bad,' Bridgette said, 'but this is awful.'

'That where you're from, Paris?'

'Not really though I went to live with an aunt and uncle there when my mother died in the summer of 1944,' Bridgette said. 'I am a widow, you see.'

'Well, I'm sorry about that,' the taxi driver said. 'But you have a lovely little boy there.'

'He is very like his father,' Bridgette said wistfully. 'I called him Finn because that was my father's name.'

'Funny name that, Finn?'

'The full name is Finbar, and it means fairhaired, so it doesn't sit well on my son at all,' Bridgette said. 'But I wanted him called for his grandfather, who was killed in the Great War before I was born.'

'You seemed to have had your share of tragedy.'

'Many are the same these days,' Bridgette said. 'My son is not the only one that will grow up fatherless, but that's the reason that I would like to find my father's family. My mother said my father spoke of them often.'

'And whereabouts do they live in Boldmere?'

'I'm . . . I'm not sure.'

468

'So where do you want me to drop you off?'

'I suppose anywhere will do.'

The taxi driver drew in to the pavement, stopped the car, turned around in the seat and said to Bridgette, 'Do you know exactly where these people live?'

Bridgette shook her head. 'I understood that it isn't a big place. I thought if I asked round someone will know them.'

'I doubt that very much,' the taxi driver said. 'It's more highly populated than that. So where are you intending to sleep tonight?'

'I thought to find somewhere.'

'There might be nowhere except some place you wouldn't want to be in,' the taxi driver said. 'Like you just saw, Birmingham has been bombed to bits. People have been living in church halls and basements, and many still are. Good decent lodging houses are full to the brim.'

'I never thought . . .'

'Well, that's how it is,' the taxi driver said. 'And you have that babby to think of as well as yourself.' He took pity on her and he said, 'Look, my mother might put you up. God knows, the house is big enough for her now – too bloody big – but she's lived there years and she don't want to move. She don't run a boarding house or owt like that, but she had a bombed-out family living with her since 1941, a woman with two little girls with her husband in the Forces. Anyroad, the man weren't demobbed five minutes till they gave the family one of them prefabs. So, at the moment she is on her own and a bit lonely, and I reckon she'll put you up all right.'

Much of what the taxi driver said was lost on Bridgette, but she did work out that he was offering her a place to stay. 'Does your mother live in Boldmere?'

'No, she lives in Orphanage Road, Erdington,' the taxi driver said. 'It isn't far away. Do you know what any of your family look like?' he asked as he began driving again. 'Have you ever met any of them?'

Bridgette shook her head helplessly and, as she realised her plight, tears stood out in her eyes. The taxi driver saw them too and he said gently, 'I think that you are all in. My old mum will sort you out, never fear.'

As the taxi driver began to head towards his mother's house, however, Bridgette ran through in her head what she had decided to tell her Irish relations when she met up with them. Finn's family were Catholics, possibly devout Catholics, and she could take bets that any Catholics from Ireland would be as disgusted as those in France if they knew the truth about Finn. They might think her some sort of strumpet, a fallen woman, and probably not the kind of person that they wanted in their family.

In France her aunt had let it be understood that Bridgette was a recent widow, and despite the fact that she wanted there to be no secrets between her and her son for now, she knew that for respectability for herself and legitimacy for him, the family in Birmingham had to believe the same thing if she and Finn were to have a chance of being accepted.

She had realised she couldn't say the name of the shop where she worked at all, in case she mentioned Xavier or the family, which meant her story didn't add up. Her name was Madame Laurent and so James's name also had to be Laurent and he had to be a soldier in the Free French Army, killed in the invasion. James had left her in mid-July so she would have to tell some fabricated tale of some injury that the fictional James had sustained and that after treatment he had had a few days' leave at home to recuperate before rejoining his unit.

This was also the tale that she realised she would have to tell to the taxi driver's mother. The driver had spelled out to her the difficulties of finding any other sort of lodgings in Birmingham at that time, and she couldn't take the risk that this woman might turn against her because of her unmarried state. What would she do then?

As it happened, Mrs Entwhistle, or Ada, as she insisted on being called, was a motherly soul who looked kindly on most people. She was also, Bridgette was to find, more interested in talking than listening, though she had been enchanted by the baby and so moved by the details that her son told her about Bridgette she readily agreed to take them both in.

'And glad to do it as well,' she said. 'Since Sandra and the nippers went I haven't known what to do with myself. Of course, when her Syd came back they needed their own place, I could see that.'

'The house is too big for you, Ma,' the taxi driver said. 'How long have we all being telling you that?'

'Oh, it's all right for you young ones,' Ada said with spirit. 'But I raised the six of you in this house and then nursed your father until he died. All my memories are here and, anyway, now Bridgette and the babby are here it will be fuller, won't it? And if I know anything, travelling makes a body hungry and a feed just now won't come amiss, so I'll get on with that and you, our Bill, get about your business while me and Bridgette get to know one another.'

Bill gave Bridgette a wink as he said, 'Bossy old cow, ain't she? Don't say I didn't warn you.'

'What a thing to say about your own mother!' Ada said, though Bridgette saw the twinkle in her eyes. 'No respect, that's your trouble, our Bill. Go and earn an honest crust, or you'll go home empty-handed to Mavis, and that won't go down a bundle.'

'Oh,' said Bridgette. 'I owe you money. I'm afraid I have little understanding of it yet.'

'Have that one on me,' Bill said. 'But Ma is right. 'Less I earn more money before I go home tonight, I might have to throw my hat in first.'

Ada was smiling as she shut the door on her son.

'I suppose that made no sense to you. Throwing your hat in first is like testing the waters, seeing how cross his Mavis is. It's just an expression. It's not something he'll do.'

'Oh,' Bridgette said, more confused than ever. She had thought she would be all right in England as she had been speaking English since she had been a child, but it was a different English here.

'You'll soon get the hang of the lingo, never fear,' Ada said, as she made her way to the kitchen. 'Let's see what I have in the cupboard that will do to stick to our ribs this evening.'

That same evening, after they had all eaten and Finn put into the bed that Bridgette would share with him later, Ada told Bridgette all about Bill and his two brothers and three sisters, and how that big old house was once full of children and noise and laughter.

'Then with most of the kids gone, the old man got ill,' she went on. 'He'd had rheumatic fever as a nipper and it had damaged his heart. He didn't know, like, when he was younger, but as he got older it got worse and I nursed him till the day he died.'

'I nursed my mother too,' Bridgette said. 'She had TB and that's when I learned about my real father,' and she went on to recount what her mother had told her. 'I was very sad for a long time when first James and then my mother died. Then, when I had Finn, I suddenly thought it was important

473

to find the family that Maman wanted me to find, for his sake as well as my own.'

Ada's eyes when they rested on Bridgette were tender as she realised the depth of the young woman's suffering and how alone she must have felt. 'It's important to know where you have come from, I can see that,' she said gently. 'But you say that you don't know where these people actually live.'

'Only that it's around here somewhere,' Bridgette said. 'You see, when Christy told me that Boldmere was an area of Sutton Coldfield and that was a small market town just outside Birmingham, I assumed that Boldmere would be smaller even than the town I was born in, where everyone knew everyone else.'

'Boldmere used to be like that – Erdington too,' Ada said. 'Now, though, I'm not too sure. You could try asking in the post office – or are they Catholics, these Sullivans?'

'Yes,' Bridgette said. 'Of course, I should try the churches.'

'Well, it can do you no harm,' Ada said. 'The nearest Catholic church to here is the Abbey, and that's not that far from this end of Boldmere either. I don't know if there is one nearer to wherever they are living because I'm not Catholic myself.'

'Oh, Ada,' Bridgette exclaimed, 'that is a genius idea. I will try this Abbey tomorrow and go from there.'

It felt better to have a plan of some sort and

Bridgette curled up with her son in a happier frame of mind that night.

However, the priest, Father Cunningham, didn't know of a Tom Sullivan. When he listened to the reason that Bridgette wanted to contact the man, he even called over two of his colleagues. They couldn't help either but suggested that Bridgette try St Nicholas's church, which was in Boldmere, and leave her address with them in case they did find out anything.

Bridgette was very despondent, but Ada was more pragmatic. 'Never mind,' she said. 'At least they told you about the other church.'

'Yes, St Nicholas's in Jockey Road, and they said that was at the bottom of Boldmere Road,' Bridgette said. 'But I can't go there until tomorrow, and what if that priest doesn't know anything either?'

'Let's cross that bridge when we come to it, shall we?' Ada said. 'We have to get your ration book too, from the Council House in Birmingham City Centre, as soon as we can. And if the priest at St Nicholas's knows nothing, do what I suggested first and try the post office.'

Bridgette didn't know if the priest did know anything because he was away on holiday and would be gone for two more weeks. The priest covering for him couldn't help her. Before going back to Ada's she walked back up Boldmere Road, and called into the post office. The man behind

475

the counter though didn't know anyone by the name of Tom Sullivan either.

'If you say he lives round here he might well call in to send letters or parcels, but I really only know the names of those collecting a pension of one kind or another. This is a busy place and we have a lot of people through the doors. We couldn't know the whys and wherefores of them all.'

'He has a point,' Ada said to Bridgette when she recounted this. 'City life is different from the country, where people might be a sight friendlier and interested in anyone that moves into the neighbourhood. Here people are left more to themselves.'

'It's a bit hopeless, isn't it, Ada?

Ada thought that it probably was, but she said, 'No, it's not hopeless, but it's a bit like looking for a needle in a haystack, though the priest in the church in Jockey Road will likely know all about the man when he comes back.'

'It's almost two weeks till I can ask him,' Bridgette said glumly.

'Well, you could use the time to acclimatise yourself to the area,' Ada suggested. 'What if we go and get your ration book tomorrow, and then get off the bus early and take a dander around Erdington.'

'If you like,' Bridgette said with a sigh.

'And keep your pecker up, girl,' Ada said. 'When you saw the size of the place, you knew it wasn't going to be easy.'

Bridgette had known that, but she hadn't known

that it was going to be almost impossible. If the priest at St Nicholas's knew nothing, then Bridgette didn't know what to do. Ada didn't charge a great deal but even so, Bridgette couldn't stay in Birmingham indefinitely, and when the money was nearly all gone, if she was no further forward then what the hell was she going to do?

On Thursday night there was a knock at the door and Ada, expecting it to be one of her children, opened it to find two men outside that she had never seen before.

'Can I help you?'

'We need to speak to a woman you have living with you, a Mrs Bridgette Laurent,' one of the men said. 'One of the priests at the Abbey asked us to call.'

It was obvious the men were Irish. Ada said, 'One of you ain't Tom Sullivan that Bridgette has been looking for?'

'No,' the first man said, 'but we met Tom. When he first came over from Ireland in 1943 he travelled with us. He was not a seasoned traveller like my brother and myself, but we put him right about a few things. What he told us on the journey might help locate him now.'

Bridgette thought so too when Ada ushered the men in and they introduced themselves as Mick and Pat Donahue. 'But how did you know I was looking for a man called Tom Sullivan?' she asked, as Ada scurried off to make tea.

'The priest came and told us,' Mick said. 'See, though we now live in Birmingham, originally we came from Donegal, like Tom, and the priest remembered that. He thought maybe we knew him and might have some idea where he's living now. The point is, though, Donegal is a big spread-out county and we had not known anything of the Sullivans there, but, as luck would have it, we travelled together when he came over first. We met in the train and did the whole journey together.'

'He talked plenty,' Pat put in. 'We thought he was one of those quiet sorts of fellows when we met him first.'

'Maybe it was the Guinness we bought him as a cure of seasickness that loosened his tongue,' Mick said, and Pat gave a chuckle and agreed. 'That must have been it right enough.'

'So what did he say?' Bridgette asked.

'He told us he had a niece and nephew in Birmingham,' Mick said. 'And that was who he was going to see. The boy was called Kevin and he had never seen him, but the girl, Molly, who hailed from Birmingham originally, had lived with him and his mother for some years after the death of her parents. Did you know any of this?'

Bridgette shook her head.

'According to what Tom told us, Molly's brother, who was only a wee boy at the time, was left in Birmingham with the grandfather,' Mick went on. 'But then the war began and when she hadn't heard from them for a few weeks Tom said nothing would satisfy her other than coming back and making sure that they were all right. Unfortunately, she found her grandfather had been killed in one of the raids and her brother was in an orphanage, but she took charge of him as soon as she could.'

'You said death of her parents, Molly said. But who were her parents?'

'Oh, we know that too,' Pat said, taking up the story, 'and that's a tale on its own. Their mother was Tom's sister Nuala.'

'Oh,' said Bridgette in disappointment. 'How awful. She used to work as a nursemaid in the Big House in Buncrana.'

'She may well have done,' Pat said. 'But the poor woman had been dead now for nearly eleven years, for Tom said this happened in 1935. Both her and her husband were killed together in a car crash.'

'The poor children, and then to split them up like that . . .'

'That isn't the end of it, though,' Pat said. 'Nuala was sent to England because of the Troubles in Ireland and she met and married a Protestant. When she wrote and told her parents this her father had a heart attack and died. She was blamed by the mother and disowned by the family.'

Ada, coming in that minute with a tray of tea, heard what Pat had said and commented, 'I think there are more wars and upsets caused by religion than any other damned thing. I keep well away from all of it and I will take my chance with my maker when my time comes. I mean, was it so bad for her to marry a Protestant?'

'Her mother seemed to think so.'

Ada shook her head as she handed around the tea. 'Point is,' she said, 'I can't think of anything that my kids would do that would make me disown them.'

'She doesn't sound a very nice woman,' Bridgette said. 'My mother told me that my father always said she was awkward and could be really nasty, and yet I am called for her.'

'You haven't a nature like hers, though,' Ada said. 'Can you imagine Finn doing summat bad enough for you not to want anything ever to do with him again?'

Bridgette shook her head. 'Not a thing.'

'Nor me neither,' said Mick. 'Though, God, they have your heart scalded sometimes. I have four of my own.'

'Do you know what happened to Molly and where is she living now?' Bridgette asked. 'I would love to meet her.'

'Of course you would,' Mick said. 'Families should stick together. You need to meet Tom as well, for he is your uncle and a nicer man you would never meet. As for Molly, she did all right for herself and found some civilian job on an RAF aerodrome near a place called Castle Bromwich. She rents a house nearby from one of the airmen and had her brother living with her as soon as she could. She has also, in her words, found someone special in her life that she wanted Tom to meet.'

'Oh, I am so glad it turned out right for her in the end,' Bridgette said. 'What of the grandmother?'

'Dead and gone long ago,' Mick said.

'The point is, though,' Pat said, 'this is all we know. I remember Tom saying Molly's father was a man called Ted Maguire, so that was her name, but if she married the man she said was so special then I don't know what she became. The man was called Mark and I only remember that because I have the son the same name, but if Tom told us his surname then neither of us has any recollection of it.'

'But if we go to this camp maybe someone will recognise the name Molly Maguire. That's, of course, if the camp still exists,' Bridgette said.

'Only one way to find out,' Ada said. 'You and me will take a dander up there first thing tomorrow.'

TWENTY-FIVE

The RAF camp was totally deserted, the fence around it buckled in many places and the gate, looking quite bedraggled, hung on its hinges. The only sign that it had ever been an aerodrome at all were the huge hangars at the very bottom of the large field and the tarmac runways crisscrossing the place. There were no Nissan huts and only piles of bricks to show that there had ever been buildings there. No one was around to ask if they remembered a Molly Maguire. Bridgette was so disappointed that she felt tears stinging her eyes.

Ada saw them and she said, 'Don't take on, bab.'

'I am trying not to,' Bridgette sniffed, 'but this was the first real lead I had. I met two people that had actually met and talked with my uncle Tom, and heard about cousins I had no idea about and I thought that this time I really might be lucky.' She shrugged. 'But no. I am once more disappointed.'

'I know,' Ada said. 'I thought we might get summat here as well.'

'I wonder if she is still in the house that she rented from the airman?' Bridgette mused.

'Maybe,' Ada said. 'And then if he survived this little lot, maybe he wanted his house back again. Anyroad, whatever he did isn't going to help us, is it, because we have no idea where the house is?'

'No,' Bridgette agreed. 'And all I can say is, thank God for Finn.'

'Yeah,' Ada said. 'He has a smile that nearly cuts his face in two and it makes you smile back almost despite yourself. How about taking him up the park for a bit?'

'Is there one near?'

'Well, Pype Hayes Park isn't that far,' Ada said. 'Just up the Chester Road. We may as well give Finn a good time, even if we feel disappointed.'

It was nice to walk on grass instead of pavements, Bridgette thought a little later. She unstrapped Finn and he toddled before them, stopping to examine everything that took his attention. But neither of them was in any sort of hurry and they let him do as he pleased. To him, everything was new and exciting, and his antics brought a smile to both women's faces.

'He needs a ball,' Ada said. 'Every boy needs a ball. Not that you could get one for love nor money during the war. Didn't think it was in the nation's interest to use rubber for balls, I suppose. Lots of things then was unobtainable and if you said owt about it people would say, "Don't you know there's a war on?" Like as if it might have slipped your memory. Things are coming back into the shops now. I bet we could get a ball for his lordship there if we tried. What d'you say?'

'A ball would be good,' Bridgette said slowly. 'But . . . but I am afraid of spending anything I don't have to spend just now.'

Ada looked at the lines of anxiety crisscrossing Bridgette's face and said reassuringly, 'I understand, and don't worry about a thing. I'll have a word with Bill and the others. One of them is sure to have an old ball knocking about.'

'I don't want you to go to any trouble.'

'What's the trouble about asking if they have got summat they don't need any more that that babby would love?' Ada said. 'Don't you think no more about it. Now,' she went on, as they approached some large tennis courts, 'if I remember right there's a children's playground not that far from here. Shall we take a gander? I bet his lordship will approve of that.'

Bridgette readily agreed. She really liked Ada. In many ways she reminded her of Marie Laurent – not that they looked that much alike, but both women had such a kindly nature. Living there also meant that Bridgette had begun to understand the Birmingham accent and humour more, so she didn't have to concentrate so hard to understand what people said. She even had a grasp on the money, though it still totally confused her at times.

What threw her was when the money could be called different things, like when a one shilling piece could be called 'a bob' and when a shiny sixpence was also known as 'a tanner,' and so on, but in the main she understood it pretty well.

Ada was quite willing to help Bridgette in her quest to find her family too, though Bridgette wondered if Ada thought it a waste of time. Bridgette wouldn't blame her if she did: she was beginning to feel that way herself. She bitterly regretted not writing to those people at the post office that Christy had told her about, and before throwing in the towel altogether she resolved to remedy that over the weekend.

A shout from Finn broke through her musings and she decided to shelve her worries and give herself over to having a good time with her son. And he did have a wonderful time. There were several safe swings for him, but as Bridgette pushed him she remembered his father saying that he always seemed to be pushing his little sister, Dolly, on the swings, and as the memory flitted across her brain, her eyes clouded over.

Ada saw it but didn't comment. She knew Bridgette was carrying some great sorrow and couldn't wonder at it, and she only wished that she could help her in some way.

When Finn eventually tired, Bridgette put him back in the pushchair and he made only a token objection.

Knowing he would be asleep in no time, Ada

said, 'I fancy looking at the gardens, if you don't mind. They used to be lovely once upon a time but in the war all the flowers was dug up and they had to grow vegetables. Half the park was given over in the same way, and I know the nation wanted feeding and that, but it weren't so nice to look at.'

'I never mind looking at flowers, but who lives in that big house?' Bridgette asked as they passed a large construction not far from the playground.

'Well, once it would have belonged to some landed gentry and all this park would have been their land. Bill goes all over, being a taxi driver, like, and he said most of the parks are the same. Don't know how it is in France.'

'I think most are public parks,' Bridgette said. 'In my small town, St-Omer, there was a public park.' And she added, 'most of our landed gentry fell to Madame Guillotine of course in the Revolution.'

'My goodness!' Ada exclaimed. 'Did they really?' Doesn't bear thinking about it does it?'

Bridgette laughed. 'No I suppose it doesn't but that's was how it was then,' she said. 'So who lives in the house now?'

'Unmarried mothers,' Ada said. 'And there was a spate of them during and after the war, I can tell you. Morals and knickers fell along with the bombs, in my opinion, and them Yanks have a lot to answer for. Many of them left our girls with more than a pair of nylon stockings.'

Bridgette felt a chill run through her, and she was immensely relieved that she hadn't told Ada the truth about her baby son. They began to walk through the flower garden, which Ada observed were being restored to their former glory, and on the other side of the gardens was a pond that she said her husband and the lads used to fish in before the war. 'That's of course if they didn't use the Cut. I didn't like the lads going down there 'cos the water runs deep, see?'

Bridgette nodded obediently as they turned away from the pond and she began pushing the pushchair up the slight incline.

Seeing her confusion, Ada laughed. 'The Cut's what Brummies call the canal,' she said. 'Anyroad, during the war they was used to transport big items, coal and the like, and the canal was all boarded over at night in case the bombers caught the gleam of water in their headlights. Birmingham made a lot of things for the war, see, and lots of factories and workshops backed onto a canal somewhere 'cos they used to tip all the waste in there. People say Birmingham has more canals than Venice. Course I've never seen Venice, nor am I likely to so I can't say it has or it hasn't. You got many canals in France?'

'In St-Omer we have a very beautiful canal, wide and tree-lined.'

'Blimey,' Ada exclaimed with a laugh. 'The Brummie cuts ain't nothing like that.'

They had reached the brow of the hill and Ada

pointed right down at the edge of the park is a little stream. It's over hung with trees and a pretty spot. We'll go down one day if you like and bring a picnic; the babby will love it. But for today I'm ready to head for home. My stomach thinks my throat's cut and I am dying for a cuppa. What about you?'

Bridgette nodded. 'I am a little hungry,' she said. 'And when Finn wakes up he will be ready to eat too, I'm sure.'

'Let's go then,' Ada said. 'And leave the stream for another day.'

It was as Bridgette tucked Finn into bed that night that she remembered the child Kevin that the two Irishmen, Pat and Mick, had mentioned.

'Maybe I could trace the others through him,' she said to Ada later as they sat together over cups of tea. 'I mean, I know his name is Kevin Maguire. I could try the schools.'

'It was eleven years ago,' Ada warned.

'Even so.'

'What I mean is, you don't know how old Kevin was in 1935 when the accident happened,' Ada said. 'The men said he was young all right, but how young? Unless he was little more than a baby, eleven years on he will have left school.'

'But they will have records,' Bridgette said, 'I am determined to try to find out.'

'Paget Road is the nearest.'

'Yes, but that isn't a Catholic School, is it?'

'No,' Ada agreed. 'That would be St Thomas's at the Abbey, I would say. There is an Irish family down the street and their children all went there.'

'Well, that's where I will go,' Bridgette said. 'And first thing Monday morning.'

In the meantime she composed the letter to the McEvoys in Buncrana. It was in a similar vein to the one she sent to Christy, except she said that she had actually arrived in Birmingham and was having trouble locating the family and could any of them help at all. She read the letter over three times and still wasn't totally happy with it but she decided it would have to do. She put it in the envelope and wrote the address with care. She hadn't much hope that the McEvoys would be able or even willing to help her, but she knew she had to try every avenue.

Father Cunningham stopped Bridgette after Mass and asked if the Donahue brothers had been any help to her.

'In a way, yes, thank you, Father,' Bridgette said, and told the priest what they had told her about Molly and Kevin. 'I went up to the aerodrome, but the place is all disbanded and deserted, and Pat and Mick said she had rented a house off a pilot but didn't know where.'

'That must have been disappointing for you,'

'Oh, it was, Father, very disappointing,' Bridgette said. 'It was later I got to thinking of

Molly's brother. When the accident happened he was much younger – they didn't know how young – and so he must have gone to school somewhere. I thought he might have gone to the secondary school here.'

'He may have done,' the priest said, 'but though the aerodrome was in Castle Bromwich, you don't know where the house actually was.'

'Well no, Father,' Bridgette conceded. 'But it couldn't be that far away if Molly had to make her way to the aerodrome to work every day.'

'No, I suppose not. What did you say the boy's name was?'

'Kevin Maguire, Father,' Bridgette said.

'I don't recognise the name at all,' the priest said. 'Of course, I have only been here two years. If you had spoken to Father Clayton or Father Monahan they might have been able to help you further. They had been here for years but Father Monahan has retired and Father Clayton moved to pastures new. Still, there will be no harm in your visiting the school. In fact I will accompany you and we will see what we can find out. When were you thinking of going?'

'Tomorrow, Father, first thing.'

The priest smiled. 'I have some dealings with the school and I know that Monday morning is the very worst time to call, for it is very busy. Why don't you call at the presbytery about two o'clock. I'm sure that that will be a more convenient time for them.'

'All right then, Father,' Bridgette said, and she turned the pram for home.

Ada had said she had to go out and couldn't mind Finn that morning. Surprisingly she was still out when Bridgette arrived home, but the kettle hadn't quite boiled when she heard a car pull up outside.

It was Bill's taxi, and Ada got out of it and so did Bill, carrying a variety of items.

'A cot for the babby,' she said in explanation to Bridgette, who had opened the door for them. There wasn't just a cot, but a truck too, full of bricks, a little tricycle and a football.

'But where did they come from?' she asked.

'Our house,' Bill said. 'Mavis was glad to get rid of them. Been cluttering the loft up long enough, she said.'

'But don't you need them any more?'

'Not likely,' Bill said. 'Our youngest is sixteen and I think Mavis would fling herself off a tall building if she found she was up the pole again, and we've stored the stuff for years. The football belongs to my lad, but he's twenty and more interested in girls than footballs just now. Said the wee fellow can have it and welcome.'

'Oh, thank you,' Bridgette said, overcome at the kindness of Bill and his mother, and Bill's wife too of course. 'I don't know what to say.'

'You have said enough,' Bill said. 'A simple thank you was all that was needed, and now if you will excuse me I'll go and assemble the cot.'

*   *   *

The following day, Ada offered to mind Finn while Bridgette went up to the Abbey School. She was only too pleased to take up her offer and she set off full of enthusiasm and hope that surely this would be it. At the Abbey School she would find Molly's address and that in turn would lead her to the rest of her family.

However, again she was to be disappointed, thought the priest, who seemed almost as keen for Bridgette to be reunited with her family as Bridgette was herself, insisted on checking back records for seven years. The secretary, who had been at the school three times as long, insisted, however, that there had been no boy called Kevin Maguire there at any time.

There were two sisters called Sullivan. Bridgette got very excited about this although the priest did warn her that it was a very popular name in Ireland. So it proved, because within minutes of talking to the girls, Bridgette knew that they were nothing to do with the family that she was trying to trace.

'So,' said the priest as they walked back to the presbytery, 'seems like it's back to the drawing board.'

'Yes, Father.'

'Have you any more irons in the fire?'

'Pardon, Father.'

'Oh, I'm sorry, my dear,' Father Cunningham said. 'That saying just means have you made any other plans?'

'Not really, Father,' Bridgette said. 'I mean, I have

sent a letter to Mrs McEvoy, who runs the post office in Buncrana, the nearest town to the cottage where my father was born and reared. Christy, who was my father's friend, said that the McEvoys were great friends with all the family. If that was the case they probably kept in touch and they would probably have all their addresses.'

'So, why didn't you write to these people before you came?' the priest asked.

Bridgette sighed. 'I don't know, Father. Why does anyone do these things that you know in hindsight aren't sensible? But anyway, I didn't think there was much point. They know nothing about me. Why would they send people's addresses to a perfect stranger?'

The priest could see Bridgette's point. 'I feel very sorry for you, Bridgette,' he said. 'And I know it doesn't help you but the same scenario is going on all over Europe. I was only reading in the paper the other day about families ripped apart through that devastating war and still searching for loved ones.'

'Yes, Father,' Bridgette said. 'And what a heartbreaking search it is.'

'Maybe he passed the eleven-plus,' Ada said later when Bridgette told her what had happened at the school.

'What's that?'

'An exam the bright kids take,' Ada said. 'None of mine were brainy enough for it, but this Kevin might have been. See, if they pass they go to a different school called a grammar school. I'm surprised the priest didn't think of that.'

'So where are these schools?'

'Well, that's just it,' Ada said. 'They are all over the place. All the kids of the Catholic family I was telling you about went to St Thomas's, bar the youngest boy and he passed for the grammar school a couple of years ago. Then apparently the parents have a choice of the school to send him too, but Catholics have to pick one called St Phillip's as their first choice because it is the only Catholic grammar school in Birmingham. It's in Edgbaston, right the other side of the city, one hell of a trek I thought it was, not that I said owt. It weren't none of my business. Anyroad, he never went there in the end. He went to King Edward's in Aston.'

'So what you are saying is that if Kevin passed the exam for grammar school, the chances of finding out where would be very difficult.'

Ada nodded sadly. 'That's just about what I am saying. Yes.'

'So, everything now hinges on the letter to Buncrana.'

'Yes, I think it does.'

'And if nothing comes of that?'

Ada was silent for a mintue or two and then she said softly, 'You've still got the babby.'

'Oh yes,' Bridgette said, suddenly scooping him up and holding him close. Finn had been playing with the bricks and he was surprised to find himself suddenly in his mother's arms. He laughed at her and patted her face, and Bridgette felt a sudden tug of love for her child. She kissed his soft little cheek. 'Without Finn I would be lost.'

'All I'm saying is, I have got right fond of you and you can stay here as long as you like—'

'Oh, but—'

'Hear me out,' Ada said. 'If you want to stay on here and get a job or summat then I will see to Finn for you.'

'Ada, you have given me a lifeline,' Bridgette said. 'I hate being beholden to people. I would have preferred to have looked for a job in Paris, to support myself and Finn. And it would have worked because my aunt would have loved to have a free hand to spoil Finn totally, but I never mentioned it because my uncle would have been scandalised. He wasn't an ogre or anything, and agreed in principle with women working, but he thought it was his place to look after me and he would have felt shamed if I had insisted on finding a job. So, I thank you for that.'

'It'd be no skin off my nose to do it, bab,' Ada said. 'In fact, it might give me a new lease of life to have the care of a little one again.'

'You wouldn't find it too much for you?'

'Not a bit of it,' Ada said. 'Not with a child like Finn anyroad, who is as sunny as the day is long.'

'All right then,' Bridgette said. 'Shall we leave it another week and then if I have had no reply to the letter, I will give up the search for the family and start looking for a job somewhere.'

'If that's what you want, bab.'

'It is,' Bridgette said with an emphatic nod. 'I can't spend my life looking for elusive family members. For Finn's sake as well as my own, I must settle somewhere, and Birmingham seems as good as any other place.'

The following day in Buncrana, Nellie McEvoy received a strange letter, so strange that when she shut the post office that evening, she told her husband, Jack, about it as they ate dinner together.

He looked at her in total amazement and then said, 'You are telling me that young Finn Sullivan was supposed to have married a French girl and he is the father of the young woman that has written to you?'

'That's what this Bridgette Laurent claims.'

'Do you believe it?'

Nellie shook her head. 'I don't know. It is almost too incredible to believe.'

'Wouldn't people have been informed if such a thing had happened?' Jack said. 'His family would have been told, surely to God. One of them would have said.'

'Maybe in wartime communications were more difficult, certainly in the Great War,' Nellie said. 'This young woman said that she has only found out that Finn was her father because her mother, who was called Gabrielle, told her almost on her deathbed. I can't help feeling that unless she believed that to be true she wouldn't have bothered to write. She is a widow now with a young child and, if Finn is her father, I would say that she is searching for her roots. I feel a bit sorry for her. Maybe it was just something her mother said, because why would she keep quiet all these years if she actually married Finn?'

'You're right.' Jack said. 'And another thing. If they had been married, as she claimed, it would have been she, not the family here, that received the telegram telling them of his death.'

'Yes,' Nellie said. 'So they couldn't be married, and that would explain this Gabrielle's silence over the years. Mind you, Bridgette Laurent might still be Finn's daughter. She believes it, anyway. She mentions Christy Byrne. He told her that some of the family was in Boldmere and she hightailed it off to England to seek them out. She said that Christy advised her to write to get the addresses of all the family before she left, but she didn't. But she won't find any of the family in Boldmere now.'

'God, I haven't seen Christy in ages,' Jack said.

'Well he seldom leaves the farm,' Nellie said. 'It's hard for him, poor fellow.'

'Maybe I should go out and see him?' Jack said, 'And see what he has to say?'

'Why worry the man over it?'

'Well, the letter could be genuine.'

'I'm not absolutely sure if it is or is not,' Nellie

497

said with a sigh. 'What I do know is that I do not feel right sending addresses to a perfect stranger.'

'You can't just ignore it, though,' Jack said. 'So what are you going to do?'

'I'm going to write to Tom,' Nellie said, 'and I will enclose this Bridgette's letter with my own. The girl is in England at the moment, so Tom can go along and check it out.'

'Yes,' said Jack. 'I think that's the best thing that you can do.'

TWENTY-SIX

On Thursday morning of that week, Ada said to Bridgette, 'Why don't you go and ask at Paget Road School? If Kevin Maguire didn't pass the eleven-plus then that's where he well might have gone. I hear what you say about him being Catholic and everything, but there could be a hundred and one reasons why he was at a normal school. Wouldn't do him any harm to check, would it?

'I don't suppose so.'

'And give you summat to think about other than a letter coming from that Irish place. If he was never at the school, you have lost nothing. I'll mind the nipper for you.'

Bridgette knew now how Ada could go on if she had a bee in her bonnet about something, though she did have a point about the school. It was better not to leave any stone unturned and yet when she left the house later she thought it would be another wild-goose chase. Ada said Paget Road School was in the middle of a council estate called Pype Hayes, and she drew her little map and so she found the school easily.

It was a very large square building. The windows were rather high and some were open. She could hear the noise of the children inside, and as she walked up the drive to the entrance, she felt her stomach quail. This, she knew, could be the end of the road as far as her search was concerned. Everything hinged on the people in the post office giving her the addresses she had asked for, she now believed.

The secretary at the school was very pleasant and Bridgette sat on a chair facing her across the desk and explained who she was and the quest to find her family. The secretary listened politely and with a measure of sympathy because she knew the young woman before her was not the only one whose family had been split asunder by the war. However, when she mentioned the name, Kevin Maguire, she took more interest. 'How old would he be now, this Kevin Maguire?' she asked.

'That I don't know,' Bridgette said. 'The men who travelled to England with my uncle Tom just said he was younger than Molly, who had been thirteen in 1935. I got the feeling that he was much younger and that was why he stayed here with his grandfather, but I don't really know.'

The secretary had got up while Bridgette had been speaking to search a filing cabinet behind her. She withdrew a file and laid it on the desk. 'We had a Kevin Maguire with us until last summer,' she said. 'I think this is the Kevin Maguire that you are after, for Molly Maguire is stated here as his guardian.'

Bridgette's stomach was doing somersaults and her face was a wreath of smiles as she said, 'You don't know what this means to me.'

'I think I do, my dear,' the secretary said. 'Your eyes speak for you. They live on the Kingsbury Road. Do you know the airfield?'

'Yes, I have been up to it,' Bridgette said. 'Molly worked there during the war.'

'Yes, she did,' the secretary said. 'Anyway, the house is this side of the airfield, one of a cluster set back from the road called The Copse, and the Maguires live in number eight.'

Bridgette felt almost breathless with excitement. All that searching had paid off and soon – very, very soon – she would meet up with members of her family.

After shaking hands warmly with the secretary, she almost floated home and told Ada excitedly what had transpired.

'It was all your doing,' she said, throwing her arms around the older woman and kissing her soundly on both cheeks. Then she snatched Finn from where he was building a tower of bricks and danced him around the room. 'Who's going to meet his new cousins then?' she cried, and though Finn didn't understand a word, he caught the excitement, and shouted and waved his arms in the air, which made both women laugh even more.

When their hilarity was spent and Bridgette had come back down to earth, Ada said. 'So when are you going to go up to the house?'

'Ooh, Ada, I would like to go now this minute,' Bridgette said, 'but the secretary told me that Kevin had left school last year so he will probably be working somewhere now, and Molly might be working too. It will kill me to wait but I think late afternoon will be the time to call.'

'And are you taking the babby with you?'

'Oh, yes,' Bridgette said. 'They are his relatives too.'

'Let's have a bite to eat then,' Ada said. 'And what I am going to do with you until it's time to set off I don't know.'

Bridgette didn't know either – the clock had never turned so slowly – but eventually she was ready with Finn strapped in his pushchair. 'Don't forget it's the number twenty-eight tram and it goes right down the Chester Road,' Ada said.

'I know, you have told me this already.'

'Doesn't hurt to go over it again,' Ada said. 'Don't forget to ask the conductor to tell you when you get to the Tyburn pub. The houses are only a step away from there.'

'We were so close the other day! I feel like I have a whole lot of butterflies in my stomach.'

'Go on with you,' Ada said. 'You're like a big kid.' But when she gave Bridgette a hug at the door her eyes were very bright. She watched her walk down the road and hoped that something would go right for her for once. And that when she found the family she had set such store by they were kind and welcoming to her.

Bridgette got off the tram and controlled the urge to run down the road, pushing Finn before her. She forced herself to walk sedately though the churning of her stomach was almost uncomfortable. She found the house with ease, a nice solid red-brick house, and she walked up the path almost apprehensively because she knew whoever opened that door wouldn't know a thing about her.

'This is it then, Finn,' she said, as she lifted the knocker, and he just laughed.

No one came to open the door, though, and Bridgette had knocked again before the woman in the adjoining house came out.

'Ain't no good you knocking there,' she said.

'Are they at work?'

'No,' the woman replied. 'They're gone.'

Disappointment hit Bridgette like a piece of lead and she repeated, 'Gone?' as if she couldn't quite believe it. 'Do you know where?'

'Back down to her sister's near Hereford somewhere,' the neighbour said. 'I don't know her address or owt.'

'Back to her sister's near Hereford,' Bridgette repeated.

The neighbour looked at Bridgette shrewdly, wondering if she was quite right in the head and then she said, 'Who you looking for anyroad?'

'Molly Maguire.'

'Oh, they just lived here through the war,' the woman said. 'It was never their house. It belonged to the Salingers, and her and the two younger girls went to stay with her sister through the war when her son, Terry, went into the RAF. It was him let the house out.'

'So where did the Maguires go after the war?'

The neighbour shrugged. 'Search me. Molly got married, but I don't know where they went after that. First thing I knew was Molly and her brother was gone and Carol Salinger was back. Anyroad, it didn't last because the kids couldn't settle and she wasn't here quite six months and they went back again and the house is up for sale now.'

'What about the son? Did he go with them?' Bridgette asked, thinking if she could trace him he might have more information about the people he had let the house out to.

The neighbour shook her head. 'I don't think so,' she said. 'Don't really know what happened to him. Someone said once they'd heard he'd started up his own business, a garage or some such thing, but I don't know. I never saw him again after he left here.'

'So there is no one that can tell me what happened to Molly Maguire, or whatever she is called now, or her brother?' Bridgette said her voice sounding so bereft that even the neighbour noticed.

'No,' she said. 'I don't think there is. Is it important?'

'To me it is probably the most important thing in the world just now,' Bridgette said sadly.

She turned the pushchair round and began walking back up the path, anxious to be away from the woman lest the urge to throw herself on the ground and howl out her frustration should overcome her. The neighbour watched her go, still not at all sure that she was all right in the head.

Bridgette couldn't believe that she had actually been to the house where Molly and Kevin had lived through the war years, and that woman had lived beside them, and yet she'd had no curiosity about where they had gone when they left the house. She wasn't aware when her tears began. She wanted to sink onto the pavement and weep out all her sadness and her desperate disappointment, to beat her fists at the unfairness of life. She would never find her family – she knew that now – and the realisation was like a hard knot in her heart.

She was unaware where she was pushing the pushchair except that it was in the vague direction of Ada's. Not that she wanted to go home yet. Ada would be all caring and everything, but Bridgette felt she really had to get it straight in her own head before she could talk about it without giving way to the tears now clogging her throat. That would just upset Ada and Finn too.

Finn, she saw, was already disturbed. He was watching her, his large dark eyes solemn, and she knew that he had picked up on her mood. Poor

505

little scrap, she thought. It's hardly his fault. If all he was going to get in his life was her she had to take a grip on herself for his sake, and when they came out at Eachelhurst Road, she could see Pype Hayes Park across the road. She made an effort and said to Finn, 'Shall we go to the park then?'

She wondered if he would recognise the word, for they had only taken him once before, but he obviously did because his eyes lit up again and he began bouncing in his pushchair. 'I suppose I can take that as a yes,' Bridgette said, and she even managed a smile for his sake.

Once in the park, Bridgette made straight for the playground. There was another young mother there with a little girl slightly older than Finn, and she was on one of the toddler swings. Finn could remember the swings too, and he began to shout and point. Bridgette lifted him into a swing next to the little girl. She looked very like her mother, she noticed, with gorgeous dark brown hair that fell around her head in curls, and deep brown eyes like Finn's, though her eyes were dancing.

She reminded Bridgette of Leonie at about the same age, and then she turned and smiled and it was as if a light was turned on inside her face. Despite her innate sadness, Bridgette found herself smiling back.

'Your daughter has a truly beautiful smile,' she said to the young woman pushing the swing beside her.

She laughed as she said, 'Which she uses to great

advantage, and when she turns it on her father he would lift the moon from the sky for her. I have to be quite firm at times because the whole family would have her ruined if I allowed it. Still,' she went on, 'as my uncle says, better that way than the other way and I suppose he's right. Yet I think it will be better when she has a brother or sister. Is yours an only one?'

'Yes,' Bridgette answered shortly. 'And he will always be because I am a widow.'

'Oh, I am sorry,' the young woman said.

Bridgette shrugged. 'There are many of us after this war.'

'Yes,' the woman agreed. 'But knowing that doesn't make it any easier to bear I should think.'

'No, it doesn't.' Bridgette said. 'Nothing really helps, and yet I'm glad I have his child. He is my consolation.'

'Yes,' the woman said gently. 'If anything had happened to my husband I would have wanted his child. He was worried about that very thing when I became pregnant, but when you love someone you want to raise their child. It's part of them, after all. And you're foreign too, aren't you?'

'Yes, I come from Northern France,' Bridgette said.

'My word,' the woman said in admiration. 'Your English is jolly good.'

'Thank you,' Bridgette said. 'I have been learning it since I was a little child. I think that makes all the difference.

'My husband said France had a terrible time in the war,' the woman said. 'He was a pilot and he used to fly over it and see the destruction. Were you in France throughout the war?'

'All through,' Bridgette replied. 'Our town was occupied by the Nazis. That was a terrible time.'

'Oh, it must have been,' the woman said sympathetically. 'I would have hated that.'

Suddenly the little girl started to gabble and the woman gave her swing a hefty push as she said with a wry smile, 'I don't know, even when they can't say much they make their wishes known.'

'I think we become attuned to them,' Bridgette said. 'I always seem to know what Finn wants.'

'Finn's an unusual name, isn't it?' said the woman, and she pushed the swing again.

'I don't really know,' Bridgette said. 'He was called after my father.'

'Oh, my little girl was called after my mother,' the other woman said. 'Her name is Nuala.'

The name resounded in Bridgette's memory. Her heart was thumping hard against her ribs and there seemed to be a roaring inside her head. She remembered that the young woman had said her husband was a pilot and she said, 'This may seem an odd question, but what is your husband's name?'

'Why do you want to know?'

'Please,' Bridgette pleaded. 'Is it Mark?'

The woman looking totally confused said, 'Yes, Mark Baxter.'

Bridgette was so agitated she was having trouble

508

breathing. Could it be possible that this was Molly Maguire, whom she had been looking for, or was it just some cruel coincidence? 'And your name is Molly and you used to be called Maguire?' she said breathlessly.

Totally mystified now, Molly nodded. 'Who are you and how do you know all this?'

'Oh my God! I can scarcely believe it,' Bridgette cried.

'What's this all about?' Molly asked again.

In answer Bridgette said, 'Did you have an uncle who enlisted in the Great War and was killed?'

'Yes,' Molly said, beginning at last to understand. 'He was called Finn and that is your son's name and you said that he was called after your father, so that means . . .'

'That means that I am your cousin,' Bridgette said.

All of a sudden it was too much: the hopes continually dashed, the leads that led nowhere, the disappointment and despair, and the realisation that very day that she would never find her family, and then to meet up coincidently with Molly Maguire in the park. She felt the tears rising up in her body like a torrent.

Molly took one look at Bridgette's face and although she was reeling herself from the things Bridgette had said she left the children swaying back and forwards on the swings, put her arms around her weeping cousin, and led her to a nearby bench, glad they had the playground to themselves.

Bridgette's distress was so profound that in the end Molly felt her own eyes fill up.

Eventually, Bridgette tried to get a grip on herself as she saw the babies watching her dolefully and, seeing her a little calmer, Molly said, 'Before my mother died she told me about Finn and how he died, and said that he had loved a girl called Gabrielle dearly. She was just a young girl herself and she thought it the most romantic thing. In fact, when Finn died, had she known anything about Gabrielle other than her first name and the fact that she lived above a baker's shop in some obscure French town or village, then she would have written and told her that he was dead. It's just amazing that years later I am talking to his daughter that I never even knew existed.'

'Like you say, it is amazing,' Bridgette said. 'Sorry about that outburst earlier, but I didn't think I would ever find you. I have felt so alone for so long that I can hardly believe it and I am almost afraid that you might just disappear in a cloud of smoke.'

'Believe me, I am far too substantial to disappear in any cloud of smoke,' Molly said with a laugh. 'But we need to go home soon, if you feel OK. It's not far and Mark will be in before long. He will want to hear and, goodness, I wonder how the others will view it. I'd love to see Uncle Tom's face.'

'I would like to go home with you, really I would,' Bridgette said, 'but I lodge with a lovely lady and she will worry if I do not return.'

'Don't worry, we'll dispatch Kevin,' Molly said. 'He's very obliging like that, my young brother, and he will explain things to her. Now we have met at last I'm not letting you out of my sight.'

Tom was living with his sister Aggie and brother-in-law Paul Simmons in Sutton Coldfield. He received few letters as all the family lived close together, so when Aggie had one for him when he came in from work one evening in mid-May, he was pleased. He recognised the writing as Nellie McEvoy's. She had written to him a few times after he'd moved to England, usually to keep him up to date with small-town gossip.

Tom slit the envelope and withdrew the letter with a smile on his face. However, when he read that the girl he had almost forgotten about, Gabrielle's daughter, Bridgette, had been in touch with Christy and was now in Birmingham searching for her family, he was totally staggered. He unfolded Bridgette's letter and read that too.

'What is it?' Aggie said. She had seen the frown puckering Tom's brow.

'It's nothing upsetting really,' Tom told his sister. 'Just surprising. Our youngest brother, Finn, was billeted for a time in a small town in Northern France after he joined the army. And there he sowed his wild oats a little too well and in 1916 was married to a French girl called Gabrielle Jobert, who was expecting his baby.'

'Did you know all about it?'

'Well, yes, but not for years afterwards. Finn enlisted with a childhood friend called Christy Byrne, and he told me of the great passion between Finn and Gabrielle.' He went on to tell Aggie and Paul everything Christy had told him of Finn's love affair, which had culminated in his hasty marriage. 'Christy wrote to Gabrielle when he arrived home, telling her of Finn's death,' Tom said. 'And later Gabrielle had a daughter she called Bridgette, after our mother.'

'He never even got to see her,' Aggie said. 'How very sad. But why didn't this Christy also write to Mammy and Daddy and tell them about Gabrielle and their grandchild?'

'Well,' said Tom, 'it would have been difficult because Finn had never told our parents about his sexual exploits. He told me and Joe, boasted of it, and told Nuala a fair bit too. But all he wrote to my parents was that he was going to Mass every Sunday, and going to confession and taking Communion on a regular basis and was as well and happy as could be expected in the circumstances. That is really all they wanted to know.'

'So it would have been a shock to them, d'you mean?' Paul said. 'Like they might not have believed it?'

'There's that, of course,' Tom said. 'But there was a bit more to it than that.' And he went on to tell them of Finn's giving the wrong date of birth to put on the certificate and why he had done it. 'My parents would know, of course, if they had wind of it,' he added, 'and could possibly declare the marriage null and void because their permission hadn't been sought.'

'From what I remember of her, Mammy would have done that,' Aggie said. 'Especially if she thought some young brazen French girl had snared her son.'

'Your memory serves you well,' Tom said. 'France, like Ireland, is a Catholic country where I should imagine having a child without a husband is the greatest sin in the world. Anyway, Christy and Gabrielle decided to leave things as they were and say nothing.'

'So when were you told?' Paul asked.

'Oh, years later,' Tom said. 'After Mammy died.'

'Did you not think to get in touch then?'

'Yes, I thought of it,' Tom said. 'But the country was at war, and France was occupied. Then we thought Gabrielle, who Christy claimed was very beautiful, had probably married again and maybe no one had told the child about her real father, especially if Gabrielle had other children. Now we know this to be true, for Bridgette wrote to Nellie McEvoy that her mother only told her the truth when she was terminally ill and Bridgette was nursing her. On her death bed her mother made Bridgette promise to contact us. She is a widow with a small son that she has called Finn and she wants him to know his Irish relatives.'

'Seems reasonable.' Paul said. 'Where is she now?'

513

'Here,' Tom said. 'In Erdington, according to her address.'

'So how did she get in touch with Nellie at the post office in Buncrana?'

'Must have been Christy advised her,' Tom said. 'She wrote to see if someone there had our addresses and of course Nellie has them all, but didn't want to send them off to a perfect stranger.'

'So what are you going to do?' Paul asked.

'Well, contact her, of course,' Tom said. 'She's as much my niece as Molly is. But I thought maybe I should at least warn the others before I do that because it will be a shock to them all. After I have eaten I will pop along to see Joe and we will go round to Molly's.'

'Me too,' Aggie decided.

'You're right,' said Tom. 'We'll all go.'

'Where do the others live?' Bridgette said as they were making their way back to Molly's house.

'Oh, no one lives far away,' Molly said. 'My house backs onto Pype Hayes Park, and if you walk diagonally down as far as the stream and come out of that gate you are in Sutton Coldfield and in a district of it called Walmley. They all live there.'

'I was surprised to hear that Tom had given up the farm and moved here,' Bridgette said. 'My father always told my mother that he was a born farmer.'

'I asked him that when he suggested coming

514

here first,' said Molly. 'I thought he might regret it, but he said that he never had a say in whether he wanted to be a farmer. He sort of fell into it because he was the eldest and would inherit. Lonely existence, though, and he thought a pointless one: he would be killing himself with the work and at the end of it there would be no one to leave it to. He had a point because he never married and Joe didn't want it.'

'My mother said that Finn talked about the family all the time,' Bridgette said. 'He always said that Joe wanted to see beyond Buncrana and he would if he plucked up enough courage.'

'Well, he did,' Molly said. 'He went to New York in 1921, loved the life there and ended up marrying the boss's daughter, Gloria. They had everything – a fine house and thriving factory – but then came something called the Wall Street Crash. I don't understand it all but it's something to do with stocks and shares and the price of them goes up and down. Joe said it was a bit of a gamble and he had nothing to do with it. But his father-in-law had gambled thousands using the house and factory as collateral, and when the prices of shares dropped so low they were worthless he realised they had lost everything. In fact it was so bad, his father-in-law shot himself.'

Bridgette gave a gasp of shock. 'What did they do?'

'It was a terrible time,' Molly said. She told Bridgette of Joe and Gloria's slide into real and

515

abject poverty, and how they had nearly starved to death in the tenements of New York, and when Ben was born it was even worse.

'It was for Ben's sake that they came to London before the war, but when the war began Joe became a volunteer fireman until he was badly injured in 1942.'

'Is he all right now?'

'Yes, he's fine,' Molly said. 'He went back to Buncrana to recover properly when the hospital was finished with him, because their flat had been destroyed by then and Gloria and Ben had been living in a church hall.'

'Did he mind going back?'

'No, I don't think so,' Molly said. 'By all accounts, it was Gloria that minded. Tom always said that none of us realised just how much.'

'Why?' Bridgette asked. 'What did she do?'

'I'll fill you in later,' Molly said. 'We're here now and if I'm not careful Mark and Kevin will be in on top of us and the dinner won't even have been started.'

However, the meal was well on its way by the time Mark put in an appearance. When Bridgette saw Nuala's eyes light up as she caught sight of her father she felt sorry for her son who would grow up without one. Then Nuala launched herself across the room shouting 'Dadeee' as loud as she could. Mark caught up his young daughter, and even while he lifted her in his arms and planted a kiss on her cheek, he was looking quizzically at

Bridgette and her son, who was playing on the floor.

Molly caught the look and said, 'Save the questions until Kevin is in and we are sitting around the table to save me repeating myself. But this is Bridgette Laurent and her son, Finn. Bridgette, this is my husband, Mark.'

Mark's eyebrows rose, but his smile was genuine and he shifted Nuala to his left hip and approached Bridgette with his hand outstretched. 'I suppose all will be explained in due course,' he said, with a smile that made his dark brown eyes twinkle. 'Till then, Bridgette Laurent, I bid you welcome.'

The handshake was as firm as Bridgette expected it to be and Mark's face was open and honest. She decided that she liked her cousin Molly's husband. 'It's quite a story,' she smiled back

'And one I will look forward to hearing,' Mark said.

Bridgette wasn't able to make a reply for at that moment a young boy came through the door and immediately Nuala was clamouring to be let down. She ran to the lad, whom Molly introduced as her brother, Kevin. He too lifted Nuala into his arms while Molly introduced Bridgette. He shook hands with Bridgette and then squatted down by Finn. 'And who's this?' he said, glancing up at Bridgette as he built a big tower of bricks.

'Finn,' said Bridgette. 'He was called after my father, who was a British soldier.'

'Was he?' Kevin said. 'Then what—'

'Sit up to the table, Kevin, and we'll tell you everything,' Molly said. When everyone was seated she placed a large casserole on a mat on the table, saying as she did so, 'Now, I would like to say that this is beef casserole, but this is austere post-war Britain, so it has plenty of vegetables, with the meat just waved over it.'

'It's what I am used to,' Bridgette said. 'During the occupation in France it was far worse, because a lot of the food was sent to Germany. Most people got used to feeling hungry.'

'We didn't go hungry exactly,' Molly said. 'We were more bored.'

'I'll say,' Kevin said with feeling. 'It was carrots and swede nearly every day. And it wasn't like served with the meal. It *was* the meal.'

There was laughter around the table. 'Yes, Kevin's not far wrong there,' Molly said. 'We had many meals that had no meat in it at all.'

'Yeah, like Woolton Pie,' Kevin said. 'That was just disgusting.'

Molly, seeing Bridgette's confused look, explained, 'The Minister for Food, Lord Woolton, devised this pie and it was considered a patriotic thing to eat it. All that was in it was potatoes, swede, carrots, onions, Marmite and oatmeal.'

'And even the crust wasn't crust,' Kevin complained. 'It was like a lump of dough on top.'

'Well, it was made with only flour and lard.'

'It was horrible.'

'It was,' Molly agreed, and added sarcastically,

'and I'm sure that Lord Woolton is such an honourable man that he has it served up to him morning, noon and night.'

There were gales of laughter around the table and Bridgette realised what a happy family they were and how easy they were with one another. She wanted herself and her son to be a part of this family more than anything else in the world, and so, at Molly's invitation, she began to tell them her story.

TWENTY-SEVEN

When they had finished the meal, Kevin was only too ready to go to tell Ada what had happened to Bridgette. He had been fascinated by the story of Finn and Bridgette's mother, Gabrielle, and as he got to his feet he said, 'You know what? I thought when Mum and Dad died, there was just me and Molly and our granddad. Now we have relations coming out of the woodwork.'

'Are you complaining about that then?' Molly asked.

'No.' Kevin had a grin on his face. 'I ain't complaining. I think it's great.'

'So do I,' Bridgette said. 'I know exactly what you mean. I didn't think that I had that many relations either.'

'Well, I'm off to fetch some more,' said Mark, as Kevin left and he slipped on his coat, but when he opened the door, he saw the rest of the Sullivans, the very ones he intended seeing, coming down the road.

'Are you on your way out, Mark?' Tom asked when they arrived at the door. 'Can you wait on a moment? I have something to tell you.'

'Molly has something to tell you too,' said Mark, throwing open the door. 'Come in. She has someone she's dying for you to meet.'

Intrigued, led by Tom they went into the living room. Bridgette was standing with Finn in her arms, but before any of them were able to say anything Molly came through from the kitchen with cups of tea, saying as she did so. 'Sorry it's got to be tea. The only coffee we can get at the moment is not coffee at all. Aunt Isobel says it's made with chicory and it's liquid and pre-sweetened, not very nice at all really.'

Then she caught sight of her them all standing there and exclaimed, 'What are you all doing here?'

'We have come to see you to tell you some news, but unless I am very much mistaken, you already know it,' Tom smiled.

'Probably,' Molly answered with a grin. She put the cups down on the coffee table and drew Bridgette forward. 'Uncle Tom,' she said, 'this is my cousin Bridgette Laurent, née Sullivan, and her son, Finn.'

Tom thought of his young brother cut down before he had even cast his eyes on his own child and he knew Bridgette to be his because she had Finn's mouth and his dark amber eyes. He stepped forward and, mindful of the child, put his arms around her. 'You're both welcome, my dear, a thousand times welcome,' he said in a voice husky with emotion. 'I am your uncle Tom, or just Tom, as you prefer.'

It was such a genuine welcome, and Bridgette had the strangest feeling that she had come home. Then Tom lifted the baby from her arms and said, 'And hallo to you, young fellow-me-lad.' He was rewarded by a beaming grin. 'You have a grand boy there,' Tom said, handing the baby back to Bridgette. 'And Finn is a fine name for him.'

'Uncle Tom, you are taking this all in your stride,' Molly said. 'You are not even the tiniest bit surprised.'

'Ah. But you see I knew about the existence of Bridgette,' Tom said. He went on to tell Molly all that he had told the others. 'Christy Byrne told me all this, but not until Mammy died,' Tom said. 'By then, though, so many years had passed we thought it better to say nothing. Finn's child, who we knew was a girl and called Bridgette, would be fully grown and maybe married with other children and oblivious of her parentage. Anyway, by then the war was on and France was occupied. The first I heard of Bridgette afterwards was from a letter that she sent to Nellie McEvoy at the post office in Buncrana, and she forwarded it to me.'

'How on earth did you know about Nellie?' Molly asked Bridgette in surprise.

'I didn't,' Bridgette said. 'I wrote to Christy Byrne because it was the only full address I had. He'd written to tell Maman of my father's death when he realised that she hadn't been told officially. When my mother made me promise on her death bed that I would search out the family, I thought of Christy straightaway. He said that the people at the post office might have an actual address for you all because you had been such good friends.'

'We were and still are good friends,' Molly said. 'The McEvoys and Uncle Tom saved my sanity when I was sent to live in Buncrana after my parents died. Nellie was a substitute mother to me when I was in great need of one.'

A shadow passed over Molly's face as she remembered that sad period in her life and then it was gone as she went on, with a glance at her husband, 'If I can ever convince that man of mine to take some time off I would like to go back to Buncrana for a little holiday and see them all again.'

'That would be a grand idea, Molly,' Tom said approvingly.

'Yeah, it would help lay some ghosts and be a chance to show Nuala off.'

'She's well worth showing off,' Bridgette said. 'She is very beautiful.'

'She is,' Aggie said. 'But then so is your son with those big dark eyes.'

'All I can say is that we are very pleased to know you at last,' Tom said to Bridgette. 'You and your son both.'

'I echo that,' Joe added. 'I'm very glad you found

us in the end. As Tom said, you are very welcome. My name is Joe and this is my wife, Isobel, and my son, Ben.'

Bridgette was puzzled for surely Molly had told her that Joe had been married to someone called Gloria. Isobel's greeted Bridgette warmly, but her eyes were on Finn and she exclaimed, 'Aggie is right, he is a beautiful baby.' She poked him gently in the stomach and said, 'And I know one thing, Finn Laurent, you will break hearts one day with those dark eyes.'

'His father's were dark like that?'

'And did he have those incredibly long lashes as well?'

'I'm afraid so,' Bridgette said with a laugh. 'Doesn't seem fair, does it?'

Finn was passed from one to the other, as all exclaimed about his dark eyes, and the sociable baby waved his arms and giggled and thoroughly enjoyed the attention. Little Nuala watched it all with a furrowed frown between her eyes and Molly laughed and said, 'Do her good to have a bit of competition.'

Ben, though, had noticed Bridgette's confusion when she had been introduced to Isobel and he said to her, 'Isobel isn't my mom, though I call her mom sometimes, and other times I call her Izzy. My mother's name was Gloria and she went to live in America with an American sailor. Dad says this summer I can go and see her for a whole month, and Kevin's coming too. I've got a baby sister called Rebecca, almost the same age as Nuala.'

Bridgette was shocked at Ben's words, but she just said, 'That will be wonderful. You must miss your mother very much.'

Ben nodded. 'I used to miss her loads, but I'm used to it now, and Izzy is nearly as good as a proper mom.' And then a cheeky grin spread over his face as he saw Molly approach and he added, 'Kevin's only got Molly. I'd rather have Izzy any day. She's not half as strict as Molly.'

'You, my lad, will get your ears boxed if you're not careful,' Molly said in mock indignation.

Ben gave Bridgette a wink and said, 'See what I mean?' and Bridgette had to bite on her bottom lip to prevent her smile.

'He's a cheeky monkey, all right,' Molly said, watching Ben cross the room. 'But to tell the truth, it's nice to see him like that. He was once a very confused and unhappy boy.'

'He said his mother lives in America,' Bridgette said.

'She does,' Molly said. 'When they were living in Buncrana, she fell for an American petty officer at the nearby naval base. Remember I said how much she hated Buncrana?'

'Yes, but hating something doesn't mean that you can go to America and leave your son behind,' Bridgette said, appalled.

'Ben was adamant that he didn't want to go with her,' Molly said. 'He was actually on the ship that would take them to New York and he jumped off before it sailed. He told Kevin that he couldn't leave his dad behind, and knew that he had made the right decision, but he was angry that he had to make any decision at all. I don't think he realised just how much he would miss his mother. Kevin, having lost his own mother at an even earlier age, helped him cope with that in the end. Anyway, now Joe has met Isobel and Ben thinks the world of her. They will be married when Joe is a free man and meanwhile they live together in a bungalow in Walmley, Sutton Coldfield.' And then she added with a smile, 'Shocking really what the older generation get up to. Come and meet Paul and Aggie.'

Again Bridgette was confused, and as she took Aggie's hand she said, 'Finn told my mother that you had disappeared when he was just a boy.'

'And he was right,' Aggie said. 'All the family know my story. Even Ben has been told now and so it's only right that you should too. I was forced to leave home because when I was fifteen I had been raped by a man called McAllister and was having his baby.'

'I don't know how it is in France,' Molly said, 'but in Ireland, the greatest sin in all the world is to be having a baby without a husband. And somehow it's always the woman's fault. This was 1901, and I imagine things were even worse then.'

'It's the same in France,' Bridgette told her, and knew she had been sensible not to tell the truth about Finn's father. It would be sure to be viewed in a bad light because she was old enough to know what she was doing. She was, though, full of sympathy for the young Aggie as she suddenly remembered that Georges had nearly raped her when she was just a year older. 'What a terrible thing to happen to you,' she cried. 'You were little more than a child. Wasn't there anyone you could have confided in?'

'He said if I told anyone he would say that I had instigated it, that I was more than willing.'

'What a rat!'

'I couldn't agree more,' Aggie said. 'And the dreadful thing is he would have been believed as well. Tom was the only one in the house when I came home that time and he helped me and we agreed to tell no one. But when I found out that I was pregnant I confronted McAllister and he sent me to his sister in Birmingham, who he said would sort me out. I was terrified because I'd never left home before, but I was even more scared of staying.'

Tom snorted. 'I wasn't scared. I was raging angry, especially when I realised that McAllister was going to get away scot-free. Then after Aggie disappeared, I saw McAllister riding out to one of the farms and, wanting to teach him a lesson, I stretched wire across trees where I knew the horse would run into it as he made his way home.'

'Did it work?'

'Oh yes, and far too well,' Tom said. 'McAllister

was thrown from his horse. He went sailing through the air and he hit his head on a tree and the blow killed him. McAllister's wife had followed me and when I told her what her husband had done, she said Aggie wasn't the first girl he had taken down, and so she helped me cover up the crime. Then, before the funeral, she wrote to his sister in Birmingham, informing her of her brother's death but the letter was returned with "Not known at this address" written across it. I was so worried for I had no idea what had happened to Aggie.'

'I obviously knew nothing of this,' Aggie said. 'But there was no one at the address when I arrived because the sister had moved.'

'Oh God, what did you do?'

'I didn't know what to do,' Aggie said. 'I was desperate. I would have probably died had it not been for prostitutes who took me in and looked after me, particularly when I lost the baby. Living there, though, sealed my fate, and for years and years. I sank into their world of prostitution, because I couldn't apply for anything more respectable without references and I owed the prostitutes loyalty and in time I took the drugs and drink they plied me with because it blurred the edges of what I was forced to do.'

'It's a dreadful tale,' Bridgette said. 'And I feel sorry for you too, Uncle Tom, having to carry such a burden.'

'Yes,' Molly said. 'And one that prevented him marrying anyone. Uncle Tom, being the man he is, holds himself totally responsible for McAllister's death. So he has never even allowed himself to get close to anyone.'

'It was safer that way,' Tom said. 'How could I risk the tale getting out? And yet I couldn't keep such a thing from any woman I wished to marry. If it became known, the sacrifice Aggie made to save the family shame by leaving home before her pregnancy should be noticed would have been in vain. McAllister's wife would have been in trouble too and if, because of my age at the time, I was spared the hangman's noose, I would probably have been transported.'

'This is awful,' Bridgette said. She turned again to Aggie. 'How did you escape in the end?'

'I wasn't on the streets straightaway,' Aggie said. 'I was taken as a paramour by one of the bosses of a club. They called it that, but really it was a posh name for a whore house. The manager wanted to marry me, but he was killed by an evil man called Finch. When I tried to break out of prostitution, he abducted me and forced me back into it. By the time I accidently bumped into Tom I was drink-sodden and addicted to the drugs Finch supplied me with. Tom weaned me off the drugs and hid me from those who were out to harm me.'

'And what happened to the man Finch?' Bridgette asked. 'Was he ever brought to trial?'

'Not through the official channels, no,' Tom said with a slight smile.

'I knew nothing of this until it was all over,'

Aggie said. 'My brothers took matters into their own hands.'

'We had to,' Tom said. 'Finch was rich and influential, and Aggie would be known as a street woman. If the police had agreed to take the case on, it would be laughed out of court. Anyway, she was too frightened of the man to testify.'

'So?'

'So, Joe and I tracked Finch down and Joe beat him up on a canal towpath.'

'No more than he deserved,' Bridgette said. 'Did he kill him?'

'No,' Tom said. 'He left him unconscious but alive on the towpath, but we had gone no distance when we heard a splash and running feet, and went back. Someone had heaved him into the canal and we watched him sink under the murky waters.'

'I would say that he was no loss,' Bridgette sighed.

'I agree,' Aggie said.

'Yes,' said Tom. 'And when we told Aggie that the man was finally dead, I saw the fear fall from her like she was shedding a skin she had lived with for years.'

'And then she met Paul?'

'Well, yes,' Tom said. 'Though Paul knew our family for some years before he met Aggie.'

'He was an officer my father saved in the Great War,' Molly said. 'And Dad went to work with him afterwards. And then when Mum and Dad died I was taken to Buncrana to live.'

'But your brother stayed here?'

Molly nodded. 'He was too ill, the doctors said, and so he was left with our grandfather.'

Bridgette, remembering what the Donahue brothers told her, said, 'I heard all this and I thought it a shame to part you both.'

'I agree with you,' Molly said, 'we should both have been left in Birmingham with Granddad. I used to wish that when I was going through it with my vindictive and spiteful grandmother. But I would have hated Kevin to go through what I did.'

Bridgette remembered that that was what Pat and Mick Donahue had said too and she looked across at Tom and he nodded as he said. 'Every word Molly said is true, for my mother gave her one hell of a life. She had done the same to me since I had been a boy and had me near scared half to death, and I had never bothered standing up for myself. When Molly came, she was such a sad and troubled young girl I had to take a grip on myself for her sake.'

'But why was she like that?' Bridgette asked.

'It was basically because my mother married a non-Catholic,' Molly said. 'She was determined that I would pay for that.' When she went on to chronicle some of the abuse and cruelty that she had suffered at the hands of her grandmother Bridgette was shocked to the core.

'Yet,' Molly continued, 'if I hadn't gone to Buncrana then I'd probably never have met Uncle

Tom or Joe or Aunt Aggie or you either, so I can't totally wish that I had never been sent there.'

'So how did you track us down in the end?' Joe wanted to know.

'I didn't know what to do at first,' Bridgette told them of her assumption that Boldmere was a small place and the fruitless searching she had done after the two men from Donegal had arrived at her door.

'But how come you are living in Orphanage Road now?' Tom asked.

'It's the taxi driver's mother's house,' Bridgette said. 'He was concerned about me when I said I had nowhere to stay. I asked him if he knew of a hotel and he said in a place as bombed to bits as Birmingham, decent hotels and guest houses would all be full and the only ones likely to have rooms free would probably be in places that wouldn't be safe for me.'

'I can say from experience that he was probably right.' Molly said with a shiver.

Bridgette raised her eyebrows, but Molly shook her head, 'My tale will keep for another time. This is your story.'

It isn't a lodging house or anything, just a house, but Ada, the taxi driver's mother, is lovely. She had the room and agreed to take me in. Ada has been trying to help me find where you all were, although I imagine sometimes she must have thought it hopeless. I know I was beginning to. It was she who suggested that I try Paget Road School and they gave your address as Kingsbury Road.'

'Of course, the Salingers' house.' Molly said. 'Terry is in partnership with Mark at the garage. Apparently his sisters liked the quiet life and they went back to the place they had been living in all through the war and put their house on the market.'

'That was the end of the road for me,' Bridgette said. 'When I wandered into the park this afternoon and by chance met Molly I was feeling so dispirited and low. I had written to the post office at Buncrana by then, but I thought it highly unlikely that they would help me.'

'They did in a way,' Tom said. 'Nellie forwarded your letter to me and it had the address where you are staying in Orphanage Road. I was only alerting the family before going to call on you. And we all came to tell Molly and found you had already met.'

'It was totally amazing how that happened,' Molly said with a smile. 'I will write to Nellie and explain everything.'

'I can only imagine what it was like to lose both parents so suddenly and so tragically,' Bridgette said. 'The Donahue brothers told me what happened to you.'

'It was a bad time,' Molly agreed. 'For all of us. But something nearly as bad happened to me when I first arrived in Birmingham.'

She stopped and Bridgette urged, 'Go on.'

Molly took a deep breath. 'When I was in Ireland Kevin and my grandfather used to write to me every week, but in October 1940 the letters stopped.

533

When I had heard nothing for three weeks, knowing the pounding that Birmingham was having, I decided to go there myself and find out what had happened to them. As I stepped on to the platform at New Street Station, the sirens screamed to warn us all of a terrifying raid that scared me rigid and two men offered to look after me. That's why I said what I did about the taxi driver. People are not always what they seem. I thought these two men were kind. They took me to a shelter, shared their food and when the raid was over, offered me an empty flat they knew of to spend what was left of that night. But I soon found out those men were anything but kind. I was soon pumped full of drugs while I was being preened for the whore house.'

Bridgette was so shocked her mouth had dropped agape. 'You too,' she gasped out. 'I can scarcely believe it.'

'Eventually, I was rescued by a lovely man called Will Mason,' Molly continued, 'who put his whole family at risk by doing that and then also harbouring me. But they tracked me down and made another attack on my life.'

'My God! Molly, how dreadful!' Bridgette cried.

Molly smiled wryly. 'It would have been far worse if it had succeeded. As it was, that's how I got together with Mark because in hospital I met his sister, Lynne. Mark came to visit his sister and through him I got a job on the airbase. So you see, every cloud has a silver lining. Then later I testified against the men who abused me and many

534

others, and I had the pleasure of seeing them gaoled for many years,'

'You are incredibly brave, Molly,' Bridgette said with a sigh. 'I am so glad that I have met up with all of you.'

'Yes, but I fear we probably won't see that much of each other,' Molly said, 'because you will have to return to Paris sometime.'

Bridgette shook her head. 'My dear aunt and uncle offered me a home straightaway when they knew my mother was dying, and Paris is lovely to visit, but I have been unable to settle there. Anyway, their elder son is now back home with his fiancée. They were parted from both boys for many years and I think need time to be together as a family.'

'Would you like to go back to the other place then?' Tom asked. 'St-Omer, wasn't it?'

Bridgette imagined the violence of the mob that would have attacked the bakery to drag her from it, and their frustration when she wasn't there causing them to set fire to her home. Just thinking about it brought a bad taste to her mouth and she knew that she could never live among such people.

She could share none of this with Tom and Molly, but they had seen her shiver of distaste as she said, 'I definitely don't want to return to St-Omer.'

'Too many bad memories, I suppose?' Molly said, and Bridgette just nodded.

'You could do worse than stay here with us,' Tom said. 'It can't be that bad, as we have all settled around here, and you would have the support of us all. I should imagine widowhood is a lonely route to travel without family support.'

'Uncle Tom has a point,' Molly said. 'But you'd hardly know what the place is like because you've seen nothing yet. Mind you,' she added, 'we can soon remedy that.'

Bridgette was not able to make any reply as just then Kevin came in, holding her shoulder bag in his hand. He said, 'That Ada is really nice and she has packed a few things for the baby in case you want to stay the night.'

'Oh, I couldn't impose like that.'

'Course you could,' Kevin said. 'I can always bunk in with Ben for a bit, can't I, Uncle Joe?'

'But will you mind doing that?' Bridgette asked Kevin.

But before he was able to make any sort of reply, Joe said, 'Mind? I'll say not. The two of them are as thick of thieves. And yes, Kevin, that will be no trouble. Anyway,' he went on, turning back to Bridgette, 'I think we have told you enough about us. It's time we learned something about you now.'

'I'd be interested in hearing,' Aggie said. 'In my years away from the family I often thought of Finn, for I loved him dearly and I didn't think he would forget me so easily. I was very upset when I heard that he had been killed in the Great War and I'm so glad that he found someone he loved as much as your mother and that you were the result of that love. That is very comforting.'

536

Bridgette was moved by the emotion in Aggie's voice, but she said, 'I hope you are not disappointed for there is little interesting to say about me, and as for my father, I only know what Maman told me, though he did write her many letters that you can read. I read them all and he became more real to me because of it.'

They all sat around the room, and Kevin and Ben made tea for everyone as Bridgette told them all she knew of her mother's courtship with Finn, the love they had so evidently shared, and showed them the locket with Finn's lock of hair inside, which she still wore around her neck, and the ring she wore on her right hand that her mother said they had used as a wedding ring.

They were interested in all that, but they also wanted to know something about the person she was now, but she knew she had to be cautious in what she said. So she told them just that she had had a troubled upbringing with Legrand, who had pretended to be her natural father, and his bullying son, Georges, and said it was one of the reasons she had left the bakery and gone to work in the dress shop. 'I married James and he enlisted as soon as war was declared,' she said. 'And later was rescued from the beaches of Dunkirk.'

It had hurt Bridgette to say that, when Xavier's body might still lie there hidden under the sand, and she bit her lip to try and prevent the tears from falling.

But the family saw her distress and Tom said,

'Please don't upset yourself, Bridgette. These memories are still painful for you and we don't need to know any more.'

However Bridgette knew it was better to go on now she had started, get all the lies out together and get the story established in her head, and so she said, 'No. It's all right. James made it to Britain and I found out later that he had joined the Free French Army under General de Gaulle. But in St-Omer times were hard after the occupation and I took up bar work.' Here again she kept the details very vague.

'James was involved in the invasion, when he injured his arm quite badly. When they patched him up he came home for a couple of days' leave to rest it properly before rejoining his unit.'

'I had been living back at the bakery since April, when Legrand fetched me to nurse my mother and by the time James was ready to leave in mid-July she had become very ill indeed. I sent a telegram to my aunt and uncle in Paris. They arrived the day I received news that James was dead.'

'Oh, my dear girl,' Aggie said. 'What a terrible thing to happen, and for your mother to be so ill too.'

Bridgette nodded. 'It was a very sad time. I remember feeling that I was filled up with sorrow. Maman died a fortnight later, the very day the American soldiers reached the town, and she made me promise on her deathbed that I would come and see Finn's family, and so here I am.'

'And it has been a delight to meet you,' Aggie said.

'Hear hear,' Tom said heartily. 'Welcome to the family, my dear.'

TWENTY-EIGHT

The family went out of their way to make Bridgette feel welcome, and within a couple of days a strong bond had grown between her and Molly. The babies got on well together most of the time and any spats were few and far between and easily resolved.

Initially, Bridgette had felt bad about leaving Ada, but when she went to see her to collect her suitcases and arrange for Mark to collect the other larger items, the older woman was all smiles.

'Don't you worry about me, ducks,' she said. 'You've done me a favour. All that searching you did for your family made me realise what's important in this life and so I am doing what the kids want and putting my house on the market and moving to somewhere much smaller nearer to them. Should have done it years ago.'

'What about all your memories tied up in the house?' Bridgette asked.

'Memories don't rely on bricks and mortar,'

Ada said. 'Memories are locked in your heart.' She patted Bridgette's arm and went on, 'You stay with your family, my duck. It's what you come to find and where you belong, and don't you give me another thought.'

'You're a very special lady,' Bridgette said. 'I only hope that your family appreciates you.'

Ada gave a chuckle and said, 'I'll probably irritate the life out of them, but that's family, ain't it? You accept each other, warts and all.'

Bridgette returned home in a reflective mood. She knew essentially that Ada was right and she felt bad to be living a lie with her own people. The longer it went on, the more entrenched it would become, and yet she could see no way out of it.

When she got home, Molly said, 'If tomorrow is a nice day, how d'you fancy a trip to Sutton Park?'

'Oh yes,' said Bridgette, remembering how she wanted to go there and take James's son to the place his father had such happy memories of and her voice had a breathless note to it as she said, 'I'd love to go. Is it far?'

'As I said before the boundary of Sutton Coldfield is no distance at all,' Molly said. 'The park though is further and we'll go by train. That will please the children anyway, and your lovely big pushchair will accommodate both of them with ease. As long as we have the weather we'll make a day of it and take a picnic.' Molly added. 'What d'you say?'

'I say that sounds a very good idea,' Bridgette said, and when she went to bed that night she prayed for good weather for the morning.

The day was fine and dry and promised to be warm. They set off for the station in high spirits and Molly was right: the children did love the train. As it chugged its way through the countryside Molly said, 'I bet you have seen nothing like this park. It's massive and there are roads running through it.'

Bridgette remembered James telling her that the park had five large lakes and that it was given to Sutton Coldfield by Henry the Eighth. Before she could stop herself, she blurted that out and Molly looked at her in amazement. 'How on earth do you know that?'

Bridgette was annoyed with herself. Whatever had possessed her to come out with something like that? She could hardly tell Molly the truth and so she said, 'I don't know. It just popped into my head.'

'Well, that's just uncanny,' Molly said, 'because you're right. It's a really special park and those who don't live in Sutton have to pay to get in. Through the war a lot of it was out of bounds because soldiers trained here and I heard that they had a POW camp there too. People say that farmers whose men had been called up and wouldn't have land girls often opted for prisoners of war to work on their farms.'

'Were they not afraid they would escape?'

'Where to?' Molly said. 'Britain is an island, don't forget. Anyway, very few tried to escape. They knew when they were well off, I suppose. It will be nice now to see the park in peacetime.'

And it was a wonderful park, just as Molly had said. They went in what she said was the main entrance, Town Gate. Just the other side of it was a children's playground where a boy was pushing his younger sister on one of the swings, and there again there was the memory of James saying that he always seemed to spend a long time pushing his sister, Dolly, on one of the swings in that park.

Apart from the boy and his sister, they had the playground to themselves but Molly said at the weekend it was swarming with children and the park was popular with courting couples too, especially on Sundays.

'So,' she said with a grin to Bridgette, 'if you stay in Birmingham and fall in love with someone, you'll know where to take him.'

'That will never happen to me,' Bridgette said. 'It isn't worth the heartache. The only man I will love is little Finn.'

'That's a sad and very final decision to make,' Molly said. 'Someone once said that it was better to have loved and lost than never to have loved at all.'

'Then I would say that person has never loved deeply and lost the person they cared for so that they only feel half a person afterwards,' Bridgette said.

'It is like you British say, that person was talking through the top of their head.'

'You mean top of their hat?' Molly corrected.

Bridgette gave a definite nod. 'Yes, and that too.' Then she caught Molly's eye and the two women burst out laughing. Bridgette realised that it was the first time in ages that she had laughed like that.

After that the day could only be a magical one. They walked by the edge of one of the large lakes and as Molly led the way into the wood at the lake's edge she pointed out the rivulets that weaved through the trees to feed the lake. 'Little streams like that are all over the park,' Molly said.

Bridgette just nodded as she took a deep breath in and smelled the fragrant blossom on many of the trees and saw the clusters of pink and white peeping out amongst the bright green leaves and the dappled sun shining down on them through their semi-canopy of foliage. The children were clamouring to be let out of the pushchair and walk, and so Molly and Bridgette unstrapped them and let them explore the woods too. They showed them the roughness of the tree bark and how to kick their feet through the decaying leaves from autumn still littering the ground, which made them both giggle. They shared in their excitement when they uncovered a pine cone or found petals from the blossom that had floated to the ground.

'Doesn't having a small child make you look at the world in a different way?' Molly said.

Bridgette nodded. 'Everything is new to them, so the mundane becomes exciting, and if you can catch a bit of that it makes you realise what a wonderful world it really is.'

'Maybe more people will see that now that the fighting has stopped,' Molly said.

Suddenly Bridgette burst out, 'Oh, look at the cows.'

The trees had thinned and Bridgette had spotted cows on the lush pastureland in front of them. They watched the people approach with large doe-like eyes. 'Oh,' exclaimed Molly in delight, 'it's nice to see them back! Mark told me all about those cows. When this park was given to the people of Sutton Coldfield, certain farmers were given permission for their cows to graze in the park. That was suspended during the war and this is a sort of sign that things are returning to normal.'

'I know exactly what you mean,' Bridgette said, as they walked past the field with the cows, onto a grassy hillock. 'It's lovely to see everything returning to a more peaceful time.'

'Shall we stay here a while?' Molly said. 'It's a good spot for a picnic. I don't know about you, but I am suddenly very hungry, and I bet Finn and Nuala won't say no to a bit of grub either.'

'I'm all for that,' Bridgette said as she took the blanket from the back of the pushchair and laid it on the ground. Soon a sizeable hole was made in the food and drink they had bought with them and Bridgette lay back on the grass, gazing at the pale blue sky, the white fluffy clouds scudding across it, and felt contentment seeping all through her as if at last she was in the right place.

She said none of this to Molly, but Molly had deduced a lot by the look on Bridgette's face and she gave her a gentle poke in the ribs and said, 'What d'you say to us peeling off our stockings and giving the babies the chance to paddle in one of the streams?'

Molly wanted to take Bridgette into Birmingham town centre and show her a place called the Bull Ring.

'Do they sell bulls?' Bridgette asked.

'No,' said Molly with a smile, 'though they probably did once. But there are stalls that sell just about anything else. I haven't been there since the war ended, to tell you the truth. I went during the war a few times once I had Kevin living with me because they used to sell rabbit, offal and horse meat, and it was off ration. Isobel and Aggie are falling over themselves to look after the babies, so we won't have to take them with us and we can go in on the tram.'

The tram stopped at a place called Steel House Lane, so called, Molly said, as they alighted, because of the police station across the road.

'And what is the other grim building on this side?' Bridgette asked.

'That's the General Hospital now,' Molly said. 'Mark's mother told me that once it had been built as a work house and you're right, it is rather grim from the outside. Come on,' she went on, linking her arm through Bridgette's, 'I'll take you up Colmore Row and show you first what used to be our Jewellery Quarter.'

As they were coming up to a road on the right she said. 'This is Whittall Street and if you look up as we pass there you will see the Catholic Cathedral of Birmingham called St Chad's at the end.'

'It has two blue spires.' Bridgette said in surprise as she caught sight of it.

'Yes and it's very grand,' Molly said. 'But not big for a city Cathedral. Not that it's much smaller than the Anglican St Phillips that we will pass in a moment.'

'I attended a Cathedral in St-Omer,' Bridgette said, 'It was called Notre Dame and that wasn't all that big either, but very beautiful inside.'

'We're coming up to Colmore Row now,' Molly said. 'What can you see behind the façade of Snow Hill Station?'

'Just a sea of rubble,' Bridgette answered.

'That was our Jewellery Quarter,' Molly said. 'Such a lot of it was burned out in the war. It was before I arrived in Birmingham but I was told that the fires were so intense the tar melted and slid into the gutters and, of course, buckled the tram-lines and the railway tracks too.'

'It sounds dreadful,' said Bridgette, and she remembered that James had said his wife, Sarah, had worked there.

547

'It must have been,' Molly said. 'St Phillip's, the Anglican cathedral, was bombed too and they must have been semi expecting that because they removed all the stained-glass windows to a place of safety before the war.'

'It does look a bit battered,' Bridget said, looking across the road to the church. 'But I like the clock tower and the blue dome above it, and the gardens around it are lovely,'

'I suppose,' Molly said. 'I was born and bred here and that means that I probably don't appreciate things as much as you do seeing them for the first time. I mean we have a pretty impressive Town Hall, at the end of this road based on a Roman temple and I have never really looked at it.'

Bridgette looked at it though and used as she had become to the historical sites of Paris, she was impressed by the grandeur of the place before they turned into New Street. 'I saw all this destruction and devastation and massive holes from the taxi the night I arrived,' Bridgette said, 'but somehow it affects you more when you are actually walking past it.'

Molly nodded. 'We're just so used to it, we hardly notice any more.'

'And where is the Bull Ring?'

'Not far now,' Molly said. 'It's just along here.' And then she added, 'Before the war you could buy anything in the Bull Ring and Saturday night was party night. I only saw it a few times but I'll never forget it. All the stalls were lit like fairy land,

and there were stilt walkers and a man tied up in chains, and another with hardly any clothes on lying on a bed of nails. There was a boxing booth too, but my parents never let me see that. And there might be someone giving a sermon. Then after a while all these men would be along with their accordions. First they would play all the jigs and reels from Ireland to get people in the mood, and then they'd do all the music-hall songs and everyone would be singing. It was always a smashing night. Anyway, we're here now and you can see the place for yourself.'

They began to walk down the cobbled incline, passing mounds of rubble. 'There used to be shops all along here as well as you can probably see.' Molly said. 'There were at least two tailors that could make up a suit for you for thirty shillings, or two guineas if you wanted a waistcoat. Dad took me in one day when he was being measured for one. And before the war there were a lot more flower sellers around too. Course, all the available land was dug up in the Dig for Victory campaign.'

Bridgette thought parts of the Bull Ring were not unlike the market in St-Omer. Barrows piled high with produce of every description swept down along the cobbled incline to a church at the bottom, which was ringed by trees. The cries of the vendors mixed with the voices of those bartering with customers and the general crush of people, and through this cacophony one strident voice could be plainly heard: an old lady standing in front of

Woolworths. She was blind and had a card around her neck saying so, and cried out incessantly, 'Carriers. Handy Carriers.'

'We'll take a look around Woolworths later, if you like,' said Molly. 'It's called the Sixpenny Store because nothing cost more than that in there.'

'I'm only just getting to grips with your money.' Bridgette said. 'But sixpence isn't much is it?'

'No,' Molly said, pulling one from her purse. 'It's also called a tanner. Come on, let's go and have a shufty in Peacocks first. It used to be great before the war because there were toys of every description. I used to love the dolls and what a variety they had then. There were dolls' houses too, with miniature furniture. I never had anything so fine. There just wasn't the money about. My dolls' house was a shoe box and my dolls more the battered variety. But Mum used to say no one could charge you for having a look. Did you have many toys?'

Bridgette shook her head. 'No, and what I did have my stepbrother, Georges, often broke or else spoiled in some way.'

'Why?'

Bridgette shrugged. 'I never knew why. I once had a doll my aunt sent to me from Paris. But Georges threw it in the fire?'

'That's a terrible thing to do,' Molly cried. 'I hope he was well and truly punished.'

Bridgette gave a bitter little laugh. 'Nothing happened to him, but I was punished for making a fuss. One day I will tell you more of what my life was like, first with my grandfather and then my stepfather, but not today. It would spoil my first visit to this Bull Ring of yours and I would like the see these toys in Peacocks.'

'If they have any,' Molly said.

The store looked pretty well stocked with toys to Bridgette's unaccustomed eye, but the scant number of dolls and basic dolls' houses didn't please Molly.

Bridgette found Woolworth's store was just as Molly had said. There was kitchenware, general household goods and things for the garden and tools for the handyman, all for sixpence or less, but they were more interested in the jewellery. They saw sparkling diamond rings, or those with red stones that glittered like rubies, and there were pearl necklaces and a wide variety of brooches, earrings and bracelets, also all for sixpence. Besides the jewelry counter was one selling hairslides and ribbons and silver backed brushes and matching combs.

They bought nothing though and wandered back into the cobbled streets. Next door to Woolworths was the Hobbies Shop where plywood models had again begun to appear in the windows now that the war was over and they stopped a moment to admire the trains yachts and cars adorning the window. 'They sell kits inside,' Molly said as they turned away. 'The shelves were virtually bare through the war, but I managed to buy Kevin and

Ben one each last Christmas. It kept them quiet I must admit, but the glue stunk to high heaven.'

They had to dodge the trams rattling along at terrific speed in front of the church that Molly said was called St Martin in the Fields. There were also large beefy horses pulling wagons behind them but they were relatively easy to avoid. There also many men with trays around their necks selling things like razor blades and shoe laces or wind up toys and another man by the church had a crate of fluffy baby chicks for sale she noticed as she crossed the street and went up the steps and into the roofless Market Hall.

It was just like any other market there, Bridgette thought. There were flower stalls and those selling clothes and material, kitchen utensils, toys, haber-dashery and junk. This latter had many interesting objects for sale. Interspersed were stalls selling meat and fish and cheese. Molly bought some cheese and horsemeat, though she said it was daylight robbery at two and six a pound. On the fruit and vegetable stalls she was delighted to see they had bananas.

'I can't really believe it,' she said to Bridgette. 'Bananas haven't been in the shops for years.'

'I wonder what Finn and Nuala will make of them,' Bridgette said.

'We'll soon find out,' Molly said. 'And I will buy a bunch for Joe and Isobel too. I bet Ben and Kevin will like the taste of bananas.'

With her purchases stowed away Molly suggested,

'What d'you say to us having a cup of tea, or coffee if you prefer it, and whatever they have in the way of cakes in Lyons Corner House before we make for home?'

'That is a very good idea,' said Bridgette. 'And by the way, I like your Bull Ring. In fact, so far I like what I've seen of Birmingham very much.'

The days slid one into another, all very pleasant, but Bridgette began to worry about her finances. If she was going to make Brimingham her home it was no longer a holiday and she needed to find a job. Her savings would not last for ever.

The following Sunday, Bridgette waited until they were all relaxing with the inevitable cup of tea after Sunday dinner at Joe and Isobel's house, and Ben and Kevin, not up to relaxing, had set off to the park with their football, before she said. 'I am thinking of looking around for a job.'

To her surprise they were all against it. 'There is no need to do that,' Tom said determinedly.

'But I can't live off you,' she complained.

'Of course you can,' Tom said. 'That's what being a family is all about.'

'There may be something due to you being a war widow,' Paul said. 'I'll help you look into it, if you like?'

Bridgette definitely did not like. If they investigated why she wasn't receiving a war widow's pension it would blow everything open.

Tom read the trepidation on her face and said,

'Don't worry about that for now. We have enough money to help you out and I think – and I am sure the other will agree – that Finn needs his mother while he is so small.'

'I certainly agree,' Molly said. 'And what would I do now without Bridgette's company? Unless, Isobel, you want Kevin to come back home now?'

'Not at all,' Isobel said. 'He's no bother at all. I hardly see either of them, with Kevin at work all day and Ben at school, and all too soon they'll be off to America for a month.'

'Yes,' Molly said, 'there's not many apprentices I know would be allowed to have a whole month's holiday.'

'Ah,' said Aggie, 'but then Paul is not a usual employer, are you?'

'No,' Paul said with a grin. 'I'm a saint, I am. But don't worry, Kevin is a good worker and everyone deserves a treat once in a while.'

Molly, for all her token grumble, was grateful to Paul for his considerate nature because she thought Kevin had had a hard enough ride in his young life but she said to Joe, 'Won't you miss Ben awfully, Uncle Joe? A month is ages.'

'Of course,' Joe said. 'But you have to remember that whatever differences Gloria and I had, she always loved Ben and always will. He didn't want to go and live with her in America and still doesn't, and Gloria had to accept that. So how can I begrudge him spending a month with her? It must be harder for her being without him most of the time.'

It must, Bridgette thought. She adored Finn and would guess that, however much Gloria loved her American, there would be a hole in her life because she no longer had her son to share it. On the other hand, though Ben wanted to see his mother and America, he had become used to being without her and was happy with his father and Isobel and the other relations. And that was what she wanted for Finn. He would grow up without a father, but he would have Tom and Joe and Mark, and, later, Kevin and Ben to model himself on.

Bridgette and Molly grew closer than ever and Bridgette became more and more certain that she had made the right decision. Both she and Molly had an extra ration book as they each had a child under five and they pooled them and would try out different recipes together that they would get from the wireless, or the *Evening Mail*, which ran a weekly recipe slot. Although some of what they produced looked less than appetising, Mark valiantly ate everything and usually declared it delicious.

Happy though she was, Bridgette had initially felt a pang of guilt about her aunt and uncle in Paris, who had been so generous to her, but as time passed their letters were all about Raoul and Monique and the wedding planned for the autumn, and Gerard, who was courting a nice girl from a good family.

Bridgette was so pleased. She knew that not that

long after the marriage, Yvette would be looking forward to the prospect of becoming a grand-mother, and she hoped she wouldn't have to wait too long.

Marie Laurent wrote that Lisette and Edmund, who had been demobbed six months before, had moved into a house of their own because Lisette was pregnant again and they needed the extra room. It was as if Bridgette had been given the green light to go ahead and choose the life she wanted to live, and this is what she told Molly.

'And, as Finn is half-French, I will teach him to speak both French and English, so that if ever I take him back to visit his French relations, he will be able to talk to them in their language.'

'That's a really good idea,' Molly said. 'I only wish that I could do something like that for Nuala.'

'You don't have to,' Bridgette said. 'I can teach Nuala just as easily.'

'You'd not mind that?'

'Why should I mind?' Bridgette said. 'It will benefit them both, I should say, and then they can rattle on to each other in French.'

'You know,' Molly said with a catch in her voice, 'I bless the day that you came into our lives, and not just because you have offered to teach my daughter French. It's strange because I know that we haven't known each other that long and yet . . . well, I think I feel as much for you as I would any sister.'

'I feel the same,' Bridgette said. 'And I think that's wonderful for both of us.'

'You certainly have kept me company, with Mark working long hours,' Molly said. 'He says everyone and their dog seems to want the cars that they put under wraps for the duration made road-worthy again for when petrol rationing is eased a little. And, of course, many of the demobbed servicemen are using their gratuity to buy new cars. But I have told Mark if he is not careful Nuala will forget who her father is.'

Bridgette knew Molly had a point. Mark was away from the house before anyone else was up and back home grey-faced with exhaustion long after the children had gone to bed. However, he had obviously taken Molly's words to heart and one Friday in early July he asked Bridgette and Molly if they would like a run out the following afternoon.

'Where to?' Molly asked.

'Sutton Coldfield,' Paul said. 'I have to deliver a Ford Prefect to a customer. I thought I might play hookey after that and spend the afternoon in Sutton Park if the weather holds and we could come back by train. What d'you say?'

'I say, yes please,' Molly said. 'And I'm sure that Bridgette is of like mind.'

'I am,' Bridgette said. 'I love Sutton Park.'

And so they were all waiting for Mark when he drove up that following afternoon in the maroon Ford Prefect. 'It's lovely,' Molly said, slipping in beside Mark with Nuala on her knee.

As they drove past Joe and Isobel's bungalow,

and then Paul and Aggie's house, Molly said, 'Why can't we have a car? Think of all the places we could go so easily on Sunday.'

'You told me one time that you never wanted a car,' Mark said.

Molly had. In fact she had been nervous of riding in cars, she presumed because her parents had been killed in one. She knew she had had to get over it, though, and she said to Mark, 'That was ages ago.'

'Well, I'll look around as soon as the petrol ration is increased,' Mark said. 'I told you this before.'

Bridgette in the back of the car wasn't really listening to the conversation she could barely hear anyway, but was pointing things out to Finn, who was sitting on her knee looking out of the window.

'I know but—'

'Believe me,' Mark said, 'it is more frustrating having a car sitting outside the house that you cannot drive because you haven't the petrol, than not having a car at all. This chap is going to find that out.'

'What's he buying it for then?'

'To have it ready, he said,' Mark told Molly. 'That's what they're all doing, and when it seems feasible I will be in a good position to buy us a really good model. Don't worry, I am keeping my eyes open.'

He drove in silence for a minute or two and then said. 'I sort of know the man who is buying this Ford, from my days in the Forces. He didn't know Terry and I owned the garage. He just called in on spec.'

'Is that why you offered to deliver it, because you know him?'

'Well, I do deliver some if it is difficult for the customer to collect,' Mark said, 'but I offered to do it this time because I thought about what you said. I missed enough of Nuala's early life and really have to make time for her now, and I have hardly got to know Finn at all.'

'So, the sky is blue, the sun is shining and when you and your RAF wallah have finished, we can take off for the park, can we?'

'Course,' Mark said. 'But this chap was never in the RAF, he was in the army.'

'So what was he doing on an RAF base?' Molly asked. 'Seconded like Will Baker, I suppose?'

'No,' Mark said. 'It was nothing like that. I mean no one was supposed to know then, it was all terribly hush-hush, but I asked him the other day when he came in to finalise details about the car and it was what we all suspected.'

'What, for heaven's sake?'

'He was an agent dropped behind the lines in France.'

'Oh, gosh!' Molly said. 'I always thought them terribly brave.'

'They were, and so were the Resistance workers that liaised with them. The information they gathered was sometimes vital for the Allies.'

Molly, knowing Mark was hopeless at the remembering people's names, said teasingly, 'You might have recognised this man's face but I bet you didn't remember his name and ended up calling him thingy.'

'No I didn't,' Mark said with a laugh. He put his name on the order form – James Carmichael.'

That name seared through Bridgette's brain and she leaned forward. 'What did you say?'

Neither Mark nor Molly noticed Bridgette's agitated tone and so Molly repeated almost nonchalantly, 'That's the name of the man who is buying this car, James Carmichael.'

'Oh God!' Bridgette almost screamed. 'Oh, Almighty Christ.'

Molly turned her head in alarm. 'What is it, Bridgette? God, you've gone as white as a sheet.'

Bridgette couldn't answer. Her mind was in such turmoil that she couldn't formulate coherent words to say to her cousin, who was now looking alarmed.

And then there was no time anyway. Mark was turning the car into a drive and someone was yanking open the front door and running towards them. Bridgette turned and looked at the man she thought she would never see again in the whole of her life. She opened her mouth to call his name but no sound came out. She fought the blackness threatening to throw its shroud upon her, but she was powerless against it, and as she sagged against the car seat, Finn slipped from her knee onto the floor.

TWENTY-NINE

When Bridgette came to she was in a bedroom and James Carmichael was in a chair beside the bed.

'Are you all right?' he said.

She shook her head almost in disbelief and, ignoring the question, said, 'The baby . . .'

'He's fine,' James said. 'My mother is in her element. She loves babies. Mark told me his name is Finn.'

'His full name is Finbar James,' Bridgette said.

James gave a gasp and said, 'I must ask you this, Bridgette. Is the child mine?'

Bridgette stared at him before saying stiffly, 'I am surprised that you even have to ask that question. Quite apart from the fact Finn has your dark hair and eyes, what sort of girl do you think I am? I slept with you only because I loved you.'

'I've offended you, and I'm sorry,' James said. 'But it's just when the letters were returned I thought—'

'What letters?'

561

'It doesn't matter,' James said almost impatiently. 'You said loved me. How do you feel about me now?'

Bridgette shook her head. 'When I thought I had lost you I thought my heart would break in two and the pain sometimes was almost unbearable, but I thought you were dead until a few moments ago, and I was trying to live my life without you in it.'

'Why were you so sure that I hadn't made it?'

'They found Charles's body,' Bridgette said. 'And I was talking to a fellow Resistance worker and he said that you were probably lying dead somewhere in the dense undergrowth, and the only reason that they hadn't found you was because they didn't know to look for another body. He hunted down and killed the two German soldiers, so there was no way of knowing whether they had killed one man or two. Not long after he had left in the ambulance with Charles he said the Germans had got wind of the shootings and were swarming all over the place. In other words, if the original two hadn't got you the others would, and even if you should still be alive you would never get through the forest on your own. What was I supposed to think, James?'

'Every word that man told you was the truth,' James said. 'And it is little wonder that you thought me dead. I didn't know that you were aware of any of it, of course, but I still wrote to you as soon as I could.'

'But what happened?' Bridgette said. 'I don't understand.'

'We stumbled unexpectedly upon two German soldiers,' James said. 'Fortunately they hadn't seen us but we knew they would if we made any sort of movement so we hid in the undergrowth and we waited for them to move off. But they didn't; they settled themselves. Charles and I just looked at one another because precious minutes were passing by and we had no idea what the two lone German soldiers were doing there. Had Charles been able to get closer to them without being seen he would have finished them off with his knife. He indicated that much to me, but there was no way that he could do that, and though we both had pistols, we dared not use them.

'Then the two German began talking to one another and Charles listened intently because he knew a smattering of German. He whispered to me that the two soldiers were waiting for re-inforcements. They must have worked out that many Resistance fighters were using the forest and they intended to flush them out. I imagine it was a sort of last-ditch attempt to kill as many as possible before the Allies should reach the town. We both knew then we had no time to lose and we had to be a good way through the forest before those reinforcements should arrive. I didn't know how it was to be achieved because the minute we tried to move forward we would be heard and hunted down.

'Suddenly Charles seemed to make a decision. He shook my hand and said, "Farewell, my friend. Kill as many Germans as you can in my memory," and he slipped away. I was so stunned I almost followed him. Then I thought that wouldn't be what he wanted and I heard him crashing through the trees, making no attempt to be quiet. He began to yell and shout, and he even fired a few shots. Of course, the Germans were off in hot pursuit, but Charles knew the forest like the back of his hand. Even so, I knew they would get him in the end.

When the first shots rang out, I wanted to go back, but I forced myself not to do that. I accepted that he had chosen to sacrifice himself for me. He had given me the gift of life and I couldn't throw that gift back in his face. I thought of you then, and the possibility of our future together, and I put as much distance between myself and the Germans and Charles as I could. I did hear more firing in the distance, and presumed they were from German guns, but that must have been the Resistance fighter you spoke of. By the time the reinforcements came I was well away.'

'Yes,' Bridgette said. 'But that same Resistance fighter told me you would never get through the forest on your own.'

'That probably would have been true,' James said, 'but Charles thought of everything. He had given me a copy of his map, a powerful torch, a pistol and a compass. He had marked the route we were to take through the forest in case we should get separated. Charles gave his life for me and I will never forget that. After that encounter, though, I tended to hide during the day and walk all night by the light of the torch so it took me some time to reach the edge of the forest. I was picked up by an American unit. When they had checked out I was who I said, they put me in a Jeep and took me back to the British lines. From there I was able to connect with my old unit.'

He looked at Bridgette, his dark eyes troubled. 'I told you this in the letters, but you didn't even open them. Were you mad with me because you found you were expecting our baby?'

'James, I never received any letters,' Bridgette insisted. 'Maman died just a fortnight after you left. I'd sent a telegram to her sister before that and she arrived in St-Omer with her husband the day I found out that Charles had died, and probably you too. Straight after Maman's funeral I went to Paris with my aunt and uncle because they thought my life was in danger.'

'Why?'

'I had lived in the same house as known collaborators and informers.'

'You were in the Resistance.'

'No one knew that, and Charles was the only contact I had,' Bridgette explained. 'After he died there was no one to verify that fact. Anyway, there was another reason. I didn't want to burden you with this at the time, but when our house was virtually the only house left unsearched when I was hiding you, they assumed that I had been pleasuring the German officers.'

'Who assumed?'

'Nasty vindictive people out to cause mischief,' Bridgette said. 'They attacked me one day as I was going in to Mass, and after that I stopped going.'

'I remember that,' James said. 'You said that your mother was too ill to be left.'

'That was an excuse,' Bridgette said. 'And of course they were there at the funeral. When Yvette's husband saw them he told me to pack everything I wanted to take with me as we were leaving for Paris early the next day. Henri said amongst some of the townsfolk the euphoria of being free was being replaced by a desire for revenge. They were looking for people to blame and one of those could be me. I thought he was being melodramatic, though he isn't prone to it, but we soon found out that he wasn't. About a week after I arrived in Paris, a letter came from Marie Laurent. The mob had come that night. Legrand and Georges were taken and later tried, found guilty and shot along with other traitors. Some women too were shot, but most were tarred and feathered. That was the fate awaiting me.'

'My poor darling,' James said, enfolding his hands over Bridgette's agitated ones. 'Thank God that you were spared that, at least, but I cannot feel sorry for your stepfather or his son. I think they probably got their just deserts.'

'I agree with you,' Bridgette said. 'But it didn't end there. They were so angry that they didn't get me that they set fire to the bakery. It's now just a shell, I've been told.'

'Oh, my love,' James sighed. He put his arms around her and held her tight and Bridgette felt her heart give a sudden flip. 'You have suffered so much, and then to find that you were pregnant . . .'

'I was glad,' Bridgette said. 'Because it was part of you, the only part I thought I would ever have.'

'You didn't hate me?' James asked.

Bridgette kissed his lips gently and then she held his face and looked deep into his eyes as she said, 'I couldn't hate you, James Carmichael, not if I tried from now until eternity. I love you far too much.'

'Oh God,' James cried, 'this is more than I ever dreamed of.' He looked deep into Bridgette's shining amber eyes and said, 'Do you mean it?'

Bridgette nodded. 'Every word.' She put her lips to his and the sweetness of that kiss took her breath away.

'Ah, Bridgette,' James said when they broke free at last. 'I love you so much. I was only half a person when I thought you wanted nothing more to do with me.'

'I was the same when I thought you dead,' Bridgette said.

'To have you back like this is truly amazing,' James told her. 'And I will never stop loving you until the breath leaves my body.'

567

This time their kiss held a promise of the years to come that they had to share. Together.

Bridgette and James left the bedroom hand in hand, and Molly ran forward and gave Bridgette a hug. 'I am so happy for you both,' she said. 'Why didn't you tell us that you were in the Resistance?' And at her startled look explained, 'James told us about that when you were out cold.'

'Did he tell you why I joined the Resistance?'

Molly shook her head and Bridgette said. 'I have told all of you lies that I am sorry for, and I think it is time to tell you the truth about everything.'

'When we were at the Bull Ring together you said that one day you would tell me about your stepfather,' Molly said. 'Many times since I have wanted to ask you about that, but I was afraid of upsetting you.'

'It's time you knew it all anyway,' Bridgette said. 'Everything that happened to me in the end was linked to the way first my grandfather and then my stepfather treated my mother and me.' She told them how her grandfather had forced her mother to marry Legrand, the threats made and the life they both had had to endure throughout that sham of a marriage. My grandfather hated both my mother and myself so much that after his death, when I was five, we found he had disinherited us both in his will and left the bakery, house and everything else to Legrand, and to Georges after his death.'

'Disinherit his own family?' Molly said. 'It's almost unbelievable.'

'Do you know all this already?' Mark asked James. He shook his head. 'Barely nothing, for all we were together many weeks.'

'I didn't want to talk about it,' Bridgette said. 'Especially as you seemed to have some sort of idyllic childhood. And talking of that, are your parents all right with Finn?'

'They're fine, honestly,' James said. 'But I will go and check on him, if you like,' he added, getting to his feet.

'I'll come with you,' Mark said. 'And see if Nuala is OK.' The two men left the room together as Molly said to Bridgette, 'Was your stepfather as bad as your grandfather?'

'Worse, if anything. He used to beat me and really lay into my mother. Georges too was a nasty, cruel bully, and I suffered at his hands until I learned to stand up for myself.'

'You told me about the time he threw your beautiful doll in the fire.'

'He was constantly doing things like that,' Bridgette said. 'The worst thing that Georges did was try to rape me when I was just sixteen. He didn't succeed but my mother knew that she couldn't totally protect me. By then I was working at the Laurents' dress shop and I moved into their house, with my mother's blessing, and later married their son, Xavier.

'When war was declared, Xavier joined the

French Army, but he was killed at Dunkirk. I was expecting my first child and when I heard of his death and I went into premature labour and my baby was stillborn. If I am honest, I joined the Resistance not to free France, but to kill as many Germans as possible. And I did kill them; and rejoiced in their deaths. Now, it's hard to believe I did those things.'

'The situations were totally different,' Mark said, coming into the room with Nuala in his arms. 'We were at war. How many German pilots did I shoot down and how many German men, women and children did our bombers kill? It was what we had to do then.'

'I suppose.'

'No suppose about it,' Mark said. 'All those in the Resistance did a sterling job and you all knew the penalty if you had been caught. The Allies greatly admired the work the French Resistance were doing.'

'Well, I'm glad we were of some use, at least,' Bridgette said. 'I only gave up the work and moved back to the bakery when Maman became so ill.'

'And then agreed to hide me when my escape route broke down,' James said, appearing with Finn, with his parents following behind him. Seeing James and Finn together, the likeness was startling and obvious.

'Finn's your son, isn't he?' Molly said.

'Yes,' James said proudly, crossing to Bridgette's side and putting an arm around her. 'I ended up staying with Bridgette some weeks and we discovered that we loved each other.'

'I'm sorry that I told such a pack of lies to you all,' Bridgette said. 'I was so afraid that you would think less of me if I told you the truth about Finn.'

'How could you think that?' Molly cried.

'Well, you said that in Ireland having a baby with no husband was considered one of the worst things a girl can do,' Bridgette said.

'Yes, but I didn't say that I agreed with it,' Molly said. 'I told you all the things that happened to Aggie, and what she was forced to do, and that was nearly my lot as well. How in God's name could we look down on you? You suffered so much too.'

'And you don't know the half of it,' said James.

He told Molly and Mark, and his parents, Audrey and Jim, about the duplicity of Legrand and his son and how they had paid for that with their lives, and how Bridgette had been tainted too.

'It was an extremely risky thing to take me in the way she did and she was very brave even to consider it because she knew the risks she was running,' James went on. 'The Germans knew that I had landed somewhere and we were working on the assumption that with Legrand and his son being so well in with the German officers, and Bridgette's mother being extremely ill, they wouldn't search the bakery. It was a gamble and could have backfired at any time, for they tore the rest of

571

the town apart. But it was noted, of course, that the bakery was untouched and so malicious lies were spread about that Bridgette had been sharing her favours with the Germans.'

Bridgette went on to detail the punishments meted out to women accused of consorting with Germans, her flight to Paris, and ended up with telling them about the vengeful mob that had set the bakery ablaze.

Then James took up the tale. 'The three letters I sent to Bridgette she never got. They were returned to me unopened as there was no house to deliver them to, and so I thought that Bridgette was no longer interested. Meanwhile, Bridgette thought I had been killed, and then found she was pregnant.'

James's voice was choked, and Bridgette looked from his emotional eyes to Finn's merry ones and felt such a rush of love for them both that it almost overwhelmed her.

'We might never have met again, James and me,' she said in a voice that shook slightly. 'Because of misunderstandings that happen in wartime, Finn might have grown up fatherless and James would never know he had a son, and you,' she went on, smiling across at James's parents, 'would have lost the opportunity to be grandparents.'

'It's unbelievable,' Mark said. 'You only met because of a quirk of fate.'

'Yes,' Bridgette said. 'And that quirk of fate only happened because I eventually did what my mother wanted and came to meet my father's family.'

James's parents looked a bit confused at Bridgette's words and so the others filled them in with details and Bridgette left them to it. She was happy to feast her eyes on the two men in her life, whom she loved so much.

James turned and saw the love light shining in his beloved Bridgette's face and he felt his heart turn over. He loved her with a depth that seem to encompass all his being and he suddenly handed Finn to his mother and kneeled down in front of her. 'My darling Bridgette,' he said, 'will you do me the honour of becoming my wife?'

'I will, James,' Bridgette said. 'I will, and gladly,'

There were cheers and hugs and handshakes all round. His father brought out a bottle of champagne that he said he was saving for a special occasion and this was about as special as it got, and when the health of the couple was drunk and the hubbub had died down, James said to his mother, 'You can go about arranging the wedding, Mum, which I know you'll be longing to do, but not just yet, because the first thing I want to do is return to St-Omer.'

'Oh, no, James,' said Bridgette. 'I want to draw a line under that period of my life.'

James shook his head. 'I don't think that that is the way to play this,' he said. 'We need to confront these lying busybodies that maligned you. I would like to give them a piece of my mind, but my French isn't good enough. Anyway, it was you they abused, so you should stand up to them.

I know how brave you are and I will be with you every step of the way. No one can hurt you any more.'

Suddenly Bridgette knew James was right. She would go back and clear her name. She had been forced to flee from Madame Pretin and her ilk, but now it was time to face them unafraid and refute the lies they had told about her.

'You're right, James,' she said. 'That is one of the first things that we must do.'

'Oh, Mark,' Molly said, clapping her hands together in delight, as a child might, 'I am so excited about all this. Shall we forgo our outing to Sutton Park? I can't wait to tell the family.'

'All right,' said Mark, good-naturedly. He added, 'You better come along with us too, James. Bridgette's uncles will probably want to give you the third degree.'

'Stop it, Mark,' Bridgette said with a laugh. 'You will have James frightened to death.' She looked at James and said, 'Uncle Tom and Uncle Joe will not do that at all, but I know the whole family would like to meet you.'

'I would be glad to come,' James said. 'And I will answer any question they want to ask. It's understandable that they want to know something about me. And don't worry, my darling, they won't scare me away. Nothing would. I would walk through hot coals if that is what it took to be with you.'

*   *   *

James was approved by the whole family and Bridgette's tale had to be told again and again. Bridgette was very relieved to see that it made no difference to the way she was treated by the others. In fact, they seemed to think that she was really heroic and she was slightly uncomfortable with this because, as she said, in wartime a person did what they had to do and she never thought of herself as anyone special.

James, on the other hand, thought Bridgette very special indeed, and he said that they had been apart long enough. There was no reason to delay the wedding for months and months. It was set for the beginning of August, before the boys set off for America, though Audrey Carmichael complained that wasn't nearly enough time to plan the wedding of her only son.

Bridgette, knowing Audrey was really upset about this, called to see her on her own the following Monday afternoon, leaving Finn with Molly.

'I do understand how you feel,' she said. 'But really, James and I don't want anything lavish. We just want to be together as soon as possible.'

Audrey saw the sincerity in Bridgette's face and when she said, 'I truly love your son so very much,' she knew she meant every word.

'I am so happy that you have called to see me,' she said. 'I'm not sure I have ever thanked you enough for saving James's life.'

'Oh, really, I didn't . . .'

'Don't be so modest, my dear,' Audrey said. 'James has told me how it was and how the storm troopers actually came into the house, and he said even then you showed such bravery and went out on to the landing to meet them.'

'I was so scared that my knees were nearly knocking together.' Bridgette smiled ruefully at the memory.

'I am not at all surprised,' Audrey said. 'You knew what would happen to you if James had been discovered. He has told us that too. You know, my dear,' she went on, 'when James was demobbed and came home, there was a sort of innate sadness about him. In fact, he was so depressed and dispirited I was quite concerned about him. He reminded me of the way he was when he heard about the death of his wife, Sarah, for he seemed to go a little mad for a time, and that wasn't helped of course when Dan was killed the following year and poor Dolly's fiancé as well.

'Dolly said that it was probably reaction to what he had had to do and that she would imagine returning to civvy street was difficult for many servicemen. And I'm sure she's right, but in James's case it seemed more than that. I tried asking him if anything was the matter, and so did his father, but he always said that he was fine. We thought in time he would maybe recover but now I know it was because he thought he had lost you.'

'I thought the same,' Bridgette said. 'And I know that he loved his first wife, as I did Xavier.

He was a wonderful man and husband, and I was incredibly sad when I heard of his death, and then for my daughter to be stillborn was very hard for me to come to terms with. But now I feel the same way about James and I am so very grateful that we can both have another crack at happiness. Having Finn is just like the icing on the cake.'

Audrey heard the longing in Bridgette's voice. She and James had been through months and months of unhappiness. No wonder they wanted no delay to the wedding, and in making difficulties she knew she was thinking of herself rather that the young people concerned, and so she patted Bridgette's hand and said, 'I know that, and you mustn't mind me. It's just a mother's pride, and how does that measure up to your happiness? If you want the wedding in so short a space of time then that's when it will be.'

Bridgette felt herself relax and Audrey, seeing this, said, 'I can't tell you how happy Jim and I are that you are joining this family, and Dolly too is delighted.'

Bridgette knew that Dolly was pleased for when they'd met she had thrown her arms around Bridgette and told her that she had always wanted a sister. Finn, of course, was the light of all their lives.

The fact that she was surrounded by people who loved her filled Bridgette with confidence, but she knew that she had to return to St-Omer with her James by her side, or that terrible business might always remain a blot on her new life.

The family weren't that sure that it was a good idea for her to return to France, especially when they heard the truth of what had happened after her flight to Paris.

'Why don't you forget all about going back to France?' Aggie said coaxingly. 'You have got away and you're free, and can make a new life for yourself here and never think of them again.'

'Aunt Aggie,' Bridgette said, 'you were once terrorised by a man named Finch, who Uncle Joe dealt with.'

'Yes.'

'If that hadn't happened, if the man still lived, would you be as happy and contented as you are today, or would you always feel that there was unfinished business?'

'I don't think I really need to answer that,' Aggie said. 'And I understand what you are saying.'

'I have good friends in St-Omer that I may want to visit,' Bridgette said. She raised her head and said firmly, 'And I will not have people whispering about me behind my back and so I need to confront them. It is the only way.'

'All I can say to that,' said Aggie, 'is that you are a braver person than I am, and your father would have been proud of you.'

THIRTY

Bridgette and James sailed for France the following week, leaving the plans for the wedding in the capable hands of James's mother aided, abetted by Isobel, Aggie and Molly. Bridgette had written to her aunt and uncle in Paris and they stopped off there for a few days.

Raoul and his fiancée, Monique, were living there too, and James greeted them all in French, but hestiantly as his skill had got rusty through lack of use. They were impressed anyway and shook him warmly by the hand. Bridgette was hugged and kissed by them all, and they positively drooled over Finn. Henri and Yvette were astounded at how much he had changed in a few months.

Bridgette had told them little details in the letter she had sent, and while Yvette and Henri had never seen James and knew nothing about him, Raoul and Monique wanted to hear everything from the beginning. Bridgette told them all about her

Resistance work, culminating in hiding James in the first place, and then thinking that he was killed as he tried to rejoin the advancing British Forces.

Yvette came in there. 'We arrived in the town to see my desperately ill sister the day that Bridgette had seen the dead body of the Resistance worker, Charles, whom she knew, who was guiding James through the forest. The man with him told her though they hadn't found James's body, the Germans had probably killed him too.'

'I thought my heart had broken,' Bridgette said.

'I can imagine,' Monique said, and was further astounded when Bridgette recounted what had happened when she left her home for Paris.

'They thought I was a collaborator, no worse, some plaything of the German officers.' Her lip curled in disgust.

James, who was pleasantly surprised how much he was able to understand, said in French, 'We're going back now to tell them they were wrong.'

Raoul and Monique could plainly see that that was what they had to do, but Henri and Yvette were worried for Bridgette.

'I must do this,' Bridgette said firmly. 'It's unfinished business. I was unable to say a word in my defence before this, or explain what I was really doing, but now, should they doubt one word of what I say, I will have James as proof.'

Again, James spoke in French. 'You mustn't worry. I will protect Bridgette. No one will ever hurt her in that way again.'

Later, as Yvette and Bridgette made coffee in the kitchen, Yvette said, 'We missed you so much when you left, but I see you were right to go.'

'If I hadn't I might never have met up with James again,' Bridgette said. 'Isn't that an awful thought? I was so convinced he was dead, I would never have gone looking for him.'

'It's wonderful that you got together,' Yvette said. 'I couldn't be more pleased, and Henri feels the same. It is obvious that you love him and he is totally besotted by both you and the boy.'

'I know,' Bridgette said. 'He is so pleased to be a father, though he regrets missing some of Finn's babyhood.'

'He has years to make up for that.'

'He intends to make the most of them,' Bridgette said. 'But this does mean, of course, that we will be living in Birmingham, in England.'

'I know that, my dear,' Yvette said. 'I accepted that a long time ago. Now you have James, and Finn has his father, and that's as it should be.'

'And you will come to my wedding?'

'Of course, my dear,' Yvette said. 'We will all be there. You just try to keep us away. And then you will return here in the late autumn for Raoul and Monique's wedding.'

'We will of course,' Bridgette said. 'Monique was saying that they intend to start a family immediately.'

'Yes,' said Yvette with a smile on her face. 'She said the same to me.'

'That will keep you busy then.'

'Ah, yes,' Yvette said. 'Busy and happy. It is by far the best way to be.'

Three days later, on a Saturday, Bridgette, James and Finn were on the train bound for St-Omer. The only people who knew they would be arriving were the Laurents. Bridgette said she wanted to arrive as unobtrusively as possible and so asked them not to meet her at the station and that they would make their own way to the house. So there was little notice taken of the young couple and child that alighted from the train. Bridgette saw no one she recognised.

Once clear of the station, though, with James pushing Finn in the pushchair, their feet automatically turned towards Rue Allen, where the bakery had once stood. Marie had been right: it was now just a blackened shell.

The dank smell of the charred embers still hung in the air and as Bridgette stood looking at it with James's arm around her, tears ran from her eyes.

'It's silly, I suppose, to cry,' she said. 'I mean, I can tell myself that it's just a building and there were many buildings destroyed in the war, but this was directed at me and me alone, and that is the thing that's so upsetting. Can you imagine the violence, the blood lust, that was running through the people who did this? They destroyed my home because they hadn't got hold of me to abuse and harass. What I find really upsetting is that it

582

wouldn't have been mindless thugs that did it,' she told James as they turned away and began walking towards the Laurents' shop. 'These were people I had known all my life. I thought this was a nice friendly town, and never could I have visualised anyone doing anything like that. Somehow this has coloured my whole attitude to most of the people here.'

She wasn't including the Laurents in that assessment, of course, and a few minutes later they saw Marie, who must have been watching out for them, running towards them with her arms outstretched. She enveloped them both in a bear hug and then unstrapped Finn and lifted him in her arms, saying as she did so, 'Aren't you a little beauty?' In answer, Finn kicked his legs and chuckled.

'Oh, he's gorgeous,' Marie said, holding him in her arms as they made their way to the shop. 'And a heartbreaker with those dark eyes.'

'That's what Isobel said as well,' Bridgette said. 'But James has those dark eyes too, and the only time he broke my heart was when I thought he was dead.'

'I remember,' Marie said. 'And I am glad that things have worked out well for you in the end. It's just wonderful. I shed tears when you wrote and told us the news, and so did Lisette.'

'When is her baby due?'

'September. And Leonie is that excited. I said to Lisette we'll be lucky if either of us gets a look in.'

'I wonder what Leonie will think of Finn.'

'She'll adore him. And Jean-Paul too,' Marie said confidently. 'They are so excited about you coming back to see us all. It's good that you stopped off in Paris too. How is everyone?'

'Oh, very well,' Bridgette said. 'Aunt Yvette has a wedding to prepare and Raoul's fiancée, Monique, is a lovely girl that she gets on so well with.' She looked at Marie and said impishly, 'When the children arrive what a doting grandmother she will make.'

'Ah, well, a little bit of spoiling from a grandmother does them no harm in the long run,' Marie said rather smugly.

Bridgette smiled. 'Well, you should know, Marie.' And the two women's eyes locked and they laughed together.

Lisette, Edmund and the children came around later, and it was lovely to see everyone again. The children had grown out of all recognition and, as Marie prophesied, were enchanted with Finn – even Jean-Paul, who was a big boy now and in double figures. Bridgette was so pleased to see Edmund again, who was so glad to be back with Lisette and his family after so many years apart.

However, throughout that evening, always in the back of Bridgette's mind was the confrontation with Madame Pretin that she was determined to have before Mass the following morning. When she told Marie and Lisette her intention she expected Marie to try to talk her out of it.

But she said, 'I don't blame you in the slightest.

That woman has had things her own way for long enough, and the accusations she levelled at you, Bridgette, were downright malicious. I'll make sure that I am there to back you up.'

'And so will I,' Lisette declared stoutly.

And so the next morning the party set out for the short walk to Notre Dame, James as usual pushing Finn in his pushchair, Bridgette by his side, and behind them Marie and Maurice.

Madame Pretin was on the steps, as Bridgette knew she would be, surrounded by the usual crones. She had her back to Bridgette, but Bridgette saw that one of her friends has spotted her and had alerted the old woman. Madame Pretin was surprised because she hadn't heard that Bridgette was even in the town, but by the time she had turned, her face had assumed its usual sour expression and her eyes glittered with spitefulness. Bridgette held her gaze, only dimly aware that Lisette, Edmund and the children had come out of a side road and were grouped around her.

She didn't stop until only about a metre separated the two woman. James with the child stayed further back as Madame Pretin spat out, 'I'm surprised that you have the effrontery to show your face here.'

'You're surprised, are you?' Bridgette said. 'Why is that exactly?'

'You know,' Madame Pretin spat out. 'We don't want your sort here. Thought we showed you that plainly enough.'

There was a murmur of agreement from the other women at this.

Bridgette said, 'You mean when you burned the bakery to the ground? But you see, the bakery wasn't mine and never would have become mine. My grandfather cut my mother and me out of the will and gifted it to Legrand and then his son, Georges. Now they are no more and I don't think they need a bakery of any sort where they are now. It's probably quite hot enough.'

'It's how we deal with traitors, and any others who were too friendly with the Germans,' said one of the other women.

'But surely you must be certain of your facts?'

'Everyone knew about Legrand and his lily-livered son.'

'And you lived with them,' Madame Pretin almost snarled. 'Eating the best of food while the rest of us starved.'

'I had no jurisdiction over Legrand,' Bridgette said. 'None whatsoever. He wasn't even my father. My real father was a soldier in the British Army and he was killed at the Somme in 1916 before I was born.'

Bridgette saw that many were surprised at that, but she wasn't finished. 'I lived back at the bakery because I needed to nurse my mother. She was very sick, and you know that and were so scared of catching her disease you never came near her and then expected to lament her passing at my expense the day we laid her to rest.'

586

'It's how it's done,' another women said. 'You have no manners.'

Bridgette laughed. 'I have no manners,' she repeated sarcastically. 'I'm sure that it is very mannerly to drag women out into the street to abuse and humiliate them on the merest say-so of another, and if I had not left for Paris that would have happened to me.'

'We know the sort of woman you were,' Madame Pretin said. 'Even early on in the Occupation you were seen fraternising with the Germans.'

Bridgette sighed. 'In 1940 my husband, Xavier, was killed on the beach at Dunkirk. When word reached me, it caused me to go into labour and my premature baby was stillborn. I wanted to pay the Germans back for taking away my husband and my child and so I joined the Resistance.'

She saw the incredulous faces around her and she said, 'What you saw as fraternisation I saw as trying to ensure safe passage across the city. Skilfully hidden in my beret there might be messages, maps or diagrams that I had to deliver. I could not risk being stopped and searched too thoroughly, so yes I used to flirt. I was advised to. Later, I also set fire to fuel dumps, cut telephone lines and laid charges on bridges, roads and railway lines.'

Some of the women looked decidedly uncomfortable now, Bridgette noticed, and some on their way to church had stopped to watch the exchange.

Even those already in the church had come out as far as the doorway.

Madame Pretin, seeing this, snapped out, 'You still haven't explained why your house wasn't searched when everyone else's was.'

'Oh,' Bridgette said. 'I must explain that, mustn't I? Well, here goes then. I gave up working with the Resistance when I went back to live at the bakery for I wouldn't put Maman at risk, but I was approached one day by a man I knew in the Resistance who asked me to hide a secret agent.'

She reached her hand back and James took hold of it, gripped it tight and came to stand beside her.

In his halting French he said, 'My name is James Carmichael and I was a secret agent dropped in France.'

'James's escape route back to Britain broke down,' Bridgette said. 'And the Germans knew a secret agent was in the area but they didn't know where. I was asked to hide him because it was thought that with Legrand and Georges so well in with the German officers, and with Maman so sick, James would be safer there than anywhere.

'Obviously, Legrand and Georges knew nothing about it. And there was no guarantee that the Germans wouldn't search the bakery,' Bridgette said. 'We just had to take the risk. And they did come into the house, and were just yards from the bedroom housing James when they were ordered out again. In the end James was with us from April to July, and we found that we loved one another.

Our son, Finn, is the fruit of that love and as we have just found each other again after the war, we are not yet married. That is the only sin I committed. I am no traitor to France.'

The priest had been drawn to the church doorway as well to see what had so interested his flock, and as Bridgette's tale drew to a close he descended the steps and said, 'Well, I would not condemn you, Bridgette Laurent. Indeed,' he extended his hand, 'I am honoured to shake your hand and that of your intended. France owes you both a debt.'

'Hear, hear,' said a voice from the crowd, and this was echoed by another. When applause began, Madame Pretin and her friends, red-faced with embarrassment, took themselves off.

Bridgette was amazed by the response, but as she looked around at the people she was aware that some averted their eyes or moved their feet nervously, and she knew Henri had been right: Madame Pretin would not do the dirty work herself; she would incite others to do it instead. And these people lauding her now, but unable to meet her gaze, were the likely protagonists that had searched for her and then set fire to her home.

They were the sort of people who would sway with the wind, join whichever side was the most popular. And despite Madame Pretin's very probable provocation and encouragement Bridgette thought that the whole atrocious act was less her fault than theirs.

It was the normal St-Omer townsfolk who had made the decision to hunt others down and administer their own brand of punishment, even though many must have known how wrong it was. Firing the bakery was the last straw, as far as Bridgette was concerned. She knew that there were quite a few neighbours she had thought she had known that she could never trust again.

The priest had turned away and was going back into the church and the crowd had begun to follow him.

'Are you coming?' Marie asked.

Bridgette shook her head. 'I am in no mood for Mass,' she said. 'Not here, anyway. Today the responses would choke me.'

'What are you in the mood for?' James asked when Marie had gone.

'Oh, I don't know,' Bridgette said, then suddenly cried, 'Yes I do. I have done what I came here to do.' She had a sudden vision of her family in Birmingham. 'I am certain now that I no longer belong here and I want to go home as soon as possible.'

'We will,' James said soothingly. 'I will see to that first thing tomorrow.' He put his arms around her and said, 'And soon we will be man and wife. Hold that thought because then our future together will begin. I can hardly wait to love you properly and be a real father to our son. We will have a honeymoon too. Europe is in such a mess it will have to be somewhere near home,

590

I think. Have you anywhere you would particularly like to go?'

'Yes,' Bridgette said. 'I would like to put in the last piece of the jigsaw and go to Buncrana in Ireland, where it all began. I want to walk the streets of the town as my father did and visit the post office and thank Nellie McEvoy, who Molly speaks so highly of. I want to go out and see the cottage where my father was born and raised. I know someone else owns it now, but Molly said she is sure we will still be able to see it from the head of the lane. And I want to call on Christy Byrne and thank him too.'

'If that is what you want to do, my darling, then that is what we will do,' James said, 'for all I want is to make you happy.'

'Well, you have succeeded in that, my darling James,' Bridgette said as she wrapped her arms around him. 'For at this moment I feel as if I am the happiest women in the world.'

Author's notes

This book is the last piece of the Sullivan jigsaw that locks into place all the books that went before it. In Buncrana, 1914, Finn Sullivan joined the Royal Inniskillens to fight in the Great War. He did it partly to bring some excitement into his mundane life, and partly because he was resentful working his butt off on a farm that would never be his. He also thought that if enough Irish men and boys volunteered then Ireland would be united once more, because that was what the British Government promised if Ireland was to help them in their fight against the Hun. Finn lost his life not quite two years later at the Battle of the Somme, July 1st 1916.

However, Finn didn't entirely sink without trace, as everyone thought, because he left behind Gabrielle who was pregnant with his child, Bridgette. When the child was born, she had no idea that Finn was her father. Gabrielle was forced into marriage with Robert Legrand – a harsh and domineering man – when Bridgette was just a baby. She thought he was her natural father, though she suffered at his hands and was mercilessly bullied by his son, George. Aged seventeen she was glad to escape their clutches to marry Xavier, a man she loved dearly. But tragically, just as the Great War had taken her father, the Second World War took her husband, and she suffered a miscarriage on hearing the news. On her mother's deathbed a few years later, Bridgette learned of her true father and, as soon as she could, she set off to find the Sullivan family. She had many disappointments in her search – they had all moved to Birmingham and knew nothing of the daughter Finn might have had.

Because much of the backdrop to this book was set in France I travelled there in May 2008 on a research trip. I could see immediately why the only way to fight would have to be in the trenches, because the landscape was so flat. We stayed in St-Omer which really was where the BEF were stationed and all the facts about the period there are as accurate as I could get them. The people were lovely and very helpful, from the librarian who searched out old maps for us to photocopy, to the lady in the small café by the hotel who had pictures of St-Omer in the Great War around the wall. She allowed us to freely take photographs – giving me a feel of the time.

We toured the town across the market square

in front of Hotel de Ville (the Town Hall) where the Saturday market used to be, visited the *Jardin Public* and saw the bandstand where Finn would wait for his beloved Gabrielle. We went into the Notre Dame Cathedral, a beautiful golden palace with huge pillars and beautiful stained glass windows, lit up by the flickering lights of many candles. We also visited the tremendous Baroque organ and golden tomb of St Erkembode, which was covered in shoes.

We didn't just stay in St-Omer, opting to travel further afield. We visited the Somme and saw some of the graveyards that abounded there and museums at Lille, Arras, Amiens, Abbeville and Albert. In Albert we saw a replica of Notre Dame Breberieres with the statue of mother and child, called The Golden Virgin locally, on top of the basilica. It was shelled on January 15th 1915 and the statue was knocked so that it was at right angles to the *basilica* but did not fall. The legend was that it wouldn't fall until the war should be coming to an end. It finally fell during an Allied bombard-ment, as they attempted and succeeded in recap-turing the town, in April 1918. In the same town, the tunnels that run underneath it have been trans-formed into a museum to document The Great War. It was here I found out what Brigade and Battalion Finn Sullivan was in, because all the men recruited in either Donegal or Fermanagh were in the same one, and this meant I could track his training. The Ulstermen were in the forefront of the attack at the Somme and the casualty lists were so high that the survivors were sent back to St-Omer for a rest. The report by Captain William Spender is a genuine one, in fact one of many such reports that can be seen on the walls in this underground museum.

The report in the paper though is a conglomerate of many such reports, as the Battle of the Somme was the first time press and newsreels had been let into the battle field. *The Times, Observer, Mail* and *Mirror* were just four I know about, though there might have been others, and of course reporters supplied more than the papers they were assigned to with written accounts and pictures.

As I began writing about the Second World War it was interesting to see things from a French point of view. When the Germans were able to ignore the Maginot Line and get through the forest, thought to be impregnable and with the Allies retreating to the beaches, the French people must have known that they were staring invasion, defeat and occupation in the face. How frightening that must have been, for they knew what was in store for them – as Hitler's armies had already rode rough shod through much of Europe.

I researched the work of the Resistance fairly well too from De Gaulle in the early days, their efforts to aggravate the enemy via the wireless from

London, to the resistance groups becoming more organised. They amalgamated for maximum effect and began to liaise and work with secret agents sent over from Britain. I also went to Eperlecque Forest where a huge concrete bunker called *Le Blockhaus* was built, and then nearer to St-Omer, La Coupole rising out of the ground like a gigantic mushroom. Both constructions were instrumental in the manufacture of the pilotless rockets V1 and V2 that sent another wave of terror across Britain.

Despite my visiting France though and the benefit of the internet I do like reference books as well and so, I also read, *The First World War* by Andrew Wren, *All Quiet on the Home Front* by Richard Van Emden and Steve Humphries, *The Soldiers War* by again Richard Van Emden, *First day at the Somme* by Martin Middlebrook and *Resistance in France* by Jean-Paul Pallud.

So with all this research why was this book not out in September like it should have been? Well, from October 2008 there was such a catalogue of disasters that my agent thought the book jinxed and I thought she wasn't far wrong. I was walking my dog one dismal evening in early October when I tripped up a step and managed to break two bones in my left wrist and stretch the tendons in my right hand so violently they tore a piece of bone from the thumb. Plastered, strapped and splinted and without the use of either thumb, washing, dressing and even squeezing the tooth-paste was well nigh impossible without help. Typing was a non starter altogether. Almost seven weeks later I had everything removed and faced three weeks of physio. The deadline was extended to March and I was on track again. In February my brother in Birmingham had a massive heart attack. Obviously I had to go, to be with the family. A week later my lovely brother was dead and after the funeral I felt completely drained. It became apparent to all that a September publication dead-line couldn't be met and I can only say I'm sorry. I know you'll all understand and I hope that you enjoyed *The Child Left Behind*.

Q&A with Anne Bennett

Q. *When did you first know you wanted to be a writer? Was it always novels that you were drawn to?*

A. I have always been an avid reader, since childhood. I did not like pure fantasy books even then, I always went for books that were more realistic – that's what I write as well. I can't remember a time when I didn't want to be a writer.

Q. *Do you think it's important to have a regular writing routine?*

A. I wouldn't dream of telling other writers how to organise their writing time, but for me it is vital to have a routine. I am an early riser and I start work straight away and work for an hour or two, before taking my dog for a long brisk walk across hills, beaches and sand dunes minutes from my home, whatever the weather. Then it is back home for breakfast and work until lunchtime. After lunch I usually check my e-mails, especially those from fans who have taken the trouble to write and comment on a book. Then I usually edit what I have done that morning and work until teatime. My husband is in a band, so the nights he is practising or at a gig I often work on into the evening too.

Q. *You say you're an 'Irish Brummie'. How do you balance these two aspects of your own background in your work?*

A. It was great being brought up as a Catholic, and I am very proud of my background. As I write about both places, the Irish claim me as an Irish writer because my parents were both Irish. The people of Birmingham claim me because I was born and bred there and write about their city and mine, which few people do. Added to that, and to a lesser extent, the Welsh claim me because I have chosen to make my home here.

Q. *Many of your novels are partly set during World War Two. Did your own family and friends experience this and is that how you came to write some of the descriptions?*

A. No, not really. My husband Denis's father was a Despatch Rider, but would never talk about it, Denis's mother was just a girl. My parents were Irish and Ireland was neutral and so they didn't have to to register for war work, though they experienced the raids and did fire watching and things like that, but they only spoke about it briefly. How people lived through those six years of deprivation and terror and tragedy and true acts of bravery have always fascinated me. And so I have listened to people who did want to talk about it, read many books, watched videos and trawled the internet. I have been left with immense respect for anyone who went through it and a feel compelled, for their sakes, to get the facts right.